BY ALEXIS HALL

Mortal Follies
A Lady for a Duke
Something Fabulous

LONDON CALLING

Boyfriend Material
Husband Material

WINNER BAKES ALL

Rosaline Palmer Takes the Cake
Paris Daillencourt Is About to Crumble

CONFOUNDING OATHS

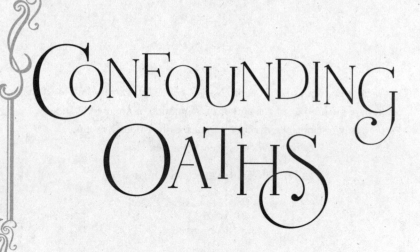

CONFOUNDING OATHS

ALEXIS HALL

NEW YORK

A Del Rey Trade Paperback Original

Copyright © 2024 by Alexis J. Hall

Published in the United States by Del Rey, an imprint of Random House, a division of Penguin Random House LLC, New York.

DEL REY and the CIRCLE colophon are registered trademarks of Penguin Random House LLC.

ISBN 978-0-593-49758-6
Ebook ISBN 978-0-593-49759-3

Printed in the United States of America on acid-free paper

randomhousebooks.com

9 8 7 6 5 4 3 2 1

Book design by Sara Bereta

To my lord Oberon,

I'm honestly not sure how much longer I can put up with this.

AUTHOR'S NOTE

Please note that *Confounding Oaths* includes a number of themes some readers may prefer not to engage with. These include, but are not limited to: sexual content, racism, colourism, discussion of the transatlantic slave trade, violence, the threat of violence and danger, murder, a missing (presumed abducted) minor, blood sacrifice (including graphic description of an animal sacrifice in chapter 21), social non-acceptance of LGBTQ+ relationships.

PROLOGUE

Introductions, gentle reader, remain in order.

Although I'm really not sure why. I assumed I would only have to write one of these damnable things, after which I fully anticipated that my lord Oberon, having accepted that whatever misunderstandings may recently have passed between us are surely as nothing compared to a timeless, ouroboran eternity of loyal and mirthful service, would welcome me back to his court with open arms.

Spoiler. He didn't. Frankly I expected to be jesting in the invisible palace at the end of the middling road sometime last February and do not know what is taking him so long.

Instead I remain here, trapped in the dreary, damp, culinarily moribund country you recently (well, recently-ish; what's a millennium or so between friends?) started calling *England* and forced to make my living by recounting for the mass market some of those stories I originally compiled for my master's delight alone.

This is the second of those stories I have chosen to share. If you have not read the first, why not? Do you personally dislike me? Are you determined to see me suffer, interminably and without even the comforts of a scribbler's income to lighten my exile?

I swear, just when I thought my contempt for your species could not sink any deeper.

If you *have*, like the discerning mortal creature I am sure you are, read my previously published work then you will know that the story in question took place in the year 1814, beginning shortly after the exile of Napoleon to Elba. This new narrative takes place just after his escape a little under a year later, in the March of 1815.

In the few months between my visits, the British burned Washington as part of the confusingly named War of 1812, eight Londoners died in a flood of beer, and a great white serpent arose in the north of England and devoured several villages. What will follow is a tale of beauty, blood sacrifice, and the wonderfully cruel business of granting wishes.

You are, I hope, here *primarily* for the cruelty. That's my specialty, after all, and if you are not you have chosen a very peculiar era to read about.

CONFOUNDING OATHS

CHAPTER ONE

I FIRST ENCOUNTERED MR. CAESAR DURING the unfortunate business with his cousin that had begun with her losing her clothes at a ball and ended with her sacrificing a British peer to an ancient goddess, fucking a disgraced noblewoman, and developing a lifelong aversion to marchpane, not necessarily in that order.

In the near year that had followed, I had been observing that lady's friends and family closely in case they should prove likewise diverting, but, thus far, they had not. Mr. Caesar in particular had proven deeply tedious. His studies for the bar had languished somewhat (and were about to begin languishing rather more for reasons you will soon discover), and he was spending the majority of his time at various London institutions that catered to a certain sort of gentleman with a certain sort of interest.

This latter point you may think would grab my attention, but I am not mortal and I am not so prurient in my outlook that mere sodomy arrests me.

Indeed I would probably have given up on Mr. Caesar as a

prospect entirely had he not, at a ball hosted by the Vicomte de Loux, punched a fellow guest in the jaw.

The blow in question would not land until later in the evening, but I mention it now in case you, like me, find balls in general rather dull unless something unexpected is happening and might, therefore, put the book down in disgust were it not for the reassurance that in a few short pages you will be able to watch an irritating man get smacked in the teeth by a slightly less irritating man whose teeth-smacking skills—if we are honest between ourselves—leave a great deal to be desired.

I begin my tale in earnest, then, clinging in the shape of a woodlouse to the ceiling of a carriage whose occupants, in descending order of age, were Mr. Caesar, his friend Miss Bickle, and his two sisters, Miss Caesar and Miss Anne. We are starting early partly to build tension ahead of the much-anticipated teeth-punching, and partly because I am given to understand that you mortals find it more enjoyable to watch other people's misfortunes if you learn a little about them first.

And on the subject of learning a little about people, there is some context surrounding the Caesars which will, over the course of the narrative, prove pertinent. Their mother, Lady Mary, had been born the youngest daughter of the Earl of Elmsley but had defied the conventions of the ton by marrying a freedman of Senegalese birth whom she had met through her work with the abolition. And whereas in the enlightened twenty-first century the marriage of a British aristocrat to a Person of Colour is a wholly unremarkable thing that results in no hostility whatsoever, in the bad old days of the 1800s it caused quite a scandal.

Isn't it wonderful to know how far your species has come?

At any rate, those are the inhabitants of the carriage and this, as best I recall it, was their conversation.

"I was wondering," Miss Bickle—a fair-haired, doe-eyed crea-ture who stubbornly remained an ingenue despite being some way into her nineteenth year—was asking the group at large, "if after the ball is over, or if the ball becomes wearisome, any of you would be interested in reading my *ction*."

"What's a *ction*?" asked Miss Caesar, who, at sixteen years of age, was now formally out in society and thus learning the fine art of pretending to care about things other people cared about. Of all her siblings, she was the one who most favoured her father, her eyes and her complexion both a deep brown that almost glowed in the waning sunlight.

Mr. Caesar—immaculately presented and patrician as ever—gave his sister a warning look. "Please don't encourage her, Mary."

"*Ction*," Miss Bickle explained, ignoring her friend's admoni-tion, "is an abbreviation of *avrection*."

Unable to quite help himself, Mr. Caesar disregarded his own advice and offered the obvious question. "And what is *avrection*?"

"Ah"—Miss Bickle's face lit up—"well, you see, that is itself an abbreviation of *avid reader fiction*. I am an avid reader of the works of the anonymous lady author of *Sense and Sensibility* and I, along with some lady friends, have formed what we call an *avidreaderdom* devoted to the wider anonymousladyauthorverse."

Miss Anne gave a thrilled gasp and tossed her fashionable ring-lets. Though she was by far the youngest in the carriage, her grasp of the mortal art of flattery was greater than any of her compan-ions. "How fascinating."

"I'm not sure I understand," admitted Miss Caesar. "What do you actually do in this . . . this . . ."

"Avidreaderdom," Miss Bickle reminded her. "We meet, and we discuss the works of the anonymous lady author—"

Mr. Caesar, growing increasingly aware that he was the only

gentleman in the carriage and beginning to wonder if this was hampering his ability to follow the conversation, continued to look sceptical. "These works you insist upon calling the *anonymousladyauthorverse*?"

"Yes." Miss Bickle had a fine line in confident nods, and she deployed one of them now.

"You don't think that's a rather silly name?"

Never having considered anything silly in her entire life, and being, I suspect, one of the few mortals who appreciated the etymology of the word, Miss Bickle was unperturbed by the criticism. "Not at all. I think it rather splendid."

The Misses Caesar, to their brother's chagrin, both agreed that it was splendid indeed.

"Although," added Miss Caesar, "I am not entirely certain how this group of yours differs from a literary salon."

"Ah, well," Miss Bickle explained, "we do not only read and discuss the works, we also write our own stories set within the wider anonymousladyauthorverse."

Miss Anne clapped her dainty hands. "Oh, how marvellous."

"Is it, in fact, marvellous?" asked Mr. Caesar. "Is it not, in fact, a slightly peculiar thing to do?"

Before Miss Bickle could either deny or embrace the peculiarity of her chosen hobby, Miss Caesar was leaning forward with fatally sincere interest and asking, "But what are these stories about?"

"For example," Miss Bickle began with the joy of an enthusiast encouraged to expound upon their area of enthusiasm, "my current *wtiitpobw*"—the look of perplexity on the faces of her audience was enough to make her clarify—"that is, *work that is in the process of being written*, is called *The Heir and the Wastrel*, and it concerns events that I imagine occurring between Mr. Wickham and Mr. Darcy in their youth."

"What sort of events?" prompted Miss Anne, with an innocence that caused her brother to chime in immediately with "Do remember that Anne is fourteen."

Miss Bickle, who had indeed overlooked the lady's age, opened her mouth, closed it again, and then said somewhat demurely: "Japes."

"And would I be able to join your avidreaderdom?" asked Miss Caesar. "I have read all of the anonymous lady author's works and might like to try my hand at writing avrections."

"Oh, that would be lovely." Miss Bickle beamed. "At the moment it's just me and Miss Penworthy."

"I *really* don't think you should be encouraging Miss Penworthy's attention," warned Mr. Caesar. "She may take it in ways you don't intend."

With casual bonhomie, Miss Bickle gave Mr. Caesar a pat on the arm. "Don't worry, we've established the parameters of our friendship very thoroughly."

A suspicion crept into Mr. Caesar's mind, and quite without any mystical influence on my part. "*How* thoroughly?"

"Very thoroughly. Exhaustively, really. Miss Penworthy can be very detail-oriented."

To Mr. Caesar's relief, the fates decreed that he would not need to pursue this line of enquiry any further, as they had arrived at their destination, the temporary London residence of Alexandre, Vicomte de Loux.

While Mr. Caesar and his lady companions disembarked, I took the shape of a sparrow and flew out into the night.

And there, in the sky, I saw a star fall.

When the vicomte had started arranging this particular ball, it had been a simple enough matter. Although he was of West Indian heritage, and that put him on the outs with certain parts of the ton no matter what he did, he was also rich and Parisian, and in the early months of 1815 all things rich and Parisian had been much sought-after.

Then Napoleon had escaped from Elba and begun his march on the capital. Which meant that the French, in the eyes of the ambitious mamas of London society, transformed overnight from the people who made the fashionable hats to the people who were trying to shoot their sons dead with muskets.

His solution to this problem had been to issue hasty invitations to as many British military officers as possible. The hope being that a sea of red coats in the ballroom would signal to his guests that he remained on the side of monarchy, serfdom, and the sceptred isle, rather than the side of liberty, equality, and subjugating Europe.

And this seemed to have worked. Because wealthy people very seldom need much excuse to take advantage of free food.

The overrepresentation of military gentlemen inspired a response of unalloyed delight from Miss Bickle, who had promised herself that she would be cruelly treated by an ill-reputed officer before she was twenty-two, and the Misses Caesar, whose plans were not quite so specific but who made up for it with the nebulous passion of youth. It inspired a response of slightly more alloyed delight from Mr. Caesar, who had a partiality to military gentlemen himself but who needed to be a little more cautious in approaching them.

Not that approaching soldiers was part of his plans for this evening. For all its gaiety, this event—like any event now his sister was of age—had a serious purpose. Mary was formally on the marriage mart and while there was no *rush* exactly—sixteen was young to marry even for that time and set—Mr. Caesar knew that years had a way of getting away from one. He was himself already in his early twenties and while gentlemen were afforded rather more latitude in these matters than ladies, he had lately begun to wonder if he would ever truly find a permanent place in the world. The bar did not suit him, and was no career for a gentleman, but his mother's inheritance and his father's speaking fees would not last the family forever. At nineteen he had assumed it would all be sorted out by now, and it most certainly was not.

Still, he endeavoured to do what he could for his sisters. In a better world, it would not have been a concern. In a better world, every lady would have the same luxury as Miss Bickle, who stood to inherit wealth so vast that her only matrimonial concern was avoiding fortune hunters. Or as his cousin Miss Mitchelmore, who had been lucky enough to fall in love with a woman of independent means. But in the world as it actually existed, people needed to eat, and that meant securing an income. And for ladies, the only acceptable way to secure an income was to marry it.

While Mr. Caesar was musing on his life's many imperfections, one of the thornier ones appeared just over his left shoulder. That imperfection was Mr. Thomas Ellersley, who the wags of the ton quite correctly whispered that Mr. Caesar had once fucked, and slightly less correctly whispered that he was still fucking.

"I swear," Mr. Ellersley purred, "you look worse every time I see you."

It was a barb on principle, but Mr. Caesar did privately feel that he'd been letting his personal grooming slide a little of late, so it stung more than it should. "Really? You look better every time I see you. But then you're usually further away."

"Quite the selection, isn't it?" observed Mr. Ellersley, perusing the crowd with one hand resting languidly and a little possessively on Mr. Caesar's back. "Who do you fancy?"

Having been scanning the room more for net worth than for rough trade, Mr. Caesar was quite without opinion. "Tonight, nobody."

"Fuck me, John, when did you get so dull?" I shall say that in our limited interactions I never especially liked Mr. Ellersley, but in this moment we shared something of a bond.

By way of answer, Mr. Caesar tilted his head towards his sisters, who were standing a little way off with Miss Bickle.

"Oh, come *on*, John"—Mr. Ellersley hooked a playful finger into the collar of Mr. Caesar's coat, the play of the nail down his neck awakening the ghosts of old passions—"why don't we give this place the slip? The girls will be fine."

It said terrible things, Mr. Caesar reflected, about the state of his soul that he found the offer mildly tempting. The choice was between duty to his family and the company of a man he disliked. To his father, he had no doubt, it would not have been a choice at all. But Mr. Caesar was not his father. He was not wholly sure who he *was*, but he knew he was not that. Still, appearances had to be maintained, so he turned his head just far enough that he could see Mr. Ellersley in his peripheral vision and, when he was sure he had the man's attention and that his profile was displayed to exactly the right advantage, raised an eyebrow.

"They'll be *fine*," Mr. Ellersley repeated. "In this . . . room full of soldiers. With . . . only Lysistrata Bickle to look after them." He flushed a little. He'd always flushed readily, Mr. Caesar recalled. "Actually I do see your point. Probably best we stick around."

A youth in a red coat sauntered over to the trio of ladies and led Miss Anne away to dance. Although her gown was a little out of fashion and her youth was very notable, she made a fine figure on the dance floor. She was delicate of feature and graceful in motion, and eyes turned to her quite naturally.

Soon enough that dance ended, and the cycle began again. Two gentlemen this time, one for Miss Anne, one for Miss Bickle. Not wishing to leave Miss Caesar wholly alone, Mr. Caesar went to her side, Mr. Ellersley following him like a spiteful shadow.

"Am I invisible?" Miss Caesar asked, and Mr. Caesar suspected she wasn't really asking *him* specifically, but he felt compelled to answer anyway.

"Gentlemen can be boors," he said. It was the kindest answer he could think of. Certainly it was kinder than telling her that the issue was not invisibility but its opposite. Miss Caesar was of a height with her younger sister, but fuller figured and broader featured. She had a beauty of her own, but in an English ballroom at the height of the Empire, her hair twisted into a style it would not hold and her gown cut for a fashion she did not fit, she was sunlight behind clouds, the sky through a narrow window.

"If I dance at all tonight," Miss Caesar continued, "it will be with some elderly gentleman who takes pity on me. And I do not want to be pitied."

Mr. Ellersley gave a soft chuckle. "A pity-dance is better than no *dance* at all."

"Oh, shut up, Tom," Mr. Caesar snapped, then immediately regretted the lapse in composure. In the great game of who-can-be-more-artfully-cruel-to-whom which Mr. Caesar had been playing with the ton his whole life, to rise was to lose.

While Miss Anne and Miss Bickle danced, Mr. Caesar glanced across the ballroom to see another of the world's great imperfections slinking into view.

Richard, Lord Hale, was his maternal uncle and failed to be the bane of his life only by virtue of his persistent absence from it. The Baron Hale had long felt that his sisters' marriages—Lady Mary's in particular—had brought shame on the family and took every opportunity to vex his nieces and nephew. He approached now in the company of an older man in military dress. A major by his insignias, a drinker by his complexion, an arse by his company. They were both, I was sure, the worst kinds of mortal, but the worst kinds of mortal so often make the best kind of sport, and so I watched their arrival with a keen anticipation.

"Uncle Richard." Mr. Caesar inclined his head the exact minimum distance required for the gesture to be considered not completely disrespectful.

"John." Lord Hale made a similarly minimalist gesture. "May I introduce Major Bloodworth; Major Bloodworth, this is my nephew Mr. Caesar, his"—the pause was so pointed you could strap it to a rifle and call it a bayonet—"*friend* Mr. Ellersley, and my niece Miss Caesar."

Mr. Ellersley and the Caesars made the obligatory *delighteds*.

"Capital," declared Major Bloodworth. Then he added: "That's the wonderful thing about the vicomte's events, isn't it? They always attract such a *colourful* crowd."

Like Mr. Ellersley, the major had opened with a barb. Unlike Mr. Ellersley, he had chosen one without the softening grace of mutuality. One that, if challenged, he would most certainly deny. And one that, bitterest of all, was as directed at Miss Caesar as much as her brother. Cold experience had taught Mr. Caesar that the best thing to do was to ignore it, and in this instance, he chose to do the best thing. "Don't they?"

"He's even invited Wellington's favourite," added Lord Hale, nodding across the dance floor. There was a definite sneer attached to the word *favourite*.

The subject of the nod and the sneer was a singular figure and, to Mr. Caesar, an immediately arresting one. Firm-jawed, dark-skinned and with just the right note of dashing, the stranger moved through the crowd with the confident disinterest of a man who cared more for battlefields than ballrooms. For a moment, Mr. Caesar found it hard to tear his gaze away.

Black men were not unknown, or even uncommon, in the British army—the Empire was, after all, an empire and its soldiers came from all corners of it—but in a system where commissions were almost always bought rather than earned it was rare for one to rise to the rank of captain. Rarer still for him to attend a ball with the gentry.

"*Captain Orestes James,*" observed Mr. Ellersley, whose interest in military matters was keen if highly specific. "They say he saved Wellesley's life at Talavera."

Major Bloodworth was unimpressed. "They *say* a lot of things. Never believe soldiers' talk."

While Mr. Caesar would, begrudgingly, admit that enlisted men were not always the most truthful of individuals, looking at the captain he found himself well able to imagine Captain James riding to the rescue of a duke. And for a moment at least it was a pleasing thing to imagine: a tall man on horseback, hands rough from swordplay, arms warrior-strong, eyes deep and soulful and . . .

This was not, he reminded himself, the time for daydreaming. There were appearances to maintain, and while he knew rationally that the ton could not read his mind, it often *behaved* as if it could. Besides, the dance was finishing, the couples were returning to their places, and he needed once more to play the stern elder brother. Miss Bickle and Miss Anne both came back to the little group, though it was merely a matter of moments before another suitor was sweeping in to carry Miss Anne away again.

"Shaping up into a regular Cleopatra, isn't she?" said Lord Hale, archly.

"Yes," mused the major. "Shame about the other one."

Now Miss Bickle was back, Miss Caesar was at least mildly distracted. Still, Mr. Caesar stiffened. "And what do you mean by that?"

Major Bloodworth smiled. "Well, she's rather like Her Majesty, isn't she?"

"I'm sorry." Mr. Caesar feigned obliviousness. "Are you insulting the queen, or my sister?"

Like many men of his class and habits, the major had an unoriginally cruel laugh. "Both, I think. They share the same Mulat—"

He got no further. Because this, oh patient reader, is the point at which Mr. Caesar punched a man in the teeth.

The punching went poorly. Mr. Caesar was no pugilist, and soon learned the hard way that human teeth are sharp, human wrists fragile, and human sensibilities dull.

All of which combined to see him, two minutes later, nursing a sprained hand and bleeding knuckles, being escorted into the Mayfair night by the vicomte. I followed in the shape of a mouse.

"I understand he was provoking, Jean"—the vicomte always insisted on using the Frenchified pronunciation, despite having otherwise perfect English—"but you made me look bad." He paused, staring at the floor a moment in a manner rather uncharacteristic of the mortal aristocracy. "You made us *all* look bad."

"Us all?" asked Mr. Caesar.

"You know what I mean."

He knew. As, reader, I presume do you. But he did not like it. "There isn't a man in that room who would have stood by and let his sister be insulted."

" 'I do confess the vices of my blood.' "

Mr. Caesar took the allusion to the so-called bard even more harshly than I normally do. "Oh, fuck off, Alexandre. I'm not Othello."

"To people like the major and your uncle," replied the vicomte, "we are each of us Othello."

Being a man of temperate character, the thought of being considered intemperate by a society that would not look past his birth inspired in Mr. Caesar ironically intemperate emotions. "And you're taking their side."

"I am taking the ton's side. Your English manners are quite strict on this issue."

With a more-English-than-the-English-will-admit exclamation of "Fuck," Mr. Caesar sat himself awkwardly on a low wall.

"Take a moment if you need it," offered the vicomte with Gallic generosity. "But then *leave*. We cannot be associated for a while."

What stung the most was how unexpected it wasn't. The vicomte, being the son of a Frenchman and a woman of the gens de couleur libres and thus, by English standards, suspect on both sides of his family, had his own concerns. And in the world of the ton, solidarity was in short supply; the gossips smelled weakness and struck without mercy.

Still, Mr. Caesar had his duties to think about. "And my sisters?"

The vicomte gave him a gentle nod. "I shall see they are safe. This is a shitty business, Jean, but I don't think anybody wants it to harm the ladies."

Personally, I doubted the truth of that. While I, despite my avowed love of cruelty, thought the Misses Caesar would make poor sport, I suspected that there were those still at the ball who absolutely did wish them ill. Of one sort or another.

"Thank you," said Mr. Caesar, though he was not feeling especially thankful. He and the vicomte were not exactly *friends*, despite
the superficial similarities in their heritage, and the man outranked
him. Still, he could not help but feel a little thrown under the
carriage.

Having been too long absent from his own ball, the vicomte
gave a rather stiff bow and went back to it, leaving Mr. Caesar
alone in the night. And bad things happen to those left alone in the
night. Especially when the *those* in question have recently offended
a rich man who kills for a living.

The March air was chill but the sky was clear, and for a few
minutes Mr. Caesar stared—as that self-aggrandising shit Oscar
would a near century later—at the stars and wondered quite how
badly he had fucked everything up for his family. His parents, distracted as they perennially were by their good works, had never
placed him under any especial pressure, but the stark reality of
their situation meant that *somebody* had to make certain that neither
he nor his sisters would starve in the wider world. Although why he
thought *he* of all people was best suited to that particular duty I
have no idea. And just as I was pondering this example of mortal
hubris, I was distracted by the annoyingly loud voice of an annoyingly loud human.

"On your feet."

Looking around, Mr. Caesar saw—to his fleeting satisfaction—
that the major was still nursing a split lip. "I'd rather sit, thank
you."

"On your feet," Major Bloodworth repeated. "Scoundrel."

There was, Mr. Caesar knew, no real point in defiance. But in
that moment he, like I, felt that pointless defiance had a charm of
its own. "I'd rather sit, thank you."

From the shadow of a nearby coach, two large men emerged.

They were not, to my expert eye, professional ruffians, but height and weight can make up for all manner of deficiencies in other areas.

"Make him stand," commanded the major, and the larger of the two large men stooped to haul Mr. Caesar up by his collar.

And I was just shifting my shape to something more airborne, in order that I might watch proceedings from a better vantage, when from the direction of the townhouse, a low, London voice asked: "Is there a problem?"

CHAPTER TWO

THE VOICE, AS I AM sure perspicacious readers have already surmised, belonged to Captain James. And never, in a long career of being rather glad to see members of His Majesty's army, had Mr. Caesar been so glad to see a member of His Majesty's army. Although admittedly, present circumstances took something of the shine off of his earlier fantasies of rescue.

"This is no concern of yours, James," spat the major. "Run back to your band of misfits."

Captain James looked from the major to Mr. Caesar, to the men, and back to the major. "No."

"Why, you insolent—Bailey, Roberts, deal with this reprobate. Then we'll get back to business."

There was something about the way Captain James stepped forwards that, to Mr. Caesar, read as a warning and, to me, read as a threat. There is a certain way of moving, you see, a certain mix of grace and confidence that is found only in a certain kind of person. Heracles had it, and Theseus. And several other over-rated pricks. This, his movements said, was a man who could slay dragons. Not that there are any of those left to be slain anymore. Possibly because people kept slaying them.

Bailey and Roberts, for the moment, unhanded Mr. Caesar and turned their attention to the captain. Turned, but did not advance.

"What are you waiting for?" demanded the major. "Thrash him."

Ignoring the commentary, the captain looked to the taller of the men. "Bailey?" he asked. "It's not Jim Bailey, is it?"

"That's me," said Jim Bailey.

"I know your sister. Good woman, does laundry off Tower Street."

Jim Bailey hesitated.

"Not sure how she'd feel about you laying hands on gentlemen and officers," the captain went on.

"Man's got to work," replied Jim Bailey, sounding genuinely apologetic. And he was right—it's by far my least favourite feature of the mortal world.

"True that," the captain said. "Well, when next you see her, tell her I'm sorry I had to do this."

Before Jim Bailey could ask what, precisely, the captain was sorry he had to do, the captain had done it. He crossed the distance between them so fast that the major was still exhorting his men to start fighting several seconds after the fight had already begun.

I am not, as longtime readers will already know, an expert in matters of violence. But even I will admit that the captain had a wonderful poetry to his actions. His initial strike against Bailey had been a precise kick to the mark, which put the man down long enough that he could focus for crucial moments on Roberts, who came swinging wildly only to find his blow caught and answered with a sharp jab to the throat.

With his job on the line, Jim Bailey came back to the fight with what I personally considered a commendable lack of enthusiasm. Putting his head down, he threw himself into a half-hearted tackle that the captain sidestepped, jerking a knee into the man's ribs as he passed.

With the largely innocent working gentlemen dispatched, or at least severely incommoded, Captain James turned his attention to the major and said: "Try your luck?"

"Certainly not," Major Bloodworth blustered. "An officer, a *real* officer, does not stoop to brawling."

Straightening his shirt, Mr. Caesar regained at least some of his composure. "You mean he gets others to brawl for him?"

While it had been intended as a slight, the major didn't take it as one. "What do you think war is, you pampered fop?"

Mr. Caesar would admit to *fop*—indeed he rather relished the descriptor—but he had never been pampered. "A place where bold men give their lives so small men can make their reputations?"

Apparently being as unsuited to words as he was to actions, the major stood staring at Mr. Caesar and Captain James, occasionally glancing to his servants in the hope that they would be inspired to new violence on his behalf. They were not.

"I have friends at court," he warned, apparently deciding that threats were always de rigueur. "You will regret this. Both of you. By God, sir"—he directed his ire now solely towards the captain—"I'll have your commission and then your hide."

When neither Captain James nor Mr. Caesar rose to the provocation, the major huffed out one last "Good day to you" and, Bailey and Roberts hobbling in his wake, clambered into his carriage and left.

The immediate danger having passed, Mr. Caesar experienced that sudden enervation which biological creatures are prone to as adrenaline abates. All at once unsteady on his feet, he sat back down rather heavily.

"You all right?" asked Captain James.

Mr. Caesar looked up at the man he didn't quite want to call his saviour although he had, strictly speaking, saved him. In any light, and from any angle, he cut a remarkable figure, the clean military lines of his infantryman's jacket at odds with a slightly unshaven jaw and eyes that said he'd seen mirth and sorrow in equal measure. Realising that he was taking far too long to answer a simple question, Mr. Caesar stumbled into a "Sorry, what, yes."

"And your sister?"

The part of Mr. Caesar that expected everything to be a slight or a feint wanted to reply with something sharp. A *has had her fill of soldiers, I suspect* or similar. But it was late, and now the shock of the fight was wearing off he was realising how tired he was. So he tried honesty. "I don't know. I'd have checked on her but Alexandre— the vicomte—wanted me out and it would have been gauche to refuse him."

"I could go back if you like, do it for you?"

Fond as he was of military men, Mr. Caesar was beginning to grow suspicious. "You seem very keen to help me."

That earned a smile. And Captain James's smile was wide, sincere, and knowing. "There's not a lad in the regiment wouldn't lamp Bloodworth one if he thought he could get away with it. That's worth a couple of good turns."

"Insults a lot of men's sisters, does he?" asked Mr. Caesar.

"Gets a lot of men killed."

Not normally one to be back-footed, Mr. Caesar found himself without an answer. Present circumstances excepted, his experience of physical danger was strictly limited to the occasional visit to a gaming hell and that one time he'd helped his cousin confront a murderously enraged goddess. "Perhaps I should have hit him harder."

"Nah." Captain James looked down at Mr. Caesar's hand, still bloody around the knuckles. "You'd have broke your hand. Keep your wrist straight next time."

"I'm hoping there won't *be* a next time."

A faintly rueful smile flickered across Captain James's face. "You don't know Major Bloodworth."

"Nor do I care to."

"Must be nice to have the choice," replied the captain, and there was the rue again. "Now, you just sit tight and I'll check on the ladies."

All in all it was, for Mr. Caesar, a bit of a personal low point. He had gone from defending his sister's honour to sitting on a wall while a man he'd just met—and a military man at that, so to be trusted only in a very narrow set of circumstances—checked on her actual well-being. And tempted as I was to lurk nearby and watch a man in a now rather disarranged cravat wallowing in self-pity, I elected instead to follow the captain inside. There was unlikely to be more violence that evening, but I hoped that I might at least hear some choice insults.

I did not hear any choice insults. But I got to see a young woman cry, and I take my victories where I may.

Miss Caesar was sobbing in Miss Bickle's arms, while the vicomte stood a little way off doing his best to refocus his guests' attention on less diverting matters. Miss Anne, meanwhile, was watching proceedings with the petulant expression of a young girl who sees no reason why somebody else's hurt feelings or bruised face should ruin her evening.

Despite the vicomte's best efforts, a small crowd was gathering. As desultory as the fight had been, it was still an order of magnitude more entertaining than a band of old toffs dancing a reel.

"I say," a redheaded fellow named Fillimore was observing, "this has been quite a scene."

"How perceptive of you," replied Miss Penworthy, who had come to discuss the works of the anonymous lady author with Miss Bickle and encountered far more excitement than she had bargained for. "Perhaps you should add that this sort of thing seldom happens."

"Well, it does not," Fillimore agreed. "I've never seen such a sight in all my days."

Lord Hale smiled a grim smile. "It's what comes of letting in the wrong sort."

"Perhaps we should let in more of the wrong sort," another guest suggested over the top of her fan. "It enlivens the evening."

This suggestion went over poorly with the rest of the gawpers. "On behalf of my sex," said an older man with wispy hair and a mild stoop, "I can safely say we'd prefer to all go home with our jaws unstruck."

A little apart from the throng, a young officer—barely more than a child to my eyes, although being ageless and caring little for the life cycles of biological organisms I find these things hard to judge—was attempting to console Miss Anne as much as a gentleman could while remaining within the bounds of propriety. "Rest assured, miss," he told her, "that no gentleman of good character will hold these events against you."

That nobody, gentleman or otherwise, of good character or ill, offered similar reassurance to anybody else was not lost on Miss

Bickle, Miss Caesar, or the newly returned Captain James, who pushed his way towards the front of the group with a relentless mission-focus that did as well for the social battlefield as the more literal one.

"You all right, miss?" he asked Miss Caesar and then, when she proved incapable of providing a coherent answer, looked to Miss Bickle and asked, "She all right?"

Miss Bickle gave a reassuring nod. "She will be. It's just all been rather beastly."

Still not especially coherent, Miss Caesar burbled something to the effect that she agreed with this characterisation.

"Your brother's outside," Captain James explained. "He wants to know if you're well, and to be told if you're staying."

Raising her head a fraction from Miss Bickle's bosom, Miss Caesar looked around, her eyes blotched red with tears. "Stay? How can we stay after such mortification?"

"How can we leave?" Miss Anne protested, and then, turning soulful eyes to the young officer, added, "We shan't leave, I promise."

Miss Bickle looked uncertain. For a lady who lived in a world of rainbows and fairy dust, navigating so prosaic a dilemma as two young women with opposed preferences was quite discomforting. "I wonder if we might not be better off going. It has been a perfectly lovely evening of course but, well, Mary is clearly distressed and—"

Having decided, probably correctly, that his ball would be a complete disaster if he didn't do something about the crying girl in the corner, the vicomte waltzed into view. "Ladies," he began in his most charmingly Gallic tones, "I can see you have had a distressing night, pray let me give you the use of my carriage to return you *home*."

The word of the host, being also the word of a vicomte or its continental equivalent, rather settled the issue, and the Misses Caesar, along with their accidental, Bickle-shaped chaperone, left with as little ceremony as could be managed given the highly ceremonial nature of the circles in which they moved.

Outside, Mr. Caesar was still waiting on the wall, and when his friend, family, and unexpected military benefactor emerged from the house, he rose hastily to greet them.

It was not, in the end, a warm greeting. Both of his sisters were, in their different ways, indignant at his role in their evening's premature end, and while Miss Bickle was more inclined to give him the benefit of the doubt, her peacemaking skills were rather limited.

"How *could* you?" Miss Caesar demanded, once she'd recovered enough to form sentences.

Doing his best to remain brotherly, Mr. Caesar looked down. "The gentleman was speaking impertinently."

"So you *hit him*?" Miss Caesar seemed about to burst once more into tears. "Well, I hope your honour was worth it."

Miss Bickle, who had heard a little more of the exchange and the subsequent discussion of it amongst the guests, did her best to come to her friend's defence. "I'm sure John had his reasons."

"*What* reasons?" asked Miss Anne, who, like her sister, had remained largely ignorant of the cause of the disturbance.

"Good reasons." That was Captain James, who had thus far been standing quietly at the back of the group. "I know the man he hit, and I've no doubt he deserved it."

The appearance of Captain James presented something of a problem for the young ladies. On the one hand, his voice made it very clear that he was no gentleman, but on the other, a red jacket *was* a red jacket and thus worthy of respect.

"What did he do?" asked Miss Anne, ever the first to play up to an officer.

There had never been an *explicit* agreement in the Caesar household that the girls should be shielded from the harsher parts of their world. But ladies were expected to be innocent, and as the elder brother, Mr. Caesar felt a strong need to preserve that innocence. So he said simply: "He spoke ill of the queen."

That, at least, his sisters could accept as a valid reason to strike a man, although both remained disgruntled that he had not thought to make this clearer at the time. Still it meant that they consented to return to the carriage and to be escorted home without further fuss. And Mr. Caesar, with aristocratic reserve, formally thanked Captain James for his assistance. For a moment they made quite the picture between them, the soldier and the gentleman. Captain James stood tall and proud and just a little wary, watching the Caesars load themselves into the carriage with eyes full of life and fire. And a scant three feet away Mr. Caesar stood ramrod straight, his courteous façade brittle as glass as he made polite reassurances that should the captain need the favour returned he need only ask.

It was not an offer he expected would be taken up, but he would prove wrong about that. As he would about so much else.

CHAPTER THREE

I SWEAR THAT I ONLY TURNED my back for five minutes and when I looked again Mr. Caesar was standing on the doorstep of Mr. Ellersley's London residence. Although if I was perturbed by this turn of events, I suspect that Mr. Caesar was even more so. He had, of course, no fit subject for his disappointment save himself, but that was perhaps part of why he had come in the first place. Having marred not only one of the few social events at which his sisters would be welcome but quite possibly their long-term prospects of a successful marriage, home was not especially appealing to him. And he knew where he *was* with Thomas Ellersley. Even if it wasn't anywhere he wanted to be.

It was an unfashionable hour—indeed an unseemly hour—to be calling but Mr. Ellersley, while always fashionable, was never seemly, and was taking brandy in the drawing room when Mr. Caesar was shown up to him.

"Well," he said, as Mr. Caesar lowered himself into an armchair, "that was a fucking mess."

Mr. Caesar poured himself a drink. "By God, I've missed your wit."

"Not half so much as I've missed your carefree demeanour. Though frankly, John, I swear you've deteriorated."

Frankly, Mr. Caesar agreed with him. In some respects, at least. "Perhaps I've acquired more cares. Between an angry goddess nearly killing my cousin and my sisters fast approaching marriageable age I have a great deal to think about."

"Isn't your sisters' future more your parents' concern?"

That raised something like a laugh. "My father has no connections, my mother burned her ties to society when she married, and my grandfather is less and less often in London."

"Still"—Mr. Ellersley swirled the brandy in his glass like a witch mixing a potion—"the old man won't let them starve, will he?"

The old man, in this context, was Mr. Caesar's grandfather, the Earl of Elmsley. A forgettable enough mortal, but a wealthy one. "He won't," Mr. Caesar agreed, "but Uncle Richard most certainly will, and Grandpapa won't be around forever."

Mr. Ellersley drained his glass and poured himself another. "You poor thing. The weight of the world truly does rest on your slender shoulders, doesn't it?"

"Oh, fuck off."

"No, no, I'm serious. I *deeply* sympathise." He did not sound like he deeply sympathised. He sounded like he found the whole subject loathsome, a position with which I sympathised myself. "Although I will say that given your doubtlessly heavy burdens you should *maybe* avoid running around smacking the gentry in the face."

Mr. Caesar didn't know what was worse. That Mr. Ellersley was an arse, or that he was in this instance a correct arse.

"Still," Mr. Ellersley went on, "it got the attention of Captain James, so there is *some* upside."

"I have no idea what you mean," lied Mr. Caesar.

"Oh, come off it, you love a soldier as much as I do and Orestes James is the *pinnacle* of British soldiery. All the dash of an officer, all the grime of the ranks, what's not to like?"

A scowl came unbidden to Mr. Caesar's face. He was used to Mr. Ellersley talking like this, of course. Once he'd even encouraged it, but for some reason this time it landed differently. "He helped me when he didn't have to. I'll thank you not to speak so wantonly of him."

Mr. Ellersley made a hollow sound that could have passed in a bad light for a laugh. "Gods and powers, John, you really have stopped being fun, haven't you? The man is a soldier; we must have fucked a hundred each and scratch the surface they're all the same. Drunken lackwits who'll suck every cock in the room if you throw them a guinea for a new jacket."

"Remind me why I thought I liked you again?" asked Mr. Caesar, genuinely uncertain.

Setting his glass down, Mr. Ellersley rose, sauntered behind Mr. Caesar, and began to massage his shoulders. "Because, Johnny, my lad, you and I are birds of a feather. You can pretend all you like but deep down you're a catty little Ganymede who hates the world, just like I am." He paused. "Also I have a truly gigantic member and you are *profoundly* shallow."

The latter point, Mr. Caesar was forced to concede. Out of his multitudinous memories of Mr. Ellersley, by far the fondest were at least member-adjacent. "I should probably go home," he told his glass of brandy. In truth he should never have come, and he tried to pretend that he wasn't sure why he had. Except he was, he just didn't like the reason.

"You should," Mr. Ellersley agreed. "But I strongly suspect that you won't."

And then he leaned around Mr. Caesar's chair and kissed him.

I left the gentlemen their privacy—I say *privacy;* the ease with which beings like myself can spy on your kind means you should never truly consider yourselves unobserved—but returned to watching over Mr. Caesar and his family the following day. Events of the preceding evening had convinced me that the gentleman's life might be on the edge of becoming interesting, and I was determined not to miss out when it did. Thus I was rather aggrieved when I returned to find him standing, quite politely, in his father's study, waiting for him to finish his correspondence.

Still, I contented myself with the hope that once the elder Mr. Caesar was done writing, they might at least have a heated exchange of words. Much as I enjoy watching mortals harm one another physically, I find emotional damage fully three times as entertaining.

While he waited for his father to be ready, Mr. Caesar found his gaze drawn, as it often was, to the portrait that hung above his father's desk. It depicted a woman who Mr. Caesar had never met, plain-featured but aristocratic and shown—as all aristocratic women were in her day—surrounded by the trappings of her high station. Thus her wrists and neck were adorned with jewels, horses gambolled in the fields behind her, and by her side knelt a young boy. He gazed up adoringly at his mistress, a pearl in his ear standing out brilliant white against his dark skin. It was the only portrait of his father that Mr. Caesar had ever seen.

He kept it, the elder Mr. Caesar had explained, to show that he was not ashamed of where he had come from. It was a boldness that his children admired on good days and resented on bad ones.

"John," the elder Mr. Caesar said at last, leaning back in his chair, "I hear you were involved in an . . . altercation last night."

Mr. Caesar nodded. "I struck a man."

"That isn't like you."

"I know."

Silence fell between them and I began to feel terribly afraid that they might continue in this nothingish back-and-forth for the rest of the encounter.

"He insulted Mary," Mr. Caesar added, hoping in vain that he would be asked to elaborate no further.

From the look on his father's face, that was still no excuse for violence. "You told your sisters that he insulted the queen."

"It seemed kinder than the truth. He insulted her by specific reference to . . ."

He did not need to finish the sentence. His father understood and had likely understood for some while. "I assume other people know of that detail?"

"Yes. Uncle Richard was there."

"Ah." The elder Mr. Caesar looked grave. "Keeping the specifics from Mary is probably for the best. She is having troubles enough, I think."

"Are you certain?" Mr. Caesar asked. He understood the impulse to protect his sister from certain harsh facts of the world, but his recent experience had taught him that things you did not understand could still hurt you.

The elder Mr. Caesar regarded his son thoughtfully. "I am never entirely certain, but . . . your mother and I always wanted to give you and your sisters an ordinary life. As much as we can. I would not compromise that thoughtlessly, and for the moment I do not see that Mary needs to know the details of an incident that, if we are fortunate, we will soon be able to put behind us."

Candidly, Mr. Caesar was not certain they *would* be able to put it behind them, especially given what had happened afterwards with the major. And for a moment he tried to decide whether bringing up the tiny matter of an irate military officer instructing his servants to beat him and then swearing nonspecific vengeance was a good idea. He concluded, in the end, that it was. While he had realistic expectations about his father's ability to intercede, they had always been honest with each other. "You should know," he said, "that the man I struck, he—well, he had his servants attack me outside the ball."

It wasn't that the elder Mr. Caesar didn't believe his son, but the facts were rather hard for him to reconcile. "You look remarkably well for it."

"I was . . . rescued?"

"Rescued?"

"By another officer."

That brought the trace of a smile to his father's lips. "Perhaps a knack for attracting mysterious saviours runs in the family."

"He—the first officer—also told me I'd regret crossing him."

The elder Mr. Caesar shrugged. "They usually do."

At this juncture, their conversation was interrupted by a knock at the door. The Caesars had only one servant, a maid of all work by the name of Nancy, who hustled in with a calling card.

"Gentleman downstairs, sir," she explained. "Military."

Having never expected to see Captain James again, Mr. Caesar was surprised, gratified, and not a little flustered as he hurried through to the drawing room to meet their guest. And he was, therefore, wonderfully disappointed when he discovered that it was not the captain at all.

"I've come to give my regards," explained the too-young officer from the previous night, who held the inconsequential rank of ensign, the inconsequential given name of Robert, and the inconsequential surname of Bygrave. "And to reassure you all that nobody in the regiment thinks any ill of you for what transpired last night."

The Misses Caesar looked up as one from their needlework.

"Oh, but you are too kind," replied Miss Anne, which earned a warm smile from the ensign. Possibly because, sitting in her window seat the sunlight slashing lines of brilliant golden-brown across her bare forearms and her curls framing her face like she was a plate in a fashionable periodical, she looked almost angelic. Or at least as angelic as you can look if you aren't a giant wheel of flaming eyes. "Far too kind," echoed Miss Caesar. And this did not earn so warm a smile.

The five members of the Caesar household arranged themselves around the room in a pattern designed to put their guest just the right amount of at his ease.

"And is last night much discussed in the regiment?" asked Lady Mary. Being an earl's daughter, the lady of the house had, despite her marriage, kept her Christian name, her title, and her propensity for pointed questions.

Mr. Bygrave nodded. "Amongst the officers at least. One doesn't fraternise with the enlisted men, so I wouldn't know about them."

"Oh, well"—Miss Anne waved a hand—"they're scarcely of consequence anyway."

The elder Mr. Caesar gave his daughter a disapproving look that she steadfastly ignored, and offered the ensign tea.

Clearly an individual of what the misguided mortals of the day considered impeccable breeding—which is to say that his ancestors had been ruthless enough to acquire wealth and canny enough not to talk about it—Mr. Bygrave settled himself into an armchair and began making meaningless chitchat with the Caesars. Or rather, with Miss Anne Caesar, the others having far less of a hold on his attention.

"Have you been very long in the army?" asked Miss Caesar, in the hope that bringing the conversation around to martial matters might encourage the ensign to spread his attention more equally.

Mr. Bygrave looked almost abashed. "A few months only. My commission came through just after old Boney abdicated so I never got the opportunity. But, well, he's back now and if His Majesty needs me, I—I trust that he shall not find me wanting."

"I am *sure* he will not," declared Miss Anne with an earnestness I found flatly irritating. "You struck me as quite the boldest gentleman at the ball last night, though it seemed unfair to say so in front of the other officers."

His abashment progressed from almost to definite. "You flatter me, Miss Anne. There were many present last night who have done far grander things than I. Though of course I aspire to someday be their equal."

Attempting once more to participate, Miss Caesar asked him what kind of grand things the other officers had done and, when Mr. Bygrave noticed her presence, he deigned to answer.

"Well, Major Bloodworth—the gentleman your brother, ah, that gentleman—he fought with Wellington at Toulouse. And then there's Captain James, of course. Although he's rather . . ."

"Rather what?" asked Mr. Caesar.

Mr. Bygrave shifted uncomfortably. "Don't mistake me. I hear he's a very fine officer in many ways, but, well, he's up from the ranks, you know. You'll notice he didn't dance at all at the ball. Never learned, you see."

"Is dancing," asked the elder Mr. Caesar, "important to leading men in battle?"

"Well, not *directly*," the ensign admitted. "But the men expect that an officer should be, that is, he should be of a certain sort."

Miss Caesar nodded. "Refined," she said.

"Educated," added Miss Anne.

"Rich?" suggested Lady Mary, with a little less sincerity than her daughters.

Mr. Bygrave smiled, not quite realising it was at his own expense. "Precisely."

This era being one of strict social convention, there was a limit to the duration any visitation could reach before it was deemed indecorous, and the refined, educated, rich Mr. Bygrave observed that limit scrupulously. He departed in a haze of pleasantries, avowing his intent to call upon the family again when next he was in the vicinity, which Miss Anne expressed the profound hope would mean "tomorrow."

"Was he not marvellous?" she asked the room in general once Mr. Bygrave was more or less out of earshot. "So genial and dashing and—"

"Well, I found him rather rude," replied Miss Caesar without much real conviction. "I don't see why he showed such favour to Anne when there were four other people present."

"In his defence" the younger Mr. Caesar said, making the subtlest effort he could to turn the conversation in a lighter direction, "I don't think I'd be entirely to his tastes."

Unfortunately the remark did not have its intended effect. Miss Caesar remained disconsolate, and Miss Anne took the opportunity to assert her inalienable right to occupy the ensign's attention.

"It is hardly my fault," she told her sister, "that gentlemen like me more than they like you. They clearly respond to my sweeter temperament."

This was decidedly not what they were responding to, and at least half the room knew it.

"It is not your temperament they admire," Miss Caesar said bluntly. "It is your face. You had the fortune to be born favouring mama. I did not."

A hush fell across the assembly. Miss Anne, if I am any judge (and as the omniscient narrator of the entire book I am), seemed about to break that hush with some indignant observation to the effect that she could not be blamed for her own prettiness, but her mother did not permit it.

"I do not think," Lady Mary said in the gentlest tone she could muster, which, despite her upbringing, was actually quite gentle, "that is necessarily a helpful way to—"

"And what would you know of it?" demanded Miss Caesar. "Gentlemen slight me at balls and in my own home. Dresses hang poorly on me. My hair will not take the fashionable style. My complexion is not fair, my features are not delicate, I dance well enough but I never get the chance to show it because nobody will ask me to dance with them."

Rising from the chair where she had been working on her own needlepoint, Lady Mary went to her daughter's side. "You are beautiful, Mary. Let nobody tell you otherwise."

"Not in the eyes of anybody who matters." Miss Caesar seemed close to weeping. "To the ton I am worse than nothing."

I have said many times that I am a connoisseur of human sorrow, and that watching mortal kind torment themselves is one of my finest pleasures. But even I found this exchange pitiable. More pitiable still was its effect on the elder Mr. Caesar, who sat stoic throughout but found himself unable to comfort his child, and for that matter on the younger Mr. Caesar, who found himself similarly affected but with less talent for stoicism.

Through it all, Miss Caesar proved quite inconsolable, and so at the first opportunity she retired to her room. And there, as the sun set, she sat by her window with tears in her eyes, and watched a star fall.

Miss Anne, in the end, got her wish. Which is suitable, for this is, after all, a story about wishes. Mr. Bygrave returned the next day, and the next, and the next after that. Indeed the sequence of events had become practically routine—Nancy would arrive announcing a military gentleman, Mr. Bygrave would appear, demonstrate his absolute besottedness with Miss Anne, and then he would depart with the impeccable manners of the set to which Lady Mary had been born and to which all three of her children, in their several ways, aspired.

Miss Anne was thus somewhat disappointed on the fourth day when Nancy once again announced a military gentleman at the door and—running downstairs in her best dress as she always did—she was met not by the lovely Mr. Bygrave but by somebody altogether shabbier. She should perhaps have expected that something was amiss when the visitor was announced rather before the fashionable hour and did not send a card, but the whole household had grown so lulled into complacency that it was only when the visitor was admitted that they realised the error.

The new guest was ill-kempt and rough-featured, and although he wore regimental red, he wore it with sufferance. When he spoke, it was with a thick Irish brogue that would have been quite unacceptable in fashionable society.

"Begging your pardon," he said to the elder Mr. Caesar, "I'm Infantryman Callaghan, and I've a message for the young master."

Mr. Caesar, who knew his son's proclivities and considered them nobody's business, fixed the visitor with a stern glare. "If you are here for money . . ."

"Nothing of the sort, sir"—the man seemed genuinely surprised—"I'm here on behalf of the captain, and he doesn't want no money neither, sir. Just, well, helped your son out of a spot of bother he did, and now that's landed him in a spot of bother himself."

"Has Major Bloodworth decided to cause trouble?" The younger Mr. Caesar had been expecting a development like this and dreading it. I, by contrast, had been hoping for it so fervently that had it not happened soon I would have seriously considered *making* it happen. Not that I do such things, of course. I am only an observer.

Callaghan nodded. "He's coming for the captain's commission. Brawling he says he was. Drunk he says he was. And seeing as he did you a turn, the captain thought as maybe you'd speak for him."

"I'm not a military man," the younger Mr. Caesar told him with genuine regret. "I'm not sure what influence I would have."

"And even if he *had* any influence," declared Miss Anne, "perhaps your captain should not have been brawling."

Lady Mary and the elder Mr. Caesar exchanged quiet looks. Neither they nor their son had explained in front of the girls *exactly* what service Captain James had performed for the family, but it should not ideally have been necessary.

"Brawling or not," said Lady Mary, "the captain came to John's aid when aid was required. It would be extremely unworthy of us to abandon him."

"It would be unworthy of us," her husband added, "to abandon anybody in need."

Miss Anne looked chastened and, with the mental flexibility of the very young, turned her position 180 degrees without missing a beat. "At the very least, I may vouch that the man was not drunk. I spoke with him and he appeared quite sober."

"I shall send word to Papa at once," said Lady Mary, "and to my sister. Though I fear time may be against us."

Mr. Caesar tried not to overly interrogate his feelings. That his parents had rallied more decisively in defence of his debt than he had was, if he wanted to be cruel to himself, both typical of them and typical of him. "I believe Maelys and Georgiana are in town also," he tried. "I shall see what they can manage."

"The hearing," Callaghan added, "is rather by way of being this afternoon, so while that all sounds wonderful we'd be exceedingly grateful if you could get a scoot on."

The logistics proved a little fiddly, with Lady Mary and her husband electing to take an emergency run to visit the earl in the hope that they could solicit his assistance personally while Nancy was dispatched with notes for the other members of the family.

As they variously departed I—being incapable, despite my preternatural swiftness, of being in two places at once—was forced to decide who to follow. And for the moment at least I chose none of them, but elected instead to remain at the family home. They had, after all, opted to leave their young daughters unattended, and I held out some hope that one or other of them would involve herself in some kind of mischief before the day was out.

They did not, while I watched. Miss Caesar divided her time between playing on the pianoforte, which she did rather pleasingly, and reading on the settee. Miss Anne took a novel and sat in a window seat, although the book seemed primarily decorative, since she mostly left it open on her knee and bombarded her sister with questions about society matters that Miss Caesar found by turns enthralling and vexatious, depending on their subject matter.

I, meanwhile, roamed the house, looking for things to steal or to break and growing increasingly uneasy.

You may already know—especially if you have ever seen a certain play that a certain mortal flagrantly stole from me some four centuries ago—that my master and his, shall we say, counterpart are locked in an aeons-ancient game of intrigue, recrimination, and rivalry. I should add, of course, that while the origins of this enmity are lost to the mists of time (or our closest analogue for it), my master is absolutely in the right and wholly justified in all of his actions.

Perhaps, then, it was merely paranoia that made me sense the hand of Titania in the way that the shadows shifted in the house, or the patterns that formed in the sunlight through the windows. Or perhaps it wasn't.

And really, would I be mentioning it if it didn't lead *somewhere*?

Once I had convinced myself that my master's hated rival posed no immediate threat to my own plans for the Caesars (such as they were: I should stress that I am purely a passive observer and would never, ever, under any circumstances interfere with the unfolding of events for my own benefit), I flew in the shape of a swallow across London. I had been relatively confident in my own ability to track Mr. Caesar even if he did not go to the place I expected, but my hunter's skills did not, in the end, need to be tested. The hearing was taking place, as military matters often did, at the Mithraeum in Walbrook.

This ancient complex had been founded nearly two millennia earlier by a cult within the then Roman army and had expanded down the centuries as generations of legionaries, mercenaries, knights, dragoons, and infantrymen had added to it little shrines and icons devoted to whichever deity they most favoured or wished to propitiate. So it contained now busts of Minerva, statues of Bacchus, rune stones to Odin, and even a small alcove dedicated to Christian saints, although ancient pacts prevented those entities from intervening in the world as directly as the old gods could.

In recent years, as the British army had grown more structured and more organised, the Mithraeum had become a somewhat more formalised space, its corridors painted bright white and portraits of kings and generals hung in any space that wasn't already being used for the veneration of less worldly idols. Some of the less popular deities had—to their largely impotent chagrin—found their temples and offering-spaces relocated to make room for offices and antechambers.

It was in one such room that Captain James now waited, and had been waiting for some hours, impatiently aware that his future depended on decisions made by men who thought nothing of him. And it was into this room that Mr. Caesar appeared, hurried and flustered.

There was, even he could not quite keep himself from admitting, a certain pleasure to seeing the captain again. Although in ideal circumstances their reunion would have involved rather more swashbuckling romance and rather less bureaucracy. Still, even an ill-advised night with the execrable Mr. Ellersley hadn't quite been enough to shake the memory of their first meeting from his mind and so it was with a certain timidity that Mr. Caesar approached the captain and nodded a greeting.

"Wasn't sure you'd come," said the captain, without rising.

"I said I would assist you if you needed me," Mr. Caesar replied, a little stiffly.

"Didn't mean you'd do it."

Mr. Caesar looked almost offended. "Sir, whatever else I may be, I am a gentleman."

"I know," replied the captain. "That's why I wasn't sure you'd come."

That was, in Mr. Caesar's experience, a fair assessment. He'd known far too many gentlemen who weren't, so he understood why a man might hold the term to little account. For his own part, he had always taken pride in being a better gentleman than better gentlemen were. This, in his estimation and my own, was an extraordinarily low bar but still one Mr. Caesar failed to clear with alarming regularity.

Since the army moved on its own time, the two men had ample opportunity to become reacquainted while whoever was in charge of proceedings did whatever they needed to do on the other side of the door. They sat side by side on a low green bench that seemed to have been designed explicitly for discomfort. A portrait of George II and a statue of Mars loomed over them from opposite sides of the room, but neither made for a light conversational companion.

"Thank you," Mr. Caesar offered. "Again. You didn't have to look out for me."

Captain James shrugged with one shoulder. "Yeah, I did. That's what you do. Man needs a beating, you beat him. Man doesn't need a beating, you stop him being beaten."

By the standards Mr. Caesar was accustomed to, it was an almost naïve principle to live by. In his own world, if a man needed a beating, you quietly put it about that he needed a beating, and if he didn't you put it about slightly more loudly, because you suspected he was saying the same about you. "Still, you put yourself in danger for me."

Despite the real peril hanging over him, Captain James laughed. "That wasn't danger, that was two servants not being paid near enough to fight a man who knows how."

"You risked your commission as well."

"I risk my commission by existing. Men like Bloodworth think I'm a threat to the army."

Though he didn't want to, Mr. Caesar felt a twinge of recognition in that. A shared knowledge of being part of something that resented him. "Even so, it was the least I could do to return the favour."

It seemed like an age had passed, and perhaps it had, for they were alone in a sparsely decorated room with little to mark the passage of time. But eventually, the door to the nearby office opened and an ancillary called them both through to the hearing.

There were three men in the room, and Mr. Caesar's heart sank as he realised he recognised all of them. One—a greying man in the uniform of a major-general—might have been a slight comfort. Mr. Caeser recognised him as Lord Hawksmoor and, although they were barely acquainted, he understood the man to be a friend of his grandfather. The other two, however, were less comforting. Major Bloodworth and Lord Hale, who familial propriety still required that Mr. Caesar address as *Uncle Richard*.

"Ah," began Lord Hawksmoor as though he hadn't been quite sure who he was expecting, "James."

"My lord." The captain bowed his head in a gesture of what seemed to be sincere respect.

"My *lord*," Major Bloodworth interrupted, in a tone that read as rather less respectful. "This reprobate was caught not four nights past brawling in the street with common servants. He is a disgrace to his country, his uniform, and his king."

Lord Hawksmoor turned his hooded eyes to Captain James. "Is this true?"

"Not a word of it, sir," the captain replied, a little overzealously from my perspective, but then my understanding of truth is rather more refined than that of mortals.

A pretriumphal gleam appeared in Lord Hale's eye. "You deny that there was a fight."

"I deny brawling, my lord. I encountered a gentleman who was being accosted by two ruffians, and I fought them off."

"And by *gentleman*," Lord Hale clarified, "you mean Mr. Caesar here."

"My grandfather is an earl," replied Mr. Caesar firmly. "And my uncle is a baron. I believe that makes me a gentleman."

Lord Hale, never original in his facial expressions, sneered. "And who is your father?"

This was an old point of contention within the family, and by this stage the Caesars had a standard response to it. "The best man my mother ever knew."

To Lord Hawksmoor, this all seemed to be drifting a little off topic. "But you *were* being accosted? And Captain James here came to your defence?"

"That's correct, my lord," confirmed Mr. Caesar.

Major Bloodworth made an unbecoming sputtering sound. "He was not *being accosted*, he was being taught an important lesson."

"What manner of lesson, precisely?" asked Lord Hawksmoor.

"Not to strike an officer of His Majesty's army," replied the major.

Lord Hawksmoor's gaze turned impassively to Mr. Caesar. "And did you?"

"The officer in question insulted my sister," Mr. Caesar explained.

The major bristled. "I *did not.*"

"I'm sorry"—Lord Hawksmoor rested his hand on his chin and gave the major a long, cool look—"it seems you might be a little more involved in this matter than I thought."

Lord Hale, if I was any judge, had expected this whole exchange to go better. But then he had also, perhaps, expected his companion to be more circumspect.

"I made"—the major launched into his version of events without consultation or consideration—"a perfectly reasonable comment about the young man's sister, a girl nobody will deny is ill-favoured—"

"I would deny it," remarked Mr. Caesar, as blithely as he could manage.

Lord Hawksmoor looked approving. "I should hope so. Man who can't stand up for his sister isn't much of a man at all in my book. And look here, Bloodworth"—he turned to the major—"even if this girl isn't so easy on the eye, that's no reason to go saying it aloud. It's unbecoming."

"But that doesn't excuse violence." Lord Hale's tone was so moralising I almost wanted to give him ass's ears there and then just to spite him. Honestly, I think it would have been an improvement.

"Well, no," conceded Lord Hawksmoor. "While many a gentleman might have felt *compelled* to strike a gentleman over such a slight, few gentlemen actually *would* strike a gentleman over it. That is *also* unbecoming."

"Certainly it isn't fit for *polite* society," added Lord Hale. "And that says nothing of the interference from"—he waved a dismissive hand in the direction of Captain James—"this individual."

"That individual protected me from serious injury," said Mr. Caesar, and he was surprised at his own conviction. Partly, of course, it was simply that he tended to assume any physical altercation would result in serious injury, but mostly it was out of an unexpected desire to protect the one who had protected him.

His uncle, however, was paying no attention. Instead he turned to Lord Hawksmoor with the conspiratorial affect that rich, powerful men used in their private dealings with other rich, powerful men. "What we have here is a private dispute between two gentlemen"—I can see the hearts of mortals as knots of coloured string, and a green skein of resentment twisted through Lord Hale at having to admit his nephew to be a gentleman—"in which a common soldier chose to intervene and, in intervening, brought disrepute on himself, his uniform, and the king's army."

Like all of the best horseshit, it was passionately delivered, and Lord Hawksmoor considered it for long enough that Captain James felt compelled to speak.

"I'm not a common soldier, my lord," he said with almost touching conviction. "I'm an officer, promoted by Wellington himself."

Lord Hawksmoor looked grave. "A fact that will remain true only so long as you continue to *comport* yourself like an officer."

"Which he has not," added the major.

"And cannot really be *expected* to," continued Lord Hale, "not being a gentleman."

If there is one thing I respect about mortals, it is their ability to invent meaningless hierarchies for themselves. My own kind do it as well, of course, but we at least have the insight to know that it is nothing more than a game.

Mostly a game. My lord Oberon, by contrast, holds his power and title by natural right and by virtue of his many fine qualities so self-evident that they need not be explicated.

Before the group could further debate the complex philosophical question of whether shouting at underfed men in a muddy field was truly a skill one needed to be born with, they were interrupted by voices from outside.

"—can't go in, his lordship's—"

"Nonsense, my son is in there and you will *absolutely* let me through."

"Now, now, Mary, fellow's just doing his job."

The harried ancillary opened the door and announced Lady Mary Caesar and her father, the Earl of Elmsley.

"Dicky," exclaimed Lord Hawksmoor, "what're you doing here?"

"Mary brought me," explained the earl. "Said there'd been a spot of bother involving young Johnny and that maybe I could clear it up."

Lord Hale gave his sister a cold look. "That was ill done, Mary. This was a matter of internal military discipline."

"Then why are you here, Richard?" asked Lady Mary, placidly. "I always thought you rather despised the army."

This was half a truth. Lord Hale had no special contempt for armed service, it was just that he seldom needed *special* contempt to consider something contemptible.

"Besides," added Mr. Caesar, "hadn't we established that this was a private matter between gentlemen?"

"I think we had, actually," confirmed Lord Hawksmoor. "Look, I'm sorry you got dragged into this, Dicky, but it really isn't the sort of thing you need to worry yourself with."

Where I come from, the resolution of this matter would have been simple. Each party would have abducted a mortal champion, transfigured them with fey sorcery into the most terrifying form possible, and then made them fight each other. The winner, naturally, would have been the contestant whose representative died most amusingly.

But in the mortal world, apparently, there were other, less sophisticated systems in place.

"The way I see it," the Earl of Elmsley said with the confidence of a man accustomed to his way of seeing being treated as fact by all around him, "this is all a very nasty business. Mary has told me what happened and while I'm sure different fellows have different perspectives, it seems to me there's no reason why we can't all just shake hands and put it behind us."

Lord Hale was looking at his father with a quintessentially human combination of despite and deference. "That may settle matters between John and Major Bloodworth, but there still remains the question—"

But his father didn't let him finish. "Of the captain? Well, far be it from me to intrude on a military matter, but as I see it, if he's good enough for Wellington he should be good enough for us."

"Yes, well." Lord Hale's habitual distaste for anybody different from himself continued to war with his instinctive respect for his social superiors. "I'm not *totally* certain I'd take character references from an Irishman."

Lord Hawksmoor pursed his lips. "Now, now, Hale. That Irishman is a peer of the realm. And a privy counsellor."

"And a Knight of the Garter," added the Earl of Elmsley.

"Field marshal of His Majesty's armies," added Captain James.

"And Knight Grand Cross of the Bath," added Mr. Caesar.

"And Count of Vimiera, Marquess of Torres Vedras, and Duke of Ciudad Rodrigo," added Lady Mary.

"Field marshal of the Hanoverian army too, come to think of it," added Captain James. "And marshal-general of the Portuguese and captain-general of the Spanish."

"And Colonel of the Horse Guards," Lady Mary finished.

"Yes, yes," conceded Lord Hale, "he has a lot of titles. But that doesn't mean we should acquiesce to him in every instance."

On that one point, Mr. Caesar was in very slight accord with his uncle. "Well, no, but I think we can probably trust him to know a good officer when he sees one."

Major Bloodworth, who had remained at least mostly silent for the majority of this exchange, could hold his peace no longer. "By God, man, I've had about my fill of your insolence."

With a serene smile, the Earl of Elmsley turned to Lord Hawksmoor. "You see, Reginald, I really think this is just a private disagreement. And I'm sure the most sensible thing is to look at this as a matter between Johnny lad and the major here. One that I'm sure they can resolve amicably and put behind them."

Amicability, to nobody's delight except mine, was far from the major's mind. Indeed his thoughts seemed to be heading down a more drastic path. In unrelated news I *may* have conjured the scent of gunpowder beneath his nose at a strategic moment. "Oh, we can put it behind us," he said with an ominous tone suggesting that he did not mean *by forgetting the whole thing ever happened.* He had approached very close to Mr. Caesar now, and was glaring at him the way a dog glares at a burglar's leg. "Will you give me *satisfaction,* sir?"

As I have intimated several times, I do not normally like Mr. Caesar. I find him stuffy in most circumstances, insufferable in

others, and fleetingly amusing only when he is frustrated. But he
earned my temporary approval when he looked the major squarely
in the eye and said, "I didn't realise your inclinations ran in that
direction."

In retrospect, Mr. Caesar realised, his response to the question
had made a duel inevitable. He had hoped that since duelling
was at the very least strongly discouraged in the armed forces and
that killing a man in a duel *was* still legally murder, Major Bloodworth might not be quite so foolish as to follow through on the
challenge.

Now he chided himself for not remembering that it was *never*
wise to bet against the foolishness of men like Major Bloodworth.
So the event had been set, nominally at least, to take place upon
Hampstead Heath at dawn three days hence. Which left Mr. Caesar with little time to prepare to fight or, as might be, to prepare
himself for the social consequences of failing to fight.

That evening, the Caesars—excluding the Earl of Elmsley, who
had a seldom-used London house to which he preferred to retire—
hosted Captain James at an informal dinner. It was, by the standards of the day, an intimate affair. Just the Caesars, Captain
James, Miss Mitchelmore, and Lady Georgiana. It was also, by the
standards of the day—or at least by the standards of the ton—
a meagre affair. The elder Mr. Caesar did not earn much from his
writing and speaking engagements, and most of Lady Mary's
inheritance was bound up with her various charitable commitments. The gossip sheets had, for a while, made great play of the
fact that the Earl of Elmsley's youngest daughter lived like a

Quaker, but, since she had persisted in taking the observation as a compliment, they had eventually stopped out of spite.

The whole concatenation of circumstances put Mr. Caesar in a tangle of conflicting thoughts and priorities that to my fairy senses was like a well-aged wine. In any other situation, he would have found the company of the captain delightful, but in any other situation, he would not have been three days from death.

"You didn't have to do this," protested Captain James as Nancy came around with the soup. Soup into which I had infiltrated myself disguised as a stray potato peeling.

"I'll say they didn't," Nancy replied. "No notice I've had, and guests for dinner all the same."

Miss Mitchelmore—still as conventionally pretty and as fashionably demure as she had been before all that messy business last year—cast Nancy an apologetic look. "I'm so sorry, we shouldn't have come. And we were no help at all with the hearing."

"But it did get us out of an evening at the opera," added Lady Georgiana. "For which I am eternally in your debt." Given her prior experience with the unnatural, it surprised me that Lady Georgiana was so casual with such language. You should *never* say you are eternally in something's debt. One day you might meet a creature that takes you seriously.

That proved a good enough segue for the younger Mr. Caesar, who turned to the captain with an expression of carefully calculated regard. Surviving society meant concealing his feelings about more or less everything, and that made it hard to conjure sincerity when it was needed. "And on the subject of debt," he tried, "it is only right that we repay you properly for your assistance."

However well it might have been meant, the captain took it otherwise. "I've no need to be bought."

"That we thank you, then," Mr. Caesar corrected himself. "You can surely have no objection to gratitude."

"Depends whose gratitude," replied the captain, with a smile I personally interpreted as promising and which Mr. Caesar couldn't quite bring himself to interpret similarly.

Miss Caesar and Miss Anne, for all they were inured to the tiresome pleasantries of their society, could be quiet no longer. Neither their servant's inconvenience nor their guest's amenability to recompense was the matter that interested them. Like me, they were here for the blood.

"Are you truly to fight a duel?" Miss Anne asked her brother.

And to that the younger Mr. Caesar had no easy answer. *Yes* was hubristic, *no* was cowardly, and the man he wanted to be hovered somewhere between the two. "Well . . ." he began, and when that seemed inadequate he added, "That is to say . . ."

"I sincerely hope he will not," put in Lady Mary. "It would be neither safe nor seemly."

Lady Georgiana was smiling the kind of smile I at once understood and appreciated. "True, but safety and seemliness are both highly overrated."

"Seemliness perhaps"—Lady Mary's tone was sharp, her advantage in years over Lady Georgiana compensating for her disadvantage in rank—"but not safety."

"People will think him a craven." Miss Caesar looked horrified at the thought. "They'll consider him less than a man."

Being accustomed to polite society thinking him less than a man already, for more reasons than he could count, this observation had for the younger Mr. Caesar the familiar discomfort of an old ulcer. "Is the major"—he turned to Captain James—"is he a very skilled swordsman?"

Captain James shrugged. "Doubt it. Though I'm sure he's had lessons. The proper officers all do."

"Do you not," asked the elder Mr. Caesar only slightly pointedly, "consider yourself a proper officer?"

"I've learned there's no sense in thinking myself something other men'll never think me."

The elder Mr. Caesar took a moment to digest the observation, nodded once, and then said, "Curious. I've learned the opposite."

"Well, I think you should do it," Lady Georgiana declared, drawing a look of harsh if loving reproof from Miss Mitchelmore. "There can't be that much to it really; just make sure the pointy end goes in the other man."

"In my experience, my lady," replied Captain James, "that's not easy to do when the other man's doing his best to kill you."

Mr. Caesar choked on his soup, and only partly because I'd slipped into his bowl and caught in his throat. "I mean . . . it won't come to that, will it? It'll be more of a . . . first blood honour-is-satisfied sort of thing?"

Captain James set down his spoon. "Maybe. Lot depends on the weapons."

To the younger Mr. Caesar's profound distress, both his sisters were looking at their new guest with rapt attention.

"If it's pistols," the captain went on, "then you'll both likely miss. But if you don't, the bullet could take your jaw off."

Mr. Caesar's hand went involuntarily to his face. He had always rather liked his jaw. Indeed he was rapidly coming to wonder if it might not be one of his best features.

"Sabres, now those are made to use from horseback. Wide blades, good for slicing." The captain made a cutting motion with his hand and the Misses Caesar gave little yelps of excitement.

"Won't likely kill you, not with one cut, but they can split you open so's the doctor'll have a hard time stitching you up again."

"Is this quite the right talk for the dinner table?" asked Lady Mary, her aristocratic upbringing briefly surfacing through decades of rebellion.

"If he's to face it," said Captain James, "he should hear about it."

Lady Mary gave a cautious nod. "Yes, but can we remember he could always choose not to face it?"

This was too much for Miss Anne. "Mama, things are hard enough for our family without John being branded a coward also."

"Better a coward than a corpse," pointed out Miss Mitchelmore.

"Not amongst men of honour," Miss Anne protested.

"You must forgive Anne," explained Miss Caesar with only the tiniest trace of bitterness. "She is being courted by an officer and she believes it makes her an expert on all things military."

Miss Anne looked shyly into her soup bowl. "I am not being courted. He merely . . . visits the family a lot."

"He visits *you*"—the trace of bitterness in Miss Caesar's voice was growing less trace-like by the moment—"because—"

"Perhaps," the younger Mr. Caesar cut in, and only partly for selfish reasons, "we might return our attention to the many ways in which I might die in the near future."

Miss Mitchelmore concealed a chuckle behind her hand. "Not pleasant, is it, John?"

It was almost a relief to be fencing with words, rather than fearing the need to fence with swords. The younger Mr. Caesar raised an eyebrow. "I was very understanding."

"You were moderately understanding and, if I may say so, rather high-handed."

"I was not high-handed."

Lady Georgiana matched Mr. Caesar's eyebrow-raise and then some. "You did keep insisting that I was trying to murder her."

"No, I insisted you were trying to seduce her and"—the younger Mr. Caesar waved a demonstrative hand—"well."

Captain James looked around the party quizzically. "I feel like I've missed something."

"Long story," unexplained Lady Georgiana. "Perhaps we should return to sharper topics?"

The younger Mr. Caesar glared at her accusingly. "You're enjoying this, aren't you?"

"Immeasurably."

"So if it's smallswords," the captain continued, "which it might be for a dispute between gentlemen, then you're in proper trouble."

"Misnamed, are they?" asked Lady Mary, who had little experience of bladecraft.

The captain shook his head. "About this long"—he held his hands a little over two feet apart—"and thin as a knitting needle. One can go right through you and it'll take you a minute to even notice."

"That's not sounding too awful at the moment," Mr. Caesar hazarded, although the fact that talk of being run through constituted *not too awful* was its own kind of awfulness. "You've not mentioned losing any parts of my anatomy yet."

The captain gave him what could almost have been a teasing look. "Oh, you'll be fine on the day. Little hole never stopped anybody. It's the fever's the problem. Thin, deep wound. Hard to clean. Hard to heal. You just get worse and worse and then they put you in the ground."

Mr. Caesar was looking decidedly queasy but was, perhaps unexpectedly, feeling queasily decided. As ghastly as it was to admit, his sister had been right. He had already brought shame on the family by starting a fight; it would only deepen that shame were he not to finish it. "That sounds flatly terrible. But even so, I think I may have to go through with it."

Paying at least some mind to the gravity of the situation, the Misses Caesar managed to restrain themselves from applauding. If only just.

"Are you sure, John?" asked the elder Mr. Caesar. "It's a lot of danger for no gain."

The younger man nodded. "If I refuse, it will go poorly for all of us. I already caused a scene at a ball, I shan't compound aggression with cowardice. That would be the worst of all possible worlds."

"The worst of all possible worlds is one where you are dead," observed Lady Mary. And though restraint was in her blood, she sounded almost impassioned, which she normally did only when speaking of her causes.

Having restrained their ghoulish enthusiasm for whole seconds, the Misses Caesar would be held back no longer.

"Will you need to learn to fence?" asked Miss Caesar. "I am sure we could afford an instructor if we made economies elsewhere."

"Perhaps Mr. Bygrave could teach you," suggested Miss Anne. "I am sure he is quite the swordsman."

"With respect," replied Captain James, "I know the lad. He's not a bad sort but he's green as a spring lawn, and though I've no doubt he's taken lessons, he'll have seen no battle."

"Then perhaps you could teach him," suggested Miss Mitchelmore with, I thought, a wickeder glint than I was used to seeing in her eye.

Captain James considered this for a moment. "Duelling's a

gentleman's art, and I'm no gentleman. I can't teach you to fence."

Everybody at the table looked, for their own reasons, disappointed. What those reasons *were*, of course, varied markedly from person to person.

"But," he continued, "I'm pretty sure I could teach you to *fight*."

CHAPTER FOUR

THE FOLLOWING MORNING A LARGE fraction of the Caesar household returned to a semblance of their normal routine while Mr. Caesar diverted from it so enormously that he even found himself out of bed before ten. But the matter of Mr. Caesar's lessons in swordplay under the tutelage of a man who, if pushed, could tear a monster's arm off and watch it bleed to death (then have similar luck with its mother and be royally screwed over by a dragon) is one to which I will return later. There are many threads to this tale that demand my attention, and I choose for now to focus on the Misses Caesar. For they, too, were about to have an unusual day, albeit a far less unusual one than their brother.

Mr. Bygrave called, as he always did, at the fashionable hour, but this time he arrived, uncharacteristically, with a guest. The gentleman he had brought with him was roughly of an age with Mr. Bygrave, lanky and tousle-haired with a faintly bewildered expression that some might find endearing but which I personally found made me want to turn him into a minnow and throw him into a horse trough.

"I was wondering," Mr. Bygrave explained to the household, "seeing as it is such a fine day, if you would be so good as to permit your lovely daughters"—he was looking exclusively at Miss Anne as he said this—"to come walk with us awhile?"

Lady Mary, who understood well enough how the game was played and understood, too, the delicacies of it, extended a cautious permission, assigning Nancy to play chaperone since she herself was running late for a meeting and with all the recent excitement had fallen a little behind on her correspondence. And so Mr. Bygrave introduced his friend as Mr. Saunders and, once it had been established that his family were rich enough to be trustworthy by default, the foursome set out into the late morning sunshine.

At the beginning of the walk, Miss Caesar did her best to enjoy herself. It was uncommon for gentlemen to seek her company in any matter and so she decided to seize the opportunity with both hands.

"It is a fine day," she began. As opening gambits went it lacked originality, but what can we expect from a mortal? Especially since *ill met by moonlight* was already taken.

"Hmm?" Mr. Saunders nodded, then added a distant "Yes."

"Have you known Mr. Bygrave long?" she followed up, noting that Mr. Bygrave and Miss Anne were already walking several paces ahead of them and engaged in an animated conversation about, as near as she could tell, nothing of consequence.

"Many years. We were at Eton together."

Miss Caesar clasped her hands together. "Oh, how marvellous. It must be so fascinating to go to Eton, to learn all those wonderful things."

"I daresay."

It occurred to Miss Caesar that Mr. Saunders was not looking at her. And she wanted to believe that this could be accounted for by the beauty of the scenery, or the interesting tableau presented by all of the other persons walking the same route at the same time. But Mr. Bygrave was experiencing no such distractions. And besides, there was nothing remotely diverting about the crowd in Hyde Park on a weekday morning. The company was always the same: a pack of self-important mortals who were far too keen on being looked at to be remotely worth seeing.

Not to be defeated, and lacking my sensible disdain for everybody not myself, Miss Caesar tried a different approach. "I have lately been reading *The Wanderer*."

That at least got Mr. Saunders to turn his head towards her. "Burney?"

"You like her work."

For the briefest of moments, Mr. Saunders's expression settled into something other than neutrality. Although it wasn't a something that Miss Caesar especially liked, or a something that changed my personal preferences re: minnows. "I neither like nor dislike it. Although regarding her latest I think I rather agree with Hazlitt. It focuses far too much on women's problems."

"You do not think women's problems a fit subject for fiction?"

No, she definitely did not like the cast his expression was taking. It was not cruel, nor even unpleasant exactly. But it had an almost didactic quality that a deep and instinctual part of her revolted against. "In a few short weeks, Bygrave there will be sent to France where he will be fighting for his life in a war that will determine the future of Europe and thus the world. *That*, I think, is a fit subject for fiction."

The polite thing to do, Miss Caesar knew, was to nod and smile and agree. To say, *Yes, that's a very good point, I hadn't thought of it that way.* But despite her sister's insistence to the contrary, she was beginning to realise that a sweet temperament was getting her nowhere. So instead she said, "And must everything be about the fate of the world?"

"For ladies?" replied Mr. Saunders, his tone lightening in a way that Miss Caesar could not help but read as patronising. Probably because it was, in fact, patronising. "Not at all. But an educated gentleman does generally expect his reading matter to engage with issues of substance."

Having no desire to continue that particular conversation, Miss Caesar quickened her pace to draw level with her sister and Mr. Bygrave.

"I was just saying to Mr. Saunders," she said very loudly, and shooting an imploring look at Miss Anne, "what a fine day we are having."

Painstakingly courteous as always, Mr. Bygrave nodded. "Oh yes, quite. Miss Anne was just sharing a remarkably similar observation."

"Actually," Miss Anne corrected him, "we were having a rather lovely conversation about the situation in France. A conversation that you're *interrupting*, Mary."

Mr. Saunders, bringing up the rear, held up his hands in a *mea culpa* gesture. "Sorry, Robert, rather fumbled that one. The chit had some terribly silly opinions about literature."

While Miss Anne was still fuming about the intrusion on her doubtlessly lovely, and not at all a cavalcade of mortal banalities, conversation about the French situation, Miss Caesar was making some swift social calculations.

"Which ball did you drop exactly?" she asked.

Standing a little way off, Nancy winced. She, too, could see exactly where this was going and also exactly who would be left picking up the pieces.

With all the elan of a midsized terrier, Mr. Bygrave did his best to smooth things over. "There were no balls. Not really. I just sort of mentioned to Saunders here that it might be nice to go for a bit of a walk and that maybe it might be nice to have some company from, you know, the gentler sex, and that—"

"And that you wanted somebody to take me, so you could have Anne?" Miss Caesar finished for him.

"When you say it like that," Mr. Bygrave protested, "it sounds far more sinister than—"

But Miss Caesar was not listening. She had turned, tears pricking her eyes, and was making for home.

We leave the ladies now and turn to their brother. Yes, such a shift at so pivotal a juncture is a rather tawdry trick, but I am an otherworldly sprite exiled to physicality in the mortal world. Tawdriness is hardly beneath me. Besides, you must surely wish also to know what was becoming of Mr. Caesar in his (I believe here it is customary to clear one's throat to signal euphemism) *fighting lessons.*

He had been collected by the captain first thing in the morning and led through London's tangled streets to one of the city's most notorious rookeries. It was called the Holy Land by some, a moniker I thought fit it well given how venal and blood-soaked the things you mortals call *holy* tend to be. They had progressed through the grey dawn light (yes, reader, I have narrated these events slightly out of their chronological order, it's another tawdry trick of the narrative) towards what a less creative wordsmith than I might call a low tavern.

Mr. Caesar was not wholly unfamiliar with the city's underworld, since society still dictated that gentlemen who wished to liaise with other gentlemen needed to do so at a discreet distance from polite company. But he had never quite found himself in a true *slum*, those blights on the city steeped in the kind of poverty that moralists chose to call sin.

Which was his loss because they're tremendous fun.

As they drew closer to their apparent destination, Mr. Caesar found himself looking up at a finely painted but ill-maintained sign naming the establishment as the Lord Wriothesly's Folly.

"Who's Lord Wriothesly?" asked Mr. Caesar, hoping that the question would not make him look foolish. Or at least would make him look no more foolish than he already looked following a strange gentleman into the worst part of London at an ungodly hour of the morning on the tenuous promise of duelling lessons.

"No fucker knows," replied the captain. This was not entirely true. I know, but I choose not to tell you.

From the outside, the Folly looked deserted, but that was largely due to the soot and dust covering the windows. Inside, cheap tallow candles replaced the inaccessible sunlight and filled the air with a brightness that could almost have been cheery were it not for Mr. Caesar's unworthy—but not unwarranted—suspicion that he might take a knife to the ribs any moment.

A gaggle of uniformed men were propping up the bar and embodying all of the pettiest accusations that the officer class lev-elled against their subordinates. Disorderly and shambolic, they were engaged in a mixture of drinking, swearing, gambling, and whoring of which I mightily approved. Especially at that time of the morning.

"Aye aye," called one—the Irishman Mr. Caesar remembered from earlier as Callaghan. "The captain's back. And still with his stripes if I'm any judge."

A cheer went up from the crowd.

"I'd say drinks were on me," the captain told them, "but are they fuck, you sack of drunken layabouts."

"Get off, you'd not have us any other way," replied a thin man with a strong Northumberland accent and strange symbols tattooed across his knuckles. Then he stopped short and, to my consternation, looked directly at me. "Hang about, lads, something's up."

Mr. Caesar was the only person in the hostelry to be surprised when the room fell silent.

"Up how?" asked Captain James, suddenly deadly serious. Worryingly serious, from my perspective.

"Something invisible walks among us," replied the northerner. "I can tell no more."

I breathed a metaphorical sigh of relief. He was, it seemed, the weaker kind of seer, attuned to the hidden world but lacking the capacity to perceive it directly. Still, from an abundance of caution I took the shape of a spider and scuttled into a high corner to watch proceedings.

"Barryson's a vitki," explained Captain James. "Or something like one. Gets warnings from Odin when the French are up to fuckery."

"Which is always," added Barryson. "They march with the gods of Old Gaul on their side, plus whichever of the Hellenes feel like backing them that day."

"As flies to wanton boys are we," said a slim man at the end of the group whose features spoke of the subcontinent but whose accent spoke of Eton.

Being, insofar as his circumstances would allow, a pink of the ton, Mr. Caesar was not unaccustomed to meeting large groups of new people, but the Folly was decidedly outside of his element. It was not that he objected to rough company, indeed he rather enjoyed it in many contexts. But the rough company he normally sought was anonymous and fleeting, not named and trying—to some extent at least—to save his life.

A young woman, fair-haired and dark-eyed, who was sitting on the knee of one of the soldiers, came gallantly to his rescue. "Do you think, Captain, you should maybe introduce us all so that your new friend's head doesn't spin off his shoulders?"

With the resigned expression of somebody who would rather ignore social niceties wherever possible, Captain James did the honours. "Mr. John Caesar," he began, "these are the scoundrels, mollies, thieves, and bastards of the Irregulars. The one who sees things he shouldn't is Barry Barryson, he says his ancestors were Vikings but I don't believe him. The fellow with the nice turn of phrase"—he indicated the man who had chosen to quote that fucker Bill—"is George Kumar, got one of his father's names but not the other, and my right-hand man on account of being the only one of these pricks as can read."

"I can read," protested Barryson. "Just not English."

The captain glared. "And when we start getting orders in runes, I'll send for you. Callaghan you've met. The one looks far too young to be holding a gun is Boy William." Here Captain James indicated a boy who had yet to speak and who really did look far too young to be holding a gun. "We none of us know how he's not dead yet."

"Me mum dipped me in a river as a baby," replied Boy William.

"Jackson there," the captain went on, pointing to the man with the lady on his lap. He was gentle-faced and wide-eyed with hands that looked too soft for a soldier's. "Is a thieving, swindling, lying, traitorous son of a whore and I'm very glad he's on our side."

"Why Captain," purred Jackson, pressing a hand to his breast, "you flatter me."

"Finally there's Sal"—he indicated the lady herself—"she's a woman in a dress, a man in uniform, and a devil in battle."

"And in bed," added Sal, casting a coquettish glance up at Mr. Caesar, "for the record."

"Duly noted," replied Mr. Caesar. "Though I'm unsure which I'll need sooner."

"That's everybody," finished the captain with a notable air of relief. "Everybody, this is Mr. John Caesar, grandson of the Earl of Elmsley, spoke for me at the hearing, and is about to duel Major Bloodworth despite best I can tell not knowing which end of a sword is sharp."

It wasn't exactly a slander, but Mr. Caesar still felt he should probably say something to that. "I assume it's the end that gets narrower?"

"The fact that you had to say *I assume*," replied Kumar, "speaks volumes."

The clearly doomed Boy William gave Mr. Caesar a look of honest respect. "Well, I think it's right brave of you, sir. Standing up for the captain's honour."

"'Specially since he's not got any," added Callaghan.

Captain James had, by now, crossed to the bar and ordered himself a drink. "I've got as much honour as any man in the British army."

"I know," Callaghan replied. "That's what I said."

Jackson, having dislodged Sal from his lap, was on his feet and stalking a circle around Mr. Caesar with a predatory shadow creeping across his naturally innocent face. "So what, you've brought him here so we can make a fighter of him?"

"I don't think I'm under any illusions in that regard," Mr. Caesar replied, turning instinctively to watch Jackson as he circled. "But I should probably at least know how to defend myself."

Keeping his eyes on Jackson, however, meant that he lost track of Sal until her boot caught him in the back of the knee, driving him to the ground and leaving him kneeling with a knife at his throat. "Lesson one," she told him. "Cheat."

I have tried, throughout my collection of this story and indeed *all* of my stories, not to have any respect for any of the mortal species. But I have to confess that the elan with which Mr. Caesar bore the chill of a blade against his carotid artery did him credit.

"I am not sure," he said very calmly and levelly, trying not to swallow, "that technique will be especially pertinent in a one-on-one duel."

Sal spun her knife away and concealed it somewhere about her person. "True enough. Boy William, get the swords."

The patrons of the Folly, happy as any group of Englishmen to receive free entertainment, obligingly cleared a wide circle in the middle of the floor. This left Mr. Caesar very aware that he was surrounded by vagabonds, common soldiers, a single officer, and (this last unbeknownst to him) a capricious fairy spirit.

"You're not going to stab me, are you?" he asked, trying to make it sound like a joke.

"Only a little," Barryson reassured him. "You'll hardly feel it."

Kumar entered the circle with a pair of light, thin blades, one of which he passed to Mr. Caesar. "You might want to start with this. It's the proper weapon for an affair of honour—"

"Fuck proper," called Sal from the sidelines.

"It's the weapon you're most likely to *face* in a duel with a gentleman," Kumar corrected. "Not that the major *is* much of a gentleman."

Already convinced he was holding the sword wrong, Mr. Caesar swung it experimentally and found he didn't much like the experience. "I'm not sure he thinks me a gentleman either."

Captain James, still moving with that strange grace of his, came to Mr. Caesar's side and guided his fingers into their proper position around the hilt. There was an intimacy to the gesture. One which tangled with Mr. Caesar's apprehensions and uncertainties in an intoxicating cocktail of wanting and fearing. "What he thinks don't matter," the captain told him. "What matters is you win."

"Or at the very least," added Jackson, "that you lose without dying."

"Now," the captain went on, "Kumar here'll show you the stance he learned at his fancy school, and you'll mirror him. It won't make a swordsman of you, but you might get out with your skin intact."

Kumar leaned his weight back on his left foot and raised his sword to shoulder height, pointing directly into Mr. Caesar's eyes. When Mr. Caesar tried to copy him, the attitude felt constrained and awkward. The blade was light enough, but by some trick of leverage a light blade at arm's length felt a lot like a heavy blade in any other context.

Still, he appreciated the captain's guiding hands on his arms and, occasionally, his hips, helping him stand as correctly as he was able. Had he been less concerned for his life he would have counted it one of the better ways to spend the morning. Especially a morning where he had been asked to rise early.

For a short while that turned into a long while they walked through the basics of thrust and parry, and Mr. Caesar tried not to think too hard about the fact that if he did any of this even a little bit wrong, he'd get two feet of steel through his intestines.

"I'm not sure," he said, after the drills had gone on long enough that he was beginning to forget how they started and to sweat rather more than he'd expected from a series of repeated but economical motions, "that I'll be able to do this right in an actual duel."

There was a general laugh from the crowd.

"That's good," the captain told him, "because you shouldn't. Not saying it doesn't work." He gave a respectful nod to Kumar. "Just that it doesn't work on a day and a half's training."

That left Mr. Caesar feeling very slightly used. While he hadn't *wanted* to be in a position where he needed to defend himself in deadly combat, the part of him that included "swords" in the ever-lengthening list of things a modern man should be good at had been taking some satisfaction in learning. "Then what precisely was the point of this exercise?"

"If you're to fight a gentleman," explained Callaghan, "you'll need to know how a gentleman fights."

Captain James nodded. "But if you're going to *beat* a gentleman, then you'll want to fight like a soldier. Like all that matters is getting out with your life."

"And how do I do that, exactly?" asked Mr. Caesar. For although it was reassuring to know he would not be required to do anything complicated, even the simplest fighting style seemed unlikely to be one he could learn in time.

Captain James held up one finger. "Keep your distance." He held up another. "If you see something sharp coming at you, get it away however you can." He held up a third. "If the other man gets close, stick something sharp at him."

"That seems less fighting like a soldier," Mr. Caesar pointed out, "than fighting like a coward."

Kumar gave a solemn nod. "All men would be cowards if they durst."

"Fuck off," replied Barryson. "What does that even mean?"

Either to assert his authority or to prevent his men falling to squabbling, the captain took charge. "It means any man with sense is afraid to die, and the ones that act like they aren't are too scared to be honest."

"There's a little more to it than that," Kumar protested. "But not very much more."

"And your three rules will win me a duel?" asked Mr. Caesar, more than a little incredulous.

"Against a bad swordsman." Captain James took the blade from Kumar's unresisting hand and moved into the circle to face Mr. Caesar. "And I'd lay money on the major being a bad swordsman. He's not fine enough to have learned well in the salle, nor base enough to have learned well in the street. Now go on, defend yourself."

And with no further warning, the captain attacked. It wasn't a particularly precise thrust, nor one with much vigour behind it, but the shock of it was enough for Mr. Caesar to leap back hurriedly, flailing with his own sword, and then, judging himself to have executed the first two techniques adequately, hold the point out in the general direction of his opponent.

"There you go," said the captain with a broad, easy smile. "That wasn't so hard, was it?"

Captain James came forward again and, again, Mr. Caesar leapt back, batted at anything long and metallic that seemed to be in his general vicinity, and then once more pointed his weapon as a deterrent. After a few more similar exchanges, a pattern seemed to be emerging.

"I'm not sure," Mr. Caesar confessed, already a little out of breath, "that I see this strategy proving viable in the long term. How am I ever supposed to hit him?"

This drew another smile from the captain. He had an annoyingly good smile, Mr. Caesar felt. A smile that said he'd seen more of life than you and so could understand more of joy. Then again, maybe Mr. Caesar was just the kind of man who assumed everybody else was doing life better than him. Although to be fair, in his case he was mostly right. "You don't. Unless he runs onto your blade, which happens more often than you'd think. Otherwise you're playing for time."

"Time for what?"

"For him to get tired," suggested Kumar.

"Or the law to show up," added Sal.

"Or—and I'm just throwing this out there . . ." That was Jackson, watching like a cat from the sidelines. "For a gang of vagabonds to appear out the early morning mist, make a grab for the gentlemen's bags and baggage, and then dash off in the direction of a local rookery, causing the whole thing to be called off by reasons of interruption."

Conventional though his life had been, Mr. Caesar understood enough of the proposal to have misgivings. "Isn't that a little deceptive?"

"Oh, it's a lot deceptive," Callaghan told him. "But you soon learn in the king's army that if it's deception or bleeding to death in a field, you choose deception."

"Fact is," said Captain James, "that when two men with blades don't know what they're doing—and I don't really think either of you are going to know what you're doing—somebody gets hurt. If we set up a distraction, things'll go better for everyone."

Mr. Caesar looked down at his hand, still gripping the hilt of his sword with the best technique he was able to grip it with. "So what was all this in aid of?"

"Stop you panicking. You need to know what it'll be like to have some bastard trying to kill you or you'll just stand there and let him. Now, we should think about how it works with a sabre. Barryson"—he turned to the vitki—"pass me something that cuts."

The lessons, such as they were, lasted all day and into the evening, with the captain growing incrementally more aggressive as time wore on and Mr. Caesar, eventually, growing confident that he could at the very least defend himself long enough for somebody more competent to intervene. Eventually exhaustion and alcohol (in different measures for different parties) overtook the assembly and matters were deemed concluded.

This, however, left Mr. Caesar stranded in by far the most perilous part of the night in by far the most perilous part of the city and only now was he beginning to realise the difficulty this placed him in.

When he raised the issue with the captain, it earned him a laugh and a grin. "Well now, what kind of officer would I be if I turned a fine gentleman like yourself out to the mercy of St. Giles?"

Mr. Caesar couldn't tell if the glint in the captain's eye was intent or just candlelight. So he opted to be indelicate. "That sounds a little like you're propositioning me."

Sat a little further along the bar, Callaghan nudged Boy William with his elbow. "Hear that, lad, the captain's slipping. It only sounds *a little* like he's propositioning him."

"Now, now," put in Sal from the opposite direction, "we're dealing with a gentleman here. You can't go up to a gentleman and just say how do you feel about getting your cock sucked, it's not done."

This kind of vulgarity was far more familiar to Mr. Caesar than anything else he'd experienced since his arrival in the Folly. When one spent one's formative years in places like Lady Quim's House of Buggery, one learned to accept a certain amount of lewd talk as ordinary. "You'll find," he said to the room in general, "that it actually depends very much on the gentleman."

"And on who's asking, I expect," added Jackson.

"Again, depends on the gentleman."

That raised a laugh from the room and allowed Mr. Caesar to feel, for a moment at least, at ease.

"And what sort of gentleman are you?" asked Captain James, not serious exactly, but the kind of playful that meant business.

It had been a long day. A very long day. And Mr. Caesar felt he had earned himself a little levity. Besides, he would need to come back here to continue preparing for the duel. Was it not easier to stay regardless? "I think," he replied, sipping the kind of beer he would have turned his nose up at in any other company, "that I am probably the same sort of gentleman as you are an officer."

You may, gentle reader, be disappointed that I have not gone into detail about that first assignation between the good Mr. Caesar and the, if I am honest, somewhat better Captain James. This is what we are here for, you might be saying, why are you skipping the good stuff?

And yes, yes, they were both terribly aesthetically pleasing gentlemen, Mr. Caesar with the taut figure of a man who is determined to wear the tightest breeches and the slimmest-fitting waistcoat fashion will allow without any untoward bulging or pouching, and the captain with the lean, battle-scarred muscle of a man whose body is a tool devoted wholly to preserving its own integrity at the expense of the bodies of its adversaries.

They also both had very fine cocks. Or so I imagine, not having

made extensive comparison. As I think I have established, the
vagaries of mortal physicality mean little to me. I am a creature of
passions from a world of whims, and sex interests me only when
there is love or hate or chaos behind it. This, as fascinating as both
gentlemen will become in the following pages, was just two men
fucking in a dark room in a slum. It was to sex what a loaf of stolen
bread is to a starving man. Not strictly of the highest quality, but
with a savour born of hunger and a worth weighed at least partly
in the knowledge that you could be hanged for it. A thousand similar encounters were taking place even then, all over London, albeit
with more malnourished participants.

I, for my part, left them to it and returned to the Caesar residence. And on the way there I saw a pale blue twinkle in the distant
sky and—in concert with my other suspicions and observations—
I felt a sudden need to hurry.

Driven, I should emphasise, purely by my duties as a chronicler
and not at all by concern for the well-being of any living human, I
went at once to Miss Caesar's chambers. I found her sitting at her
dresser, staring at herself in the mirror and tallying all the ways in
which her society found her deficient. As somebody who finds *all*
mortals deficient, I thought it a foolish exercise. Why fret, after all,
over the tone of one's skin or the shape of one's nose when the
entire human body is an absurd one-way trip to the grave?

Taking up a well-used brush, she began slowly to work on her
hair. Fond as she was of literature, she had seen in her mind's eye a
hundred heroines sitting as she was now, brushing their luxurious
tresses in the moonlight. In a quiet way, it was the quintessential
image of girlhood, at least as she had learned it.

In real life, it did not work that way. In real life her tresses
fought her at every step. If she was gentle with them, they sprang
back to their natural shape with a stubbornness that I personally

appreciated even if she did not. If she was rough—and she grew increasingly rough as time went on—then far from attaining the lustre that all the ladies' journals promised, either they grew brittle and snapped or the brush snagged and became immobile. She had once broken one, and not quite known how to explain it. Indeed there was much she found hard to explain; her mother she was sure meant well but they were so different in so many ways, and it was not done for a young lady to bother her father with such concerns.

I have told you, readers, that I am a student of mortal hearts, and what I saw in Miss Caesar's heart that evening was a still, simple sadness so private that even I felt a little uncomfortable chronicling it.

But that was, perhaps, an un-fairy-like weakness. In general it is when you mortals are at your most vulnerable that we come to you and offer our services.

So it was this evening. For when Miss Caesar turned from her glass to her window, tears still pricking her eyes I watched her watch the star streak across the heavens. And to think, she believed it only a beautiful celestial phenomenon.

But I am of the Other Court. I saw the wheels of the carriage, I saw the train of its rider streaming behind her.

She has no name save what she wears in the moment, but then neither do any of my kind. Her colour is blue, her stock in trade is wishes and hearts' desires. She goes simply by *Lady* when she goes by anything at all, and on this night she rode a beam of moonlight, all invisible, into Miss Caesar's bedchamber.

"Oh," she said on seeing me. "It's you."

"And I would be very grateful if you would *leave*," I told her.

She looked from me to Miss Caesar, and back again. "Whyever would you want that? I'm about to make this girl's life *much* more entertaining."

"It interferes with my plans."

The Lady smiled at me in a way I intensely misliked. "Say that twice more."

"I could, but I choose not to."

For some reason, she reached a conclusion from this. "Does Lord Oberon know how badly you're slipping?"

This was outrageous slander. "I am as loyal a partisan for my court as ever," I told her with absolute and unimpeachable honesty, "which is why I will not tolerate Titania's interference with mortals in whom my lord has a declared interest."

And again she smiled. Her smile was ethereal, and to mortals entirely enchanting. It gave me chills. "Then stop me, wanderer."

I did not.

Motes of stardust gathered around her, a sound of chimes filled the air, and she materialised.

Miss Caesar looked up, eyes wide and glistening.

"Why do you weep, child?" asked the Lady. There were forms to this kind of bargain, and this was how it had to begin.

"Because I am alone," the girl replied, "because gentlemen scorn me, because ladies mock me. Because I have neither wealth nor beauty. My sister has the favour of an officer, even my *brother* has gentlemen running to his protection. And what have I?"

"You," the Lady replied, "have a patron."

Miss Caesar dabbed at her eyes with a prettily embroidered handkerchief. "Who *are* you?"

"A friend."

To her credit, Miss Caesar had the wherewithal to look suspicious. "What manner of friend?"

"The very best."

To her further credit, her suspicions were not allayed by this. "Are you a fairy?"

"Some have said so."

"That means yes," I added, although Miss Caesar could not hear me, and was forbidden from hearing me by old bargains.

Miss Caesar twisted her handkerchief between her fingertips. "Cousin Maelys says magical things are dangerous, and we should stay away from them."

"Cousin Maelys is right," I told her—of course, reader, I was being untruthful in this matter. Magical things are perfectly safe and you should run towards them with enthusiasm. But I had an agent of Titania's to vex and that undermined my natural honesty.

"I know of your cousin Maelys," replied the Lady. And she did. My stories get around. "Her encounter was with a mortal curse and a divinity of this world. My people are something else entirely."

To my wholly selfish relief, Miss Caesar was treating this with the caution it deserved. "What do you want from me?"

And at this the Lady laughed. You are imagining a sound, no doubt. Imagine it *better*, clearer, more musical, more wondrous in its beauty. We can, as a species, be so very enticing when we wish to be and the music of our merriment is a weapon we have used against your kind for millennia.

"I want nothing," the Lady replied. This was a lie. "Save to know what you wish."

"Do not," I said uselessly to a world that was incapable of perceiving me, "wish for anything. Or at the very least be—"

I abhor cliché, and thus it was to some extent fortunate that I never got to complete the phrase.

Because Miss Caesar replied: "I wish that I was beautiful."

CHAPTER FIVE

THE FOLLOWING MORNING, MR. CAESAR awoke in a tangle of long limbs and inadequate blankets as the sun began to slant in through the cracks in the shutters, but even had this not stirred him, the banging at the door would have.

"Captain"—the voice was Callaghan's by its lilt, and by the fact that it was definitely him; I went outside in my mist shape and checked—"there's a man here looking for your . . . for the guest."

Concerned that one of his more persistent exes or more irritating enemies had somehow tracked him down, Mr. Caesar called out a blearily irritated "Who is it?" before flopping his head back onto the nothing that passed for a pillow.

"Unless I'm by way of being extremely mistaken," Callaghan explained, "it's your father."

Most interlopers Mr. Caesar would have happily greeted with a polite *fuck off,* but if something had dragged the elder Mr. Caesar all the way to St. Giles at so early an hour it was certainly important. "Stall," he said. "And tell him I'm—fuck—just tell him I'll be there soon."

Ordinarily, when Mr. Caesar had an assignation with a soldier, he left before morning. He also ordinarily dressed down for the occasion so that he would not be faced, as he was now, with having to retie a cravat in an emergency.

"Your old man normally do this?" asked Captain James, propped up on his elbows and watching Mr. Caesar from the bed.

"No. Which is why I'm concerned."

"And he's happy with you . . . ?" Captain James waved a hand in the air between them. "Because I've fallen foul of angry fathers before and I'd rather not again."

As it happened, Mr. Caesar had never explicitly discussed his sexuality with his father, but nor had either of his parents given him the sense that they were anything but supportive if—on those occasions that he fell in with less savoury sorts—appropriately wary. "My father cares about honesty, justice, and the abolition. He's never complained about where I spend the night."

He seemed, however, to be complaining now. Because despite Callaghan's attempts to delay him, he was banging on the door himself. "John, what's keeping you?"

What was keeping Mr. Caesar was, in point of fact, the extreme tightness of his breeches, which he had hoped to be able to put on at his leisure and when slightly less sweaty. "For a man with no valet," he replied—slightly regretting the remark because it was hardly his father's fault they had so few servants—"I think you'll find I'm doing remarkably well."

"I'm coming in."

"We are not decent."

"And I do not care. This is important."

It was no use. In Mr. Caesar's experience his father had two modes: contemplative and unstoppable. He wasn't being contemplative. The door opened, and he strode in, leaving his son just time to fasten his breeches and the captain just time to make no effort to react at all.

"Mary is gone," the elder Mr. Caesar said with a stoicism that the mortals of the era would have considered admirable.

"Gone?"

"Gone."

"Gone?"

"Yes, John," the elder Mr. Caesar's tone was steadier than mine would have been at this point in the exchange. "Gone."

"What do you mean, *gone*?"

"Far be it from me to butt in," said Captain James, "but I assume he means she's not there."

The elder Mr. Caesar nodded. "When Nancy went to wake her this morning she found the room empty and the window ajar."

The news of his sister's disappearance disturbed Mr. Caesar so much that he didn't even try to tie his cravat, he just bundled it up and held it. "We must look for her."

"I know. That is why I am here. Your mother, for understandable reasons, is refusing to leave Anne alone and we have sent Nancy to inform the earl. That leaves you and I to pursue . . . other possibilities."

The tone in his father's voice did not fill Mr. Caesar with confidence. "You surely don't think some harm could have befallen her?"

"I do not wish to." Mortal hearts are an open book to me, and so despite the elder Mr. Caesar's measured demeanour it was plain to me how *badly* he did not wish to. "But I must consider it."

On the other side of the room, Captain James was dressing with military efficiency. "I'll send a lad to have a word with the river police in case of the worst. And I'll put out that she's looked for. It's the older one right? The one that was upset at the ball?"

Both Misters Caesar looked at the captain with a mix of gratitude and suspicion. "You don't have to," said the younger. "I mean,
it's not your problem."

"A young woman gone missing is everyone's problem." It was
sentiments like this that made me dislike the captain. The fact that
people like him exist is probably good for the overall survival of
your species even if it *is* terrible for your entertainment value.

"Commendable," observed the elder Mr. Caesar. "But——"

"No buts. Me and my men can shake some trees, see if anybody
knows anything. You two stick to places she would have gone."

The elder Mr. Caesar nodded. "I will check hospitals and"—he
looked grave—"mortuaries. John, I suggest you see if she has gone
to Maelys or Miss Bickle. She trusts them, so if she has run away
she may have gone there."

Despite the seriousness of the situation, Mr. Caesar couldn't
help wincing. "You realise if she's not with Lizzie, and I do go and
speak to her, she'll only insist that Mary has been taken away by
fairies?"

"She might"—the elder Mr. Caesar patted his son heavily on
the shoulder—"but you should probably tell her anyway."

A nasty thought entered the younger Mr. Caesar's mind. "You
don't think—could some gentleman have taken advantage of her?
One we did not know about?"

"Perhaps," said the elder Mr. Caesar, though his expression said
he doubted it. "Although she and her sister went walking with two
gentlemen yesterday and on her return she . . . she did not seem
besotted, let us put it that way."

"I'll tell the lads to keep an eye out for the usual sorts regardless," offered the captain. "If it is that kind of abduction then
there's places people tend to go. Especially if they're army."

Thanking Captain James once more for his unnecessarily

generous offer of assistance, the Misters Caesar hurried out into the city to begin a search that would, of course, be entirely fruitless.

Because the younger Mr. Caesar had been correct. Had he asked Miss Bickle, she would certainly have told him that his sister had been abducted by fairies. And she would have been absolutely right.

Twenty minutes later, Mr. Caesar was in the Bickles' London townhouse, pacing the floor like a highly strung showcat and trying his best to filter thoughts that were a mix of deep dread for his forthcoming duel, mild triumph at having bagged an exceptionally fine officer, still deeper dread for his sister, and, deepest of all, frustration with his present interlocutor.

"She has *not*," he said for the fifth time, "been abducted by fairies."

"Well, I think that *very* closed-minded of you," Miss Bickle replied. Not that any of her companions would listen to her because they, like all mortals, were utter fools.

Miss Mitchelmore looked sceptical. Mr. Caesar had collected her first, in order that he might have an ally in the inevitable fairy conversation. "I'm not sure *closed-minded* is quite the right term," she said. "I think *justifiably uncertain* might be better."

With a defiant spirit that continued to do her credit, Miss Bickle stuck out her chin. "Then what alternative theories do you have? Either of you."

"Anything but fairies," suggested Miss Mitchelmore, quite incorrectly. "She may simply have run away."

"Or been taken by ruffians," added Mr. Caesar. And then, not able to stop his mind escalating matters unnecessarily, he added, "Or run away and *then* been taken by ruffians."

Miss Bickle was pacing also—like Mr. Caesar she had an excess of energy, but unlike him she tended to find amusing uses for it. "Mary is young, and has had one or two upsets recently, but I don't think she's the kind to run away from home."

"You ran away from home when you were her age," Miss Mitchelmore pointed out. "Twice."

"*Exactly.*" Miss Bickle enjoyed looking triumphant, and did so at the slightest opportunity. This was one such. "So I should know very well if Mary is the kind of girl to do the same, and she is not. As for ruffians, was there any sign of struggle?"

Mr. Caesar considered this. "Father didn't say. But I'm sure he would have if there had been. At least if there had been anything obvious."

"So she has simply vanished," concluded Miss Bickle.

"It seems so." Mr. Caesar did not like the direction this conversation was going.

"Into thin air."

"Yes." He *definitely* did not like the direction this conversation was going.

Another opportunity presented itself, and Miss Bickle looked triumphant once more. "As if, one might almost say, *by magic.*"

Miss Mitchelmore, the only one of the three whose response to a stressful situation was to remain seated and spare the carpets, looked up. "I hate to say it, John, but I fear she might be making sense."

"There! Maelys agrees with me."

On the verge of being right, Miss Mitchelmore did as your kind so often do and corrected herself at the last moment. "*Agrees* is a strong word, but perhaps we should—I mean—it would do no harm to rule it out."

Mr. Caesar momentarily stopped pacing in order to glare. He tended to do this, which sometimes led me to wonder if perhaps his eyes and legs were connected to some intricate gear system that permitted only one or the other to function. "Which we would do how, precisely?"

"I could speak with Mother Mason," suggested Miss Mitchelmore. "Although she lives some days away. Or perhaps Tabitha—I understand the Galli are sometimes called to London to consult with the Undersecretary of State for Oracular Affairs."

A wayward and only partially unwelcome thought crept into Mr. Caesar's mind. "I *do* know of another mystically sensitive individual. Although he's a little rough around the edges."

"How rough?" asked Miss Bickle with wholly appropriate glee.

"He's from Newcastle."

"Oh, I say." Miss Bickle put a hand to her chest. "That may be a little *too* rough."

"And where did you meet this . . . mystically sensitive pitman?" asked Miss Mitchelmore.

"He isn't a pitman, he's a soldier," explained Mr. Caesar. "And I met him last night while Captain James was instructing me in swordplay."

Mr. Caesar remembered, a little too late, that this was the other hazard of bringing Miss Bickle into their circle. She had not hitherto known of the duel and he would, on balance, have preferred that she go on not knowing.

"Why were you being instructed in swordplay?" she asked, her expression that of a woman who was concocting a hundred theories, each more scandalous than the last. "Have you taken a commission? Have you been press-ganged? Are you to fight a duel of honour?"

Mr. Caesar nodded.

"You've been press-ganged?" Miss Bickle looked sorrowful. "How beastly. I really feel we should abolish the practice."

Mr. Caesar pinched the bridge of his nose. "I am to fight a duel of honour."

Inside Miss Bickle's mind, the possibilities unspooled themselves into a tangle of conflicts. "Did you insult a man's wife? Seduce his brother? Quarrel at a club about whether a window should be left open? Have a stern disagreement over a horse?"

"It's the major," Mr. Caesar told her. "Which might perhaps have been a more obvious conclusion to reach than the thing with the window?"

"More obvious," agreed Miss Bickle. "But much less interesting."

As ever, Mr. Caesar knew he would regret it. As ever, he asked. "How is it less interesting?"

"Well, because you wouldn't really be duelling over the window. That would just be the public pretence concealing what in fact would be a matter of the deepest personal passion the details of which are too devilish by far to be discussed by daylight."

"Your imagination," said Miss Mitchelmore, "is sometimes worryingly specific."

Miss Bickle gave a solemn nod. "Reality so often disappoints one." She didn't know how right she was. You haven't truly been disappointed by reality until you have been exiled to it.

"Well, then I am sorry my upcoming life-or-death struggle is insufficiently romantic for you," replied Mr. Caesar, acidly.

Irony, however, was wasted on Miss Bickle. "Don't be. It's still the most romantic thing that has happened this month. After all, you struck a man in defence of a lady."

"That lady was my sister," Mr. Caesar pointed out. "I'm not entirely sure it counts."

"You struck a man in defence of a lady, and were subsequently called out by him. Being no kind of shot or swordsman"—

"You're making me look rather poor here, Lizzie."

—"you threw yourself on the mercy of a gallant captain who has taken you under his wing and who I am sure will fall in love with you if he's the kind of captain who is interested in gentlemen, which I am sure some captains are because, well, it only stands to reason."

This was all too much. Even if Mr. Caesar had been the sort to share these kinds of flights of fancy (and he was not), even if he had been at risk of developing that kind of attachment to the captain (and he told himself he was not), now was the worst possible time to be thinking of it. At this juncture his and Miss Bickle's mutual pacings brought them face-to-face, which gave Mr. Caesar ample opportunity to gaze his disapproval directly at his friend. "Lizzie. Stop it. Nobody is falling in love with anybody. Nobody is having any kind of grand adventure. My sister is missing and we need to do something about it. And since"—he pursed his lips, not quite able to admit he was going to have to say what he was about to say—"your theory about supernatural abduction is actually our best bet, that means finding some kind of magician. And I happen to know one who lives locally."

Miss Bickle had already called for her pelisse. "Then what are we waiting for? We simply must find this magician of yours without delay."

"There is no *we* here," Mr. Caesar insisted. "The gentleman I intend to consult is staying at an inn in St. Gi—"

He should have known better. Far better. Miss Bickle squeaked with delight. "Oh, John, are we to go to a rookery? To immerse ourselves in the grime and grit of real London?"

"Mayfair is quite real enough for me, thank you," said Miss Mitchelmore. But, just as Mr. Caesar was beginning to relax, she added, "Still, I agree that we should go with you."

This felt to Mr. Caesar like an issue on which he should stand firm. "St. Giles is not a place for ladies."

"Are half its residents not ladies?" asked Miss Mitchelmore, arching an eyebrow. I suspect this was a habit she had acquired from her lover, like behavioural syphilis.

"Not ladies of quality."

Miss Bickle was still grinning. "Oh, that's perfectly all right then. I'm not a lady of quality, I'm just very rich. In terms of heritage I'm as common as a church mouse."

This was not going the way Mr. Caesar wanted. Although were he honest with himself, he would have had to admit it was going the way he expected. And it was certainly going the way *I* wanted, which is my chief concern. "I could not guarantee your safety."

"Nor could we guarantee yours," replied Miss Mitchelmore. "But we have both been in danger before, and if we bring Lizzie then we shall have the use both of her grandfather's coach and of his large, heavily armed servants, who I suspect will see us secure enough."

There was little counterargument Mr. Caesar could make to that. He had not been relishing the thought of returning to St. Giles unescorted and the kind of entourage the elder Mr. Bickle would insist upon providing for his granddaughter would be a comfort indeed.

So he relented, and the three set out for St. Giles with your humble narrator, in my shape of mists and shadows, trailing in their wake.

They arrived at the Folly a little before noon, the late morning light rather spoiling the atmosphere of malevolence that at least one of their number had come there expecting.

"It's nicer than I thought it would be," observed Miss Bickle, disappointed. "Although it also smells worse."

Not having any sensical reply to that, Mr. Caesar led his lady companions, along with two of the four men who had come to guard them, into Lord Wriothesly's Folly. To his concern, it was a mostly different crowd from the one he had seen the previous evening, although in truth he had paid little attention to the ununiformed patrons.

The one red jacket in the room belonged to a young man who was leaning on the bar and watching the world with an expression of laconic disinterest that Mr. Caesar and I both greatly approved of.

"Sal?" Mr. Caesar said to the young soldier, hoping that he wasn't making an embarrassing error.

"Hello, sailor," Sal replied. "Can't get enough of us, eh? Sorry to hear about your sister, but if we find anything we'll tell the captain and he'll tell you. You've no need to come back to the slums."

The mix of greeting, reassurance, and implied rebuke in the space of two breaths gave Mr. Caesar a certain degree of social whiplash. "I'm here to see Barryson," he explained.

Sal yelled through to somebody who yelled through to somebody who was presumably going to rouse Barryson from a back room and I, from an abundance of caution, adopted an insectoid shape to aid my concealment. Then Sal turned back to Mr. Caesar with a lazy smile. "So who're your friends?"

Conscious that the ladies' virtues were potentially at stake, although equally conscious that each of them had the option to be more lax about their reputation than was typical, Mr. Caesar tried to keep introductions formal. "Sal, this is Miss Bickle and Miss Mitchelmore"—it struck him that given the company and Captain James's willingness to be on first-name terms with servants, it was best to introduce the men as well—"and these are . . ." He became rapidly conscious of a flaw in that plan. "Two gentlemen who work for Miss Bickle."

"Harris," said one.

"Hawkins," said the other.

"Which is pleasingly alliterative," added Mr. Caesar, who immediately regretted it.

With a level of gallantry that Mr. Caesar felt sure either of his sisters would have found head-turning, Sal kissed each of the ladies' hands (that is, he kissed one hand of each lady, not each hand of every lady; if there is ambiguity in that sentence it is the consequence of your limited mortal language, not of my intent) then bowed warmly to each of the gentlemen. "Charmed," he said, "on all counts."

"Hawey," called a voice from the back as Barryson emerged from whatever bowels the Folly possessed, "what you yelling for?"

Mr. Caesar looked contrite, or as contrite as it was possible to look while maintaining a patrician façade. "I'm sorry to disturb you. But as I believe you've been told, my sister is missing."

"Bad business that," observed Barryson.

"And my friend here"—Mr. Caesar indicated Miss Bickle—"is of the opinion that she might have been"—here an unwarranted embarrassment overtook his tongue—"abducted by fairies."

At the mention of fairies, Barryson's wild eyes scanned the room and I inched myself into a crack in a ceiling beam. "Could be," he said. "You bring watchers with you, John Caesar. There's an otherworldly air about all three of yez."

Miss Mitchelmore paled ever so slightly. "Oh, John, you don't think—this couldn't be because of me, could it? Did I somehow draw supernatural attention to your family?"

She did, of course. Just not the supernatural attention that was causing their present difficulties.

"We can't assume that yet," Mr. Caesar told her, "and even if we could it would still not be your fault."

"Perhaps," admitted Miss Mitchelmore. "But Georgiana swore off love for a lifetime rather than expose others to mystical peril. I might at least have thought about the possibility of my situation affecting those I care for."

Mr. Caesar's sometimes overbearing attitude towards his cousin had its advantages, and this was one of the rare moments in which it could be almost a comfort. "If you had, what would you have done to prevent this? Tied witch knots in her hair? Hung myrtle and wild roses over her window? Warned her to beware of fair ladies on white horses and handsome knights with sweet-sounding horns?"

Miss Mitchelmore conceded that she would not, indeed, have known which if any of those things would have proven efficacious (for the record, the answer is "two of them"; the others will kill you immediately) and that she would therefore have been no actual help in protecting Miss Caesar from supernatural danger. But she conceded it grudgingly.

It was agreed amongst those present (or most of those present; Harris and Hawkins had little say in the matter) that to determine if the unfortunate Miss Caesar had indeed been taken by my people then Barryson would need to examine the room from which she had disappeared. They returned, as a foursome (a sixsome, counting the servants, but who does?) to the carriage, and set out back through London en route to the Caesar residence.

We now encounter a slight problem. Mr. Caesar's plan, to recruit the services of a known seer in order to determine what might have become of his sister, was a good one. But since that involved determining whether there had been supernatural interference with the family in general, the sister in particular, and her room most particularly of all, I was conscious that my own presence might disrupt his divination.

Not that I cared. Or at least, not that I cared for reasons that you mortals will understand. My concern was entirely in thwarting my master's rival. I was loyal then, O my dread lord, and I remain loyal now. Ever your servant. Ever safeguarding your interests even when you do not know it.

Just saying.

But this left me with something of a quandary. My duty as a storyteller is to record every significant event that transpires and to relay it to you, my beloved readers, without embellishment or deception. My duty as a zealous (ever zealous, ever faithful, ever committed) servant of my lord was to permit this interference in Titania's plans to proceed. The deciding factor, in this case, was that I suspected staying out of the way would lead, eventually, to a better story.

As a consequence, I was not actually present in the room where the divination took place. But I have reconstructed it as best I can from my own speculations.

"Hoo hoo," said Barryson, standing mortally by the window with a mortal look on his face. "Well, this be a right pickle you do be in and no mistake. Fortunately, I have somehow conceived the vainglorious notion that having read a few runic scribblings by dead Norsemen, I am fully qualified to tangle with the immortal powers of the cosmos."

"I think this is a bad idea," said Mr. Caesar, looking mortal and priggish. "And disapprove strongly even though it is to my direct personal benefit and I am literally asking you to do it."

"Well, I think magic is fun," countered Miss Bickle. "And should like us to do more of it because my beliefs are extremely sensible and will get nobody killed. Of that I am certain."

"And I think our first priority should be assisting Mary," opined Miss Mitchelmore, "who you both seem to have forgotten in all of this."

Then Barryson reached into—oh, I don't know, a bag or something, whatever mortals carry things with—and drew out a sheaf of white wooden strips inscribed with symbols of divination. These he cast into the air and, eyes closed, selected from amongst their number. Even a floor down and three rooms sideways I could feel an unpleasant sense of being watched, of human perception interfacing with laws and systems with which your kind were never meant to interact.

"Bibbity boo," he said, "magic magic magic, probably something about Odin. Yup, definitely fairies."

"Oh." Miss Bickle looked oddly disappointed. "Somehow that feels rather anticlimactic."

". . . eels rather anticlimactic," the genuine, nonspeculative Miss Bickle was saying in the hallway.

"Magic often does," explained Barryson. "It's not all raising hanged men from the dead."

Miss Bickle gasped. "*Can* you raise hanged men from the dead?"

"I can, but there's not a huge amount of call for it, know what I mean?"

I made my way in my spider's shape to rejoin the companions, which took rather longer than travelling in a larger form. It's amazing how big a sitting room becomes when one is less than an inch across.

"What troubles me," Mr. Caesar was saying when I arrived, "is that I haven't the slightest clue what to do now. If she has, as you say, been taken by fairies, what recourse does that leave us?"

Miss Mitchelmore took her cousin's hands and looked up at him reassuringly. "We will find a way to rescue her. I am sure of it."

"People always do," said Miss Bickle with her typical confidence. "You might have to go on a very long journey, or fight an ogre, or hold on to her while she changes into lots of things you don't really want to be holding on to. But you'll win in the end. That's how it works."

For some reason, mortals often found Miss Bickle's unwavering faith in the beneficence of my people wearing but, on this one occasion, Mr. Caesar seemed to take the sensible position that she was extremely right and comforting.

"Thank you," he said. "And thank you as well, Barryson. This was beyond the call of duty, truly."

Barryson gave a sly grin. "No worries, I'm sure you'd do the same for my sister."

Since it had not occurred to Mr. Caesar that Barryson had a sister, or that he really had any life at all beyond being a soldier, that observation reproved him a little. Although only a little; he was, after all, still an earl's grandson. "If the lady ever needs"— he hesitated—"anything I am qualified to provide, please don't hesitate."

"Know any single dukes?" Barryson asked.

If he'd tried, Mr. Caesar could have named at least one, but this seemed to be going to dangerous places. "I fear relationships between untitled ladies and dukes seldom end as well as the popular imagination would have you believe."

"True enough." Barryson shouldered the bag that he was indeed carrying (you see, my descriptions were entirely accurate) and made for the door. "I'll tell the captain they can stop searching the river. Oh and, will you be wanting him to second for you?"

Mr. Caesar blinked. "Second?"

"In the duel."

The tiny matter of his sister's abduction had driven the tiny matter of the duel from Mr. Caesar's mind. "Ah. Yes. That. I suppose his seconding would indeed be valued and, well, is there still a plan for Jackson to . . ."

"Fuck the whole thing up so you don't die? Yeah."

Miss Bickle adopted an expression of approving outrage. "Are you going to cheat in a duel? Are you becoming a rakehell? Do say you're becoming a rakehell."

It was, perhaps, illustrative of Mr. Caesar's vexed relationship with the ton that *rakehell* was never a title to which he had felt able to aspire. Gentlemen with fairer fortunes, fairer skin, and more interest in the fairer sex might have been able to get away with cocking a snook at a world that at once despised and admired them. Mr. Caesar, by contrast, needed to reserve his defiance for dark rooms and closed doors and—very, very occasionally— punching annoying men in the teeth. "I am doing what it takes to secure my survival. And with current circumstances, the sooner I get this silly business with the major out of the way the better."

"John!" Miss Bickle's look of outrage grew rather less

approving. "A duel is not a silly business. It is terribly romantic and exciting."

Barryson shook his head. "Nae, miss, it's silly. Now holmgang, that's a different matter."

Ever eager for stories of iron-thewed men doing sweaty things to each other, Miss Bickle gave Barryson a wide-eyed *tell me more* look, but Mr. Caesar preempted it by opening the door and saying, "Well, we shouldn't keep you."

A conclusion that Miss Bickle found dismaying enough that she pouted for the rest of the evening.

CHAPTER SIX

THEY SHARED THE GOOD OR, if you prefer, bad news with Lady Mary and Miss Anne at once, and with the elder Mr. Caesar the moment he returned home that evening.

"What does this mean?" was his first, and eminently understandable, question.

With a wisdom that few besides me understood her to possess, Miss Bickle kept her personal theories on what it would mean silent.

The younger Mr. Caesar, however, did not have that luxury. "It means that she is presently beyond our reach. At least, beyond our reach by any method that I know of. But it also means that she is not dead."

"Can you be sure of that?" asked Lady Mary, who despite several reassurances on this front had been all anxiety since that afternoon.

"Reasonably." It was not the answer the younger Mr. Caesar wanted to give, but they had never been a family that lied to one another. "As a rule, gods kill, fairies steal."

He was oversimplifying, but that did largely capture the essence of it.

"Our best hope, I think," put in Miss Mitchelmore, "is to speak with the Ambassador." For those readers who have had the ill manners to ignore my previous published work, the Ambassador to which she referred was the Ambassador from the Other Court, a mortal man in service to my master with whom she had dealt a little in the past. "He would have knowledge at least, even if he were not inclined to help us."

Less of an oversimplification, and largely true. And there was an element of solidarity between changelings that they might have been able to play upon.

"Do we have any idea how to actually contact him?" asked the younger Mr. Caesar.

To Miss Bickle, this was a trifling concern. "Well, no, but I am sure something will come up. Trust the system, John."

"Is there a system?" the younger Mr. Caesar asked, without a trace of uncertainty.

"Well, no, but I feel one should trust it anyway."

For the past two hours, Lady Mary had been pretending to work at needlepoint while actually twisting a needle between her fingers and wondering why she had been confronted with a problem so wholly beyond her resources. Now she looked up at her son with an almost pleading air. "At least tell me you are no longer going to fight that pointless duel."

"Things will go worse for us if I do not."

"Will they?" Lady Mary seemed wholly unconvinced. "Or will it only be worse for your pride?"

Privately, Mr. Caesar was unsure. It was what he told himself, certainly. But how was he to know what he believed and what he had merely been told he should believe? A gentleman did not back down from a challenge. A gentleman did not lie with other gentle-men. A gentleman was always courteous and well presented. A gentleman did not let his sister come to harm. He had failed in so many areas that he was not sure he could bear to fail in another. "We may need to take actions that require connections. If I am thought a coward as well as a ruffian, it will make maintaining those connections harder. I need to do this."

The logic was sound, and although none amongst the company liked the reasoning, they accepted it readily enough. And the same logic led to the conclusion that it would be best if the younger Mr. Caesar got an early night. Or at least, he got what passed for an early night in his circumstances, which was a night of lying in bed staring at nothing, trying to keep his thoughts from running to all of the terrible things that lay either behind or before him. He found himself wishing, absurdly, that the captain was there. Which was not a wish he was accustomed to making about men he'd fucked. If anything he was more accustomed to wishing they'd leave.

So silence fell early over the household, a quiet, waiting sort of silence broken only by the scribbling of the elder Mr. Caesar's pen nib in his study where he, like his son, tried not to dwell on the pre-sent misfortune and his role within it. And, like his son, he failed.

There were no more falling stars that night. Which suggested to me that the Lady was busy. Perhaps she had found in Miss Caesar what she had been looking for. A project she could work on. Even if I had been the sort to show concern for mortals, which I am not, I would have felt no fear for the girl. For her life at least. The Lady's way is only to give, and to give nothing that is not asked for.

Which is, of course, its own kind of cruelty.

Mr. Caesar made his way to Hampstead Heath alone in the small hours of the morning. Well, alone save for a swallow flying overhead and observing his every action with the meticulous attention to detail of a master narrativist.

He was, he realised, somewhat taking his life in his hands not only in fighting this duel but in approaching it. The patrols had largely suppressed the threat of highwaymen but there was still the danger of more regular footpads, to say nothing of such prosaic perils as falling in a ditch, breaking one's ankle, or staining one's jacket. And those were only the perils that mortals *know* about. If you had seen half the things that I have seen lurking in the shadows of even the tamest of wild places, I swear you would none of you ever leave your houses.

Still he made the walk across not-especially-rough ground in not-especially-deep darkness unscathed, and was rewarded with the gratifying sight of Captain James and the somewhat less gratifying sight of Major Bloodworth already waiting for him. The major, it seemed, had enlisted Mr. Bygrave to be his own second, probably because Lord Hale was not the kind of man who would get out of bed for a dawn rendezvous unless he stood to profit from it personally. Of course, by acquiescing to this arrangement, Mr. Bygrave was risking direct involvement in the death of the brother of a girl he was making at least some attempt to court. A fact that bespoke either an amusing obliviousness or a commendable callousness on his part. I lean towards the former.

There stood also with the company a man who Mr. Caesar belatedly realised was a military doctor, and it was his presence more than anything else that brought home to him the reality of what he proposed to do or, more to the point, to risk having done to him. The captain's slightly too enthusiastic descriptions of the things different kinds of blades could do to a human body crept up in him and hooked into his mind like ill-mannered spiders.

"Wear these" was Captain James's only greeting, slapping a pair of heavy leather gauntlets against Mr. Caesar's chest.

Mr. Caesar looked at his own gloves, which were a rather fine kidskin although he'd had the foresight not to wear his best pair. "Aren't they a little—"

"They're a little more likely to dull a cut, put them on."

He obeyed. Or, not being a man who relished the thought of obedience, was persuaded to take the suggested course of action independently.

While Mr. Caesar was making this small alteration to his attire, Mr. Bygrave came scurrying over. "Major Bloodworth wishes me to say," he began, juddering to a halt, "that you can still be reconciled if you apologise."

"Happily," replied Mr. Caesar. "As soon as he apologises to me."

Mr. Bygrave looked uncertain. "What would he need to apologise to you for?"

It was not entirely unreasonable that the lad didn't know. Mr. Caesar had deliberately kept the details from both of his sisters. Not that it had helped Mary, in retrospect. "For having his men accost me?" Mr. Caesar suggested. "But more pertinently for what he said about my sister."

"What did he say about your sister?" asked Mr. Bygrave.

"He . . . implied that she was ill-favoured."

Mr. Bygrave adopted a look of shock that Miss Bickle would have been proud of. "Surely not, Anne is one of the—"

"Not Anne. Mary."

The look of shock vanished. "Oh, well—I mean, look, military men can be indelicate and well . . ."

"Well?" asked Captain James, his voice soft and level.

"Well, I'd never say as much aloud, but not every girl can be a beauty."

It was, I feel, testimony to the general evenness of Mr. Caesar's temperament that he felt no desire to strike the gentleman. "He insulted her by specific reference to her . . . heritage."

Sometimes, you can see a gentleman walking towards a cliff edge from so far away you have time to fetch your trombone and start playing an appropriately farcical tune. This, with Mr. Bygrave, was one such time. "I suppose," he began. It was not an auspicious beginning. "That is . . . from the major's perspective you have to concede that African ladies do, on average, look—"

"Choose your next words well," warned Captain James. "And when you do, remember two things."

"What things?" asked Mr. Bygrave obligingly.

"Number one. That what you say next isn't just about Mary, it's about my mother. And her mother. And her mother's mother. Number two, that one day in the very near future I might be in a position where I must decide whether or not it's worth saving your life."

Mr. Bygrave blinked, unused to such frank discussion of death from the officer class but cowed as much by Captain James's heroic reputation as anything else. "Of course," he said, "I'm sorry. And I meant no offence."

"See how easy that was?" replied the captain. "Now, why don't you run off and see if the major'll do the same."

Mr. Bygrave dashed back to speak with the major but, as he did, I lost interest, because I saw a single star streak across the heavens, and heard a music like glass chimes in a gentle breeze, and felt the breath of the Lady on my neck.

"I am working," I told her.

"So you continue to tell yourself."

In my peripheral vision I watched Mr. Caesar walk over to the major and say . . . something. It was hard for me to make out while so distracted. "I have events to observe."

"Don't you just. I wonder if you realise how interesting those events are about to become."

I did not wonder. I was beginning to know for certain. The Lady had chosen to interject herself into my story and there was nothing I could do about it without sending the narrative careening off onto paths I could not predict.

"It's an officer's weapon"—the major was saying—"which you'd know if you'd ever fought for your country. Go on then, you upjumped vagabond, take one."

"The big reveal," the Lady told me, "is coming in three."

Mr. Caesar's fingers closed on a narrow-bladed cut-and-thrust sword . . .

"Two."

. . . and he retreated, uncertain, to a mark that Captain James was holding for him. . . .

"One."

. . . "En garde, *sir*," the major began with a sneer. . . .

"And here we go."

. . . A gentle blue light filled the air, and from the shadow beneath two trees emerged Miss Caesar. And all eyes turned to her because, as she had wished, she was beautiful.

You mortals like to say that beauty is subjective, but you are, in this as in so many things, wrong. There is a beauty beyond words, beyond physicality, beyond truth itself. When Miss Caesar stepped forward from those shadows she was beautiful like a sunrise. Beautiful like a thunderstorm. Beautiful like a city on fire.

She looked, in some ways, much as she always had. She was no taller or shorter, her eyes and mouth and nose were in the same place as they had ever been. But her whole body was glass. Pure, brilliant, colourless glass that caught the starlight and danced it and amplified it until she seemed to glow from within like angels are meant to but, sadly, do not.

Those who had known her more closely, and who had the wherewithal to see the parts of her rather than the remarkable whole, might have noticed one or two other changes. She looked rather more carved, rather less living. Glass leaves and crystal roses, wound wicked-edged and gleaming through her hair—or the glass that it had become—and twined to her shoulders on sparkling briars. She was robed not in the simple nightdress she had left in, but a gown of some strange vitreous silk, which scattered the light within her enough to allow for modesty, insofar as such things mattered to glass women.

I hated to admit it, but the Lady had *excelled* herself.

The arrival of Miss Caesar seemed to have put all thought of quarrel out of the gentlemen's minds. Both the major and Mr. Caesar lowered their blades and for a long minute just stared. Mr. Bygrave was, if anything, still more affected, gazing slack-jawed and rapt at the visitation.

"Effective, isn't she?" observed the Lady.

"Thoroughly. What do you intend to do with her now?"

"Observe."

In that regard the Lady's function was much like mine, although she was far more a setter-in-motion than I. Far more a meddler.

Mr. Caesar broke free first, familial affection falling under the same category of exemptions to our powers that covers true love, purity of heart, and seventh sons of seventh sons. Calling his sister's name, he stumbled towards her, still not entirely in command of his faculties.

"John?" Miss Caesar's voice, like her face, had changed little but utterly. It was as clear and as cool as crystal, sparkling like sunlight on deceptively fast water. "How did you come to be here?"

"How did you?" he asked.

And Miss Caesar had no reply. She just looked down at her hands as if seeing them—and for that matter seeing through them—for the first time. "I am not sure. I . . . I believe I made a wish."

"But are you all right?"

She nodded. "I think so. But"—she turned her eyes up to her brother, eyes that had now no iris or pupil but swirled instead with an endless depth of pearlescent mist. Still, there was hope there, for those who had the skill to read it—"am I beautiful?"

"You have always been beautiful," replied Mr. Caesar with fraternal conviction.

But this drew only laughter from the lady (the young lady, that is, uncapitalised, not the Lady, who was still watching by my side, although now I make the comparison there were similarities). And her laughter, like her voice, like her body, had become a thing of weaponised marvel. Of lethal delight. "Oh, John." She reached out a hand and touched him gently on the arm, and though he tried to hide it I saw the tiniest shudder run through him at the coldness of it. "You don't have to lie to me anymore."

And before he could protest, or indeed make any reply at all, she turned away to face the three men who remained. "Greetings," she said. And in my experience she had never been a *greetings* sort of person before her transformation. But time—even a short time—amongst our courts alters mortals and makes them, in some ways, more like us. Which is to say, more fun.

At the sound of the young lady's voice, the major and Mr. Bygrave sank at once to their knees. Captain James retained his composure thanks to the other exemption that providence saw fit to weave into our magics, that which protects persons of irritatingly heroic character.

Still at least slightly confused by the sight of four men on a heath at dawn with two swords between them, Miss Caesar asked the pertinent question. "What was happening here?"

In the tangle of his heart, the major knew that something was wrong, but there is a dazzling power to captured starlight, and he was, deep down, a man easily dazzled. "I was to duel your brother," he explained, almost as though fighting his own lips and larynx. "I had offered you insult, my lady, a choice I now deeply regret."

Like a saint in an old painting, Miss Caesar approached the major with an air of endless beneficence. Where she walked, stardust sparkled in her footprints a moment. "Rise," she said.

And he rose.

"You are forgiven," she told him. "Now go. We shall quarrel no further."

Somewhere deep in the knot of bile the major called a heart, I could see something rebelling against the power of the Beauty Incomparable. He had known, after all, for certain and for a lifetime that men such as himself were to be deferred to, not defied. But for now, at least, he surrendered to the glory of the Other Court and, averting his eyes, retreated.

"As for you"—she turned her attention to Mr. Bygrave, who was still on one knee and staring fixedly at the grass—"perhaps at our next ball, we shall dance."

With no further comment she swept past him, her gown a cascade of silver motes inside a shell of nothing. She did not make it far before Captain James interposed himself.

"And where're you off to now, miss?"

"Town," she replied with a certainty that surprised even her. "I wish to be among people."

"It's dawn," the captain reminded her, "and you've people at home."

Mr. Caesar had, by this point, caught up with them. "We should get you back at once," he agreed. "Mother and father have been beside themselves."

Time is different where we live—

"Do you absolutely have to tell them every little thing?" asked the Lady, but I ignored her.

—and so it was not surprising to me that Miss Caesar looked uncomprehending. "It has not been so long, surely?"

"A full day, Mary." Mr. Caesar's tone was sharp. It was, I suppose, the kind of sharpness that comes only from affection, but that distinction is so often lost on people. I myself find sharpness of all kinds delightful and appreciate the variety. "We have been frantic. The captain's whole squadron has been out looking for you. They spoke to the river police."

Another feature of our magics is that they can make mortals callous. So perhaps that was the reason that Miss Caesar seemed unmoved by her brother's admonition. Or perhaps it was just that she was sixteen. "Well, I am back now," she said, "and I was in no danger. The Lady took care of me."

"Nice to get credit for your work, isn't it?" the Lady said to me.

"Actually, I prefer to remain anonymous. That's why I let that awful mortal slap his name on—"

"Yes, yes, let's not talk about that particular incident now. You win some, we win some."

I took my eyes off my charges for a half a second to challenge her. "Which ones have you won?"

"This one," the Lady replied, "for a start."

When I looked back, the mortals were already leaving, Miss Caesar gliding with inhuman grace in the direction of town—although admittedly one direction out of the heath was as good as any other for that purpose—while her escorts kept pace and did their best to steer her.

Their best, by and large, proved lacking.

It is often said by chroniclers of this era that there are two Londons, and that they change places at sunrise. This is of course an oversimplification. There are, to my certain knowledge, at least 234 distinct Londons, some visible to mortals, some not, some literal, some metaphorical, some that if you enter you will never leave. But I do not wish to overload your fragile human minds, so let us keep to the more encompassable convention, that the capital of the Empire is merely a dual city, and that its nocturnal inhabitants change places with its diurnal ones at their appointed hours, passing only briefly through the shadows of the demimonde between.

So it was this daily changeover through which the trio now walked, chancers and cutpurses stumbling to bed while clerks and costermongers stumbled into work. As the sun rose, its rays caught Miss Caesar's new form and danced about within her, becoming a swirling, lambent permanence which would, when she moved just so, radiate out from her like a blessing from a particularly casual god.

She was, to put it bluntly, a distraction, and when she had been the proximal cause of two carts ploughing slowly but dangerously into each other, Mr. Caesar and the captain renewed their efforts to persuade her homewards.

"Look at it like this," the captain tried, "it's morning. Nobody worth seeing is out in the morning."

Mr. Caesar nodded. "He's right, this is hardly the visiting hour. Indeed it's hardly the breakfast hour."

"And proper rogues only come out at night," added Captain James, unhelpfully to Mr. Caesar's eyes.

Stopping in the middle of the street and causing, as a result, a tremendous snarl in the foot traffic, Miss Caesar observed the crowds and did, indeed, find them wanting. "I suppose," she conceded, "it would be rather fine to see Anne." She smirked to herself. "What will she think?"

In large part, Mr. Caesar already knew what Anne thought. She had made her opinions about how selfish Mary had been in running away quite plain over the last day, although he chose to attribute this mostly to displaced anxiety.

So with Captain James clearing away the gawpers and Mr. Caesar leading his sister gently by the arm, the three of them set out for home.

They arrived to find a house not in uproar exactly—neither the elder Mr. Caesar nor Lady Mary were given to uproar—but an obvious state of agitated expectation. And I will confess to the slightest pang of professional jealousy in this matter. Because the Lady had indeed orchestrated a wonderful chaos. And that is the entire purpose of our people.

When they came at last to the drawing room of the Caesar household, Lady Mary rose to her feet, embraced her son with an in my opinion uncreative cry of "John, I thought you'd been killed," and then stared over his shoulder at the transparent vessel of luminance that was her eldest daughter. "Mary?"

Miss Caesar nodded. "It's me."

"John said"—the elder Mr. Caesar remained sitting as he spoke—"that you had been taken by fairies."

"I made a wish," Miss Caesar replied. That this statement by itself did not evoke horror amongst all present is testimony to how little mortals understand of the truths beyond their reality.

Her father gave her a look that was not disapproving but spoke of a deep, private concern. "And you wished for this?"

"I wished for beauty."

From her window seat, Miss Anne made a sound of profound grievance. "Well, isn't that just like you."

"Just like me?" The tone Miss Caesar had been aiming for was, I think, hurt, but in her new fairy-touched shape her every word was touched with mirth, and so it came out cutting. "Whatever do you mean?"

With the aggrieved fury of all her fourteen years, Miss Anne gave her sister a look of withering accusation. "You couldn't let me have even one thing. You had to be the pretty one as well."

"Not wishing to speak out of turn," said Captain James very gently, "I don't think that's what we should be worrying about right now."

"Well, of course you don't," replied Miss Anne. "You're not even a proper officer. How would you understand these things?"

By the door, Nancy cleared her throat. "Saving your presence, miss, and yours, miss"—she bobbed curtseys to both of her young mistresses—"I wouldn't know a proper officer from an improper one, but he's right. I knew a lass made a wish once and it went bad for everybody."

Reader, I have left the following exchange intact out of my peerless personal integrity, but I should remind you that incidents like the ones described in these pages represent an unrepresentative minority of mortal-fairy interactions. The vast majority of them end extremely satisfactorily for both parties and with hardly anybody dead, transformed to sea-foam, or ruing their choices until death and beyond.

"What did she wish for?" asked Lady Mary, releasing her son from her embrace.

"For her brother to not die of the scarlatina."

"And did he?" asked Mr. Caesar.

"No," replied Nancy. And there was an ominousness to the syllable which begged for follow-up.

"Did he . . ." Lady Mary was trying her very best to formulate a question whose answer would not be devastating to hear. "Did he die of something else instead?"

Nancy nodded. "Shot by three Bow Street Runners."

For a moment the detail meant nothing to anybody present. But then Miss Anne, who paid rather more attention to lurid rumours and broadside ballads than most of her family, put her hands to her mouth. "You mean he was the Red Death of Clapham?"

Mr. Caesar turned to his youngest child. "What is that, precisely?"

"He was a spirit," Miss Anne explained, still slightly too shocked to recount the tale properly, "or a demon, or a monster of some kind. His touch spread the scarlet fever and he killed twenty men before they found him and—"

"I do not," Miss Caesar insisted, "spread scarlet fever. I am just"—she stood for a moment looking down at herself, at the light spilling out from where her heart had been—"I'm just me."

And that observation hushed the room. Presumably because nobody wanted to voice the doubts they were experiencing over that exact question.

Lady Mary, aware that on that matter at least her silence was speaking as loudly as any admonition, crossed the sitting room to wrap her arms warmly around her daughter. But this nauseatingly affectionate action was cut off by a cry of pain, and she withdrew, blood flowing freely from lacerations on her palm.

"Mama?" Miss Caesar looked quite distraught, as might any child in such a situation.

Lady Mary, still nursing her injury, couldn't quite look her daughter in the eye. "Don't worry, it's just—those leaves are very sharp."

Cautiously, Miss Caesar raised her fingers to her hair. But glass does not cut glass and so she felt nothing. "I didn't mean to," she tried.

"No doubt." The elder Mr. Caesar had yet to move, but he stood now to inspect his wife's injury. "Nancy, this looks deep, you may need to fetch a doctor."

Miss Caesar looked close to tears. Close to, but not actually crying, and I wondered, idly, if she still could. "I'm sorry," she said, "I'm sorry."

"You should be," snapped Miss Anne from the window. "Look what you've done."

That earned her a harsh "That's enough, Anne" from Lady Mary, but it was too late. There is little that hardens the heart like a reprimand from a younger sibling.

Nancy returned with water, lint, and bandages, and Lady Mary sat down, a little unsteady, her husband supporting her.

"This is not Mary's fault," the elder Mr. Caesar told his daughter with a certainty honed over years of public speaking. "This is something that was done to her."

It was, by all accounts, a reasonable statement, but he had reckoned without the wilfulness he and his wife had, with some consideration, instilled in all of their children.

"It was not," insisted Miss Caesar. "This is what I wanted. What I asked for. The Lady—"

"Who is this Lady?" asked the younger Mr. Caesar. He knew in general, of course. Just not in particular.

"My patron."

Miss Anne gave an uncharitable giggle. "Mary, that makes you sound like—like a woman of questionable reputation."

"Anne"—Lady Mary gave the girl a very reproving look—"you have been warned."

"But she does sound dangerous," the younger Mr. Caesar observed. "Mary, what do you really know about this"—his hesitation to use the word *person* wounded me to my core; fairies are people too—"individual?"

"I know," replied Miss Caesar, "that she heard me when nobody else would. That she helped me when nobody else would."

Lady Mary's hand tightened around the bindings on her wound. "Are you really sure that this is help?"

Miss Caesar's eyes being pupilless, I could not quite tell where she was looking, although her focus seemed to be on the blood still seeping through her mother's bandages. But she had come a long way, and passed a timeless while amongst the Other Court, and so whatever doubts or uncertainties she may even then have harboured she still answered: "Yes."

And in the moment, she meant it.

CHAPTER SEVEN

S TRICTLY SPEAKING, MR. CAESAR HAD no reason to return
to the Folly. The captain and his men had done more
than enough for his family already, and even when
Mr. Caesar was in a mood for rough trade he did not ordinarily
frequent quite such dangerous locales.

He had tried, on his way over, to ignore the figures huddled in
doorways. Or at the very least to view them with compassion, as his
parents might, rather than fear. But having come close to dying at
the end of a blade once already he could not help but see knives up
every ragged sleeve and in the folds of every torn skirt.

Had he not recently spent the night with Mr. Ellersley, he would
have considered this quite the most self-destructive thing he had
ever done.

It was early evening when Mr. Caesar arrived at the Folly, and
so he found the place crowded but not raucous. Which was a
shame. I for one would have preferred at least a touch of raucousness. Poking his head through the door, he scanned the room for
the captain and, finding him absent, realised that he had not planned

for that contingency. Of late he had been spending much of his time feeling a fool, although for reasons he could not quite articulate it was a foolishness he did not find wholly unpleasant.

As he stood dithering on the threshold, a voice called to him from a corner of the room. "Staying, or leaving?"

The voice had enough of Eton about it that it could only have belonged to Kumar. And sure enough, it did. While around him the ne'er-do-wells of St. Giles went about their business, he was sitting quietly beside them reading what from Mr. Caesar's angle appeared to be a copy of Voltaire's *Candide*.

Now that he had been seen, Mr. Caesar had little choice but to choose *staying* from the offered alternatives. And I stayed with him, in the hope that he might amuse me by getting himself stabbed.

Kumar folded his book closed. "Take a seat. We don't often get gentlemen here. It's almost refreshing."

"You don't consider yourself a gentleman?" asked Mr. Caesar. What people did or did not consider themselves was, he knew, a thorny question, but Kumar had a gentleman's manners and a gentleman's education.

"I'm a gentleman's bastard, it's quite a different thing. We're more likely to wind up in the army, for a start."

Mr. Caesar nodded his understanding. "But for the indelicacies of the wealthy I'm sure the regiments would be empty."

A smile played across Kumar's lips. "I see why the captain likes you. He's always had a weakness for a sharp tongue."

"Oh yes?" Mr. Caesar's tone became instantly guarded. It didn't seem decorous to ask further questions, but he wanted to rather badly.

"That and a challenge," Kumar added. And I could not help feeling that a tale hung thereby, though it was not one I had collected. "I assume it *is* him you came here looking for."

"Would you believe me if I said I was just keen to mingle with the salt of the earth and the pride of the British army?"

"Not for a moment."

"Good, because it would be a spectacular lie."

Kumar drummed his fingers on the cover of his copy of *Candide*. "Well, he should be along presently. He doesn't like to let us go too long unobserved. You never know *what* we'd get up to."

A pale shadow detached itself from the wall a few feet away, and Mr. Caesar saw Jackson, who must have been listening in the whole time.

"I could almost take that," Jackson said, "for a besmirchment of my honour."

"And what honour would that be?" asked Kumar, breezily.

Jackson grinned knives. "That's why I said *almost*."

While he had been comfortable-ish conversing with Kumar, there was something about Jackson that still unsettled Mr. Caesar. Perhaps it was the perpetual undercurrent of murder.

To his relief, before he needed to choose a reply, the captain returned to the Folly and fixed the little group with a suspicious look.

"Something up?" he asked. Which gave Mr. Caesar a momentary pang of guilt since it did not, in general, bode well for one's relationships when the other party assumed you only wanted them when you wanted something *from* them.

Mr. Caesar shook his head with a little too much emphasis. "No more than usually. Which is to say that my sister is still in thrall to an unknown fairy, my best hope of assisting her lies in a plan that my least reliable friend is formulating to chase down a changeling we have met all of twice, and I am profoundly helpless to do anything to assist anybody until she has gathered herself."

"A sharp tongue," Kumar stage-whispered, "a challenge, and helplessness. You're on *very* good ground."

Either not hearing or pretending not to, the captain carried on with his not-exactly-interrogation. "So you're here for what, the beer?"

"I thought I might . . ." I was, I had to admit, *aching* to hear how Mr. Caesar finished that sentence. I had no idea what he thought he might.

"Might what?" asked Captain James with half a smile. "Take me to the opera?"

Kumar and Jackson burst into guffaws.

"Oh, you *should.*" Kumar was capable, it seemed, of smiling quite wickedly if he had to. "Captain, I would love to know your thoughts on *Fidelio.*"

"Fuck off," replied Captain James. Which was a shame because I *also* would have loved to hear his thoughts on *Fidelio.*

But despite everything, Mr. Caesar—perhaps from a lack of any other options—responded with a clear if ominous "Why not? We're a stone's throw from Covent Garden and it might be a welcome distraction."

Something glimmered in the captain's eyes. Something I found extremely promising. "All right," he said. "But I'd better not be letting myself in for anything awful."

He was. That isn't foreshadowing. I've just never been a fan of opera.

Dedicated as I am to my calling, I drew the line at hours of singing in German, so I reconvened with the captain and Mr. Caesar as they were being disgorged, along with a hundred other patrons, into the streets of Covent Garden following the performance.

"What the fuck," the captain was asking, "was that all about?"

Mr. Caesar took a strengthening breath. "Well, you see, it tells the story of Fidelio who is a . . . a very faithful man . . . hence his name. But he's torn between his duty to, I suppose, his country? And his love for . . ."

"You haven't got a clue, have you?"

Sheepishly, Mr. Caesar shook his head. "Not really, no."

"Do you even know which one Fidelio was?"

"The tall one? Probably the one who did the most singing? The thing about opera is that nobody really goes for the show. They go to watch other people and gossip."

The captain considered this. "Seems an expensive way to go about it. I'd have thought you could do that anywhere you liked for free."

"But at the opera," Mr. Caesar explained, "you can do it exclusively to the sorts of people who can afford to go to the opera."

Had any further illustration been needed of the opera's primary social function, it was provided at once by a cry of "John, fancy seeing you here." A cry that emanated from an extraordinarily well-turned-out Mr. Ellersley. "And with company, no less. So good to see you showing your appreciation for the fine bodies of our fighting men."

"I think you mean 'our fine body of fighting men,'" Mr. Caesar corrected him, knowing full well that it hadn't been an error.

"Oh, do I?"

"Who's this?" asked the captain, his hand going at once to a sword he wasn't wearing.

"Old friend," replied Mr. Caesar with a studied laconicity. "And I cannot overemphasise the word *old*."

Mr. Ellersley curled his lips into a smile that Mr. Caesar had always been unsure if he wanted to kiss or punch. Although given how poorly punching had gone for him lately, he'd probably made the better choice overall. "Claws in, prince of cats. I just wanted to see how you found the show."

He did not, Mr. Caesar knew full well, want to see how he had found the show. "Delightful," he said. "So delightful that it almost distracted me from what Lord Wilmslowe was doing with that lady he swears is his niece."

"Oh, well deflected," replied Mr. Ellersley. And there was that smile again. "Although thinking about it, if she *is* his niece that makes things substantially more interesting."

I sometimes almost liked Mr. Ellersley.

Captain James, not especially interested in being caught up in a duel of manners between bitter exes, fell back on his training and looked for the nearest path of escape. "Do you reckon that if we put a sprint on we could make it somewhere fun before we get trampled by theatre folk?"

"Oh don't *go*." A gleam came to Mr. Ellersley's eye. "Why don't you bring the captain to the club? I'm sure he'd go down wonderfully."

This kind of sniping was to be expected from Thomas Ellersley and normally Mr. Caesar would have taken it in stride. But the joke was not entirely at his expense, and while the captain, in any other circumstance, was worth twenty Ellersleys, to the opera crowd he was an upjumped slum rat from the ranks whose words would by definition be worthless.

"I think you'll find," Mr. Caesar began, but then his words ran uncharacteristically dry. *That is but one of many areas in which he is your superior* had been the retort that sprang instantly to mind. But that would have been for *his* defence, not the captain's. One could hardly defend a gentleman from the intimation that he was your catamite by praising his sexual technique. "I mean to say——" was the next fateful stumble.

"Shall I send a man ahead?" Mr. Ellersley continued. "Or do you want to surprise them?"

It should not have been this difficult. All he needed to do was to take what the other gentleman had just said, turn it around, and fire it back in a way that made him look foolish. He'd done it a thousand times. But never once in a way that required him to think about the well-being of another party.

"Having a bad evening?" Mr. Ellersley continued innocently. "You're usually much better sport. What *has* this creature been doing to you?"

He was failing. He was failing at the one thing he was meant to be good at. So Mr. Caesar took a deep breath, looked Mr. Ellersley in the eye and said: "Tom. Fuck off." Then before his brain could process the damage to his reputation as a wit and a gadabout, he turned to the captain. "Come on, let's go somewhere that isn't miserable."

"Paying your respects to the men in uniform?" Mr. Ellersley shot after them, having at least partially recovered from the sheer effrontery of having been dismissed so curtly.

"You know," Mr. Caesar returned over his shoulder. "I think I actually might."

So they went back to the Folly. It was not the kind of place Mr. Caesar would normally have gone after the opera, but it was nearby and it was mercifully free of the Mr. Ellersleys of the world.

The hour having grown later, the inn had grown more vibrant and the Irregulars were in attendance in greater numbers. Captain James threw himself down at the bar with Mr. Caesar companionably close beside him. He could probably have sat closer— the clientele of the Folly seemed to give zero fucks about who was and wasn't a bugger—but long habit kept him at a deniable distance.

"How was the show?" asked Kumar with a waggish tone, sidling up alongside the newcomers.

"Still got no idea," replied Captain James. "But according to this one"—he jerked a thumb at Mr. Caesar—"seeing the show isn't the point. On the other hand we did get to watch a rich man getting up to something that might have been incest."

Feeling some need to come across as less of a total cultural vacuum, Mr. Caesar made a tokenistic effort to defend himself. "Obviously we *also* appreciated the music," he said. "Which was very . . . sweeping."

Sal slipped herself onto the captain's lap, a gesture which stirred irrational jealousy in Mr. Caesar despite its being clearly a more familial gesture than a carnal one. "Was Anna Milder still in the title role?" she asked.

"It was *Fidelio*," replied Mr. Caesar with a fatal lack of thought.

"John reckons he was probably the tall one," added the captain with still more fatal helpfulness.

Sal smirked. "Fidelio is a girl."

"Are you sure?" She was clearly sure. And Mr. Caesar knew she was sure. And she knew he knew she was sure, and I knew that they both knew that they both knew. I found opera in general as dull as an ill-used sabre, but *this* was showing all signs of being a delightful evening.

Captain James made a perfunctory attempt to suppress a grin. "Sal used to be on stage. She knows what she's talking about."

"It's a gentleman's name," protested Mr. Caesar, rather limply.

Sal heaved the sigh of a woman who has needed to explain opera to people many, many times. "*Fidelio* is the story of a young woman named Leonore who disguises herself as a boy named Fidelio in order to search for her husband who has been cruelly imprisoned by the wicked Pizarro."

"So not," the captain faux-asked, "about a very faithful man who is torn between duty to his country and something something something?"

Ordinarily accustomed to the restrictions of his linens, Mr. Caesar was grown uncharacteristically hot in the collar region. "In my defence, I don't speak a word of German."

And Captain James laughed. And the Irregulars laughed. And in spite of himself, Mr. Caesar laughed. It was only later in the evening that it would strike him how rarely he had done that of late.

They fucked again that night, obviously. And although it was not unknown for Mr. Caesar to dally with the same soldier more than once, it was *different* this time. Partly, probably, because they had just been to the opera. And partly because the captain was an officer and so not so unambiguously below his own station as to make things simple. And partly because . . . because of a whole mess of unseemly human concepts that my people do not truck with.

Afterwards they lay sweat-slicked and satisfied on sheets that Mr. Caesar would not normally have touched with a barge pole that was on fire.

"So who was that feller at the opera?" asked the captain, staring at the ceiling cradling Mr. Caesar's head against his shoulder.

"An old friend. Of the"—he waved a hand—"intimate variety."

"He's a prick."

"He is. And I'm sorry you became the target of his . . . prickishness."

Although he tried to look blasé, I could still read the memory of discomfort in the captain's heart. "It's fine. You had my back, that's what matters."

"In an ideal world, your back wouldn't need having."

The captain's lips curled into a rueful smile. "In an ideal world, a lot of good men would still be alive who aren't. Don't see the sense in worrying about ideal worlds." For a moment, they lay in silence, then the captain continued "What were you doing with a shit like that anyway?"

"We suited each other."

Captain James turned his head sideways. "You're not a shit, Caesar. You pretend to be, but you're not."

"Thank you, that's the nicest thing anybody has ever said to me."

"You know the sad thing," the captain replied. "I think that might actually be true."

That wasn't a road Mr. Caesar was especially keen to go down. And it wasn't true in the absolute sense. Within his family, at least, affection had always been freely given, at least until he and his sisters had reached the age of considering such things beneath them. Outside of it, however, that was rather a different story. "I suppose we all have our . . . difficult former lovers," Mr. Caesar mused, in the hope that it would prompt the captain to change the subject.

"True. Had one try to sell me out to the French once. That was pretty difficult."

"What happened?"

"Shot him."

Mr. Caesar had been hoping for a touch more detail, and said as much.

"He had debts," the captain explained. "From gambling. And Bonaparte has spies. Not a gambler, are you?"

"Never more than I can afford to lose. Which in practice means never very much at all."

"Good." The captain gave the best approximation of a nod he could give while horizontal. "Because I've still got the pistol."

It was, Mr. Caesar was sure, mostly a joke. "Even if I owed a fortune, I don't think Napoleon would find me useful enough to subvert."

"Then we should be all right," said the captain. Apparently to himself as much as anybody.

After that they lapsed into a relaxed silence, the furtive night-time sounds of St. Giles drifting in from outside in a way that, in any other company, would have left Mr. Caesar determined to be a mile away at least but with Captain James beside him seemed almost comforting.

"I don't suppose," Mr. Caesar said eventually, "that you'd like to join me for a picnic tomorrow?"

"The opera and a picnic?" The captain laughed again, and Mr. Caesar let himself enjoy it. "You're trying to turn me respectable."

"I say *picnic*. It's more sort of an ill-fated effort to make contact with the Ambassador from the Other Court concocted by a young lady who leaves far too much to chance. But she *is* bringing a hamper."

"Oh." The captain made a great play of suasion. "Well, if there's a hamper, you can count me in."

It was not the kind of mockery Mr. Caesar was used to, being gentler and less grounded in specific knowledge of his personal weaknesses. But it was the kind he could get used to. So he leaned over to the captain and demonstrated his gratitude.

CHAPTER EIGHT

"Y OU SHOULD PROBABLY KNOW," I told the Ambassador the following day over a light supper of poet's tears and chrysanthemums, "that you're about to have some mortals looking for you."

"You can say *people*, Robin," he chided me. "And I am technically mortal as well."

I wasn't about to let that stand. "We're all technically mortal. Even the great lords and ladies of our courts can die in theory."

"So I've heard, but I don't believe it."

I wasn't entirely sure I did. And certainly I have not been spreading any rumours about specific instances. My lord Oberon in particular has always held his current throne, came by it by entirely fair means, and has no blood on his hands whatsoever. And no ichor either. "Gods have died. Titans have been cast down. Even the eternal is impermanent."

The Ambassador drained his glass. "Why are you really here?"

"A friendly visit."

"Say that twice more."

I feigned a sigh—it is a habit, I think, I have picked up from too long observing humans. "The Lady has taken an interest in a girl in whom I have also taken an interest. Her brother will be looking for you. And he will have solicited the assistance of a mortal champion—"

"Do they still make those?" asked the Ambassador casually.

"Once or twice a generation. And they're each as infuriating as the last. But that aside, he will want you to undo what has been done. Or tell him how to undo it. And I wanted to make sure that you were ready to give him an answer that will . . . be to the advantage of our mutual lord."

In the Ambassador's lily-woven bower beyond space and time, something that was pretending very hard to be sunlight slanted down through things that were pretending very hard to be trees, dappling him with gold. Long ago (as you reckon it) he was the source of a quarrel between my master and his lady, and has since that day dwelt in the Other Court from which he has, from time to time, journeyed out to carry word between the human world and the fairy kingdom.

"You mean you want me to use this opportunity to fuck with Titania."

I shrugged. Another mortal affectation. "It is both of our duty, and the Lady is her creature."

"And how exactly will this mortal locate me?" asked the Ambassador, not quite suspicious. One is suspicious only when one is uncertain.

"I couldn't possibly imagine."

The thing that was pretending to be the wind sighed a melody. "My my," said the Ambassador. "I have guests. What a remarkable coincidence."

Knowing that he would not receive visitors in the space beyond

(I had encouraged him to, but he kept raising objections about things like "being able to get out again" and "grip on reality" and "inexperience with nonlinear time" like the utter killjoy he is) I went out to see who it was. I, of course, had no forewarning as to the identity of the intruders because I had no involvement with any sequence of events that could have led to anybody being present.

"Remind me again," Mr. Caesar was saying to Miss Bickle, "how you know this will work?"

"It came to me in a dream," she told him, with ironclad surety.

"And you're certain," said Captain James, who made up the final third of their party, Miss Mitchelmore being otherwise employed with her lover, "that this is the right tree?"

The tree in question was old and gnarled, its branches spreading wide and forming, if one so fancied it, the top and side of a frame or a portal. Daffodils, just in season, strewed the ground beneath, although their exact position was never quite the same the second time one looked.

"I am positive. It was most vivid. I have never felt anything like it, and you should know I have exceedingly vivid dreams all the time."

Mr. Caesar did, in fact, know this. Indeed he had been treated to detailed narrations of several of Miss Bickle's more vivid dreams and had agreed to this little jaunt partly in the hope that he would be treated to no more.

"I'm extraordinarily sorry about this," said Mr. Caesar. "I'm aware that it's a rather odd thing to be doing."

The captain shrugged. "Still better than the opera."

"So now," Miss Bickle explained, "we just place the offerings"— she lifted the hamper that she had brought for the purpose—"on the right spot beneath the boughs."

Mr. Caesar was still looking profoundly sceptical. "And you're sure that teacakes, clotted cream, mature cheese, and a decanter of brandy are appropriate for conjuring an otherworldly intermediary?"

"They seem a fine enough present to me," said Miss Bickle, her lips turning artfully downwards into an aggrieved frown. "And I don't see you stepping forth with any better ideas."

Captain James made a thoughtful expression. "Blood of a virgin? A handful of grave dust?"

After a moment's consideration, Miss Bickle screwed up her nose. "Why would anybody want anything like that? None of those are pleasant at all. Anyway, we have placed the offering, now all that remains is to say the words."

"The words," Mr. Caesar pointed out once again, "that came to you in a dream."

"Yes." Miss Bickle nodded emphatically. "Those words." Because she was the best kind of human being, Miss Bickle paused for an appropriately dramatic time and then said, loudly and clearly: "By the compact of three veils and nine cyphers, I request audience."

For a moment nothing happened. And then for another moment.

Captain James gave Miss Bickle a regretful look. "I don't think it worked, miss."

Being, once again, possessed of a perspicacity that most of her kind lack, Miss Bickle beamed. "Oh, but it wouldn't, you see, until somebody said that it hadn't. But now you've said it didn't, so I'm sure it shall."

The captain glanced confusedly at Mr. Caesar but the only reply he received was "I'm sorry, I have no idea either."

"She means," said the Ambassador, stepping out from behind the tree trunk, "that we like to keep you waiting."

Without hesitation, Miss Bickle scooped up the hamper. "We bring offerings."

"We bring cheese," clarified Mr. Caesar.

"But she's rich," explained the captain, "so it's probably good."

"It's Cornish," explained Miss Bickle. "From a little village near my grandfather's country house. I do not believe it to be famous, but I think it very fine regardless."

The Ambassador took the hamper. "And the teacakes?"

"Homemade," Miss Bickle told him. "Well, made by our cook. But I understand she's fearfully talented."

Holding the basket over one arm, the Ambassador crumbled a corner from one of the cheeses and sampled it. "Acceptable. Now, I assume you're here about your sister?"

It was a trick that never ceased to delight one member of the party nor to infuriate another.

"And how do you know that?" asked Mr. Caesar, warily.

"He's from the *otherworld*, John," Miss Bickle stage-whispered. "They *know things* there."

"We have sources, certainly." The Ambassador cast me a sly glance over Miss Bickle's head.

"What sources?" asked Mr. Caesar, not so easily placated as his friend.

"A little bird. But if you are intending to ask what I *think* you are intending to ask, then you should know it will be dangerous."

"I'd have gone with 'fraught with danger,'" I told him.

"How dangerous?" asked Captain James.

This display of caution earned my contempt and an exclamation of shock from Miss Bickle. "You're a military man, surely you should say, 'I laugh in the face of danger.' I believe there are rules."

"In my experience, miss, them as laugh in the face of danger get a musket ball down the throat. Now, tell us what we can expect. And be detailed. Very detailed."

Being, as he so recently reminded me, technically mortal, the

Ambassador was not capable of a *truly* withering stare, but he made the best approximation he could. "He was right, you *are* supremely irritating."

Mr. Caesar's inevitable response of "Who was right?" was roundly ignored by everybody present except for your humble narrator since I am both the *who* in question and mystically bound to record every detail I observe for later explication.

When it became clear that he was not going to derail the conversation onto any other topic—a common strategy and necessary for survival in the Other Court if you don't want one casual suggestion to see you spending a thousand years transformed into a living croquet set—the Ambassador continued. "What happened to your sister was the work of a being we call *the Lady*—"

"How gnomic." Mr. Caesar's tone was as arch as his eyebrow.

"Do you want this information or not? She is a servant of Titania and as such I have no influence over her whatsoever. If you wished, you could assault her court and see if you could force some kind of concession"—

"A bold strategy," I added, "and highly recommended."

—"but that would be extraordinarily likely to result in your deaths."

"Spoil-sport."

"A better approach"—the Ambassador persisted in ignoring me; if anything his millennia amongst our kind had only permitted him to hone his vexatious spirit—"would be to lure her out and ensnare her, which will prove difficult."

Always the kind to see the potential in the most restrictive of situations, Miss Bickle went at once to: "But not impossible?"

"Find her in the mortal world, however you may, and bind her at the neck and wrists with a yellow cord. This will trap her in material form, which will cause her to diminish swiftly." Would that it were swifter, reader. I have found myself diminishing by inches. "Old compacts decree that she must exchange a single service for her freedom. Reversing what she did to your sister would be well within her capabilities."

Cynical to a fault, Mr. Caesar asked: "And would she be able to seek retribution afterwards?"

I do hate it when they ask the sensible questions.

"It's considered a little gauche," the Ambassador replied. "And the Lady's power is mostly in wishing."

Mr. Caesar's eyebrow had been raised for most of this exchange and was getting few opportunities to lower itself. "*Mostly?*"

"Well, she could also hit you with a rock or something."

Captain James gave the Ambassador a long, hard stare.

"She might also have the capacity to inspire inanimate objects to motion," he admitted. "Which she could, for example, use to hit you with a rock."

"I don't like *might*," said Mr. Caesar. "Does she or doesn't she?"

The captain gave the slightest shake of his head. "It's fine. Might means does. Always. Have to plan for the worst."

"So we plan for a situation where my own cravat might choke me to death?"

"Better than *not* planning for a situation where your own cravat might choke you to death," pointed out Miss Bickle.

"Also"—Captain James was smiling now, almost slyly. For all I despise heroic mortals, those with capacity for slyness do intrigue me—"the plan for that would be don't wear a cravat."

As Mr. Caesar's hand had gone instinctively to his jaw when the captain had been describing the effects of pistol shot, so now it went to his throat.

"Truly," the captain continued, "war is hell."

Being the person present least distracted by Mr. Caesar's

cravat-related misgivings, Miss Bickle—continuing the group's run of asking the awkward questions—asked another awkward question. "But how do we find her?"

"I suspect," the Ambassador replied, "that she will find you."

"Please don't tell them how to see us when we don't wish to be seen," I reminded him. "That would make my job extremely difficult."

The Ambassador hefted the hamper into his arms. "All in all, I think you've had more than"—he counted swiftly—"three blocks of cheese, a decanter of brandy, and some teacakes' worth of information from me."

"They are exceedingly good teacakes," Miss Bickle tried, always one to take an unnecessary risk, which, reader, I strongly urge you to do also.

"And it is exceedingly good information."

Without waiting for reply, the Ambassador stepped behind the tree and vanished. Miss Bickle naturally followed him but found herself looping around the trunk and back to her companions.

"I should have told him the hamper was an offering also," she said to nobody in particular. "He may have answered more questions." Our kind are not quite so basely transactional, but I will always commend Miss Bickle for thinking in the right direction.

Having achieved their goal, at least the largest fraction of their goal that they could muster, Mr. Caesar, his friend since childhood, and the military gentleman he'd fucked and taken to the opera in that order gathered up their belongings and made their way out of the park.

On the way their talk turned to short-term tactics and long-term strategies.

"We'll see the lady home," suggested Captain James, "then I'll head back to the Folly and see if the lads are up for a fairy hunt."

Miss Bickle, who had drifted away from the conversation to gaze at the sunlight, the grass, the trees, passing wasps, and any-thing else nearby that could conceivably be gazed at, brought her attention back to the company with some effort. "Oh, you needn't escort me. I go for walks unaccompanied quite often when I am in Cornwall."

"Cornwall isn't London," insisted Mr. Caesar. "And given how many terrible things have happened to ladies of my acquaintance in the last year, I will not leave you to roam the streets alone."

Miss Bickle was not an easily rankled person, so the implication that she could not take care of herself caused her no especial con-cern. "Oh, John," she said with an indulgent smile, "it's sweet that you're being protective, but, well, your presence didn't prevent either of the first two terrible things happening, did it?"

It was a fine day and had followed a fine night, but the words still struck Mr. Caesar like a knife, all the sharper for having been meant entirely without malice.

"Even if it didn't," the captain replied on his behalf, "it might stop you getting a blade in your ribs. And it'll make the gentleman feel better, so how about you let us take you and then if you want to go for a stroll you slip out after we've gone and nobody's the wiser."

This, Miss Bickle agreed, was an eminently sensible compro-mise, and a short while later she was delivered safely to her grand-father's city residence. That left Captain James and Mr. Caesar alone on a major public thoroughfare, trying to navigate parting.

"I can see you back as well, if you want," the captain offered. "Wouldn't want you getting stabbed either."

"I think we're out of the worst parts of town now."

"Maybe." Captain James gave half a shrug. "But you might get lost."

They remained standing for a moment. Then Mr. Caesar said: "Actually, if it's all the same to you, I might accompany you to the Folly. I'm not sure I can quite face returning home while I still don't know what we're going to do about Mary." This was, in a sense, true. Although it was far from his only reason. As a shape-shifter I understand the appeal of wanting to be somebody else for a time. It is one of the few things about Mr. Caesar I can empathise with. "Besides, if there's a plan to be made about this Lady character I should probably be part of it."

Once again, I dislike Captain James on principle, but the look in his eye warmed me. "Then," he said, "I shall have Mistress Quickley make you up a room."

Rather than being a euphemism, Mistress Quickley was indeed the moniker of the proprietress of the Lord Wriothesly's Folly—although almost certainly an adopted one. Adopted, I note with some distaste, from that bastard from Stratford. But I should not hold this against the lady herself. Mistress Quickley was, by Mr. Caesar's doubtless impeccable judgement, a woman of the flash sort whose fingers were in far too many pies. That also not being a euphemism. She was welcoming enough, and when Mr. Caesar explained that he would need to be boarded while he and the Irregulars worked on what he called a *personal issue,* she asked no questions save about payment and offered instead to send a runner to tell his family he would not be returning.

"They *might* rob you," Jackson explained, leaning back against the bar and twirling an old-fashioned plug bayonet against the surface with his free hand. "But I'll have a word and let them know you've nothing worth taking."

"You wouldn't even be lying," said Barryson, who was lazily etching some symbols into a table that I worried were a runic ward to prevent me from accessing the Folly but which, on closer inspection, proved to be a generously proportioned cock and balls. "I've been to their house, there's hardly anything."

Callaghan made a great show of disappointment. "And there's us thinking the captain's bagged himself a rich one."

"Excuse me"—Mr. Caesar was finding it curiously easy to adapt to soldier's banter; it wasn't so very different from a molly-house— "nobody has bagged anybody. And I am not rich. I am . . . adequate."

Sal settled herself into Mr. Caesar's lap and gazed deep into his eyes. "And what does that make us, sweet thing? *Inadequate?*"

"Boy William is," said Jackson. He had the kind of lips that made a sneer look like a blown kiss.

"Piss off," replied Boy William.

Captain James gave him a stern look. "Not in front of the children."

"*I'm* the children," Boy William protested.

Sal slipped herself free of Mr. Caesar and draped her hands across Boy William's shoulders. "Then *that,*" she said, "makes it even *worse.*"

"What I don't quite understand," Callaghan wondered aloud, in a way that implied strongly to Mr. Caesar that he absolutely understood, but wanted to talk about it, "is if you're not rich—"

"How's he afford all that fancy neckwear?" asked Jackson. "There'd be money in that if you could filch it."

"How did you get the captain off at the hearing?" Callaghan finished.

That was, at least, a relatively easy thing to answer. "My

grandfather's an earl," Mr. Caesar explained. "But the money goes mostly to his eldest son, not to my mother. And my father has no wealth of his own. I get the occasional invitation but fewer than, for example, my uncle. He'll be at the Earl of Semweir's ball this evening. None of my immediate family will."

Captain James clapped Mr. Caesar on the back. "Hear that, you lot, he's a man of the people. Sometimes an earl will have a ball and he *won't* be invited."

"I'm aware it's a . . . somewhat trivial concern. But it affects my sisters very strongly."

"You know what my sister does?" asked Callaghan.

There was, Mr. Caesar reflected, no good answer. And he was sure Callaghan knew that. "I assume the answer is something very different to 'attends balls.'"

"Though it may still have *something* to do with balls," added Jackson.

This interjection did, at least, direct Callaghan's attention in a different direction. "Fuck off, she's a charwoman."

"Not a lot of balls then?" asked Mr. Caesar.

Callaghan shook his head. "Not a lot, no."

"At any rate," Mr. Caesar continued, "it is a matter that has affected one of my sisters so strongly that she has fallen under the sway of a fairy creature"—please, reader, do not call us *fairy creatures*, it is belittling—"and so while I am sure her life is still better than that of many of her age and sex—"

"Easy there," Callaghan raised his drink towards Mr. Caesar in a gesture of comradeship. "I was only joshing with you. No man ever has to explain why he wants to watch out for his sister."

Sal gave a polite cough.

"No woman neither," added Callaghan. "Point is if my

sister—she's a Mary, too, by the by, that's what comes of the same name going to a queen and also the mother of God—was in that sort of trouble there's nothing I wouldn't do to bring her back."

The captain patted Callaghan warmly on the shoulder. "If it was your sister the fairies wouldn't stand a chance."

And again Mr. Caesar noticed the difference: it was a joke, yes, but not meant to wound. Which was presumably why Callaghan just nodded and said, "True enough. She's a formidable woman."

"I think we can all agree," purred Jackson, who was sitting just outside the group and nursing his drink like he was concerned it might be poisoned, "that not one of us will judge you for looking after your own."

"Thank y—" Mr. Caesar managed.

"Just as I'm sure you wouldn't judge us for looking after ours."

Even coming from Jackson, a man Mr. Caesar had been told outright was a thief, a liar, and a killer, it stung a little. Primarily because it was so plainly factual. "I would not. You've all been very kind, but I assure you I am *very* aware that I'm an outsider here."

"And that you've brought danger on us," added Jackson.

That, too, was an uncomfortable thought. "That danger has passed now, surely?"

Sal laid her hands on his shoulders. Mr. Caesar wasn't quite sure when she'd appeared behind him. "From what I saw you humiliated a British officer, insulted him, let him call you out, then humiliated him again by magic. No, I don't think this is over."

Letting his head flop forward like a broken doll, Mr. Caesar emitted a low but sincere "Fuck."

"Not your fault," Captain James reassured him. "Bloodworth's always hated me. You were just the excuse. And if he comes for us"—he looked pointedly at the Irregulars—"we'll be ready for him."

That was some comfort to Mr. Caesar, but only some. Ideally, he felt, they should not have needed to be ready for anything at all.

But as grim a turn as the conversation had taken, the Irregulars were practical people, and if they had ever allowed themselves to dwell too long on the bleakness of their situation they would have all died from despair and French musketry long ago. So Barryson hijacked the mood with a story about a girl he'd known in Jarrow and the little band went back to drinking and laughing and trying not to worry too much about who was going to try to kill them next.

For Mr. Caesar it was a curiously—one might almost say unfamiliarly—pleasant evening. Although from time to time he would catch Jackson watching him coldly from across the room, more often he would catch the eye of the captain, and they would smile at one another. And not in the threatening way that men of Mr. Caesar's set so often smiled. Despite the real physical danger he had been in just the day before and the only slightly less real physical danger he stood in now, surrounded by people who made their livings killing or stealing or (worst of all) doing honest labour, he found himself almost able to relax. It was a strange experience. And not an unwelcome one.

Which was, I am sure, terribly healthy for him, but it was sadly lacking in entertainment for *me*. That was the trouble with low taverns, so few of them bothered to maintain a proper standard of lowness. There had been a time when hardly an hour would pass in a place like this without a knife fight. I miss those days. Or at least I missed them. Now I'm stuck in a physical body I'm rather glad they're over.

Towards the end of the evening, the party's conversation turned to their plans for tracking the Lady and since I expected them to make limited progress in that area for reasons of having no idea what they were dealing with, I elected to leave. There were, after all, other threads to this tale that I needed to follow.

If the Irregulars offered scant hope of entertainment, I held out slightly more hope for the Caesars, who would soon be receiving word that their son had chosen to spend the evening with vagabonds rather than his family. Thanks to my uncanny alacrity and impeccable narrative timing, I caught up with the messenger just in time. She approached the Caesar residence with the sharp, cautious air of somebody who was accustomed to being unwelcome in the parts of the city that had streetlights and knocked at the door. Nancy greeted her, and I saw there pass between them the curious recognition of mutual hierarchy that, in that day, existed even amongst the lowest orders. A maid in a lady's house, even a lady who lived like a Quaker, outranked a girl from the slums.

A letter was passed and I, wearing the shape of a bumblebee, slipped in the door as it was closing. From the street, Nancy ran it upstairs and put it in the hand of Lady Mary, who read it, rose at once, and went to fetch her husband.

"John is not returning this evening," she told him, when he emerged from his study. "He says he has a plan that will help, but that it requires him to remain at—he says the Folly. Do you know what that is?"

There were few secrets between the Caesars, and so the elder Mr. Caesar nodded and told the truth. "It is an inn in St. Giles, frequented by soldiers and criminals."

"Then I'm sure John shall like it very well," said Miss Anne, looking up from her novel. "Such company suits him."

"Anne." Lady Mary glared at her daughter. "While I am also not . . . overjoyed that John has chosen to absent himself at such a difficult moment, you should not speak of your brother that way."

Standing in the centre of the room in a flawless attitude of otherworldly grace, Miss Caesar turned as slowly and inexorably as public opinion. "The difficult moment has passed, Mama. And besides, Anne is just being shrewish because she's upset that Mr. Bygrave hasn't called."

"I am not being shrewish," Miss Anne protested. "I say it suits him because it does. John has behaved very ill of late."

Mr. Caesar, who knew more of his son's recent activities than either of his daughters, was not quite willing to let that stand. "He has made difficult choices," he said, "and while they are not the choices I would have made they are still his to make."

The lesson that the lives and decisions of others are complex and best left unjudged unless one is very certain of one's awareness and standing settled onto Miss Anne like snow and then, like snow, melted away. Whereupon it was replaced by a wholly different thought. So she sighed only a little theatrically and segued into a matter closer to her heart. "I do think this absence very unkind of Mr. Bygrave. I had grown used to his visits."

"Perhaps somebody else has caught his fancy," suggested Miss Caesar, a spiral of light dancing delightedly inside her.

Miss Anne's lips trembled and a single tear glistened artfully in the corner of her eye. "Mama, make Mary stop being beastly. She has already driven John away and——"

But it was not Lady Mary who intervened. "That is enough," said Mr. Caesar with finality. "You are sisters. You will behave like it."

"She may not even be my sister anymore," replied Anne. "She may be something else entirely."

Lady Mary glared at her daughter. "Your father said that was enough. If the next words out of your mouth aren't all rainbows and butterflies then you will not attend another ball or speak with another gentleman until you are thirty."

The injustice of this clearly burned Miss Anne like wet fire, but she did at least keep her silence.

"I am still me," said Miss Caesar, a little plaintively. And were I the sentimental sort I might have wondered who she was trying to convince.

"I am sure of it," her father said. And it didn't sound like he was trying to reassure her so much as that he was stating an immutable truth of the cosmos. "Who you are is the one thing that can never be taken away. And had you not come back to us, we would have found you. Something is trying to separate this family, and I will not permit it."

Sunlight glittered off the glass roses in Miss Caesar's hair. "The Lady is not trying to hurt us, Papa, she is trying to help me."

Mr. Caesar's face was stone. "She came in the night. And she took you. That is not the action of somebody who wishes you well. It is the action of somebody who wishes to use you."

"She seems to have done very finely for it," said Miss Anne, immediately following up with: "Which is a pleasant thing to say. I was paying her a compliment."

Miss Caesar bobbed an eerily fluid curtsey. "Thank you, Anne."

"Perhaps I should find a way to be carried off by fairies too," Miss Anne mused. "It seems—"

"Anne." The tone of warning in Lady Mary's voice would have registered with even the most obtuse of debutantes, but still more notable was the fact that her husband very quietly turned and left the room.

Miss Anne's gaze followed her father as he left. "Is Papa very upset, do you think? I meant only—"

"Whatever you meant," said Lady Mary, "your father does not like talk of his children . . . disappearing."

For a moment a look of contrition flickered across Miss Anne's face. "I suppose," she tried, "it is not so very bad if Mr. Bygrave doesn't visit so often. I am still young, after all."

"You should not expect him today at any rate," pointed out Lady Mary. "He will be at the Earl of Semweir's ball tonight. He's of good family; it should be more than enough to secure him an invitation."

"Whereas we," Miss Anne ask-stated, "are not of good family?"

The Caesars had tried, as best they could, to shelter their children, especially Miss Anne, from the worst realities of the world they lived in (those realities they knew of, at least; if they understood what horrors lurked beneath the soap bubble of material reality they would have had quite a different order of problem). And Lady Mary took some small comfort in the fact that if their youngest daughter had grown up naïve and a little selfish then that was, at least, a task in which they had succeeded. "Not," she said at last, "in many people's eyes."

The light inside Miss Caesar's body faded a moment and she asked: "Why did you marry Papa?"

And for an equal moment, Lady Mary was silent. It was not a topic of which she spoke often, at least not to her children "Because I was in love with him," she began. And then she hesitated again because love was not considered a very sensible basis for marriage, and while her daughters doubtless wanted the fairy tale (I heartily

approve of this usage, by the way; fairy tales are indeed a fine thing
and always to be relied upon) for themselves, they would very much
have preferred their mother marry money. "And because I knew
that if he could live the kind of life that he had lived and still be the
kind of man he is, then I would have nothing to fear so long as I
was beside him."

In spite of her instinctive desire to scorn everything that origi-
nated with her parents, Miss Anne pressed her hands to her bosom.
"Oh, Mama, how romantic. It could almost be the subject of a
novel."

"Not," Lady Mary replied, more sorrowfully than she had
intended, "one that would be well received amongst the monied
classes." To think, reader. How terrible it must have been to live
in a world where writers of fiction have to contend with such
considerations.

"Because you married beneath yourself?" asked Miss Caesar.
Her tone would once have been icy, but since her transformation
every inflection of her voice was accentuated and it cut like, well,
like glass. "That is"—she retracted hastily—"I don't mean . . .
Uncle Richard would say you—"

Perhaps because her daughter was now literally made of a brittle substance, Lady Mary replied with care. Or as much care as she
could while indulging her distaste for compromise. "Your father is
not beneath anybody. But yes, Uncle Richard would disagree, as do
most of his friends, and most of polite society. The Vicomte de
Loux they will accept, but things are different in France. Besides,
there are other rules for men, and in his case it was his mother who
came from . . . less acceptable stock."

Miss Anne looked down at her hands. She had long, slim fingers that she was now twining nervously. Her hands, like the rest of
her, were much admired in the ton but as she progressed through

her fourteenth year she was beginning to notice how often words like *exotic* made their way onto her admirers' lips. "Still," she said aloud, "it is hard for us sometimes. And when one's future may be limited by a thing over which one has no control."

"I know," replied Lady Mary. And she did indeed know. She would indeed have given much to stop knowing, just for a day or two. "But I cannot regret my choices. Nor that I had you, or John. And besides"—she forced herself to be cheerful—"there will be other balls."

Right on cue—a cue I had been expecting for some while thanks to my marvellous sensitivity to the ephemeral but had concealed from you, dear reader, for dramatic purpose—the street outside clattered with hoofbeats and rang with the sound of harness bells.

Without being asked, for she was in many ways a well-trained girl, Nancy went to the door to see what the matter might be and, a few minutes later, returned with a puzzled expression.

"There's a carriage," she said. "With footmen. Strange footmen. And a lady in a blue gown."

The light within Miss Caesar kindled once more. "She's here?"

The same words *she's here* were echoed by Miss Anne and Lady Mary with very different inflections.

"She is," said a voice from the hallway. It was by far the pleasantest voice any of the mortals there present had ever heard, being sunlight and hope spun into sounds. Though they heard the Lady, they did not at first see her, since she was preceded by her footmen, the ones that Nancy had denounced as "strange."

Whether they were strange or not depended, of course, on your perspective. I have seen plenty of white-eyed servants with digitigrade legs and an extra joint in each finger. But then I go to a far better type of party than the average human. Their livery, like most of their mistress's belongings, was the palest of blues and they announced her arrival with slender trumpets made from a type of bone that, for the sake of my audience's sensibilities, I shall not identify.

The commotion was enough to stir the elder Mr. Caesar once more from his study, and so he was treated to the full splendour of the Lady's entrance. She shimmered into the room like a fallen star, which, in many ways, she was.

"What are you doing in my house?" demanded the elder Mr. Caesar with a commendable fortitude for a mortal confronted with one of Titania's more insidious servants.

"My duty," the Lady replied. "I have a bargain with your daughter, and I would see my side of it upheld."

Miss Caesar was already gliding towards the Lady while Miss Anne watched her with profound jealousy and Lady Mary watched her with profound horror.

"Leave her be," Mr. Caesar demanded. Which was useless. We are not amenable to *demands.*

The Lady blithely ignored him, as she was ignoring me. I was, I will freely admit, very tempted to attempt to distract her purely for my own amusement, but I was concerned that if her composure broke she would address me, and that would compromise my mission. She extended a hand, smiled beatifically at Miss Caesar, and said—because, dear reader, some incantations are mandatory, "My dear, you *shall* go to the ball."

"Mary"—Lady Mary called after her daughter—"please, don't go with this . . . creature."

Realising that the Lady was not going to listen to reason (and why should she when so little in this cosmos is even remotely rational?), Mr. Caesar decided, with some reluctance, to resort to physical intervention. He did not get very far. Although the Lady made no word nor gesture that was perceptible to mortal kind, she bid two nearby chairs to assist her, and assist her they did, skittering across the floor to intercede themselves between her and her would-be inconveniencer. When he vaulted, with a frankly unexpected agility, over them she resorted to more drastic measures. A sewing-basket slid from beneath a settee and a single long needle aimed itself directly at Mr. Caesar's throat.

"I do not wish to be uncouth," she said, "but where I come from a deal is a deal."

Miss Caesar looked from the Lady to her father and back to the Lady, and for a moment even I did not know which she would choose.

"It's all right, Papa," she said carefully. "I—this is what I want. There's no need to . . ."

She didn't finish the sentence, but went with the fairy. I fell into step beside her and left with them.

"I shan't be any trouble," I promised mostly to remind the Lady that I could if I pleased. "But you surely appreciate that *this* branch of the story is likely to be far more interesting than the one happening back at the house."

She did not reply, of course. But she cast me an evil look out the corner of her eye and made a valiant if doomed effort to shut the carriage door before I could slip through it.

The carriage itself was a wondrous thing, at least by mortal standards (the steeds and chariots of my master are, of course, more wondrous still, but I am adjusting my assessments to the limited experience of my audience). It was silver spun from moonlight, drawn by four white horses whose eyes burned with a pale fire and whose harnesses were strung with bells that were each a star.

Miss Caesar settled down on a seat upholstered in pale blue silk and watched as her parents' house receded into the distance. Her expression was harder to read now that her face was made of glass, and her heart harder to read now that it had been replaced with a ball of borrowed light, but I sensed ambivalence from her.

"Papa will—you would not have hurt him?" she asked.

"Of course not," said the Lady. Though she said it only once. "But he was trying to keep you from your destiny. And destiny, child, is not a thing with which one toys."

I knew, as I am sure the Lady did, that it was a specious argument at best. A vapid appeal to large-sounding ideas in order to cover up an unpleasant truth.

But the lure of a life of beauty was tempting, especially to a young woman in a world where beauty was the only currency a lady really had of her own. And so Miss Caesar permitted herself to be convinced. And to be carried through the streets of London to the fashionable residence of the Earl of Semweir.

CHAPTER NINE

THE EARL OF SEMWEIR WAS one of the more disgustingly wealthy gentlemen in London. Of course I say disgustingly wealthy, but that is to do the man an injustice. By the standards of his era his wealth was eminently respectable, meaning his distant ancestors had stolen it from other Englishmen long enough ago that it didn't count, and his more recent ancestors had increased it by stealing from people who were *not* English, and so that didn't count either.

Indeed his house was so respectable that it was ordinarily entirely closed to the Caesars. Lady Mary might, perhaps, have been welcome on her own account had she left the entirety of her family at home, but since she would never have wished to enter such a house in the first place, the point was moot. While Lady Mary would have scrupled at attending a ball at which neither her husband nor her children would ever have been welcome, however, her eldest daughter had the giddiness of youth, a sheltered upbringing, and fairy magic guiding her away from such considerations.

It was not the grandest house Miss Caesar had ever seen—her

grandfather's residence, being in the countryside and thus having more land to sprawl over, was larger, as was the Duke of Annadale's ancestral-ish residence of Leighfield—but it was by far the most splendid building she had ever been invited to within the confines of the city.

"And you are certain we shall be admitted?" she asked the Lady, her eyes wide with wonder.

"Quite certain." The Lady gave no further explanation. She simply willed the carriage to halt, and the door to open, and disembarked. Making *another* determined attempt to stop me following her by slamming the door in my face as I tried to leave. Unfortunately for her its windows were transparent and in the days before my exile I could take the form of sunlight if I wished, and so I did.

The door of the great house (Inching, it was called, though the name will largely not matter) was attended by two footmen who approached the newcomers with the initial intent of informing them that they had not been invited but who, at the sight of Miss Caesar and her escort, fell to deference, opening the doors wide and letting Miss Caesar, the Lady, and the things that posed as her servants walk past quite unimpeded.

By the year 1815 the practice of guests at a ball, or any public event, being introduced by fanfare had long since died out, but this did not stop the Lady, whose servants heralded her arrival, and that of her protégé, with the uncanny piping of their bone trumpets. I found the sound pleasant enough, but then I am accustomed to the music of the otherworlds.

For any mortal to so interrupt a dance in progress (for the Lady had come, as it would now be termed, fashionably late) would be an unforgivable social transgression. But transgression is the lifeblood of our kind and so it was quite overlooked.

What was not overlooked, however, was Miss Caesar. Like the sunlight and the starlight before it, her body of unearthly glass captured the candlelight of the ballroom and whirled it into a cavalcade of pale motes that coursed through her and wrapped around her like the finest gown ever spun by hands mortal or immortal.

You cannot know, reader, how much it pains me to admit it, but the Lady was very, very good at her job.

When the trumpeters finished trumpeting, the whole room fell into an eerie silence, broken only by the ringing *tap-tap-tap* of Miss Caesar's glass feet on the ballroom floor. The Lady and I stood back and watched and she, content with her work, permitted herself to fade from view.

"You have to admit," she said, more challengingly than I thought warranted, "she looks wonderful."

I nodded. "For how long?"

"Long enough."

Had I cared, and of course I did not, I would have found the answer ominous.

From the great silent crowd a young man came forwards. It was Mr. Bygrave, still in uniform—even an earl liked to have the occasional respectable soldier in his home—and looking now at Miss Caesar with a very similar rapt admiration to that with which he had once looked at her sister.

"Miss Caesar," he said, with remarkable composure for a man beholding the Beauty Incomparable, "would you be so good as to give me this dance?"

And although she had no card to mark, Miss Caesar nodded, and gave him her hand, and the band struck up a waltz.

At the same time (well, not quite the same time, but the distance from Inching to the Folly was not so very long and I *am* so very fast) that Miss Caesar's glass slippers were *tap-tap-tapping* through the waltz at one of the ton's more exclusive private balls, glass of a different sort was becoming important to her brother.

That glass was window glass. It was important because it had shattered. It had shattered because something had been thrown through it. The thing that had been thrown through it was the severed head of a bull.

The many and various insalubrious inhabitants of the Folly scrambled. For the civilian occupants, that meant making for the exits; for the military men (and for Sal, who was currently a lady), it meant finding cover and arming themselves.

Without a word from anybody in the regiment, Jackson skirted the edge of the room with his head down and a pistol he'd acquired from the-god-of-your-choice-knows-where drawn. With the caution conveniently shared by professional soldiers and professional criminals, he risked a glance through the least grimy corner of the unshattered window.

"Red robes," he said, "white masks."

"Mithraists?" asked Kumar, who had readied a musket and trained it at the door.

Jackson still had his eyes on the intruders. "The fuck should I know? Do I look like a professor of comparative religion at a celebrated university?"

"It'll be the major," replied the captain, with bitter confidence. "Every rich bastard in His Majesty's army's in at least two cults."

. . . Back at Inching (I am swift, reader, so very swift), Miss Caesar danced with Mr. Bygrave, their hands joined above their heads, the music and the lights swirling inside her. . . .

In my fleeting absence, the door had been breached, and the

robed men had come forth with fire and sabre and pistol. It had not, in the first instance, gone well for them, because while the musket was not so accurate as the rifle, the Irregulars were good shots and Kumar caught one in the chest, Callaghan got another in the shoulder, and the captain, with his pistol, took a third through the mask.

. . . In the ballroom all was harmony and wonder. The first waltz had ended and, sensible even now of the mores of society, Miss Caesar chose another man to dance with. Mr. Bygrave, after all, she could return to later, if he truly favoured her. . . .

The civilians, having learned in lives harder than they were long to take care of themselves, were scrambling for back doors and side windows, with Barryson and Boy William assisting the best they could. Mr. Caesar, aghast at the violence, shrank back against one wall next to Mistress Quickley. She, by contrast, was rather less aghast, at least at the battle. The damage to her property, on the other hand, distinctly soured her.

"Get 'em out," she was demanding of the combatants, "and someone do something about them fires."

There was, within Mr. Caesar, a war between his fear of injury and his fear of ignominy. He had no desire to lose any part of his face to a stray blade, but the thought that men were doing battle while he stood by and watched squirmed within him like maggots made of shame. So he set his jaw, snatched up a bundle of rags, tried not to think too much about the mess he was making of his gloves, and remained resolutely rooted to the spot.

"What you waiting for?" asked Mistress Quickley. "If this place goes up we're all fucked."

Being no more a man of science than he was a man of war, Mr. Caesar had no real sense of how likely it was that the fires would burn out of control. But since if it *did* he would either burn himself or feel like an utter heel for allowing it to happen, he made up his mind to advance. Though out of deference to the blades, he did so crawling.

Within arm's reach, the captain was doing battle with one of the larger cultists, and Mr. Caesar—who, unlike his sister, still had a heart—roiled with a complex mix of admiration and dread. Admiration at the man's uncanny grace in motion. Dread partly that something might befall his new . . . associate, but mostly at the fact there were swords passing scant inches over his head.

. . . In the ballroom, his sister's face was turned upwards as she gazed with empty eyes at her dancing partner. She had already forgotten his name, and he was not entirely certain that he knew hers. And it did not matter. Here and now she was the personification of beauty. Wonder in crystal. The fragile all-and-nothing in which every dream reflected . . .

The cult, if cult it was, had come in force. And while they fought with black powder and steel, the Irregulars knew well enough that if their attackers were men of consequence—even *minimal* consequence—they could not leave them dead. Or at least not many of them.

So they made a fighting retreat, their own lives and the lives of the locals their first priority.

. . . Another waltz. It was a new dance, or new by the standards of the higher aristocracy, whose tastes ran conservative, and so not normally danced at the better balls. But tonight was perfect. The Lady had seen to that. As perfect as cut glass . . .

The Irregulars were military men and fell back with military precision. Mr. Caesar was a gentleman who seldom rose before ten and, having smothered what fires he could, fell back with haste.

It was not, therefore, so terribly surprising that he found

himself staring down the barrel of a gun while the rest of the party were efficiently moving to safety.

"You, we have been asked to collect," said a soft voice that Mr. Caesar didn't recognise.

Few of either the Irregulars or the attackers remained in the fight now. Just the man with the soft voice and another masked man behind him—this one thankfully sans pistol. Not clear what else to do, Mr. Caesar raised his hands. "Asked by whom?" he tried, hoping it might at least buy him time while also not being a shot-in-the-face level of defiance.

Unfortunately the soft-voiced man didn't deign to answer, he just flicked the barrel of his pistol sideways in a *come with me* gesture and began to escort Mr. Caesar out of the burst-open door.

"I wouldn't," said the captain.

. . . Another dance. Another gentleman. This one shorter, less handsome, too old definitely, far too old; her feet clicked cold and hard on the dance floor. . . .

The soft-voiced man had only half turned, and Mr. Caesar had barely turned at all but was craning his neck over his shoulder to look at Captain James and, if at all possible, convey with his eyes how very, very important it was that this exchange go smoothly.

"I have the gentleman at gunpoint," the soft-voiced man pointed out. "And that is a slow blade you are carrying."

Captain James's blade was indeed longer and heavier than the sabres the other men were wielding. If you wish to insert your own observation about the relative values of length and dexterity at this juncture, reader, you may do so. But I hope you feel bad about it.

"Slow it might be," the captain agreed with an easy, oddly charming smile, "but I took this off a French cuirassier and though it's not made for fencer's tricks, it'll split you open right enough."

"Orestes," Mr. Caesar half whispered, "he has a gun."

Captain James extended his arm just a half inch further. "So he does." Still smiling, he gave his enemy a challenging look. "Go on then. Shoot him."

"I fail to see how this is helping," observed Mr. Caesar, his voice trembling only the slightest amount.

Ignoring Mr. Caesar's panic, Captain James continued to stand very steady and composed.

All around them, the Folly had grown quiet, and when the soft-voiced man cocked his pistol the click, muted as it was, echoed around the tiny room.

. . . All around her the music had grown quiet, and when she crossed the floor to take her next partner, the click of her feet echoed like lies. . . .

"Takes a while to reload does a pistol," said Captain James almost conversationally. "And I'm pretty sure you had your shot when you came in."

The mask made his expression unreadable, but the soft-voiced man's tone was playful. "Really? Bet his life?"

And to Mr. Caesar's great chagrin, Captain James said: "Yeah."

. . . Even the earl himself danced with her in the end. He was no marriage prospect, of course, being too old and already wed, but she was sensible of the honour nonetheless. . . .

The soft-voiced man pulled the trigger, and the hammer fell.

. . . Miss Caesar turned and turned and turned. . . .

His mouth dry and his body tense, Mr. Caesar waited for the bullet to hit. Although he did not consider himself a brave man, the fact that Mr. Caesar witnessed the gentle click of the pistol without soiling his breeches spoke either to some hidden depth of courage or a devotion to his tailoring bordering on the fanatical.

"Told you," said the captain. "Now, do you want to run, or do you want to see if you've better luck than the French cuirassier?"

From what I read of his heart, the soft-voiced man was no coward, but his bluff had been called and he had the wisdom to concede defeat. So the robed men retreated, and Mr. Caesar, the captain, and the remainder of the Irregulars decided that they, too, would be better off elsewhere.

As, reader, did I.

CHAPTER TEN

Miss Caesar's evening ended like a dream, the music at last dying with the dawn light, and the Lady, permitting herself to be visible once more, guiding her out into the carriage. The carriage which, I feel honour-bound to point out, had not transformed into any kind of vegetable overnight. The works of Titania's court are, of course, vastly inferior to those of my master, but that must be judged against the exceptional standards of fairy craft in general.

She nestled into place alongside her otherworldly patroness and, in a fit of whimsy, I took on the form of a tiny lapdog and leapt in after them. There, from my position alongside Miss Caesar's slippered feet, I was able to make out hairline cracks beginning to form at her ankles. But then what would one expect if one insists on dancing in glass shoes?

My chosen guise had been, to some extent, a calculated gamble. The Lady, of course, knew I was there, but I hoped that if I chose a sufficiently adorable form her client would defend me and the Lady would, by the laws that bind her as surely as my laws bind me, be prevented from arranging my expulsion.

And to test my theory, I sprang into Miss Caesar's lap, narrowly avoiding a sharp kick that the Lady had been aiming at me.

"Oh, how lovely," Miss Caesar exclaimed, looking down at me with restful happiness. "Although I am not sure I shall be permitted to keep him."

The Lady glared at me sourly. She was a very sour being, I felt. "On the contrary, you will find him impossible to get rid of."

I looked up innocently and shook my doggy head. "*Rrruff?*"

"What's his name?" asked Miss Caesar. And I realised just slightly too late what a poor choice this might have been.

"He's your dog," the Lady replied with an I've-got-you-now-you-fucker smile, "why don't *you* name him?"

Names have power, reader. Being given a name has power.

"I think"—Miss Caesar made a sound of musing that I did not at all like—"that I shall call him Ferdinand."

I attempted to signal my displeasure at this moniker, but it was to no avail. It had taken hold already and although it would bind me but little (names have power, reader, but not *absolute* power), it was a restriction I resented. As Ferdinand, I curled into Miss Caesar's lap and she stroked her fingers through my fur. Her hands were cold by mortal standards, but since I have danced with the North Wind's daughter in the Ice-Caves of the Utter Far my mileage, as you might say, varied.

While the sun was inching its way above the horizon, its soft rays dancing through Miss Caesar as all light now did, the carriage proceeded through the streets of London towards her home. In this much, at least, the Lady had not been lying. Her plan was not to take the child away. At least not directly. She only wanted her to go to the ball.

"You enjoyed yourself, I trust?" the Lady asked.

Miss Caesar nodded. "Very much."

"Then you shall be delighted to know that there will be more such dances in your future."

She should indeed have been delighted. But having no heart muted her capacity for joy. "And will Mr. Bygrave . . ."

The Lady didn't let her finish the sentence before breaking into a peal of beautiful laughter. "Forget him, child. You can do better now. *So much* better."

No lady of the era, however humble and pious, would be quite able to resist the obvious question. "How much better?"

"As much as you like. I have given you the Beauty Incomparable and with it you can have anybody you wish. Kings. Princes. Princesses if they take your fancy."

"They do not," Miss Caesar replied at once. "That is, I love my cousin, but—they do not. And I do not think I want to be a queen."

Mortal as she remained, despite her transformation, Miss Caesar did not catch the look of scorn in the Lady's eye. But I did. "As you wish. Still, you can set your sights higher than an ensign."

"He is a good man," Miss Caesar replied almost reflexively. "And from a good family."

"And your sister likes him." The reply was calculated. Not cruel exactly; cruelty has a different connotation for my people than for yours.

Certainly it was calculated well enough that it silenced Miss Caesar a moment. And made her denial sound weak when she made it.

"Come, come." The Lady patted Miss Caesar on the knee, and I took the chance to snap at her fingers. "It is no crime to desire what others have."

Hard as she was for me to read now, I could sense through her hands how dearly the girl wanted to believe that. Which meant she probably would, eventually. "Not a crime. But envy is a sin."

"According to one faith. There are many."

The mortals of England were strange about religion. They knew, of course, that the gods of the ancients were real, physical beings while having no such reassurance about the one their Church claimed to speak for, yet they persisted in believing in him anyway. So it was in this spirit of human perversity that Miss Caesar took the talk of polytheism rather more to heart than the act of turning her into a statue of living glass.

"I shall not have you lead me astray," she protested.

"Really?" The Lady adopted a tone that I knew well, having so often used it myself. "But *astray* is where all of the *best* things are."

And though I am loath to admit it, she was right in this also.

"I like Mr. Bygrave on his own account," Miss Caesar replied. And in the moment at least I believed that she believed it.

The Lady, for her part, patted Miss Caesar's hand in an almost motherly fashion. "As you say, child," she replied. "As you say."

They returned to the Caesar house to find it not in uproar precisely, but in a level of disharmony uncommon in the era. The night-long absence of Miss Caesar had been trying enough, but it had been punctuated around midnight by the arrival of her brother, Captain James, and a limited subsection of the Irregulars, bearing news of the robed men and the attack on the Folly. Should you be concerned for the remaining soldiers, dear reader, rest assured that they were making their own arrangements back in St. Giles. Or perhaps they had gone to stay on a nice farm in the country.

There had followed a short debriefing in which both parties had apprised one another on the flavour of fuckedness that had descended upon them, and they had then, mutually, attempted to game through the ways in which those fuckednesses intersected and exacerbated one another.

This exercise had lasted until three, at which point the younger Mr. Caesar had retired—not, in this instance, with Captain James; there were some things one did not do in the house of one's father—leaving his parents to wait up anxiously while various soldiers littered the drawing room like toys discarded by a gigantic schoolchild.

When Nancy, who was not technically expected to go to bed before the household and thus getting rather the worst end of this deal, showed the returning Miss Caesar through to where her parents were waiting, the young lady reacted to the scene before her with less surprise than one might expect for a girl of her age and experience. Then again, she had just been transported to a ball by a fairy, so her tolerance for the unusual was likely heightened.

The arrival of Miss Caesar and the Lady provoked a flurry of motion amongst those still awake. Lady Mary (my apologies, reader, there happen to be a number of ladies present) rushed forward, moved to embrace her daughter, remembered what happened last time, and caught her by the hands instead. The elder Mr. Caesar rose more cautiously, with his eyes firmly on the more supernatural of the pair, and Captain James let his hand drift slowly to his sword.

"I am safe, Mama," Miss Caesar said, finding that it is hard to sound reassuring when your voice is a song from the cold side of eternity. "I danced and was—they saw me."

Although he had maintained his calm throughout the arrival and had shown admirable willingness to overlook the bit with the needle and the direct threat on his life, this last observation proved too much for the elder Mr. Caesar. "They did not see you, Mary. They saw glass."

"Glass," the Lady replied—not, it seemed, trusting her protégé to think or act for herself—"is beauty."

With the occasionally prim defiance that gave her such a Quakerish reputation, Lady Mary folded her arms. "Beauty is character."

The Lady curled her lips into a smile of exquisite cruelty. "That is a lie we tell ugly people to comfort them. Your daughter made a bargain, it will be kept. To her benefit."

Crouching behind the divan with a pistol ready, Callaghan mustered his strength of will and disagreed. "That's what King George said to me and the lads, we've very few of us felt he held up his end of the deal."

"She says I might marry a duke," Miss Caesar protested.

"I would sooner you married a tanner and were happy," replied her mother, "than a prince and were not."

A creature of her society to the core, Miss Caesar saw no sense in the assertion. "I do not know what happiness there can be in poverty."

"To be fair to the girl," observed Sal, who uniquely amongst the soldiers had not taken cover; she was resting in the window seat with a shiv concealed in her skirts, "she has a point. Poverty is fucking terrible."

Captain James glanced at her for a half a heartbeat before turning his attention back to the Lady. "It is, but she's not talking about proper poverty. She's talking about only having one servant."

This, Miss Caesar would not abide. "If I cannot marry, I may be able to afford *no* servants."

Sal barked an unimpressed laugh. "Imagine."

"What shall I do for money if I cannot find a suitable husband?" Miss Caesar continued, demonstrating a persistent failure to—if you will forgive the anachronistic phrasing—read the room.

"Scrub floors?" suggested Callaghan.

"Take in laundry?" offered the captain.

"On Saturdays," Sal said, "there's Jewish folk need errands run. On account of the Sabbath."

"You're a well-brought-up lady," the captain tried again, "you could probably be a schoolmistress."

"Or," said Jackson, half-melted into the shadow of the doorway, "you could just sell your body."

Outraged as only a young woman infused with fairy majesty can *be* outraged, Miss Caesar glowered. "I would *never.*"

Shielded from the worst of the Lady's magic by cynicism and disinterest, Jackson raised an eyebrow. "Really? It doesn't sound that different from your first plan to me."

"More risk of the clap?" Sal observed.

"Depends on the duke."

While the Irregulars had been debating the various careers open to unwed women in the year of some people's lord 1815, the elder Mr. Caesar had been ruminating on the situation. When he spoke at last, it was over a room that fell swiftly silent.

"Mary," he said, "we are glad you have returned, and we want you to be happy. But this family knows as well as any that magic is treacherous. As are smiling strangers."

Still in the shape of Ferdinand the lapdog, I gave a gentle *ruff* of approval.

"My Lady," he continued, addressing the individual who went only by that moniker, "I thank you for returning our daughter to us

safely. And I trust that you will continue to do so, should you pro-
cure her further . . . *invitations*."

For a man with no especial knowledge of the Other Court, the
elder Mr. Caesar had done a remarkably efficient job of crafting an
insult. We hate to be thanked, at least with words, and we hate to
have our future actions predicted even more. We know the power
of even simple foretelling and take it seriously in a way your kind
do not.

In reply, the Lady smiled her most magnanimous smile. And
like all of her smiles it embodied the adjective that describes it with
a completeness that mortal flesh cannot replicate. "Think nothing
of it. And I assure you, sir, that your daughter will come to no
harm while she is by my side."

"Good." Mr. Caesar nodded with a confidence that belied his
circumspection. "But I ask you to go now. The hour is late, and the
household has been much disrupted."

Disrupting households is, in point of fact, one of the twelve
most beloved pastimes of my species. But while I *personally* find
delayed gratification to be the wholly inferior variety, the Lady was
made of different stuff, and played longer games.

So she swept a perfect curtsey, assured Miss Caesar that she
would return, and vanished into the night.

When she was gone the soldiers stood down, and the whole
company breathed a collective sigh of relief.

"Mary," Lady Mary told her daughter, "it might be best if you
went to your room."

So she went. And I, like a good little dog, followed her.

The dog disguise would, I was sure, eventually grow tiresome.
But puppies were stolen or ran away all the time, and while her
naming me would have given Miss Caesar the power to call me

back, I took comfort in the fact that she was unlikely to know the proper forms.

Upstairs, she stood in the centre of her bedchamber and looked down at me.

"Oh, Ferdy," she said, addressing herself as much as me. Not using the full name was a good sign. Nobody has ever said *nicknames* have power. "Why won't they just let me be happy?"

"*Rruff?*"

"Perhaps," she replied. What she thought I'd said I have no idea; maybe she was simply playing along. "But it seems so unfair. Mama and Papa are so overprotective."

"*Rruff.*"

"That's as may be, but I am not responsible for their uncertainties."

A vanity sat in one corner of the lady's room, a mirror above it, and she crossed over to it now and looked at herself, much as she had on the night the Lady first visited her. I remained at floor height, not wishing to accidentally reveal my true reflection.

Still, keen observer of humanity as I am, I could make out much despite my position. She was watching herself now with a melancholy that denied itself. Her reflection in the mirror was glass on glass on glass, fragments and echoes and motes of pale light.

Had she still breathed, I feel sure she would have sighed. Perhaps even let out an *ah me* as is, I believe, traditional. Instead she looked down and said, "Ferdy, I have chosen right, have I not? Whatever Mama and Papa may say?"

But I was already gone. From her sight, at least.

After all, this lady is not the only person our story is about.

I have, I think, already told you that my kind rarely watch mortals sleep (at least not from *outside* their dreams), since unconscious you are dull unless we are doing the supernatural equivalent of drawing a phallus on your foreheads with a magic marker. (This, you might recall, was essentially the plot of my best publicised escapade, albeit one for which I received no credit.)

But I went to check on Mr. Caesar anyway, because it seemed likely to me that he would be stirring soon.

And my timing, as ever, was flawless. You may think it vulgar, reader, that I keep reminding you of my own perfection, but your sensibilities mean little to me and I am extremely skilled at what I do.

Indeed so flawless was my timing that I arrived outside Mr. Caesar's bedchamber exactly in time to witness the approach of Captain James, and passed through it in my shape of mists and shadows just in time to witness Mr. Caesar, who somehow made even his nightshirt look immaculate, stirring with the ill grace of an earl's grandson asked to rise earlier than he is accustomed.

"What is it, Nancy?" he asked.

"Not Nancy," came the reply.

"Here to apologise for telling a man to shoot me?" asked Mr. Caesar, more acidly than he really felt. If there was one man he would trust to make such a life-and-death call, it was Orestes James.

"There was no way he'd reloaded that pistol," replied the captain. "Well, not much of a way. Anyway I thought you'd want to know your sister's back."

Abstractly, Mr. Caesar wanted to know this very much. In the moment, he wanted primarily to sleep for at least another two hours. "Is she well?"

"She's made of glass, John, how well can she be?" The use of

Mr. Caesar's Christian name was a little informal given their relative stations. Then again, they'd fucked.

"Allowing for that."

"Whole, and seems to have her own will."

Thanking whatever gods he was comfortable thanking for small mercies, Mr. Caesar rose and inched the door open. "You should probably come in. It's not done to have conversations through doors."

As he entered Mr. Caesar's bedchamber, Captain James was shaking his head. "You're a strange man."

"I really don't think I am."

Without waiting to be asked, Captain James sat down on the edge of Mr. Caesar's bed. "You punch a man in the jaw at a ball, you suck cock like a trooper—and I've met a lot of troopers—but then you turn around and say 'It's not done' about a chat through a bit of wood."

"That's different."

Captain James made no reply, but the expression on his face said *Why?*

"I'm at home now."

"And you're not yourself at home?"

As much as Mr. Caesar wished it could be, it wasn't that simple. "I'm one of my selves at home."

"How many've you got?" asked the captain, skirting the edge of playfulness.

"Two. Three? A hundred? I'm a gentleman and a molly and an Englishman though half the ton won't believe it and an African though I've never set foot on the Continent. I'm an earl's grandson, which means nothing except when it means everything, and a freedman's son, which means everything except when it means nothing. I'm my sisters' protector except I can't protect them and the last hope of my family name except I shan't marry. I'm a dandy who doesn't wear cotton and can ill afford to follow fashion, and a lawyer-in-training whose social set looks down on the law."

Deciding playfulness was not the right direction, Captain James just said, "Must be hard."

"It's the same for you, surely."

Captain James shrugged. "I'm a soldier."

"Yes, but——"

"My dad was a soldier. My mum was a soldier's wife. I serve with soldiers, fight with soldiers against soldiers. When I die I'll die a soldier and I'll rot with soldiers."

In some ways it took Mr. Caesar longer to wrap his mind around this than it had for him to accept his sister becoming a living vitreous statue. "It can't be that straightforward. What about other officers?"

"Fuck other officers."

"What about everybody else?"

"My everybody else isn't the same as your everybody else."

Mr. Caesar looked sceptical. "Isn't everybody's everybody else the same as everybody else's everybody else?" He checked himself. "Fuck, you've got me talking like Lizzie."

"Your everybody else," the captain explained, "is a bunch of rich bastards who've got everything and spend their whole lives scheming against each other to get more. My everybody else is regular people. And regular people have too much going on to care who you fuck or where your parents came from."

To Mr. Caesar, especially in that moment, it sounded unimaginably pleasant. Or perhaps just unimaginable.

"I'm not saying people aren't pricks sometimes," the captain continued. And there was a steadiness in his voice that Mr. Caesar wanted to cling to like a drowning man might cling to a piece of driftwood. "But I've never had to split myself in two. Your lot'll never let me in. My lot'll never let me down. You know where you are with that."

Mr. Caesar allowed the conversation to lull into silence. What, after all, could he say? That a world without contradictions was so alien to him that the mere description of it was humbling? Ordinarily in his assignations that kind of break in the conversation would be the cue to start fucking or leaving. Which had been— well, it had been *a* way to live a life. And it was the way that unmarried men were expected to live. Albeit they were generally expected to be seeking a different flavour of conquest.

"Thank you," Mr. Caesar said at last. "For caring. Mary isn't at all your responsibility."

When he wanted it to, Captain James's smile could be all kinds of wicked. "I've always had a weakness for a damsel in distress."

"I'm not sure I'd call her that."

"Wasn't talking about her."

Mr. Caesar did not look affronted, but he looked close to the front. "I'm not sure I care for *damsel*. I'm not that kind of Ganymede."

"Dandy in distress then?"

This was better, but not by much. "Nor am I *in distress*."

"When we first met," the captain reminded him, "you were getting drug up off your feet by two men who'd have thrashed you bloody without breaking a sweat."

"That might, I confess, have constituted a modicum of distress," conceded Mr. Caesar. "But I had your back at the hearing. And I don't think I was entirely useless in the attack on the Folly."

Captain James laughed. "Hold on, I'll send a runner to Wellington, let him know we've another for the front. 'Send John Caesar over right away, he's not entirely useless.'"

"That fire could have burned out of control."

"Or just burned out."

Deeply conscious that he was beginning to sound petulant, but not quite able to stop himself, Mr. Caesar said: "I thought I was tolerably courageous."

"Tolerably," agreed Captain James. "And there's officers who'd have done less."

Sensing a blessed opportunity to turn the conversation to other men's deficiencies, Mr. Caesar pounced. "Like Major Bloodworth?"

"And half the rest."

Not quite sure if theirs was yet a placing-a-reassuring-hand relationship, Mr. Caesar kept his hands very much to himself. "It was him tonight, wasn't it? The men in red."

Captain James nodded. "Probably wasn't with them, but rich fucks are up to their neck in cult bollocks. I think they learn it at them posh schools they go to."

"Having been to a posh school"—Mr. Caesar looked uncomfortable—"there were definite whispers, but I never saw anything myself. Then again I wouldn't have been invited. Wrong connections." With a frustrated groan he flopped back onto the bed. "Do you think," he asked the ceiling, "that if we sent the major a very polite letter he'd agree to stop trying to kill us until after I've worked out how to stop my sister being a statue?"

Captain James looked down at him and, apparently less concerned about propriety or the thorny question of what kind of relationship the two of them actually had, brushed his fingertips lightly over Mr. Caesar's arm in a way that wasn't quite friendly but wasn't quite sexual. "Shouldn't think so. He's not a very polite man."

Though the sun was well risen, Mr. Caesar shut his eyes and pretended it wasn't. "I think," he said aloud, "that I am going to ignore all of this until the morning."

"It is morning," Captain James reminded him.

"Proper morning. Proper morning involves bacon."

Laughed out for the night, the captain just exhaled amusedly. "Where I'm from, proper morning is a thousand Frenchmen coming over the hill with drums and muskets."

Mr. Caesar rolled over. "Where I'm from, I suspect we get a lot more sleep."

When Captain James rose to leave, Mr. Caesar felt rather than saw the motion. "You could stay," he suggested to the empty air.

"What about propriety?"

"I meant more . . . for company. Besides, Nancy will thank me for keeping your boots off the upholstery."

The captain sat back down. "You don't pay that girl enough."

"How do you know what we pay her?"

"I don't, but I know it's not enough. Balls to all hours, fairies, soldiers. She's had a right time of it."

Sleepily, Mr. Caesar murmured something about looking into it and, reasoning that little more would be achieved that evening, I let them be. The Caesars were, after all, not the only family I was observing at that time.

But those are different tales, for different occasions.

CHAPTER ELEVEN

B Y NOW, READER, YOU SHOULD know that little delights me more than chaos. And so I found the scene that unfolded in the Caesar household the following morning very delightful indeed. Poor Nancy—I say poor Nancy, but she is not the focus of this story and you should, therefore, discount her needs and feelings entirely; discounting the needs and feelings of others is a vital life skill and you should practice it early and often. Nancy, the inconsequential maid-of-all-work, had been required, on two hours' sleep, to rise, assist her various mistresses in dressing (the vitrification of Miss Caesar was a blessing in this regard since her clothes appeared now to be part of her person), and then start work on the breakfast.

She was, in this, either assisted or hindered, depending on how you might consider it, by the enthusiastic support of the captain's enlisted men.

"I do know," Callaghan was insisting to her, "how to boil an egg."

Nancy looked at him suspiciously. "Not men's work, sir. Nor guests'."

Sal, whose current presentation rendered one of those objections invalid if not the other, pried a pan of water from Nancy's stubbornly resisting fingers. "We're not guests. We're a pack of armed bastards burst into your house unannounced because one of us is fucking your master."

At that, Nancy coloured deeply. "Mistress Sally!"

"Just Sal. And I'm nobody's mistress."

Lurking in one corner and pointedly not offering to help anybody with anything, Jackson choked out a half laugh. "Sal, my dear, you're *everybody's* mistress."

"You'll not deter us, miss," Callaghan continued, ignoring the badinage that crossed the room. "We've been trained not to be deterred, you see. Leave the eggs to me and Sal, you just work on the bread, and Jackson over there will start seeing to the coffee."

From the look on his face, Jackson had no intention of seeing to the coffee. But from the look on Callaghan's face the coffee would be seen to whether Jackson willed it or no.

Leaving the downstairs to its downstairs business, I made my way up through the breakfast parlour, where Miss Anne was still remonstrating with her mother about the current state of the household.

"I thought you *liked* soldiers," Lady Mary pointed out with only the faintest of smirks.

"Officers," Miss Anne replied. "Gentlemen. Not *infantrymen*. I am sure they will have no conversation. And one of them is clearly Irish."

Her father looked up from his letters. "And what is wrong with the Irish?"

For the briefest of moments, Miss Anne adopted the perplexed expression of one asked to justify an unexamined assumption. "Well," she tried, "they just cause so many problems."

"Do they?" asked the elder Mr. Caesar, placidly.

Miss Anne nodded. "That's what Mr. Bygrave says."

"I thought you'd gone off Mr. Bygrave," observed Lady Mary.

At that, Miss Anne's face fell. "I think he's gone off me."

Her father, however, was not quite ready to change the subject. "Try to remember, Anne, that those who mistrust the Irish also mistrust me."

"Don't be silly, Papa," replied Miss Anne with a confidence born of limited experience. "Mr. Bygrave has never been anything but cordial to you."

"A man can be very cordial when another man has a pretty daughter."

This piety was boring me, and so I continued upwards. Miss Caesar, I suspected, would be doing nothing interesting until the Lady returned, and so I went to call instead on her brother.

The sun being well up, even Mr. Caesar's exhaustion and ideological commitment to the life of a gentleman could not quite keep him abed. The presence of Captain James might have provided him with some incentive, but the captain was already stirring restlessly, moving the arrangement from romantic to pointed.

Once the early morning birdsong was drowned out by the hoofbeats and cries of a busy London street, Captain James could justify indolence no longer. He swung himself out of bed, grabbed his jacket, and was instantly ready to face the day. Mr. Caesar propped himself up on his elbows and looked over at him.

"Going so soon?"

"We should be up. Have to keep moving."

Mr. Caesar looked sceptical. "Do we, actually?"

"Got a fairy to catch and a cult to outrun."

Accepting, albeit grudgingly, the necessity of activity, Mr. Caesar peeled himself out of bed and began to dress. Then he continued dressing. And continued to continue dressing.

Already jacketed and booted, Captain James watched with growing disbelief. "Do you do this every day?"

"Unless I'm in chambers. Then there's a wig."

Captain James considered the spectacle before him. Mr. Caesar had dealt with stockings and breeches and was now taking a moment to ensure that these latter garments hugged the contours of his thighs in the way that fashion dictated before moving on to the complex layers that would adorn his upper body. "Shouldn't you have somebody to help you with this?"

"We can't afford a valet, and it would be both unfair and unseemly to ask Nancy."

With an indulgent half smile, Captain James picked up Mr. Caesar's shirt and held it out for him in a passing imitation of a gentleman's personal gentleman.

"You don't have to—"

"I do if I want to get out of here before noon."

So Mr. Caesar let himself be helped into his shirt. Then his waistcoat. Then his tailcoat. And while this would have been perfectly ordinary behaviour had his assistant been an employee, it was different when it was a man he had lain with, and who had saved him from violence. There was an intimacy to the interaction to which he was unaccustomed. The warmth of the captain's hands as he smoothed—inexpertly, if Mr. Caesar was honest—the creases from his clothes. The scent of him as he helped to settle his jacket.

"You'll need to do your own cravat," Captain James whispered in his ear.

This came as something of a relief; Mr. Caesar would never have trusted anybody else to tie his neckcloth.

Standing in front of a full-length mirror with Captain James behind him, Mr. Caesar tried to focus on his knots. It was proving more difficult than he expected. This, then, was another experience to which he was unaccustomed. As an avowed sodomite, Mr. Caesar had been with many men, had even liked some of them as people, but he had never *once* had a lover who could distract him from his personal grooming.

"Pretty soon," said the captain, far too close to be convenient but nowhere near close enough, "you and me are going to need to have a tough conversation."

A little embarrassed at the intensity of his own response, Mr. Caesar shuddered. "About what?"

"About whether we're using your sister as bait."

The fact that Mary's predicament had not, in that exact moment, been the first thing on his mind made Mr. Caesar feel like a terrible brother. Then again, if it had been he would have felt like a failure as a gentleman. "I'm sorry, I must have misheard. I could have sworn you said we needed to talk about using my sister as bait."

"Yes."

"Out of the question," replied Mr. Caesar with the kind of instantaneous decisiveness that implied he was uncomfortably aware of how easily he could be swayed from the decision.

"You want to catch the Lady, you need to know where she is. The only thing we know she comes out for is your sister."

He was, of course, right. That is, he was right about the limitations of his and Mr. Caesar's fragile mortal knowledge. He was wrong that Miss Caesar was the only thing that could lure the Lady into the material world, but the other things that could draw her out were by turns secret, illegal, drenched in blood, and in several cases all three.

Captain James let his hands come to rest on Mr. Caesar's shoulders. "She'll be safe. I promise."

"She's made of glass. I'm not sure how safe she can possibly be. Besides, I'm very uncertain she'd go along with it. She still says this is what she wants."

"Boy William thought he wanted to be a soldier. He's learning different."

"Then perhaps Mary will learn differently as well? And perhaps all she needs is time."

Standing close behind Mr. Caesar and laying his hands on Mr. Caesar's hips, Captain James frowned. "It might be what she needs. It might not be what she's got. I've had little experience with magic, but I've not met an enemy yet gives you the space you need to fuck about."

The part of Mr. Caesar that sincerely wished he could shirk every responsibility and live his entire life locked in a private room with a well-tailored coat and a well-proportioned soldier sincerely wished that the captain wasn't right, and that his rightness didn't mean they would need to go downstairs for breakfast and broach some very, very difficult subjects with the family.

But he was. And it did. So they did.

The Caesars' breakfast parlour was not well set up for entertaining. But since the only people being entertained were common soldiers and a single disreputable officer, this was less of a concern than it might otherwise have been.

Nancy had done her best to keep control of the service, but she was outnumbered by infantrymen who through forceful refusal to countenance formality had caused the whole arrangement to devolve into a kind of affable chaos. Which is not the best kind of chaos, but is certainly the best kind of affability.

"I must say," observed Lady Mary with a restraint that betrayed her upbringing, "this coffee is rather—I am not sure we usually have it this strong."

"It is vile," agreed Miss Anne, with a lack of restraint that betrayed her youth and general worldview. "And bitter. Nobody of refinement could possibly—"

"Anne." If the elder Mr. Caesar was growing weary of admonishing his daughter he gave no sign of it, addressing the girl with a properly reserved affection. "This is how it is served on the Continent. I assume Mr.—" He gave Jackson a *sorry-didn't-catch-your-name* look.

"Jackson."

"Mr. Jackson acquired his taste in Spain defending us from Napoleon. It is ill-mannered to chide him for it."

"Also," added Sal, dusting toast crumbs from her lips, "English coffee tastes like pisswater."

"It is *also*"—the elder Mr. Caesar turned his gaze to the guest— "ill-mannered to speak of *pisswater* in front of your host's fourteen-year-old daughter."

Unusually, Sal looked genuinely chastened. "Sorry."

The apology was enough for the elder Mr. Caesar but not for his daughter. "See the people you've connected us to, John. Were you a better brother you would—"

Ordinarily indulgent of his younger sister, Mr. Caesar was not, on this morning, in a mood to indulge. "Were I a better brother I would not have let Mary be taken by fairies, but I did, and I am now attempting to rectify the issue."

"I was not taken," Miss Caesar protested. "I am here. And I am well."

"You've never been *well*," sniped Miss Anne from across the table where she was picking politely at a boiled egg.

In an effort to play peacemaker, Lady Mary laid down her coffee and intervened. "Whatever your sister may have been in the past," she tried, then turned to her other daughter, "Mary, you must understand that we are concerned for your well-being now?"

In her new state of crystal brilliance, it was hard for Miss Caesar to look huffy. Hard, but not impossible. "And where was that concern when the whole ton was sneering at me?"

"The men who would sneer at you," said the elder Mr. Caesar, "are not worthy of you."

At that, Miss Caesar let out a tiny scream. She had intended it primarily as a gesture of frustration but, through a throat that rang like a wineglass, the sound became piercing and otherworldly.

The rest of the company set down their cutlery with a range of clinks.

"I'm wondering," offered Callaghan, "if you might not be so well as you think you are."

A staunch adherent to the doctrine of me against my sister; me and my sister against my cousin; me, my sister, and my cousin against every other bastard, Miss Anne glared at the infantryman. "What Mary *means*," she said, "is that whatever fine words Papa might say, it does not help us secure our futures."

"Your future," replied Lady Mary firmly, "is secure. Neither your brother nor your grandfather will see you starve, even if you do not marry."

"Grandpapa will have no say in matters once Uncle Richard

inherits," pointed out Miss Anne with a shrewdness born of self-interest. "And John will have a lawyer's salary, not a gentleman's income."

"And *not starving* is a rather poor standard to wish for one's daughters," added Miss Caesar, insensible of the irony of the complaint now that she was beyond biological nutrition.

Captain James gave her a quiet smile. "With respect, lady, for some it's the most they can hope for."

If Miss Caesar was mollified by this, it was impossible to tell owing to her—for want of a better word—glassy demeanour. Miss Anne, however, was most certainly not. "You see, Papa, how low we are sinking. We are eating breakfast with the sort of people who think starvation to be an ordinary thing."

The elder Mr. Caesar folded his hands tightly together in front of him. "Anne, go to my study and wait."

"But—"

"Go to my study," he repeated. "And wait."

Although Miss Anne could be wilful, much of her wilfulness was grounded in a set of social expectations that also included obedience. So she rose, shot one last, poisonous glance at the insufficiently ranked soldiery, and departed, taking a defiant slice of toast with her.

"Now," the elder Mr. Caesar continued, turning to his other daughter, "we still need to discuss your situation."

"There is no *situation*, Papa," insisted Miss Caesar. "I have made a bargain and I am satisfied with it."

A coffee cup gripped delicately between her fingers, Lady Mary gave Miss Caesar a cool look. "You are not of age to marry without your parents' approval, child. Why on earth do you think yourself able to consent to a pact with an otherworldly potentate?"

"There is no age limit on wishes," Miss Caesar retorted, only a little stubbornly.

Jackson, who had not eaten, choosing instead to sustain himself on a single cup of very strong coffee, shot a calculating glance over the table. "No age limit on making them, no legal protection for taking them away. You think my sort are untrustworthy, miss, but I'll tell you we've nothing on the good folk."

His use of our polite name aside, this was slander.

"Whether you will it or no," the younger Mr. Caesar said, although both of his parents and most of the soldiers wished he hadn't—no persuasive argument begins *whether you will it or no*, "we shall find a way to disentangle you from this."

Sunlight, streaming now through the window, sparkled in the razor roses that wound through Miss Caesar's hair. "I do *not* will it. And I shall be no part of whatever schemes you might be hatching."

Before Mr. Caesar could respond, or before anybody else could tell him quite how badly he'd ballsed up, his sister turned on her heel, called for Nancy to get the door, and swept out into the London morning.

And suspecting that hers would be the more entertaining venture, I followed.

It was, in theory, unseemly for a young woman to be walking unescorted in London, but between a parlour full of soldiers and her physical transformation into colourless mineral, seemliness was rather less of a priority for Miss Caesar than once it was.

So with the spring sunlight shining past, upon, and through her, Miss Caesar made her way to Hyde Park. It was somewhat earlier than the fashionable hour for promenading, but that was not any great impediment in itself—she was there for the air rather than the company, and given her new status as a one-girl spectacle of the age, an excess of solitude was never going to be a concern for her.

Indeed she found herself attracting quite a following as she made her way along the banks of the Serpentine. The swans on the lake, most of whom really were just swans and not supernatural beings cunningly transfigured into a guise pleasing to mortals, drifted along in pace with her, and those walkers who had chosen to brave the early morning (or at least the early morning by the standards of that particular set, which was to say anytime more than an hour before noon) found themselves gathering behind her in an enraptured crowd.

When she stopped by the water's edge, flocks of swimming birds hopped out to gather around her, as though she were casting them bread. A not-terribly-discreet distance away, the crowd gathered, and gossiped, and wondered. But, if we're being honest, mostly gossiped.

Kneeling down with that eerily fluid grace she had possessed since her transformation, Miss Caesar gazed into the water and found her reflection broken and unfamiliar. She dipped her fingertips into the water and watched her face vanish into ripples. It felt appropriate somehow. The whole experience felt so much like nothing. Neither the cool of the water nor the warmth of the sun moved her as they once might have. Each was information without context. Sound without sense. Light without colour. Had she not firmly made up her mind to be satisfied, she would have been otherwise.

"Are you all right?" asked a voice behind her.

Rising and turning, she saw Mr. Bygrave. He looked a little

flushed, either from the exertion of the walk or the complexities of approaching an unescorted gentlewoman. "Quite all right," she said at once, not bothering to actually interrogate her own subjective all-rightness. "It is a beautiful day, is it not?"

Mr. Bygrave nodded his agreement and once their consensus on the beauty of the day had been established, he made the slightly bolder suggestion that Miss Caesar might like to be accompanied on her perambulations. This she felt she would like very much, and so they progressed in company around the Serpentine, conversing as they went.

I would recount a little of their conversation for you, reader, but while I am bound to recount my observations honestly (well, honestly-ish) I am also sensible of my need for your good approval. And believe me when I say that you would *not* thank me for sharing the details of that stultifying dialogue with you.

In candour I could scarce believe it. He was a military man and, while he had seen no battle yet, was surely conscious that he would be sailing away to fight and perhaps die against the French. She, meanwhile, had lately been granted a supernatural capacity to sway the hearts of mortals and her entire body had been physiologically transfigured. Yet somehow they conspired to speak entirely of trivia. Of the weather, and the pretty way the light played on the water. Of *ducks.* I swear I have never heard anybody express so many thoughts about ducks. In other contexts, that would be perfectly acceptable—the Swan Queen and her courtiers are indeed fascinating people, and the intrigues that the Mallard Prince gets up to when mortals aren't watching are scandalous to a level that human society would consider abominable. But they knew nothing of that, and so their remarks were restricted to such banalities as "Oh, look, that one's dabbling" and "Do you think it too early in the year for ducklings?"

Dross.

But while it was torment itself for me to listen to, to Miss Caesar it was . . . something other. England is a banal country and English society is grounded in banality, and so to speak of nothing with a man who had little to no conversation, and not once to be asked if she might, perhaps, be prevailed upon to introduce anybody to her sister, was a kind of acceptance she had long yearned for.

"I have lately," she attempted, once the weather and duck-related conversation had grown too circular even for her, "been reading *The Wanderer.*"

Mr. Bygrave looked enraptured. "I'm not familiar with it. But may I say that the way the light shimmers from your eyes is the most remarkable thing I have ever beheld?"

With a shyness she did not even have to counterfeit, Miss Caesar looked down a moment. "You may say so," she said, "and indeed I like your saying it very much."

Propriety held that a lady should not promenade alone, but it held also that a lady should be cautious as to the amount of time she spent in the company of any gentleman to whom she was neither married nor related. But time, my friends, time is a slippery thing in the best of circumstances, and for those who have been touched by the powers of fairy kind it becomes positively liquid, pooling and swirling and running away from one in wholly unexpected ways.

The unutterable ennui of Miss Caesar and Mr. Bygrave's conversation drove me back to the house where—now that both of the younger ladies had absented themselves—the matter of how to use an innocent girl to lure a creature of sapphire light and malice into an ambush was very much back on the table.

An hour or two after breakfast, the debate had been joined—if not necessarily enhanced—by the arrival of Miss Bickle, who had been making her rounds and, on finding the Caesar household overrun by common soldiers, decided that fashionable visiting could go hang.

It was at her suggestion that the party had sent for Miss Mitchelmore and Lady Georgiana, partly because Miss Bickle felt it would be—in her words—*jolly* and partly because they were the only people the Caesars knew who had any direct experience of thwarting supernatural malfeasance.

"Flattered as I am," Lady Georgiana was saying, "you do recall that I am not *actually* a witch, despite the rumours."

"Yes," conceded the elder Mr. Caesar, "but between you, you have defied a goddess. A fairy should be small challenge by comparison."

Normally I would object to the slight against the prowess of my people, but we enjoy being underestimated, so I will let it slide. By all means, readers, continue to fear us less than you fear gods. Such complacency will in no way be your undoing. I guarantee it.

And while I personally chose to make no objection, Captain James had no such reservations. "First rule of war, no small challenges."

"The *first* rule of war," Callaghan replied, "is wear comfortable boots. But no small challenges come soon after."

Lady Mary, who had insisted on being part of the council if her husband was, had been listening to the conversation intently and was only now prepared to speak her misgivings. "I am still uncomfortable about two elements of the proposed strategy. Proceeding without Mary's consent gives me pause, and sending a band of, well—"

"Armed bastards?" suggested Jackson, letting his face settle back into its natural smirk.

Lady Mary nodded. "Precisely. Sending a group of such people to a society event in the hope of incapacitating a guest seems extraordinarily likely to go wrong."

"And if we had any other option," Mr. Caesar told his mother, trying to sound authoritative and coming closer to success than I would have expected him to, "then we would surely take it. But there is one thing we have seen the Lady reveal herself for, and it is to bring Mary to a ball."

Although her recent experiences had made her rather less concerned with appearances than once she was, Miss Mitchelmore could not help but consider the obvious complaint. "Will it not make rather a scene?"

Sal batted her eyelashes. "Oh no, not at all. Swift and silent. Like a wind at night."

If she'd been at all intending to be taken seriously, the effect was rather spoiled by the captain's laughter. "It's a fight. There'll be gunshots."

"Gunshots," the elder Mr. Caesar pointed out, "around my daughter who is currently made of glass."

"The plan would be to lure the Lady away," explained Jackson. "Though what would lure her, that's another thing."

At last, the discussion had moved to Miss Bickle's area of expertise. Or at least to what Miss Bickle believed her area of expertise to be. "Oh, but that should be simple. The list of things fairies want is actually rather short when you start enumerating it. There's saucers of milk. People's firstborn children. Promises freely given.

Things that you think are one thing but are actually a different thing and the thing it turns out to be is usually your"—she stopped and looked bemused—"actually, thinking about it, children come up rather a lot."

Lady Georgiana, still standing, partly because the table was growing crowded and partly because it let her play her fingers through Miss Mitchelmore's hair, frowned cautiously. "I should stress that I am not *advocating* such a course of action. But I believe that sourcing a disposable child would prove . . . not entirely impossible."

"Sourcing from where?" asked Lady Mary, although my personal suspicion was that she either already knew the answer or did not want to know it.

"Desperate women?" Lady Georgiana's tone was matter-of-fact. "Workhouses? It's not a common practice, but it's far from unheard of. You can buy a wife similarly if you've a fancy."

The elder Mr. Caesar shook his head. "We are to buy *nobody*. There is little I would not do to protect my daughter, but that is a line we do not cross."

"Then I suppose," said Miss Bickle after a short silence, "we are left with milk."

That this discussion was going better than Mr. Caesar had expected was a damning indictment of his expectations. "I refuse to believe," he said, "that a wish-granting spirit of otherworldly beauty and inhuman wit will be lured from her places of safety by *milk.*"

Miss Bickle blinked. "Milk is good for you. And we have some very fine milk in Cornwall."

"What if we kept the milk for a backup?" suggested Captain James, leaning back in his chair and stretching like the world's least domesticated cat. "And thought more about giving her something she can sink her teeth into."

Lady Mary raised an interposing hand. "I concur with my husband. We cannot stoop to deliberately imperilling children."

"Never been in a textile mill, my lady?" asked Callaghan.

If he'd expected to shock his hostess, or to catch her out, he was bitterly disappointed. "I have, in fact. Many millworkers are friends of the abolition and I hope that the abolition is a friend to the millworker. I may not walk the streets naked in protest, but I am fully sensible of where my clothing comes from."

Easily distracted as ever, Miss Bickle stared intensely at something nobody else could see in a corner of the room. "I declare," she declared, "it sometimes feels as if there is truly no morally sound way of purchasing goods or services under our present social and economic system, and I rather feel there should be an efficient way to express that idea."

Sal smiled at her in a way that I might have been inclined to call flirtatious. "No ethical consumerism under colonialism?"

"Please don't encourage her," warned Mr. Caesar, "half her speech consists of made-up words already."

"Those aren't made-up words," Miss Bickle insisted, "they're perfectly well-formed words whose meaning is plain."

The elder Mr. Caesar leaned forwards. "The impossibility of perfection in an imperfect world aside, can we all agree that it would be wrong to sacrifice one child to save another?"

There was a chorus of agreement from everybody except Jackson.

"I mean, you say *wrong*," he opined. "Comes out a wash from where I see it."

"Where you see it from," replied Captain James, "is a very dark place."

"Safest place to be."

Her head resting against her lover's body, Miss Mitchelmore

craned her neck upwards to look at her. "Good Lord, Georgiana, somebody's said something cynical and you haven't even *tried* to outdo them. It's almost like you've grown as a person."

"I know, I'm disgusted with myself."

As the ranking officer, albeit ranking officer in charge of less than half the company, Captain James did his best to wrangle the discussion back in the direction of a plan. "Children are out," he agreed. "But we might need somebody who looks like a victim. Somebody who seems innocent, trusting, and like they'd jump at the chance to be snatched away by some shit from another world."

Miss Bickle's eyes grew wide as she stared at her companions. "But where would we find such a person?"

And the rest of the party stared back.

Satisfied that the team who were planning to go toe-to-toe with a mysterious being of unknown and subtle power had the beginnings of a plan, albeit one that stood a better-than-average chance of getting them killed, I lost interest and went to check on Miss Caesar.

She was still walking with Mr. Bygrave—something that would have been quite unforgivable had she been at all in a position to care for the opinions of the ton—and I recognised in him that enraptured look that mortals got when confronted with the Beauty Incomparable.

The sun was setting over Kensington Gardens, but its last rays danced inside Miss Caesar and spilled out of her as she walked, like the opposite of shadows.

"It's dark," Mr. Bygrave observed as if in a daze.

"Yes."

"We must have lost track of time."

"Yes."

Their voices echoed, as if from far away. An effect attributable entirely to the romantic atmosphere and not at all to the intervention of any—

"Going rather well, isn't it?" asked the Lady, freshly arrived from a place at ninety degrees to the mortal world.

"My compliments."

I watched the couple awhile. They were both, in their own ways, lost in the magic of it all. Which was, by and large, exactly where my people want your people—the more befuddled and confounded you are, the more it amuses us. Of course, having watched the young lady and her family for so long I could not quite help—but I am digressing. My kind are beings of whim who hold cruelty an art, comedy a virtue, and find our deepest delight in the combination of the two.

"What do you have planned for her?" I caught myself asking.

"Watch," she told me. "And find out."

That was the trouble with Titania's court. No professional courtesy.

"I should probably return you to your father," Mr. Bygrave continued, rather hesitantly.

With equal hesitancy, Miss Caesar nodded.

"It is not proper"—he flushed, gazing enraptured at the quasi-animate marvel that was Miss Caesar's new form—"but I should very much, that is—"

He got no further, because she kissed him.

It was a chaste affair by modern standards, but shocking by those of the day. Although of course the extent to which the standards of the day still applied when one was a fairy-wrought being of otherworldly substance was very much debatable.

Since she had no heart, I could read Miss Caesar's feelings on the exchange less well than those of most mortals, but I could still see triumph in her, and validation, and hope.

And, simmering beneath it all, questions.

CHAPTER TWELVE

A FTER THE KISS, WHICH LASTED only two-thirds of a
heartbeat—enchantment is powerful but in so many
ways society is more powerful still—Miss Caesar and Mr. Bygrave
returned immediately to their senses. He straightened his jacket
and she moved to straighten her dress, though no mortal power
was capable of disarranging so marvellous a garment.

Unable to justify any further dalliance, Mr. Bygrave made good
his promise to escort Miss Caesar back home, not realising until
after he had parted from her that his gloves had been cut when his
fingertips brushed the glass roses, and that blood was now seeping
through the fine cloth.

When Miss Caesar had returned to the bosom of her family, it
was to less admonition than she had received last time. While her
parents and brother had been concerned for her well-being, the
conclusion that there was nothing they could do until the transformation and all of its attendant consequences were reversed had
kept them from excessive panic.

Still, a tension remained in the household. The elder Mr.

Caesar spent longer at his correspondence, Lady Mary longer at her meetings, and Mr. Caesar longer visiting the Folly. Only Miss Anne was without means of escape from the realities of family life, and even she grew more given to lurking in her bedchamber.

Those members of the family who were directly involved in the plan against the Lady had eventually selected Lady Etheridge's forthcoming ball as the best opportunity for striking at their enemy. It had the advantage of proximity, being the next event on the calendar, and also of being one to which the Caesars would actually be invited. Not only was Lady Etheridge of too low rank to risk insulting the Earl of Elmsley by excluding his grandchildren, but she was at any rate a friend of the abolition and so held fewer objections to Lady Mary's choice of husband than many in the ton.

It was during my observations of Mr. Caesar's (and Miss Bickle's, since she had found herself with rather a central role in proceedings) planning sessions alongside his new associates that I discovered quite how much at odds the Lady's schemes and my own could wind up being. One of the first difficulties our intrepid band would need to overcome was their quarry's ability, common to all my people, to vanish from sight and slip our mortal guises at will. And it was through their discussions around this matter that I learned that Barryson possessed, or at least believed himself to possess, the knowledge of seeing-runes.

"The thing with elves," he explained to the assembly, the night before the plan was to be executed, "is that they think they're smarter than we are."

In our defence, we are. And in case you are concerned, reader, *elf* is also an acceptable term for our kind and is considered pejorative only if used in conjunction with the words *Santa* or *Keebler* (the history behind that last sponsorship agreement is long, sordid, and leaves neither of our species looking our best selves).

"She'll not expect us to be able to see her," he continued, "but the ones making the grab, they'll have runes painted on their eyes to show them hidden things. Which might take some getting used to, but I'll do it early."

Miss Bickle, whose father did not know where she was but was too wrapped up in poetry to care, squealed delightedly. "Oh *do*. I should so love to be shown hidden things."

"Not you," Barryson clarified. "She'll know if you can see her, and the runes are obvious. Means you're not getting them either." He nodded to Mr. Caesar and the captain. "Can't go to a ball with paint on your eyes."

Mr. Caesar gave an easy smile. "That rather depends on the ball."

"There's a ball John refuses to take me to," Miss Bickle explained, "where apparently gentlemen do that sort of thing *all the time*."

"Which is why you're not coming," confirmed Mr. Caesar, lapsing briefly back into the elder-brotherly tone that he otherwise shed around the Irregulars. "It's called the Gentleman's Ball for a reason."

Captain James frowned into his beer. "I don't like going in blind. If she can vanish on us, I should be able to see her."

At the other end of the table, Kumar had been making notes and drawing diagrams, but he looked up now. "Barryson's right. We need you on the inside. You'll have to rely on the rest of us for the catch."

Within the strict camaraderie of the regiment, *rely on the rest of us* had almost the power of a magical incantation, and the captain accepted it with good grace.

Miss Bickle, however, was not so easily put off. "Well, it seems very unfair to me that I should play so central a part in the scheme yet get to see no wonders as a consequence."

"Now, now." Sal laid a hand on the back of Miss Bickle's chair. He was a soldier today, a fact that Miss Bickle had not let pass her by. "I've offered to show you wonders and you've refused."

"I did not refuse," she protested, "I had refusal thrust upon me."

Mr. Caesar continued to do his very best to look severe. "It's bad enough that you're here, Lizzie; it would be unforgivably remiss of me if I were to allow you to be despoiled by a common infantryman while you were under my protection."

"But I should so like to be at least a *little* despoiled," replied Miss Bickle.

"And," Jackson added, "Sal is no common infantryman."

"I am," offered Callaghan helpfully. "Common as dirt. Though the wife has made it very clear my despoiling days are over."

What little authority Mr. Caesar had, he was sure, was fast slipping away. "Nobody is despoiling Lizzie. Nobody is painting anything on Lizzie's eyes. And anybody who gives her any ideas to the contrary will live with the consequences."

Moving silent as a pike through a lake, Jackson came to Mr. Caesar's side. "What consequences might those be?" he asked with the low menace of a man used to the law of eat-or-be-eaten.

"I'm sure you could paint *something* on my eyes," Miss Bickle mused. "It's far more acceptable for ladies, you know, and I might even start a trend. And think what a coup that would be. You could abandon soldiering entirely and launch a line of ladieswear."

Mr. Caesar nodded illustratively. "*Those* consequences. Nobody should ever give Lizzie ideas. She has far too many of her own already."

The night of the ball arrived and, with it, the Lady in her silver carriage. I had been wondering if, or perhaps hoping that, she would choose to miss this particular event. Since Miss Caesar had been invited to the dance already an escort to it would be less likely to engender gratitude and thus would play less into the purposes of a fairy abductor. But consistency was a virtue also, and while none of my kind are virtuous as you mortals understand, we make play of it from time to time in order that we might earn your trust.

Except for me. My virtues are entirely genuine.

Miss Caesar, therefore, proceeded in the Lady's conveyance while Mr. Caesar, Miss Bickle, and Miss Anne proceeded in theirs. Or rather, in the Earl of Elmsley's—Nancy was a skilled young woman, but the role of coachman was beyond her and at any rate the Caesars could not afford to keep their own carriage or horses.

Wishing, on this day, to avoid the society of the Lady, partly out of a desire not to interfere in a scheme that might see her brought low, and partly out of a more general social distaste, I rode with the mortal party. In the shape of a spider, I clung to a corner of the carriage, and huddled.

"Why so glum, Anne?" asked Miss Bickle, who had chosen that evening to dress in the manner of a milkmaid, complete with a pail that nobody could dissuade her from carrying. It was, of course, a choice considered gauche in the eyes of the ton, but Miss Bickle's inordinate wealth made her gaucheness surprisingly forgivable.

Miss Anne was gazing forlornly out of the window, wearing a look of tragedy that only a conventionally pretty fourteen-year-old could properly execute. "Mr. Bygrave has quite lost interest in me," she explained. "He has eyes only for Mary now."

"Well . . ." Miss Bickle showed every sign of considering her words carefully, which she did from time to time—it was one of her less appealing qualities. "She *is* the elder. And you are both young enough that there will be plenty more—"

"There will *not* be plenty more," Miss Anne complained, "because I am quite sure Mary will take away any gentleman who shows the slightest interest in me."

"Mary is . . ." If anything, Mr. Caesar was choosing his words yet more carefully than Miss Bickle. "She is going through a lot right now. Coming out was difficult for her and it is only natural that all this"—he waved a hand—"magical intervention has gone to her head a little."

For some unfathomable reason, Miss Anne was not in a mood to show empathy for her older sister. "It is unfair."

"Yes," agreed Mr. Caesar. "It is. But it was also unfair that gentlemen used to slight her in favour of you."

"That's different," replied Miss Anne with typical consistency.

Mr. Caesar arched a practised eyebrow. "How?"

To which Miss Anne was able to answer only: "It just is."

With which eloquence they arrived at the London home of Lady Etheridge to find the ball already in full swing, and already to some extent disrupted by the appearance of the Lady and her exquisite creation.

Lady Etheridge was many, many steps further down the curiously fine-grained social hierarchy of the day than the Earl of Semweir and her ball was consequently less lavish. The candles were fewer and slightly cheaper, the guests were of a lesser pedigree, and the floor of the ballroom wasn't chalked. Still, it remained a fine enough occasion for those who attended, and all the finer for its having, at its centre, the remarkable creature of glass.

The dancing was already under way when Mr. Caesar, Miss Bickle, and Miss Anne entered, and the relative anonymity this

afforded them suited Mr. Caesar's purpose, if not that of his sister.
Miss Bickle it at least afforded an opportunity to put down her
milk-pail without attracting undue comment. The three of them
settled discreetly into a corner, Miss Bickle and Miss Anne looking
available, Mr. Caesar looking watchful, and the three of them waiting to be approached by appropriate suitors.

Their first visitor was not a suitor at all—at least not for the
ladies—but Captain James. He sidled up to the group making, I
thought, excellent accommodation for the Lady's preternatural
hearing and murmured to Mr. Caesar without looking directly at
him that things were in motion and people were in place. From
there Mr. Caesar made a polite observation about the quality of
the dancing and moved over to relay the same information to Miss
Bickle, who dutifully took up her milk-pail and awaited further
instructions.

"I really, *really* don't think you will need that," Mr. Caesar told
her.

"Perhaps I shall not," she conceded. "But I see no harm in its
presence. And maybe a little milk will distract"—she cast a meaningful glance in the direction of the Lady, who was still watching
her protégé with the smug air of one watching a plan unfold to
perfection—"in the event that she attempts to make off with me."

Knowing better than to attempt to dissuade his friend from a
course of action already decided, Mr. Caesar let the matter rest
and turned his attention to the young officer approaching his sister.
The flesh-and-blood sister, that is.

He was tall, fair-haired, and handsome in a way only a certain
kind of man can be. His eyes were a piercing blue and his cheekbones were so high and sharp that other men could have shaved
with them. Had I not been able to hear the disgusting workings of
his biological organs as they pumped his blood and mulched his

dinner, I might almost have thought he came from my own land. By his side walked Lady Etheridge, whose duty as hostess was to make certain that nobody spoke to anybody to whom they had not been formally introduced.

"Miss Anne," she said with the light grace of the perennial hostess, "might I introduce you to Lieutenant Reyne."

He gave a low bow. "It seems wrong so fine a young woman should stand alone while others dance. May I have your hand for the next set?"

"I would be delighted," Miss Anne replied.

"Then I shall return when the couples change." His tone was soft when he spoke, and his smile winning. And while Mr. Caesar took note of him—for reason of his sister, I should say, not for any other reason that he might sometimes take note of soldiers—I personally was rapidly losing interest. It took an especially mortal kind of banality to think that the question of who a particular lady danced with mattered in any way, to anybody.

Besides, I had an ambush to watch.

The Irregulars had taken up positions in the garden square across the road from Lady Etheridge's fashionable residence. Jackson, dressed as a reasonable facsimile of a society gentleman, walked alongside Sal, dressed as a reasonable facsimile of a society lady, around the perimeter of the garden while Barryson lounged beneath a tree, Kumar lurked in the branches above him, and Boy William, looking deeply uncomfortable in borrowed livery, ran back and forth across the garden in the guise of a page.

Adopting the appropriately ominous form of a raven, I swooped low over the garden and took up a position in a different tree. I took this approach because I wished to know two things—how effective Barryson's seeing-runes would prove to be, and how adept the Irregulars would be at concealing their efficacy, should it become necessary.

The answers, it seemed, were "extremely" and "it varied distinctly." Boy William, with the poor impulse control of his limited years, stared at me quite openly and gawped like a guppy. At the other extreme, Sal and Jackson showed no sign of noting me at all.

"Not her," Barryson called up to Kumar, who I was a little disquieted to note had already trained his musket on me. "In fact," he mused partly to himself, "I reckon this is the one as has been watching us a while."

I cawed a noncommittal *caw* back.

The various soldiers settled into their positions and their roles, while inside the dancers continued to whirl away the evening or, quite frequently—given the kinds of dance that were fashionable in the day—walk-up-and-down-in-straight-lines away their evening.

Eventually, having decided that the time was right for her to take on her new role as bait, Miss Bickle emerged from the house, still carrying her milk-pail, and went waltzing through the garden as though she had no idea where she was or what was going on. Which may well have been true.

The plan, such as it was, had the virtue of simplicity and the vice of relying entirely on the Lady drifting away from the ball at the promise of an innocent debutante and a drink of milk. To the great good fortune of the planners, our kind are indeed selfish, opportunistic, and easily distracted.

The Lady descended from the house in a shimmer of pale blue and silver. Birdsong followed in her wake and the stars above shone just that little bit brighter to illuminate her. She swept into the garden trailing fairy dust and walked all smiles and secret offerings towards Miss Bickle, who was still staring fixedly at the sky, as though renaming constellations.

"Are you lost, child?" asked the Lady.

Whether from supreme art or genuine distraction, it took Miss Bickle a moment to acknowledge the Lady's presence. "Oh no, I'm just enjoying the evening. And I'm not a child, I'm almost twenty."

And the Lady laughed like bells. "All your people are children to my people. Tell me, she of the almost twenty years and the enjoyable evening, do you know what I am?"

Miss Bickle nodded enthusiastically. "Yes. You're a fairy. And I have *so* longed to meet a fairy. I have told all of my friends that what I long for more than anything in the *world* is to meet a fairy."

"Then"—the Lady's smile was every cat and every shark and every lie all folded together—"I am glad to have granted your wish. And quite without cost."

The thought of having had a wish granted by a fairy, even as part of an elaborate scheme to ensnare said fairy in a yellow cord, was sincerely delightful to Miss Bickle, and she beamed like a saint or a fool. "Would you like some milk?"

It was the milk, perhaps, that made the Lady wonder if she had been anticipated. The milk and the dawning awareness that the other inhabitants of the park were watching more warily than mortals should.

"Perhaps," the Lady suggested, "you would like to take my hand. I can show you remarkable things, child. If you trust me."

I have spoken often about the good credit that Miss Bickle's tendency to think well of my people does her, and so it was with grudging approval that I watched her hold out her hand to let the Lady take her away to an unknown but marvellous fate.

She didn't quite make contact before Jackson and Sal, as

casually as if they had been any couple out for a walk, sauntered over to intervene.

"A fine night," Jackson observed in an accent that was not his own. Not that the one he usually spoke in was his own either.

"Very fine," Miss Bickle agreed, snatching her hand back at the last second and bobbing a curtsey. "This lady was just about to take me somewhere extremely interesting."

Jackson nodded. "How generous of her. Tell me, is the invitation an open one, or was there something about this girl that caught your eye in particular?"

"It's the milk," Miss Bickle explained.

"It is not the milk," the Lady replied.

While this exchange was taking place, Mr. Caesar and the captain were just entering the square from the house-side, and Sal was sidling around in the other direction, her hands straying to her skirts where a long yellow ribbon was artfully concealed.

My kind are swift in our actions, and attacking us relies on swift execution and precise timing. Timing that the Irregulars *almost* missed. But right on cue, Kumar lined up his shot, and fired.

The musket-ball caught the Lady in the temple, a shot that would have been fatal to any mortal and even to a creature of the Other Court was a distraction and an impediment. Her blood, a deep indigo blue like a spilled inkwell, trickled down the side of her face, arcing across her cheekbones and staining her lips.

Being shot in the head threw the Lady off for just long enough that the captain could advance upon her, sword drawn, Barryson could begin whatever incantations he felt would be helpful in this situation, and Sal could position herself for the complex operation of binding a resisting supernatural being at the throat and wrists with a single length of cord not at all designed for the purpose.

It was not, however, long enough that the Lady was unable to shift to a space orthogonal to the garden and conceal herself, or so she thought, from mortal sight.

The captain could see nothing any longer, but if the Lady had thought herself safe from the other Irregulars she was to be proven quite, quite wrong. Unfortunately if the Irregulars thought themselves to have an insurmountable advantage they were quite, quite wronger.

From his position in the tree, Kumar was in no place to take a safe shot with Miss Bickle and the others so close, while Barryson's words of binding, chanted as he walked widdershins around the melee, were proving similarly ineffective. Jackson's sword, meanwhile, came alive in his hands, twisted out of his grip, and levelled against his throat. All around the square, faces were appearing in windows, and from the door of Lady Etheridge's residence, guests were beginning to spill outside to investigate the commotion.

Choosing her moment, Sal extended a length of ribbon between her hands like a garrotte and moved forwards with impressive swiftness, for a mortal.

Between the ribbon taking hold and whatever sorcery Barryson was weaving, the Lady dropped back into visibility. Her animation of other people's swords, however, remained resolutely intact.

Keeping his grip on his own weapon, Captain James did his best to neutralise Jackson's but found it a losing endeavour since a blade moving under its own power had nothing to incapacitate. Still, repeated strikes against the metal sufficed to keep it distracted long enough for Jackson himself to join Sal and a finally emergent Boy William in piling onto the Lady in the hopes of restraining her long enough to tie her hands as well as her throat.

I, in this situation, would have been shape-shifting. But the Lady was not that sort. She travelled as a fair woman in blue, or as light, and nothing else. And the light option was curtailed by the band at her throat.

Steadfastly neutral in the conflict as I was—I ordinarily favour my own over mortals, but Titania's court is an enemy of my master and thus an enemy to me also—I watched through the dispassionate eyes of a carrion bird and judged this particular conflict to be a win for humanity. Unprepared for runecraft, overly reliant on enchantments, and with a ball of lead still lodged somewhere where, had she been mortal, her brain would have been, the Lady had a number of disadvantages any one of which could have proved critical.

Of course, she had also a single, crucial trump card.

Miss Caesar broke free from the ever-expanding crowd of onlookers and raced past both her brother and the captain in an effort to pry the other Irregulars from her patroness. Although she was beyond biological limitations, her new body had been built for beauty rather than strength, and so her capacity to overpower was limited. But glass had its own dangers, and the leaves that wound through her hair cut deep into Jackson and Boy William as they tried to pull her away. And for a moment I quite lost track of the combatants in a mess of blue and yellow and blood and mirrors and—

"Mary." Mr. Caesar tried to address his sister with a tone of command, but he lacked his father's gravitas. He was also deeply conscious that he had, despite the warnings, come out wearing a cravat. "Step away and let us finish this."

In the tangle of limbs and multicoloured bloods, Sal managed to tie one of the Lady's wrists to her throat, restricting her enough that Jackson's sword fell lifeless to the floor and Mr. Caesar's imminent fears for his airway were at least somewhat abated.

"There is nothing *to* finish," Miss Caesar pleaded. "Except this terrible scene that you and your new friends are making in front of half the ton."

Materialising like an unwelcome spirit, Mr. Ellersley drifted to the front of the crowd. "This is more than a scene," he said, and Mr. Caesar had the unwelcome impression that he was saying it to a very general audience. "This is a criminal disturbance."

Whether from a distaste for civilian interruption or lingering resentment from earlier run-ins, Captain James glared at the newcomer. "Don't recall asking you."

Her strength recovering rapidly and the new presence of Miss Caesar vastly restricting the Irregulars' capacity for violence, the Lady shook Sal off at last, though ritual and old compacts forbade her from unbinding herself. "My protégé did not ask your assistance either," she pointed out, her voice just a fraction weaker and more mortal than it was when she was untied. "Yet you interfered."

"Respectfully," the captain told her, "shut up."

With a decorous cough, the Lady expectorated the musket ball into her palm, spattering it with bright blue blood drops. Then she turned to Miss Caesar. "Be a dear," she said, "and untie these."

While the literal undoing of all their hard work was the source of some concern for Mr. Caesar, his attention was caught by something differently disturbing. Fine cracks spiderwebbed up from his sister's ankles and midway up her calves, visible through and in the strange fabric of her dress. "Mary," he said again, but more gently now, "you are not well."

One knot undone, Mary turned. "I shall be the judge of whether I am well, John. You are my brother, not my keeper."

"Let us *stop this.*" Far from authoritative, Mr. Caesar's tone was imploring now. He had not, perhaps, quite understood until now how close he was to losing one of his sisters.

Paying him no mind, Miss Caesar hooked her delicate glass

fingernails into the knot at the Lady's throat and tugged the ribbon free.

Stepping back a little, although not, I couldn't help but notice, so far that she could be shot without risk of hitting Miss Caesar, the Lady gave a satisfied nod. "Well, hasn't this been a wonderful evening. I believe it is best that I bid you all adieu."

And then, unbound, she did indeed become starlight. As did her carriage, her coachmen, and the last wisps of enchantment that had fallen over the evening, save those that still lingered within Miss Caesar.

For a moment, the glass girl stood staring at her brother and his companions, wearing an expression of rank betrayal. And then, before he or anybody else could make apology or explanation, she turned and fled weeping into the night.

And where her tears fell, they shattered.

CHAPTER THIRTEEN

THE ONLY THING THE GOOD folk of the ton liked more than a ball was a ball abruptly interrupted by the misfortunes of others, and in this Lady Etheridge had served them admirably.

Mr. Caesar had made a concerted effort to pursue his sister through the streets but, lacking my swiftness, he had soon lost her in the crowds that never truly left the metropolis. He petered to a stop at the end of the road, a combination of social embarrassment, physical fatigue, and despair making the chase all but pointless. He stood, head bowed and shoulders slumped, while Miss Bickle and the Irregulars caught up with him. When they had, Miss Bickle put a reassuring hand on his arm and made sympathetic noises, while Captain James started issuing orders.

"Barryson, Boy William—take the park. Sal and Jackson, down St. James's. Kumar and Callaghan, north and see if you can't head her off. If you find her, one stay on her, the other come back to the Folly."

None of them spoke a reply, they just fell in line, fanned out, and vanished into the city. And no sooner had they vanished than

Mr. Ellersley swooped down upon Mr. Caesar and the captain, flanked by a pair of extremely impatient-looking night watchmen.

"There!" Mr. Ellersley pointed an artificially trembling finger at Captain James. "There's the ruffian. I *demand* he be dragged to the watch-house at once."

Never having quite shaken the rookery dweller's fear of the law, the captain eyed the watchmen cautiously. "Bit busy right now."

The taller of the two watchmen gave a frankly jobsworthy frown. "Busy don't come into it. Gentleman here says you was making an affray. There's statutes about making an affray."

"There you go"—Mr. Ellersley smiled like a particularly petty shark—"Statutes. Can't argue with statutes."

A vein in Mr. Caesar's head was beginning to throb. "Tom, can you not see that this is—this is the *opposite* of the appropriate time."

The watchmen had already moved forwards to seize the captain and, contrary to his normally dashing idiom, he was making no attempt to resist them.

"You think it's appropriate for common soldiers to let off guns in the middle of Mayfair?" asked Mr. Ellersley, his tone sugar cut with strychnine.

Mr. Caesar bristled. "Captain James is *not* a common soldier."

That *almost* brought the watchmen up short. It was, after all, true that the captain wore an officer's uniform, and most officers outranked most thief-takers in most ways. But Mr. Ellersley assuaged their misgivings with a sharp: "He looks pretty *common* to me."

With a deep sigh, Captain James cast Mr. Caesar a reassuring look. "Don't worry, it won't be my first night in the cells."

"Why," replied Mr. Ellersley, "does that *not* surprise me?"

"Tom," Mr. Caesar tried again, "*please* don't do this. It's low even for you."

As pleas went, what it lacked in tact, it made up for in no way whatsoever. Mr. Ellersley sneered. "If you're trying to reenter my good graces, you're making a poor showing of it."

"I'm trying to"—Mr. Caesar stumbled, he wasn't sure *what* he was trying to, or how he was trying to do it—"Gods and powers, Tom, why are you *being* like this?"

Mr. Ellersley's sneer became a scowl. "Because I *am* like this. As are you. It's time to stop pretending to be somebody you aren't."

"Tom—"

"I *know* you, John. I understand you. I'm really the only one who does."

I have said many times, readers, how much I despise your species for all its many vanities and weaknesses. But what I saw in Mr. Ellersley now was a wonderfully fairy-like passion. If there is one thing my people hold to be an eternal truth it is that there is no better way to show affection for a thing than to destroy it utterly.

Mr. Caesar, naturally, did not see it this way. Indeed, he was so lacking in perspective that he stood, dumbfounded, while his former lover gave the final nod to the watchmen.

"Now gentlemen"—said Mr. Ellersley—"I suggest you do your duty."

With the grudging efficiency of poor men in terrible jobs, the two thief-takers began leading Captain James away to their watchhouse. A hot blend of shame, embarrassment, and fear was prickling its way up Mr. Caesar's spine and making its way to the base of his skull. There was so, *so* much wrong with this situation and so, *so* little he could do about it. He could almost taste blood.

"*Do you,*" Mr. Caesar turned on the watchmen with pure instinct and adrenaline. "Have *any idea* who I *am?*"

As opening gambits went it had been risky, but to two men of low birth whose professional lives mostly involved getting pushed into the mud by rich gadabouts, it was practically a mystical incantation.

"My grandfather is the Earl of Elmsley," *not here right now but that isn't important,* "my uncle is the Vicomte Hale" *who hates me and actively wishes me ill, but that isn't important either* "and my cousin is the Duchess of Annadale" *that one is almost entirely a lie, but let it slide.* "This man"—he took a step towards the watchmen, one of whom was actively trembling—"is performing vital service for my family and you have no *conception* of the enemies you will make if you impede him."

For all the watchmen knew, Mr. Caesar's list of names could have been a recipe for soup or the playbill of an unpopular theatre, but he delivered it with such hauteur and confidence that they released the captain at once and fell back to an appropriately deferent distance.

"Oh, come *on,*" tried Mr. Ellersley, "you can't actually—"

"And as for *you*"—Mr. Caesar rounded on his former lover with a fury that came at least six parts from desperation—"go home. Or to your club. Or to Paris. Or to Hell for all I care. I am *finished* with you, Thomas."

Mr. Ellersley's mouth remained hanging open for a few moments, then he snapped it shut, gave a stiff little bow and said simply. "Caesar."

"Ellersley," replied Mr. Caesar with a curt nod.

The clash of politesse lasted a few seconds more, and then Mr. Ellersley lowered his gaze and retreated, taking the watchmen with him. No sooner was he out of sight than the swell of aristocratic rage that had been keeping Mr. Caesar afloat abated and he slumped like an understuffed doll.

Captain James looked at him with two kinds of concern. "Where the fuck did that come from?"

"My uncle," Mr. Caesar admitted. "And my mother, sometimes. Occasionally my grandfather."

For a moment, the captain considered this. "I'll be honest, it's a little bit scary."

Mr. Caesar nodded. "I know. I've been on the other end of it more times than I'm comfortable with."

"Still. Good to have in your back pocket." Captain James looked back towards the Etheridge residence, where a crowd of rich mortals was still in mid-gossip. "Now I reckon you should take the ladies home."

The fact that his *other* sister was also at that moment unaccounted for did not help with Mr. Caesar's turbulent blend of emotions, but it was at least galvanising. He nodded and then, restricting himself to the manner of address that could be considered at least *deniable* in public, placed a comradely hand on the captain's shoulder. "Of course. And—" But there was no *and*, not really. There was no corollary that would undo the fact that he had once again let down his family and his new companions both. "And thank you," he finished.

"It's fine," replied the captain. "And thanks too. For sorting out those watchmen."

Unaccustomed to being thanked, or at least to being thanked sincerely, Mr. Caesar couldn't think of a sensible reply. Besides, with gawkers and rubberneckers surrounding them, there was little more that could be said or done, and so Mr. Caesar returned to the crowd to search for his other sister and Captain James set off for the Folly.

Mercifully—well, mercifully for Mr. Caesar, rather less mercifully for those of us with greater appetites for chaos—locating Miss Anne was rather simpler. She had elected to cling to Lieutenant Reyne, with whom she had danced twice and thus considered herself quite well acquainted. And the lieutenant for his part delivered the girl to her brother swiftly and without complaint, but expressing his deep regrets that the evening had been cut so short. Miss Bickle, for her part, had mercifully restrained her urge to wander off, and rejoined the group as Miss Anne was saying her goodbyes.

Having accomplished as much as he reasonably could—and having failed to accomplish rather more—Mr. Caesar was just returning to the carriage with his various feminine charges when he was interrupted by the young Mr. Bygrave.

"Is she—Miss Caesar, is she safe?" There was genuine concern in his voice, although I suspected that a good proportion of that was lingering enchantment.

Profoundly not in the mood to entertain young gentlemen, Mr. Caesar glanced down. "I do not know."

"Then should you not be searching for her?"

The practical answer was that he should not, because he had equal responsibilities to both of his sisters. The less practical answer was that he should, because the greater claim to protection lay with the lady in greater peril. The answer he gave was "I do not know."

"Then should *I* look for her?" asked Mr. Bygrave, and my hypothetical ears (I was still a raven, so I had ears of a sort, just not externally) pricked up at this. If he began roving the streets now, his chances of dying in an interesting way were excellent, and while it might prove tangential to the overall thrust of the narrative, your people and mine share a taste for unnecessary bloodshed.

Thus I was delighted when Mr. Caesar's reply was "Do as you wish."

As the Caesars' carriage rolled off into the night, I took flight, tracing wide circles over London and—with bird sight and fairy sight both—observing each of my various subjects as they moved through the city.

Thus I saw Mr. Caesar and his charges returning home by a straight route, Mr. Bygrave wandering with little aim or purpose,

further and further from the paths he knew, and Miss Caesar flee-
ing like—and I apologise profusely for this analogy because it is
profoundly, as I believe those mortals of the generations born
between the end of the twentieth and the start of the twenty-first
century would call it, *basic*—Cinderella from the ball.

It was, of course, entirely outside my remit as a dispassionate
observer to guide, direct, or (perish the thought) *misdirect* any of
these wanderers. So I absolutely did not.

In the end, the carriage reached its destination before anything
murderous happened to either of the other two, and so I reverted
to mists and followed the occupants inside. There Mr. Caesar, Miss
Anne, and Miss Bickle were met by the elder Caesars who, if I was
any judge (and since I am the narrator I am, in a sense, the only
judge who matters), had been waiting in the same spots without
moving since their children had left.

They said nothing as the ballgoers entered, and they did not
need to. There was only one question to be asked and only one
answer to be given.

"We failed," Mr. Caesar told them. "*I* failed. And Mary fled.
Captain James and the others are looking for her now."

Miss Anne flopped into the window seat. "It was ill done on all
fronts. John was wrong to interrupt the ball and Mary was wrong
to flee from it. Things could have been *so* fine had you left well
enough alone."

"Your sister being under an enchantment," Lady Mary pointed
out, "is not *well enough*."

In the spun-sugar labyrinth of her heart, Miss Bickle was struggling to reconcile a set of conflicting impulses that she very much
did not wish to reconcile. "I *think*," she began tentatively, "that it
might be quite bad actually. Possibly even very bad. Which seems
so unfair because enchantments should by all rights be enchanting,

not horrible." She frowned with such exaggerated sorrow that she looked like a theatrical mask depicting tragedy. "Why must things always be more horrible in reality than they are in concept?"

"That depends on who you ask," Lady Mary replied. "Some would say it has to do with original sin. Others would suggest that we, as a society, have an unfortunate habit of making things worse than they need to be."

Miss Anne, having recovered from any shock or disappointment she might have experienced earlier in the evening, was now settling comfortably into the happy familiarity of complaining about her sibling. "Well, as I see it, Mary has made her bed and should lie in it."

"If it please you, miss," observed Nancy, who had been maintaining the traditional invisibility of the serving classes, "she's not."

This was, it seemed, new information to the elder Mr. Caesar. "What do you mean?"

"Her bed. She's not slept in it. And you've seen her not eating. Whatever's happened to her it's not right, and though it's not my place to say I'd not call it her fault neither."

"Well, who else's fault is it?" demanded Miss Anne, with entirely predictable petulance.

"Not everything is somebody's fault," the younger Mr. Caesar told her. "And I don't think you'd be such a pill about this if it weren't for Mr. Bygrave."

Despite being young himself, and having had two younger sisters for many years, Mr. Caesar appeared still to have vastly overestimated the constancy of youth. "Oh, but I don't give a fig for *him*," Miss Anne replied, breezily. "Lieutenant Reyne is a finer man by far, do you not think?"

"He is certainly handsome," agreed Miss Bickle, unhelpfully.

"And *many* years your senior," added the elder Mr. Caesar.

Miss Anne looked affronted. "Certainly he cannot be more than two and twenty."

"And you are fourteen," her brother reminded her. His tone was reproving but, worn out after the night's events, his heart was not entirely in it.

The look of affront remained attached to Miss Anne like a stubborn tick. "So was Juliet."

"Did you, by any chance, watch the *second* half of that play as well as the first?" asked the younger Mr. Caesar.

It should, I think, go without saying that I would personally advise the reader to take dating advice from any being in the cosmos before they listened to the bastard bard.

The question of the precise minimum age at which happy mothers can be made being if not resolved then at least momentarily set aside, Mr. Caesar bowed a stiff farewell to his parents and made for the door.

"And where are you going?" asked his father.

"The Folly."

The elder Mr. Caesar's disapproval was seldom spoken aloud, and seldom needed to be.

"If any of the men hear word of Mary, they will report back there," his son replied. It was an excuse, and with the possible exception of Miss Anne, the whole room knew it.

"Ah." The elder Mr. Caesar rose from his chair. "Then I shall spare you the journey. I need a walk anyway."

"There's no need, Papa," Mr. Caesar insisted. "That is—"

"That is, you would rather be there than here?" asked Lady Mary. There was no accusation in her tone, just a terrible certainty. One that had the virtue of accuracy.

"Not at all," Mr. Caesar protested (and yes, that talentless

fuckstain Bill has a line about that too). "It is merely that the gentlemen there know me and they do not know you and . . ."

"John." The elder Mr. Caesar was speaking sternly now. "I am
sure these past days have been hard for you, but—"

"*Days?* Try *years*, Papa." The words were out of Mr. Caesar's
mouth before he could subject them to his usual scrutiny. And once
they had begun he found they would not stop. "Have you any conception of what it is like living in your shadow and Mama's? To
have everybody I meet say, 'Oh, you must be that one's son'? To
know they're saying the same and worse about my sisters and that
I can do nothing about it?"

It was perhaps the longest thing of significance he had ever said
to his parents. Possibly to anybody, or anybody other than the captain. And though he saw how it stung he could not quite bring
himself to regret it.

Still, the words hung in the air like gunsmoke.

"Your father and I have . . . we have done our best to give you
ordinary lives," said Lady Mary. The elder Mr. Caesar, it seemed,
was not able to reply at all.

"Well, you have failed," snapped Mr. Caesar. "Had you not,
Mary would still be—"

"Would still be what?" asked his father as if those four words
were the most he could manage without cracking.

And belatedly, the regret came. Of all mortal emotions it is the
one that tastes sweetest to my kind, although in this instance I
found my palate oddly dulled. "I didn't mean—"

"Perhaps not," replied Lady Mary. "Or perhaps you meant
exactly what you said."

A sour taste was growing in Mr. Caesar's mouth. "I do not—
I did not—there's just so much in my life, in Anne's and Mary's
lives, that was decided for us before we were even born and—"

Lady Mary regarded her son with a look that bordered on the edge of betrayal. "We know," she said, softly. Though as she continued the softness ebbed away. "We have always known. And yes, when your father and I chose each other we chose for you as well, and I would tell you I was sorry if I could, but I will not because it would be a lie."

Beside her, the elder Mr. Caesar was silent. Two steps from defeated.

"You and your sisters," Lady Mary continued, "are the only things that matter to us. The truest things in our world. And we need you now, this family needs you."

A serpent was crawling beneath Mr. Caesar's skin, a sense like nausea moving with it. "And I—" he said, hesitantly. "I need space. I need to think."

The elder Mr. Caesar found his voice at last. "John," he said. "I have always trusted you to know what is right. For you, and for those around you. I trust you to make the right decision now."

The younger Mr. Caesar looked at his parents and sister, and what he saw looking back at him was twenty years of hope and love and expectation and disappointment that in that moment he could not face up to. So he said, "I'm sorry."

And he left.

And so did I.

London is a dangerous city for a young woman alone, and whether it becomes more so or less so if that young woman is also made of a notoriously fragile substance and illuminated with an inner glory that by turns entices and ensnares is left as an exercise for the reader.

I caught up with Miss Caesar as she was wandering from a mildly dangerous part of London-by-night into an extraordinarily dangerous part of it. Were I given to speculation (and I am not; I speak only truth in its most absolute and unvarnished sense) I might also have thought some force was guiding her, be it destiny or something more sinister.

And this time it really *wasn't* me.

Not that it was any of those other times either.

The streets were narrower now, and lit only by the moon. So the light that radiated from within Miss Caesar stood out like a candle in a darkened field. And like a candle it drew moths.

And by moths, I mean men with knives.

I should of course take this opportunity to remind my enlightened, modern readers that the average inhabitant of the London slums in this era was no less moral than the average inhabitant of Mayfair or the Houses of Parliament. Or indeed of your own great halls of power in your own countries in your own age. But then I suspect you will also need little reminding of how low a bar that truly is.

Thus it should not come as too great a surprise to know that the arrival of an obviously magical being with vast potential resale value encouraged at least some of the denizens of the less seemly parts of the city to put self-interest above self-preservation and try to acquire her.

"Lost, lady?" was the somewhat unoriginal opening line of their leader, a short, quick-eyed man with a mole on his left cheek.

Sheltered though her life had been, and young though she was, Miss Caesar was no fool. She took a step back and watched the stranger warily. "I am quite all right, thank you."

Taking a step back, it transpired, was not the wise precaution it seemed, because it brought her into contact with another gentleman, this one taller, more scarred, and more heavily built. "You don't seem all right. What do you say we find you somewhere to stay?"

Vulnerable as a glass girl intrinsically is, Miss Caesar had one advantage that she would not have possessed were she still flesh. Surprised by the arrival of the second man, she turned her head sharply, causing one of her glass roses to slash a thin red line across his face. And vulnerable, sheltered, and out of her element as she was, she had the wherewithal to take the opportunity afforded when he swore and recoiled in pain to take at once to her heels.

She had not, unfortunately, had the wherewithal to remain in the parts of the city she knew. So she fled blindly through unfamiliar streets, pursued by rough gentlemen who would not let a little thing like lacerating glass deter them for long.

Those of you who read my last novel might recall the surprisingly dramatic but assuredly very genuine moment when Miss Mitchelmore, being pursued by otherworldly enemies, stumbled at the last moment and fell, only to be rescued by an individual of dubious character.

Would you believe that it happened again? One would imagine that such charming parallelism could not possibly occur in real life. But as I watched, I saw Miss Caesar stumble, fall, find herself helpless as the men with knives closed in upon her.

What are the chances?

Except as she fell, she fell forward, and rather than crashing onto the cobblestones, she found herself caught in the arms of a woman she had never met. Tall and dark-skinned, she wore a headdress in the Egyptian style that had been briefly popular some fourteen years earlier when Napoleon moved into Alexandria. Her dress was long and decorated in white and gold, which, frankly, did not make it especially suitable for London's muddy streets. For a moment, I thought her eyes found me, but she made no mention of my presence.

The armed ruffians who had been pursuing Miss Caesar stopped short.

"Go," she told them. "You are not welcome here."

And, unwelcome, they went.

The heart Miss Caesar did not have was beating fast, causing the light within her to flicker like a candle flame or, if you prefer a more anachronistic analogy, a strobe. Eyes glimmering like stars and wide with gratitude, she gazed up at her rescuer. "Thank you," she said, "but . . . where am I?"

And the stranger smiled, and let her inside.

The building into which Miss Caesar had been led was one part temple, one part gaming hell. The walls were lined with frescoes in a range of styles from ancient to neoclassical and everywhere statues of Tyche and Fortuna gazed benevolently (and not so benevolently) down at tables where crowds of mostly men, their prospects mostly good, were playing at hazard and at games of dice as ancient as empires.

"You are here," said her rescuer. "And it is the only place you need to be."

Having, perhaps, decided at last that having her destiny decided entirely by mysterious women who appeared from nowhere was a suboptimal way to live her life, Miss Caesar rallied a little of her older defiance. "That is not an answer."

"You are in the house of prosperity. The home of Isis-Fortuna."

Miss Caesar looked unconvinced. "This seems to be little more than a den of degenerate gamblers."

"And you seem little more than a glass doll who dances for the pleasure of others." The stranger smiled. "Are you?"

In a more navigable world, Miss Caesar would have had an answer for that. "I am a person, not a building." A cheer went up from a nearby table. "And the nature of your clientele is plain."

"Three points," called a man from another table, his accent as cut glass as Miss Caesar's body, "and the game."

"Our clientele are men whose hands you would smile and bat your eyelids for if you met them in a different room," the stranger said. "All gentlemen are degenerates."

Miss Caesar stiffened. Or at least would have stiffened, were she not already rigid. "My father is not a degenerate."

"Your father is not a gentleman."

"And what do you know of my family?" asked Miss Caesar, worried that the answer would be *Quite a lot actually.*

"I know that your mother is the youngest daughter of the Earl of Elmsley, though the first to marry. I know that your father was a Frenchman's property, an Englishman's war prize, and an Englishwoman's bauble, then at last a free man in a kingdom that claims its air is freedom. Though many of us see that for a lie."

The stranger's accent, Miss Caesar could not help but notice, had a tendency to drift; though it was always London at its heart its register shifted from the gutter to the ballroom and back again depending on her subject.

"I know your brother is a dandy and a molly and dances in between worlds that will never accept him, and your sister, in the eyes of your society, is a bright jewel like a diamond from the Peacock Throne. And I know who you are, Miss Mary Caesar, more than you do yourself. And what you gave away to be what you are now."

Honestly, readers, I find this kind of trickery a little gauche. It is an easy thing for mortal witches to discover the biographical details of those they wish to impress and it is, I would argue, a vulgar thing for mortals to be impressed by such flimflammery. It bespeaks a self-regard that is unbecoming in such unremarkable beings as yourselves.

For a being like me, of course, it is a different thing entirely.

"Have you been spying on me?" asked Miss Caesar. It was the wrong question, but mortals persist in asking it anyway.

"Fate has been spying on you. I have been spying on fate."

Miss Caesar's eyes narrowed, white light spilling from between her fine glass-fibre lashes. "Then I should at least know your name."

"Should you?"

"It would be polite."

"I am a witch, child. And a woman of business. Politeness interests me only if it gets me what I want. But you may call me Amenirdis."

Speak the name of a thing three times and it will emerge. Sometimes. But in this instance the name that conjured and the conjured entity were far less related. No sooner had Amenirdis shared her moniker (it was not the name of her birth, probably; witches and fairies wear names as casually as hats) than the door opened once more and Mr. Bygrave burst in. Ignoring the entreaties of a sharply dressed croupier trying to invite him to a gaming table, he searched the room for Miss Caesar and, finding little difficulty in the task, for she stood out like—well, like a glowing glass girl in a magical gaming hell, he pushed his way through the crowds towards her.

He had acquired, in his journey through the city, a number of scrapes and bruises. The same people who had harassed Miss Caesar would undoubtedly have tried their luck with a young and callow officer, but having a sword and no purse, Mr. Bygrave had proved uninteresting prey and survived his journey with minimal jostling.

Of course, that was before he decided to *draw* said sword and point it at the hostess of the temple.

"Unhand her," he demanded despite the fact that Amenirdis's hands were nowhere near Miss Caesar.

"Or?" asked Amenirdis, staring down the blade with commendable apathy. "Will you murder me in cold blood?"

"It is no murder to rescue a lady from a . . ." He stumbled, his list of pejoratives running short in the circumstances.

Amenirdis walked slowly forward and put one fingertip on the point of Mr. Bygrave's sword. "Set this aside. You will have no need of it here."

Faced with running through an unarmed woman (albeit one who likely had defences of her own the like of which Mr. Bygrave could not possibly comprehend) or sheathing his weapon, Mr. Bygrave chose peace. Miss Caesar, however, hurried to his side.

"I have come to find you," he explicated quite unnecessarily. "Your family will want to know that you are safe."

"She was quite safe," Amenirdis told him. "And she will be better if she stays."

Raucous laughter at some unrelated joke echoed around the hall, and Miss Caesar slipped her arm into Mr. Bygrave's. "If I am not a prisoner," she said, "then I shall leave."

With that enigmatic smile common to all witches, Amenirdis nodded. "You are not a prisoner. Go if you will. You know where to find me."

Without waiting for any further discussion, Mr. Bygrave drew Miss Caesar back into the streets, and I was about to follow, but I was checked by the voice of the witch.

"And what do you want, aboatia?"

I turned. "A story. And for what it's worth the mmoatia are not quite the same as my—"

Amenirdis shrugged. "You live in forests, disguise yourselves as animals, and play tricks on people. What kind of story?"

"One that pleases my master and vexes Titania, who I *sincerely* hope you aren't going to tell me is one of the ten thousand names of Isis."

"Do I need to?"

One of the more complicated things about taking one of my extremely true and directly personally experienced narratives and wrangling them into linear shape for mortal consumption is that it is not only time but identity itself that works fundamentally differently for our people. In the play that I once gave an otherwise talentless glover's son I am called *Robin Goodfellow* amongst other things. But that is as much a name for a species as an individual and may be used plurally for all of my kind just as *hobgoblin* may (though not, please, to my face). We are ideas as much as people and people as much as ideas, which makes keeping track of the relationships between us and then communicating those relationships to three-dimensional beings an utter chore.

"Is this going to make things difficult?" I asked her. "I'm just a dispassionate observer. Whatever purposes you and the Lady have in mind, I'm more than happy for you to fight it out amongst yourselves."

With a studied casualness, Amenirdis picked up a deck of playing cards from a table nearby. She cut the deck and turned over the top card to reveal the seven of spades. "For some reason," she told me, "I do not consider you trustworthy."

"I would offer to swear oaths to the effect that I am here only to observe, but I doubt that you would trust those either."

Amenirdis nodded. "Never trust the word of a shape-shifter. Oaths mean nothing to a creature that can say 'I' and mean a hundred different things."

"I do so *hate it* when mortals work that out."

"I've had a long time to study." She turned another card. The two of clubs. "Continue watching, spirit. But interfere with me or this place, and it will end badly for you."

To which I responded with my most winning smile. "I am eternal, little witch. I have no endings, good or bad."

In hindsight, it was probably an unfortunate thing to have said. The gods have such a pissing awful sense of irony.

CHAPTER FOURTEEN

THE IRREGULARS WERE MAKING THEIR way back towards the Folly in ones and twos, reporting on their failure to locate the elusive Miss Caesar. How they missed somebody who literally glowed, I am not certain, but then the army has never been the most selective of employers and I suppose that London *is* rather large.

Having discharged their duties as they saw them, the soldiers retired to their own various nighttime activities, which for the most part meant either drinking, fucking, or sleeping, although Kumar retired rather pointedly with a book instead. By the small hours only Mr. Caesar and Captain James were left propping up the bar, Mr. Caesar staring disconsolately into a mug of weak beer and speaking little.

"She'll be found," Captain James told him. "If the men don't then the family will."

For a long time, Mr. Caesar made no reply. Then at last he responded with a morose, if accurate: "People disappear in this city every day."

"Not earls' granddaughters."

Mr. Caesar had no reply to that.

"We can go back out," suggested the captain, "if you want. Though we'll not have much chance tonight I don't think."

"No"—defeated, Mr. Caesar could barely even bring himself to shake his head—"no, I do not believe we would do any good."

The door opened and, conjuring hope from nowhere, Mr. Caesar turned towards it. Not expectant, but alert. He had responded like this to every guest who had entered all evening, finding sometimes one of the Irregulars with discouraging news, sometimes a complete stranger looking for a drink or a bed or a combination of the two.

This time, however, the new arrival was his father.

"She is back," he announced from halfway across the room. "I thought you should know."

Guilt is an alien emotion to my species (we are, indeed, capable of feeling only six things: mirth, anger, curiosity, two sensations that have no equivalents for mortals, and one I choose not to name), but I have seen it often in humans, and I recognised it in Mr. Caesar now. "There was no need, Papa," he said. "That is—you have come a long way."

Not wanting to have this conversation from across a floor full of drunk strangers, the elder Mr. Caesar approached his son. "And who should I have sent? Your mother? Your sister? Nancy is a good girl, but we do not pay her enough to carry messages at this time of night or to this part of the city."

"You still didn't have to come yourself. I would have—"

"Come back eventually?"

"Tomorrow, Father," Mr. Caesar insisted. "I would have come back tomorrow." It wasn't a lie. It was a prediction on the basis of minimal evidence.

The elder Mr. Caesar gave a slow nod. "Well, now you have no need. Be safe, John."

And he departed, leaving his son not quite able to follow, not quite able to ask him to stay. Sat at a bar he wasn't sure he wanted to be in, thinking thoughts he wasn't sure he wanted to think, about a life he was only half-sure he wanted to be living. Since waking that morning, he had managed to drive away both a sister and a father and he could face no more demands, no more expectations, and no more choices.

"I believe," he said at last, "I may be done for the evening."

With that, he rose and made his way up to the, by his standards at least, rather squalid room he had taken to staying in when he had a mind to escape to the Folly. Halfway up the staircase, he turned, and noticed that Captain James was following close behind, like a friend or a lover.

"Not tonight," he told him. "I've a lot on my mind and am in no mood to fuck a soldier."

Before the captain could reply, Mr. Caesar—perhaps knowing he had not been entirely tactful—turned and fled to the room.

In more polite company, that would have been the end of it. But he was not in polite company, he was in the company of infantrymen. So as he tried to hide in bed, a persistent pounding at the door dismissed all his hopes of oblivion. Still, with gentlemanly resolve, he did his best to ignore it.

"Do you really think I'd let you say that then walk away?" asked Captain James through the door.

"You think it's your place to *let* me do anything?" Once again it had been the wrong thing to say, but sometimes saying the wrong thing felt so *right*.

"Oh no you don't. You want to play the lordling with society brats and thief-catchers that's one thing, they were asking for it. You don't play it with me."

"Go away, Orestes."

"Captain James to you, Caesar."

"Go away, *Captain.*"

The doors in the Folly could, if necessary, be bolted from the inside. But Mr. Caesar was not of a mind to pay attention to details and was, in any case, accustomed to propriety providing greater protection.

It did not, in this case, provide greater protection.

The door opened and Captain James slipped through. With the courtesy of a dangerous man, he kept a respectful distance from his sometimes-lover, but still his displeasure was evident to anybody with eyes to see. Even those limited by mortal perception.

"That's a very strange definition of *away,*" Mr. Caesar complained. "I might almost categorise it as *towards.*"

"Don't be pretty with me. I've not the patience."

Mr. Caesar let his head thunk back on the pillow and gave a hollow laugh. "And you think I do. It may have escaped your notice, Orestes"—

"Captain James."

—"but I've had *rather a trying day.*"

His arms folded hard against a chest that somebody who was interested in such things might find distracting, the captain leaned against the wall, a careful study in idle power. "We tried. We failed. That's war."

"Well, I'm not a warrior. I'm a gentleman."

"And I'm a soldier, not a fucking rent boy."

Mr. Caesar heaved a theatrical sigh. "Then I suppose we both have our limitations. Perhaps we can address them in the morning."

If Mr. Caesar had expected that to be the end of it (and I could not tell if he did, because he could not tell himself), he was to be sorely disappointed. Captain James did not move from his place by the wall.

"I am *grateful*," Mr. Caesar continued, "for everything you have done for Mary. But I wish now to be alone."

"I don't want your gratitude." There was an atypical sharpness in Captain James's voice. "What I've done for Mary I'd do for anyone. Man or woman; French or English; Black, White, rich or poor. I learned to fight for my king, but I'd rather fight for them as need it."

Rolling over so as to face away from the captain, Mr. Caesar carried on talking to the wall. "Then why are you here?"

"Why are you?"

The list of reasons that Mr. Caesar was choosing, in those particular circumstances, to hide away in a low tavern frequented by soldiers and vagabonds was long and rambling. But it could be condensed down to a convenient five words. "I needed to get away."

And that, at last, broke Captain James's stoicism. He crossed the room with a warrior's swiftness, put a hand on Mr. Caesar's shoulder, and flipped him back to face him. "This isn't *away*, Caesar. It's *here*. It's my life. It's Callaghan's life, and Boy William's life, and Kumar's and Sal's. And you're welcome to stay with us if you're *with us*, but not if you're just trying not to be somewhere else."

The sensible thing to do, Mr. Caesar was aware, was to stay. To accept that yes, he had been taking the support of the captain and his fellows somewhat for granted. To admit that some part of him was, in fact, running *to* as much as running *from*. To say that he was afraid and ashamed and tired and sorry.

But pride was hereditary in the aristocracy and Mr. Caesar

chose this particular moment to be, once more, the grandson of an earl rather than any of his many other selves. So he rose, pulled on his shoes, and bid the captain a cold "Very well."

"Don't be an arse, Caesar. It's late, it's dark, and you don't know the streets."

Gathering his cravat, since he did not have the time to retie it, Mr. Caesar looked back, an image of civility. "A gentleman does not stay where he is not welcome."

"A gentleman doesn't last two minutes in St. Giles at this time of night."

Pride, as I say, was hereditary in the aristocracy. Which is in some ways a strike against the Darwinian theory because it is most definitely not a trait for which nature selects. Mr. Caesar gave a firm nod, bid the captain good evening, and left.

And, reader, you may be certain that I followed.

By the year of some people's lord 1815 the gas lamps were beginning to light the London streets, but they were restricted to the parts of the city about which the government gave a shit. Which meant that the only light in the streets of St. Giles came from the candles that burned in the windows of the few locals who could afford the luxury.

It was a clear night, which was a blessing. But moon and stars do not by themselves give humans any great ability to see what is in front of them (then again, neither does broad daylight much of the time; you are such a limited species). So Mr. Caesar stumbled over uneven streets in shoes better suited for a ballroom, and as he travelled he caught the attention of every ne'er-do-well, sometimes-does-well, and could-do-better in the district.

His cravat, loosely gripped in one hand, was yanked from his grasp by a small child who struck from the shadows and vanished back to the same with no more warning than a cheery "'Scuse me, mister."

And while he was mourning its loss, kicking himself for his stubbornness, and wondering whether it was a blessing or curse that he'd not brought his purse, he felt the cold press of a pistol barrel in his back and heard a soft, familiar voice whisper, "Perhaps you would be so good as to come with me."

Had events fallen out in a more convenient manner this would have been a delightful moment to jump away and begin following Miss Caesar, leaving the reader to wonder what terrible fate might have befallen her brother in the meantime. But they did not fall out conveniently, and when I went to check on the lady (briefly adopting the shape of her dog, Ferdinand) I found her . . . not sleeping, she did not sleep anymore, but standing in her room statue-still and silent. She expressed some little pleasure at seeing me, but since she did not feel inclined, at that time, to speak her thoughts aloud to a convenient canine, I gave her up as a bad job, slunk under the bed, and reemerged in my mist-and-shadow shape to follow her hapless sibling.

It took a little searching to track him down again, but my innate advantages of speed and perspicacity made it a far simpler job for me than it would be for a lesser being.

He was by the river, on a muddy bank near water that, at more sociable hours, would be a staging ground for eel-trappers and river-dredgers trying to eke a living from the open sewer of the Thames. Now, however, it was home to four men in red. Three robed and masked, one decidedly not.

The major sneered. "I said you hadn't seen the last of me, Caesar."

Relatively certain that he had less than an hour to live, Mr. Caesar saw little to be gained through politeness. "Yes, then you tried to have Captain James discharged, and failed. Then you challenged me to a duel, and failed. You'll forgive me for not taking your threats seriously."

"The duel was ruined by witchcraft," blustered the major, hand drifting to his spadroon as if he'd half a mind to demand a rematch there and then.

"And," added the soft-voiced man, "you'd be well advised to hold your tongue."

"Aren't you planning to shoot me anyway?" Mr. Caesar asked over his shoulder.

The soft-voiced man nodded. "Eventually."

"But first," the major continued, "I need to be sure you know quite how misguided you have been."

The only misguided thing Mr. Caesar felt he had done, and even that he hated to admit, was to leave the Folly in the dead of night. "If you mean hitting you, I regret only that I didn't keep my wrist straighter."

For a moment the gun moved away, and the soft-voiced man delivered Mr. Caesar a sharp clout to the back of the head that made his vision blur and his stomach lurch.

"You will learn," the major said with the most measured tone Mr. Caesar had ever heard from him, "to respect your betters."

"I am an earl's grandson," Mr. Caesar replied. "Socially, I outrank you."

This was strictly untrue. Nobility did not travel far down the distaff line, and while Mr. Caesar's direct connection to the Earl of Elmsley was advantageous it conveyed no formal honour on him.

The major, however, was not especially interested in the details of the matter. "*I* am an officer of His Majesty's army. *You* are the misbegotten whelp of a wilful harlot who—"

One of the many things I taught that bastard Will during our short acquaintance was the power of the *your mother* joke (he used it only once, in *Titus Andronicus*), and so I was very aware of both the efficacy and the artlessness of this particular barb.

Indeed it proved efficacious to the point of being counterproductive, for it so provoked Mr. Caesar that he rounded on Major Bloodworth in spite of the gun in his back and, since a quick death was not the reason he had been brought there, he did so without consequence. "My mother," he said with an almost admirable boldness, "is an English gentlewoman and you will speak of her according to her station."

"Come now, must we really stand on formalities here?" asked the soft-voiced man.

Latching on to debate partly as survival strategy and partly because he had always been an argumentative soul, Mr. Caesar replied, "It is not formality to defend one's mother from insult."

"True," returned the soft-voiced man, "but I still think it a little pointless, given the circumstances."

Perhaps because the repartee had evolved to a level he could no longer follow with his tiny human brain, the major was growing impatient. "Enough of this, take him to the water and shoot him."

Mr. Caesar was further from the gunman now, but that just meant he had a better view of the pistol.

"I strongly suggest that you move," the soft-voiced man suggested strongly.

With a resignation that substituted well for courage, Mr. Caesar smiled. "I'm comfortable where I am, thank you."

Unfortunately, while bravado can take a man a certain distance, there does come a point where physical strength, fleetness of foot, or the capacity to transform into moonlight become far more important. The two robed men who had thus far taken little interest in proceedings seized him and dragged him towards the river. I, for my part, considered transforming into an aquatic being to watch from a better position, but decided in the end that invisible and airborne afforded greater opportunity. Besides, I thought I had seen something moving beneath the surface, and it troubled me.

Having no practical defence against the manhandling of ruffians, Mr. Caesar was dragged to the water's edge and forced to his knees.

"Poseidon," began the soft-voiced man, although that appellation was no longer quite so apt, for he spoke stridently now, and with a sorcerer's confidence, "earth-shaker, averter of disasters, lord of horses, giver of safety—"

"Can you *please* just get on with it?" interrupted the major. "You don't have to say every single name of every single god."

And for an instant, the pistol was withdrawn.

"We are not here for your vengeance," replied the soft-voiced man. "We are here for the war, the king, and the gods, in that order."

Mr. Caesar permitted himself to glance up at the major. "Still taking orders from other men, Bloodworth? You should come to one of my clubs, you'd be wildly popu—"

He got no further. And there was also, at around the same time, a gunshot. But for all I love to frame events in the most dramatic manner possible, I cannot quite—under the exacting terms of my oaths and bindings—pretend that the shot came before the interruption. Something swift and deadly reached up from the insalubrious waters of the Thames and dragged Mr. Caesar down and, if not away from danger, at least away from danger of shooting and into danger of drowning.

Now the man was fully submerged, I briefly reconsidered my plan to watch from above, but that was before I saw Captain James rise from the waters like a uniformed leviathan, seize the first of the soldier-cultists by his robes, and, in the most honoured tradition of the London-trained combatant, headbutt him.

The masked men being, by and large, the sort trained in the fencing salles of the ton rather than the streets of the rookeries, the attack caught the first of them entirely off guard, or at least sufficiently off guard that Captain James was able to capitalise by twisting a short blow into his gut and, when that drove the wind from him, wrenching him around into a human shield.

"I have a second pistol," the soft-voiced man pointed out.

"And I've got your friend," replied Captain James who, while unarmed, had a grip on his opponent's carotid artery that would, with the application of a little pressure, prove extremely disagreeable.

The soft-voiced man seemed to consider this a moment. Then he raised the pistol. "Poseidon, we the army of King George grant you the blood of this man that our fleets will find calm seas, our cavalrymen strong steeds, and our people victory over France. Sorry, Charles."

Captain James moved sideways at the same time the gun fired, catching the hapless cultist square in the forehead and pitching him into the Thames.

"You're a fucking maniac," observed the captain, taking the opportunity to close with the soft-voiced man before he could either reload or find alternative armament.

"Not mania," the soldier-sorcerer replied. "Religion. Religion and grand strategy."

If Captain James had any interest in further exposition (spoilers, reader, he did not) he quelled it and moved instead to strike his opponent on the jaw. But while the rest of the cult (if cult it was;

these things are ambiguous in a world torn between cosmologies) had proved weak-willed and unskilled, the soft-voiced man had technique honed in battle and a drive rooted in divinity.

On the periphery of the fight, Major Bloodworth noted the three-to-one odds and the fact that he was the only man with a sword, and found those details to his liking. Drawing his spadroon, he rushed forwards for glory.

This, it turned out, was a mistake. The banks of the Thames were not made for rushing, and while Captain James was somewhat occupied with a more worthy opponent, he had not lived as long as he had in His Majesty's service by ignoring incoming blades.

So when the major slipped in the mud, his balance faltering just as his sword came down to strike, the captain was able to shift his weight, catch the major's forearm against his own, and then, with a motion so swift that even I could barely track it, lever the blade from his grip. And this, in the eyes of all present, shifted the calculus of the fight decisively.

"How about," Captain James suggested, "you all run back home and we pretend this never happened?"

The soft-voiced man and the last remaining soldier-cultist were silent. Major Bloodworth was not. "You have my sword, James."

"Which is why I get to make the rules."

"It is my property. Return it to me."

Captain James turned the weapon slightly in his hand. It was a fine weapon in certain ways, the blade stained blue to half its length and decorated with gold along all of it. "Don't think I will."

"So you're a thief, as well as a ruffian, a blackamoor, and a sodomite."

To a man more mired in the values of the ton, any one of those appellations would have been like a knife to the kidney. To the captain, they were merely words. "I'm a soldier," he replied. "And the first thing King George taught me was that when you beat a man, you can take what's his. You want your sword, come and get it."

Kneeling in the mud at the point of a blade, the major was in no way inclined to try to take anything. Of course, he was also not inclined to admit defeat to a man he perceived as his inferior, but in this specific context self-preservation overcame propriety. He rose, rankling inwardly at the need to put his hands in the mud, spat on the ground, and then left, taking the other men with him.

The soft-voiced man followed, but not before making a strangely formal bow to the captain.

When the strangers had gone, the captain made his way to the water's edge where Mr. Caesar was struggling to extract himself from the river. He bent down, proffered a hand, and, when it was accepted, hauled him up.

"I am *soaking*," Mr. Caesar complained. "And I am filthy. And I smell like actual shit."

"The smell's the river, it'll fade as we walk. Also you're alive."

"You could have saved me in a way that kept me dry."

The captain shrugged. "Could have. But this was safest. Besides, you needed a good drenching."

"I did not need a good drenching."

"I can always put you back."

Although Mr. Caesar was relatively certain that the captain would not, in fact, put him back, he stopped protesting nevertheless, and remained silent all the way to the Folly.

CHAPTER FIFTEEN

T HE SCENT OF HUMAN FAECES did, as Captain James had predicted, fade as they made their way further from the river, but the chill of the water and the clinging damp of the mud stayed with Mr. Caesar all the way back to his room.

"I don't suppose there's a chance of a bath?" he asked, wrestling off his shoes and tipping the remains of the river from them.

Captain James answered that with a look.

"I was only asking."

"Going to draw your own water? Carry your own tub?"

Mr. Caesar thought it over. "I'll pass."

Now that the rescue was over, a lot of the bonhomie had drained from Captain James's manner. "That all you can say? *I'll pass?*"

"I'll pass, but thank you for the offer?" Somewhere inside the gordian mess of his heart, Mr. Caesar knew that this wasn't quite what the captain was looking for.

"Oh, fuck off, Caesar."

Mr. Caesar bristled. "I'm sorry. I'm tired. Can we save this con-versation for tomorrow?"

It was the wrong thing to say. Even with an *I'm sorry* at the beginning. I mean, I'm an inhuman trickster from a culture that cherishes shamelessness and even I could craft a better apology. "No." The captain was standing very still, his arms folded. Some-how he managed to make being drenched in glorified sewer water seem commanding. "You talk to me like I'm some fucking cata-mite. You storm out like you're some fucking child. And then you leave it to me to save your fucking life and then you want me to wait until you've had a nap before we have it out?"

"I'm sorry," Mr. Caesar said again. His tone suggested other-wise, but neither his words nor his delivery precisely conveyed the chaos that was festering in his head.

"You're not though," replied the captain. "Are you? You just want me to shut up. I'd thought you were different, but I'm starting to see that you're just like every other rich fucker I've ever met, you just don't have the money to make it look good."

It would be churlish of me to suggest that the accusation of not looking good was what struck closest to Mr. Caesar's heart. But not *that* churlish. "I have had," he said, "a very hard day."

"And you think I haven't? You think the men haven't?"

"No." Defiance had never suited Mr. Caesar, at least not real defiance rather than the kind of acerbic counterfeit of it you saw in the ton, and the last of it drained away now, leaving only a damp morass of shame. Which was unfortunately still paralleled by a damp morass of Thames water. "I—that is, you've—I've been awful."

"You have."

"I mean utterly awful."

"Yeah."

"And not just to you." Mr. Caesar flopped back onto the bed, leaving the sheets damp and not much caring. "Fuck me, if I'd not tried to order Mary around, she might have let us finish the job."

Captain James looked doubtful. "Maybe, but plans go wrong all the time, no sense in dwelling."

Unfortunately, dwelling was very much where Mr. Caesar was at this moment. "My father," he said, "crossed the world twice, won his own freedom, and chose to fight for the freedom of others. My mother turned her back on her birthright for love and what was right. I can't even treat a lover well or reach my sister when she needs me."

"Can you do me a favour"—Captain James came closer and sat down beside Mr. Caesar—"and not put me and your sister in the same box? It feels wrong."

There was a world where Mr. Caesar would have laughed at that. "I know you're trying to be amusing, but—"

"I'm not," replied the captain. Then, in a spirit of honesty that I thoroughly condemn, he added, "Well, maybe a bit. But this is still important. What's between you and your family is for you and your family. And if you want me to be part of it, *really* part of it— then I will. But I'll not be where you hide from your other life. You need to be with me because of who I am, not who I'm not."

"Who you are is—God, it's such a fucking cliché to say I've never known anybody like you, but it's—I mean, you've met the kind of men I—we're shits. That's the sordid truth of it. We're just shits, and you should stay far, far away from us."

"That sounds like an excuse," the captain told him in a tone that was veering away from sympathy and closer to *tired of your nonsense.*

"It's not. I—fuck—I should go. I'm never going to be able to be the kind of man you—"

With a sigh that was almost a growl, Captain James took Mr. Caesar's face firmly but not forcefully and turned it so they were eye to eye. "John," he said, "I'm going to say this once. Stop being a prick."

Blinking back tears of which he was deeply ashamed, Mr. Caesar said, tremulously, "I don't know how."

"You do," the captain told him. "You do."

"I don't."

"Just tonight," replied Captain James, "I've seen you be a brother, a lover, a lord, a son, a fool, a dandy, and a dozen other things besides. You've got a face for every room you walk into and you change them like you change your cravats. Just pick one you can be proud of."

Put like that, it almost seemed simple. But over the years Mr. Caesar had learned not to hope for simple. "And how do I know," he asked, almost in a whisper, "which face is the right one."

Captain James cupped his cheek and looked into his eyes with an intensity that from anybody else would have made Mr. Caesar want to turn away in fear or shame or sheer self-protection. "The one I'm looking at now seems all right."

And then, reader, he kissed him.

"I don't deserve—" Mr. Caesar began.

"Fuck what you deserve."

"But—"

The captain sigh-growled again and placed a hand over Mr. Caesar's heart. "Somewhere in here," he said, "there's a good man trying to get out. Fucking let him."

And that, reader, was the problem (or the rub, if you want to bring *him* into this). It seemed to Mr. Caesar that there were no good men inside him, just a hundred confused men trying to do what was right in ways that overlapped and disagreed and contradicted. "I'm not sure I can," he said.

Captain James let out a disappointed breath.

"But—" Reaching up, Mr. Caesar brushed the back of his fingers across the captain's cheek. "You make me want to try. If—if that will be enough. If it *can* be enough."

And the captain nodded. "You'd better bloody mean it."

"I do." Mr. Caesar nodded, almost desperate. "Orestes, please, I—no matter what, I cannot help but be different for having known you."

The captain kissed him again. And this time Mr. Caesar kissed back. As I have intimated elsewhere in this and other volumes, the precise mechanics of mortal intimacy are of little interest to me, but when they involve risks or fears or prices they become far closer to my personal area of expertise.

And prices and fears there were here in abundance—and not only because they were still in a part of the city where you stood a reasonable chance of having your throat slit in the night. As Captain James peeled off his sodden shirt and bore Mr. Caesar to the bed, he gambled that this man, unlike every other member of his class that the captain had encountered in his life, would prove constant, or at least constant enough, and not abandon him the moment he was no longer useful. And as Mr. Caesar reached up with hands and mouth and body and begged wordlessly to be drowned, he gambled that the soldier wanted him for something other than money or influence or advancement, that he could be an ally rather than a rival. And of course both men were trusting that the other would not turn them over to the magistrate for sodomy, which remained a rare but constant threat.

So they came together in a tangle of fragile trust and searching. Limbs and bedsheets and sweat and questions in a room that two months ago Mr. Caesar would never have dreamed of spending more than an hour in but which now became a sanctuary from a world crawling with enemies, only some of them unnatural.

"I've never asked how you got these," Mr. Caesar mused, a little later, letting his fingertips play over Captain James's many scars.

"Did you ever care?"

The question was at least slightly shaming, because there had definitely been nights when he hadn't cared at all. And not only with the captain, but every time he'd been with a fighting man. "I should," he replied, "and I do."

Captain James guided Mr. Caesar's hand to a mark on his arm. "Musket ball at Vimeiro"—up to his shoulder—"another at Talavera"—down to his chest where the mark was longer—"sabre at Ciudad Rodrigo"—he shifted his grip and let Mr. Caesar's hand come around to his back—"lash in a British camp."

"You were flogged?"

The captain nodded. "Insubordination."

"Doesn't surprise me."

"Officer was taking liberties with the locals. Tried to stop it. Failed."

As a man whose greatest achievement to date was finding the perfect way to put on breeches without visible creases, Mr. Caesar couldn't help but find that a little humbling. "I'm sorry."

In the dark, the captain's voice was all Mr. Caesar had to go by, and his voice was giving away very little. "I was lucky. Could easily have hanged if things had gone further."

"And"—a thought had struck Mr. Caesar and he couldn't help but voice it—"was the officer . . ."

The captain laughed low and merry in the shadows. "No, it

wasn't Bloodworth. That particular officer didn't make it through the next battle."

"No?"

"Excellent shots, the French."

They held each other in silence awhile, Mr. Caesar tracing the lines of Captain James's scars and the captain breathing slow and steady and quiet.

But the talk of the major had sent Mr. Caesar's mind elsewhere, and so he asked: "What *happened* tonight?"

"With us or with them?"

Both were valid questions, but Mr. Caesar had meant the latter. The former he was trying hard to put behind him. "The men who tried to kill me."

"That's your answer then. Some men tried to kill you."

"It sounded like they were trying to *sacrifice* me. I was under the impression that people did not *get* sacrificed in the nineteenth century. It seems barbaric."

That earned another laugh, albeit one of harsher character. "I spend my life nearly dying for a cause I don't give a shit about. Your own father was abducted, branded, and sold to make some bastard rich. You don't think our fearless leaders would spill a bit of blood to get the gods on their side?"

"There are laws," Mr. Caesar protested.

"There's laws against murder too; want to know how many men I've killed for the king?"

A grim fascination took hold of Mr. Caesar. "How many?"

"No idea. Too much smoke and noise to tell who shot who. And with a sword all you know is that you're standing and the other man isn't. You've no idea if he lives or dies."

"Do you think they'll come back?"

Lazily, Captain James reached into his pile of discarded clothing and picked up the major's sword. "Bloodworth'll want this, but from what I saw I don't think he's really in charge. I think that's the other one. Or maybe it's just that the one with the rank isn't the same as the one with the plan."

Mr. Caesar laid his head on the captain's chest. It was disquieting to realise he was surrounded by enemies of which he knew nothing, though not, perhaps, as disquieting as being with a man who wanted him to be better.

But that is a very sentimental notion; I am almost ashamed of myself for recording it. Indeed I bothered myself so much that I withdrew, and attended to other matters that it pleases me to conceal from you.

The following morning, an at least partially contrite Mr. Caesar rose extremely early by his standards and expressed to his lover his intent to return home and have a frank conversation with his father.

"You want me to come with you?" asked the captain in a tone that the part of Mr. Caesar that was used to everything being an elaborate social trap assumed was an elaborate social trap.

"If you wish," he replied. "I think my parents like you, although my sisters have their misgivings. But I would understand if you had business of your own."

"Until His Majesty calls me to France," replied the captain, with an edge in his voice that I, at least, noted, "I've got time."

"And after that?" Mr. Caesar asked.

"Then I'll be gone. And then I'll be back, or I'll be dead."

It was not a possibility that Mr. Caesar was, in that moment, of a mind to countenance. "You'll be back, I am sure."

Captain James shrugged. "I might. But if I don't I'd rather not spend the next few weeks talking about it or arguing. Let's get you home."

The walk across London in the early morning was unfamiliar to Mr. Caesar but far more pleasant than he felt it had any right to be. Yes, the streets were crowded and filthy, and yes, his clothes were still rather damp, he was missing his cravat, and he could feel every cracked cobblestone and broken bottle through the soles of his shoes, but there was a liberation to it. And having already been accosted at gunpoint once, he found himself with little to fear that he had not already experienced.

Unfortunately, as the sun rose and the crowds thinned and they passed into the more socially acceptable parts of the city, that confidence began to wane. On the streets of St. Giles, his dishevelment was invisible and even his heritage relatively unremarkable. On the streets of Mayfair, he and the captain stood out like stars amongst the respectable couples taking their pre-breakfast walks and the well-groomed servants running early morning errands.

At the Caesar house, Nancy opened the door and Mr. Caesar arrived just in time for breakfast, earning a look of mild disapproval from Lady Mary, who felt it inconsiderate to bring a guest unannounced to a meal.

"It's no trouble, ma'am," Nancy reassured her. "I'll get another round of toast on and see about some more coffee."

The entire family had gathered for breakfast, despite the fact that the elder Mr. Caesar ate sparingly and Miss Caesar of late ate not at all. The atmosphere would almost have been pleasant had recent events not been casting so long and deep a shadow over the household.

"So who found you?" Captain James asked Miss Caesar with unrefined directness.

"Mr. Bygrave," she replied, with the very slightest look of smugness directed at her sister. "He was very gallant, and to have gone to such lengths I feel he must be quite besotted with me."

"Well, he would be besotted with me also," Miss Anne replied, "had I the advantage of fairy magic."

In Mr. Caesar's heart, a new impulse towards openness warred with old habits and lost. "Perhaps he likes her for her temperament."

"Her temperament is vile," Miss Anne insisted. "And besides, men may pretend to value temperament, but I am sure they do not. Madeleine Worthing is as sweet-natured a lady as can be but nobody ever wishes to dance with her."

"And Miss Bickle," added Miss Caesar, "is the flightiest creature on God's earth, but gentlemen line up for her favours."

Sliding easily into old patterns, Mr. Caesar smiled. "Now, now, that isn't just because she's pretty. She's also extremely rich."

"Not helping, John," warned Lady Mary. "And I hope you don't think that you've avoided our asking why you look like you recently lost a fight with a lake."

With an instinctive protectiveness, Captain James set down his coffee cup. "Because we did," he said. "Only it was the Thames, and we won."

The elder Mr. Caesar raised an eyebrow. "You won a fight with the Thames?"

"With four men," clarified Mr. Caesar the younger, "on the banks of the Thames. And when Orestes says *we* won he's doing me a kindness. He rescued me."

"Again?" asked Lady Mary, a little archly. "He seems to be making a habit of it."

"It worked out well enough for Cousin Maelys," pointed out Miss Anne.

Mr. Caesar looked uncomfortable. "If it's all the same to those present, I think I'd rather avoid following Maelys's example."

Calmly, the elder Mr. Caesar turned to Captain James. "Maelys was the victim of a mysterious curse last year," he explained, "and Lady Georgiana Landrake saved her life a number of times. They are now . . . good friends."

"They're fucking," Mr. Caesar clarified. "Believe me, Papa, he knows how these things work and we needn't be coy around him."

Lady Mary half smiled across the breakfast parlour. "In my experience, good friends are far more important than lovers and one is not necessarily the other."

Almost playful, the captain shot Mr. Caesar a sidelong glance. "So why don't you want to follow her example?"

"She nearly died of leprosy," Mr. Caesar told him. "And she now lives half the year in Yorkshire, which is a fate I would find frankly intolerable."

The elder Mr. Caesar had finished a single slice of toast and cup of coffee and was now fixing his son with a steady gaze. "You might also remember that you were extremely suspicious of mysterious rescuers when Maelys encountered one."

Mr. Caesar squirmed uncomfortably. "Well, I learned my lesson. And besides, Orestes is a British officer."

"Not," Captain James said, "that you should ever trust an officer." He turned to the elder Mr. Caesar and Lady Mary. "The four men were soldiers. Bloodworth was with them."

Setting her coffee down with an unsteady *clink*, Lady Mary blanched. "John, this is becoming serious and I am beginning to mislike it."

"Then I shall be sure to write the major a letter asking him to kindly stop trying to kill me," replied Mr. Caesar coolly.

This went over poorly with the whole of the rest of the family, but especially with Miss Caesar who folded her glass arms across her chest and said, "There now, he interferes in my life and can barely take care of his own. You would be a better brother if you attended first to your own difficulties."

Miss Anne, who would never agree with Mary unless it was in criticism of some third party, was about to voice her concurrence when Captain James interrupted.

"It's not my place to say," he offered, "but as I see it, a brother who puts your needs above his own is a fine one to have."

Mr. Caesar shot him a look of profound gratitude, though privately he did not think it had turned out very finely for his sisters so far.

"You're right," Miss Anne replied, "it's not your place to say."

With a deliberate grace, the elder Mr. Caesar brought his hands to rest on the table in front of him. "Children." He seldom called his children *children*, partly because John had attained legal majority some while ago and partly because no child likes to be called a child. "I will have no more of this. We are under attack, and if we do not stand with one another, who else will stand with us?"

"Everybody would be standing with us," insisted Miss Anne, "if John had not made such—"

Now it was Lady Mary's turn. "No, Anne. They would not. At best they would stand against us more politely."

The Misses Caesar were not quite willing to formally concede the point, but their parents took their silence for at least the beginnings of understanding, and the conversation was soon interrupted by Nancy, who appeared bearing Mr. Bygrave's card.

The family had observed enough of Mr. Bygrave to know that his visit would consist of little more than him sitting in a chair and staring rapt at Miss Caesar while the light danced through her at fascinating angles. And so they retired to their various rooms—save Lady Mary, who, out of deference to conventions not entirely applicable to her situation, remained behind to chaperone, and Captain James, who had no room to go to.

Mr. Caesar, however, took the opportunity to follow his father into his office and wait, hands folded behind his back, to be acknowledged.

Which, eventually, he was.

"Yes, John?"

The relationship between the Misters Caesar was a complex one, as relations between fathers and sons often are, and so the younger gentleman found it a little difficult to say what he had come to say, as simple as it was. "I just wanted to tell you . . ." he tried, then stopped and adopted a different approach. "What I mean is, although I don't think I need to explain—you were— I shouldn't have—the family needs me and I shouldn't have run."

"No," the elder Mr. Caesar agreed, "you shouldn't have. But I understand why you did. There is"—he looked down at his correspondence for a moment, then back up at his son—"a lot that you have to navigate. I wish that it were otherwise."

The younger Mr. Caesar bowed his head. "I . . . I do not, I think. I would choose no other father than you, nor any other mother than Mama. Despite everything I don't even think I'd choose other sisters than Mary and—"

On cue, Miss Anne's voice echoed through from the drawing room. "But *why not?*"

Sighing, the elder Mr. Caesar rose to his feet. "If you will excuse me, it seems the peace has not lasted."

The two gentlemen returned to join the party, where Lady

Mary was holding a differently styled calling card, Mr. Bygrave was indeed just watching Miss Caesar in silence, and Miss Anne was making a petulant protest.

"Is there some concern?" asked the younger Mr. Caesar.

"Mama is denying my guest," Miss Anne explained. "When she allowed Mary's."

Lady Mary handed the card to her husband. "The guest is Lieutenant Reyne. I do not think him a suitable suitor for Anne. Indeed I am not sure she is of an age where *any* suitor is suitable."

This went down still more poorly with Miss Anne than the exclusion of a single suitor. "I am *fourteen*," she insisted. "Margaret Beaufort married Edmund Tudor when she was *twelve*."

"Sometimes, Anne," Lady Mary observed, "I am concerned at quite how encyclopaedic your knowledge of child brides is."

At last the quarrel drew the attention of Mr. Bygrave, who wrenched his attention away from Miss Caesar. "I am not greatly familiar with Lieutenant Reyne," he said, "but I know him to be from a good family, if not a very wealthy one."

"And though I agree he's old for the girl," added Captain James, "I've heard he's a good officer. Doesn't waste lives needlessly."

"You see?" Miss Anne looked triumphant. "All the military men support me."

"And it would be very vulgar," Miss Caesar added, "to say that we are not accepting visitors when we have plainly already accepted one."

Grudgingly, the Caesars acceded to this logic. They could scarcely pretend not to be at home with an existing guest. So the lieutenant was permitted to ascend, and for a short while he sat decorously beside Miss Anne, paying her flattering attention and speaking artfully of nothing. At the very least, however, his skill in this matter exceeded that of Mr. Bygrave. The lieutenant had developed the technique of disguising his nothings as somethings, and that made all the difference.

Since the existing dispute was settled and the elders of the family were present to watch over their daughters' collective virtues, Mr. Caesar felt little need to resist when Captain James uncurled from the seat he'd been lounging in, tapped Mr. Caesar lightly on the shoulder, and led him away into an adjoining room.

"I should remind you," Mr. Caesar told him, playfully, "that we are in my parents' house and—"

But the captain placed a finger over Mr. Caesar's lips, and not in a flirtatious way. "Listen," he whispered.

They could just about make out voices from the adjoining room, the numbing hum of pleasantries constrained by manufactured propriety and newer-than-imagined traditions.

"Miss Caesar, would you care for a turn about the room?" was Mr. Bygrave.

"I declare, you have the most marvellous stories" was Miss Anne.

And, "Nothing, I assure you, compared to those of the men I have served with" was, by process of elimination, Lieutenant Reyne. It was a rather fine voice, to my ear. To Mr. Caesar's it was mellifluous, soft, and familiar.

A voice he had heard at least twice before.

"It can't be," Mr. Caesar replied, sotto voce.

"It can, and I'd bet a month's wages it is."

"Still," Miss Anne was saying, "you must have seen such wonders."

There might have been laughter there, from Lieutenant Reyne, but it was muffled by the door and the distance. "War is many things," the soft-voiced man replied. "But it is seldom wonderful. It is a banquet for gods who delight in blood and chaos."

To give the man his due, he was *good*. Not only was he entirely accurate about the nature of this world's divine custodians but he had judged his audience well. There was little that appealed to Miss Anne more than tales of blood and chaos.

Tales, of course, being so very different from reality.

As she was soon to discover.

CHAPTER SIXTEEN

K NOWING, OR AT LEAST STRONGLY suspecting, that his youngest sister's new suitor was a bloodthirsty cultist who had already sacrificed at least one man to Poseidon was little help to Mr. Caesar, because he had no sense of how to appropriately act on the information.

Having left the room, he and the captain could not very well slink back into it without looking very obviously like they'd been having a secret confabulation, and Mr. Caesar at least had no faith in his skills as an actor.

So they pretended that they had been intending to go for a walk all along, a perfectly acceptable thing for gentlemen to do. Of course, generally gentlemen going for walks were not wearing clothes still damp and muddy from a dip in the Thames, but in that moment at least they had far weightier issues on their minds.

"Quick solution," Captain James offered, "we just get some of the lads together and kill him."

Mr. Caesar looked doubtful. "I was hoping for something a little less murderous."

"Such as?"

"We approach a magistrate and tell him what is happening."

The expression on the captain's face encapsulated *I can't tell if you're joking* with remarkable efficacy. "You want to tell a magistrate that a respected officer from a good background goes around sacrificing people to the old powers?"

"It has the advantage of truth."

"And the disadvantage of sounding like bollocks."

Mr. Caesar pursed his lips, not fond of disorder even when his family's lives weren't on the line. "There's a body, surely that constitutes evidence."

"There's a body. River police might find it, might not. And the god might have taken it; they do sometimes."

They had rambled, in the end, in the direction of Hyde Park, which made an incongruously pleasant backdrop for such sinister matters. Although given their recent experiences, the cool waters of the Serpentine looked far more ominous than they would on any other day.

"I had thought it bad enough to have one sister in unknowable peril," Mr. Caesar mused aloud. "Having two feels exceedingly unfair."

"Not a fair world," the captain semi-agreed. "But we do what we can. You should tell her at least."

Mr. Caesar gave a hollow laugh. "And from what you've seen of Anne do you think she'd believe me?"

"Your parents would, and they could watch her."

"I will inform Papa directly," Mr. Caesar agreed, "but for Anne I think it might be wiser to work through an intermediary."

Less comfortable in a ballroom than a battlefield, the captain looked uncertain. "Who?"

"She trusts Lizzie."

"The silly one?"

"Yes," Mr. Caesar conceded. "The silly one."

It was an apt assessment, but there is a time, reader, when silliness is called for, and that time is most assuredly when one is in deepest danger. The roots of *silliness*, after all, are prosperity, happiness, and good fortune. And in adversity, one needs all of those things.

The Bickle residence was an unfashionably furnished house in a fashionable part of town, filled with an eclectic mix of objects that passed for art and often ringing with the loudly declaimed words of the lyric poets. The captain and Mr. Caesar were met at the door by a footman in ill-chosen livery and shown through to the drawing room where Miss Bickle was playing an unrecognisable discord on one of two pianofortes.

There Mr. Caesar explained the overnight developments to Miss Bickle, who listened with her eyes and mouth growing gradually rounder in amazement until they were, at last, perfectly circular.

"Oh, but John," she exclaimed when he was finished, "this is remarkable. Are you truly being pursued by a shadowy cadre of masked strangers bent on your destruction?"

"I seem to be," Mr. Caesar replied. "But much like Maelys's experience with the goddess, it is far less amusing when one is directly threatened by it."

In abstract, Miss Bickle knew this. In specific, not so much. "But the *intrigue*, the *romance*, the *danger*."

Mr. Caesar did his best to sound stern and didn't quite manage it. "Intrigue and danger are *bad* and romance can be achieved in safer ways. And now a man we know to be a murderer has set his sights on Anne and we don't know why."

"Perhaps he wishes to make her his partner in crime?" Miss Bickle suggested, treating the glass as half-full as always. Although possibly as half-full of murder in this particular case.

"Or to sacrifice her to one of the Olympians?" counter-suggested Captain James. "Like he nearly did with John?"

Miss Bickle's face fell dramatically. "Oh yes, that might also be a possibility. But I hope not. It would be terribly shabby of him."

"Yes," Mr. Caesar agreed, "the shabbiness of murdering my sister is my primary concern also. But I think she would listen to a warning if it came from you."

That made Miss Bickle, who was a generous being at heart, much as I am, profoundly happy. "Then I shall speak with her at once. Or"—she made a considering sort of face which, like all of her faces, typified the action to an almost unnatural extent— "perhaps it would be best to sneak it upon her under the pretence of some other matter. I have been meaning to invite her and Mary both to my avidreadermeets."

"Your what?" asked Captain James with the blithe innocence of somebody who did not know Miss Bickle at all.

"It's short for *avidreaderdom meetings*," Miss Bickle explained, "and an *avidreaderdom* is a group of—"

Mr. Caesar shook his head. "No time, Lizzie. Anyway, Mary surely won't wish to attend after you helped us try to capture the Lady."

With the sorrowful air of one who cannot fathom why those around her fail to grasp simple things, Miss Bickle laid a gentle hand on his arm. "Oh, John, you don't understand anything, do you?"

"I think I do, actually."

Partially gallant, Captain James nodded. "Some things, certainly."

"Mary isn't cross with you because of what we tried to do to the Lady. She's cross with you because you're her brother. I'm her friend. It's a very different thing."

"I have behaved towards her exactly as a brother ought," Mr. Caesar replied with a reflexive defensiveness. "If Mary finds that bothersome—"

"Then she would be entirely ordinary?" suggested Miss Bickle.

At this, Mr. Caesar frowned. "It seems there is something fundamentally wrong with the world when it is ordinary for a girl to resent her brother acting like her brother."

"I think . . ." Miss Bickle's tone was hesitant, almost awkward. "I think there *might* be something fundamentally wrong with the world. Actually. In fact."

Captain James shrugged. "World's a big place. Be strange if it weren't broken in parts."

Flopping with long-practised decorousness onto an ill-chosen sofa, Mr. Caesar let out a despairing exhalation. "Have I truly been that terrible a brother?"

"I don't think you've been terrible," replied Miss Bickle, whose reassurance was tempered in its reassuringness by the fact that she was congenitally incapable of thinking ill of anybody. "I just think that . . . well . . . maybe what qualifies as good brothering if your aim is for your sister to marry respectably and achieve the approval of men like Lord Hale might be different from what qualifies as good brothering if you . . . um . . . care whether she's happy or not?"

This was not entirely what Mr. Caesar wanted to hear. But as he looked up at the captain, who had listened to Miss Bickle with silent agreement, he began to suspect that it was what he *needed* to hear. "So what should I do differently?"

Miss Bickle smiled warmly. "I have no idea. I've never had a sister and I don't think having one is very easy. But for *now* we'll see if I can at least persuade Anne to stop accepting the attentions of a known murderer."

The fact that even this seemed likely to fail did not, Mr. Caesar reflected, bode well for his or anybody's wider relationship with his sister. Even so, the plan was agreed and the avidreadermeet was set for some two days' time. The delay rankled at Mr. Caesar, but he, the captain, Miss Bickle, and—when he revealed the danger to his parents—the elder Caesars all agreed that it was better to take things slowly and hope for a positive reaction than to rush them and risk driving Anne into the arms of a killer.

It was even, tentatively, agreed that Lieutenant Reyne would be permitted to keep visiting, despite the peril that clearly presented, in order that his suspicion might not be roused. Fortunately, or perhaps unfortunately, depending on how one measured such things, the gentleman was playing his hand carefully, and did not visit the next day, nor the day after.

Mr. Caesar himself was absent from the avidreadermeet, since Miss Bickle had felt his presence wouldn't be conducive to the proper atmosphere, and he had agreed that in this particular situation he could best contribute by absence.

So in the end the gathering was smallish, intimate-ish, and slanted towards the distaff. Miss Bickle hosted with her typical enthusiasm, and guests included Miss Penworthy, Miss Mitchelmore, and both of the Misses Caesar. Since this was the first time Miss Penworthy had encountered the Beauty Incomparable at close hand, it made the beginning of the evening somewhat awkward. For the mortals at least. I was merely hoping for unexpected developments.

"Erica," Miss Mitchelmore chided, "stop staring, it's rude."

Miss Penworthy did not stop staring.

"Erica," Miss Mitchelmore repeated.

"Miss Caesar," Miss Penworthy began, "I don't suppose you would like to take a turn about the room? And perhaps stop somewhere discreet along the way?"

Seeing no alternative, Miss Mitchelmore retrieved a pin from a nearby cushion and jabbed Miss Penworthy on the arm. "*Erica.*"

"Sorry"—a shimmer was fading from Miss Penworthy's eyes, and she shook her head as if clearing water from her ears—"don't know what came over me. But you do both look lovely."

Conditioned to respond positively to any compliment, even from ladies, the Misses Caesar smiled and bobbed curtseys in response, and settled into the group, which was forming a rough circle around Miss Bickle.

"Ahem," she said. She wasn't actually clearing her throat, but she enjoyed saying *ahem*. "Welcome to the seventeenth Anonymous Lady Author of *Sense and Sensibility* Avidreadermeet. This is a space where we avid readers of the works of the anonymous lady author of *Sense and Sensibility* can share our thoughts, theories, and avrections."

Miss Anne looked grave. "Will it be terribly inconvenient if we haven't brought anything? I had only a little notice and wasn't quite sure what an avid reader fiction was meant to look like."

"It's all right," Miss Mitchelmore reassured her, "Lizzie and Erica will have quite enough material for all of us."

This was Miss Penworthy's cue to begin. "On which subject, I do indeed have a new story to share." She stood, collected a sheaf of papers, and began to read. " 'The Other Bennet Girl:

Kitty-dash-Caroline, Kitty-dash-Charlotte, Kitty-dash-Original-Lady-Character, Cordial-Acquaintances-to-Intimate-Relations, Antagonistic-Acquaintances-to-Intimate-Relations.'"

"Is this preamble really necessary?" asked Miss Mitchelmore. "You do it every time and we're all here so I don't know who it's in aid of."

Miss Bickle gave her friend a look of endlessly patient incomprehension. "The categories make it easier to find stories you might like. So I could say to Erica, 'I very much enjoyed your recent Antagonistic-Acquaintances-to-Intimate-Relations story, do you have any more like it?'"

"And I could say, 'Yes, I have several,'" added Miss Penworthy.

Miss Mitchelmore looked at the piles of documents at Miss Penworthy's side. "That, at least, does not surprise me."

"You know." Miss Bickle was already drifting onto another tangent. "It is such a shame that Lady Georgiana has never been able to attend one of these gatherings. It's so queer that she keeps having other commitments."

Miss Anne, who had come to the avidreadermeet to hear stories, not to discuss her cousin's lover's social engagements, looked up at Miss Penworthy prettily. "Perhaps you could continue reading for us?"

And Miss Penworthy needed no further encouragement. "'The distaste Miss Kitty Bennet had felt at Caroline Bingley's mistreatment of her sister,'" she began, "'was matched only by the yearning she felt as . . .'"

I shall leave off the rest of this narrative. You are here for my definitely completely true story that I have compiled through great personal exertion. I will not share these pages with lesser scribblers. Suffice to say that Miss Penworthy's tale was carefully constructed, enthusiastically delivered, and contained a number of details that the anonymous lady author of *Sense and Sensibility* had necessarily elided for fear of the censors.

That tale was followed by the third story in Miss Bickle's *Fanny Price Investigates,* in which the eponymous lady, having successfully resolved the murder of George Wickham in the previous volume, was asked by a dashing Yeoman Warder to investigate the theft of the crown jewels.

I personally found the piece extremely entertaining, although Miss Mitchelmore declared it to be slightly overcomplicated, and Miss Caesar questioned its connectedness to the wider works of the anonymous lady author.

"I confess," Miss Bickle conceded, "that Fanny Price, Lady Investigator may have diverged slightly from her origins."

Seized by the instinct to say something more positive, Miss Anne observed that although she had found the plot a little hard to follow, the dashing Yeoman Warder had been exceptionally dashing, and that seemed to be the most important thing.

Mr. Caesar was absent, but in his stead I was forced to wonder if Miss Bickle was, perhaps, a secret genius. Because the segue from this into a wider discussion of gentlemen, dashing gentlemen, and at last military gentlemen was seamless.

"I think one of the more interesting things we might learn," Miss Bickle said, settling down in front of the unseasonably roaring fire that she insisted on having at every avidreadermeet, "from the works of the anonymous lady author of *Sense and Sensibility* is that gentlemen are not *always* to be trusted."

"Not worth the bother at all," agreed Miss Penworthy.

Miss Mitchelmore frowned. "Perfectly reasonable as a sex. Often unpleasant as individuals."

Unfortunately, Miss Anne took quite the wrong message from this. "Very true. For example, Mr. Bygrave proved *very* inconstant in his affections. But I have now caught the eye of a more seasoned officer, and I expect him to be much the better choice."

Miss Caesar glared at her sister as only a young woman made entirely from glass can glare. "Mr. Bygrave has proven very constant to *me*, Anne. Perhaps we simply have more compatible temperaments."

"Perhaps you placed him under an *enchantment*." Miss Anne had been sitting quietly throughout the reading of the avrections and was now slipping into an airing of grievances.

Glancing at Miss Caesar across the drawing room, Miss Penworthy flushed slightly. "That does seem likely. You *are* quite enchanting."

"Erica," Miss Mitchelmore reminded her.

"Sorry."

Miss Bickle made a valiant attempt to drag things back to the topic at hand. "The thing *is*, Anne . . ." She cast a meaningful glance at Miss Mitchelmore.

"I say, Erica," Miss Mitchelmore volunteered entirely unprompted, "would you like to take a turn about the garden? I hear Mr. Bickle keeps an excellent gardener."

The look of excitement in Miss Penworthy's eyes was bright but fleeting.

"An actual turn," Miss Mitchelmore clarified, "about an actual garden."

"Oh." Miss Penworthy's face fell. "Well then, I suppose yes, but under sufferance."

Smiling as sweetly as only a woman from a society in which sweetness is an economic necessity can, Miss Mitchelmore turned to Miss Caesar. "Mary? Join us."

There was, I am sure, some part of the heart Miss Caesar no longer had that yearned to know what salacious thing Miss Bickle wished to share with her sister, but Miss Mitchelmore was her elder and at least loosely socially associated with a duke's daughter, and so she acquiesced regardless.

And I shall break here, reader. For although the question of Lieutenant Reyne's murderousness (or unmurderousness; one should not jump to conclusions, after all) was a pressing one, the gardens were fine indeed.

Being a Romantic at heart in the capitalised, yearning for bucolic simplicity sense, Mr. Bickle had arranged for the gardens of his London townhouse to look as wild, free, and natural as possible, and his landscape gardener had executed that brief with merciless diligence. Every innocent flower was in its artfully chosen spot, and the bowers beneath which the Misses Caesar, Mitchelmore, and Penworthy now walked had been twined ruthlessly with ivy to give them a false impression of antiquity.

"It is *such* a beautiful night," observed Miss Penworthy. "Such a night, in fact, that one's mind turns to—"

"*No,*" insisted Miss Mitchelmore.

Miss Penworthy pouted. Her time associating with Miss Bickle had seemingly enhanced her pouting abilities substantially. "You're no fun."

"What do nights like this turn one's mind to?" asked Miss Caesar, all innocence.

Starlight gleamed in Miss Penworthy's eyes. "Romance."

"Erica," Miss Mitchelmore warned. "I am in a perfectly satisfying relationship with a woman who only *probably* won't have you killed for flirting with me. And Mary is courting an officer."

Miss Caesar did not sigh. Lacking lungs, she lacked the reflex. Instead she froze a moment, and with her animating spark abated. Even her gown grew still and solid, so she became for the passing of a few seconds a statue in earnest.

"Mary?" With an expression of concern, Miss Mitchelmore brought her face close to her cousin's and scrutinised it for signs of life.

Brought back to herself, Miss Caesar blinked, and the suddenness of the motion made Miss Mitchelmore start backwards. "I'm sorry," Miss Caesar said, "I was distracted. I am not—I think I am finding courting less pleasant than I expected."

Miss Mitchelmore frowned. "Less pleasant how?"

"Don't mistake me," protested Miss Caesar reflexively, "it is very flattering to be so . . . to not be overlooked. But I think I was hoping there would be more."

"More?" asked Miss Mitchelmore, holding up one finger to silence Miss Penworthy, who had been about to launch into a longish explanation of the *more* that could be offered to any lady willing to have an open mind.

"We walk, and it is . . . perfectly nice. And we talk. But . . . I asked him if he had read *The Wanderer* and he said he had not."

Miss Mitchelmore bit her lip. That the younger women saw her as an experienced lover and the kind to offer advice was pleasant in some ways, intimidating in others. "You cannot expect a gentleman to have read every book, Mary."

"No," Miss Caesar agreed. "But that was *all* he said. And I think—if you were to ask such a question to Lady Georgiana, what would she say?"

The swiftness with which Miss Mitchelmore answered was, in some ways, an answer of its own. "She would say, 'Maelys, I hope you aren't going to recommend me something sentimental.' Although actually I think she's rather an admirer of Burney. But in *general* that's what she'd say."

Miss Caesar took this in resignedly. "That's what I thought. I mean, not that exactly. Just—it's hard to explain."

Knowing the importance of encouragement but also the dangers of pressure, Miss Mitchelmore made a very supportive but very nonspecific *go on* kind of sound.

"I think what I *wanted* . . . when I"—Miss Caesar held up one hand to the sky and let the starlight sparkle through it—"when I asked for this . . . what I wanted was to be looked at like other girls."

Miss Penworthy, who had kept her flirtatiousness under a bushel for fifteen whole seconds and was feeling the effort acutely, could keep silent no longer. "I look at a lot of girls, Mary. I don't think I look at any of them as I do you."

"But you would," Miss Caesar replied, "if they were"—she made a fluttering movement with her fingers, and light danced about her hand in gold-and-silver motes—"like this."

"Well, yes." Miss Penworthy nodded. "But they *aren't*."

While Miss Penworthy seemed not quite to have grasped the thrust of the argument, Miss Mitchelmore was more understanding. Then again she usually was; it was one of the things I liked least about her. "You mean that to him you could be *any* girl. As long as she was—" She imitated the fluttering, although the light did not respond in the same way.

Miss Caesar nodded. "'I hope you aren't going to recommend me something sentimental' is something only Lady Georgiana could say to only you. And I think that's—I suppose that's what I want love to be."

"I think that is very wise," said Miss Mitchelmore. "But just because you do not find what you are seeking with the first gentleman who shows an interest does not mean you will never find it."

"No, but"—Miss Caesar cast her eyes down—"before the wish, all people saw in me was my heritage. Now all they see is the magic. At least the first of those was my own."

Perfectly contented to be seeing the magic, Miss Penworthy gave a sharp grin. "If it helps, *love* isn't the only thing in life. After all, it *is* the nineteenth century, ladies are doing all *sorts* of things now."

Miss Caesar lifted the hem of her skirt and showed her friends the spiderweb of cracks that were spreading across it. "How many of those things," she asked, "can you do in a body made of glass, that is slowly breaking?"

And to that, neither Miss Mitchelmore nor Miss Penworthy had an answer.

With my usual impeccable timing, I returned to the drawing room just as Miss Bickle fixed Miss Anne with her gravest, most urgent look and said, "Anne, Lieutenant Reyne is a murderer."

Thunder crashed outside. Which was unusual, because as I had established previously it was a fine evening. But, well, I am not sometimes above providing a little ambiance.

Miss Anne shuddered. "Oh, how thrilling."

I could see, from my vantage and with my mysterious senses, every strand of Miss Bickle's reason fighting against the instinct to agree. "I think he might have tried to murder your brother."

That appeared to strike Miss Anne as rather less thrilling. "That seems very unlikely. I know him well."

"How well?" asked Miss Bickle, looking disarmingly innocent.

"We have danced several times, and he has visited me on more than one occasion."

This was, even by the standards of a society that expected men and women to interact occasionally and cordially, not any great standard of intimacy.

"I know it is hard to countenance," Miss Bickle offered, "but I think perhaps it is possible to dance with a gentleman without knowing that he has attempted to kill one's brother." It may surprise the reader a little (although it did not surprise me in the slightest) that Mr. Caesar had indeed chosen his messenger well. Miss Bickle lived in a world of bright colours and high dramas, but she inhabited it so fully that it was hard for others—especially those others who were fourteen—not to be drawn into it.

Thus, for Miss Anne, uncertainty began slipping slowly into denial on the way to getting a clue. "He is of good character, and good family."

"Oh, but the worst villains always are," pointed out Miss Bickle, now on slightly firmer ground. "After all, a villain who one *knows* to be a villain is scarcely a great villain at all. Why, look at Mr. Wickham. He was *very* plausible in his manners, but he treated poor Lydia quite cruelly."

That analogy, at least, got through. "But surely even Wickham would not have murdered anybody."

"Well, no," conceded Miss Bickle. "The anonymous lady author is rather reticent about such matters. But I certainly would not put it past him."

Miss Anne had grown quiet. She was staring down at her hands and looking a little closer to weeping than she had a moment ago. "You must be mistaken," she said without conviction.

"And if I am not?"

Long, pretty eyelashes blinking back tears, Miss Anne looked up. "Do you think he will try again?"

"I do not know. I just want to make sure that you are being safe."

Belatedly, a thought occurred to Miss Anne. "How do you know this?"

"Captain James told me. He recognised his voice."

Old aristocratic instincts flared, and Miss Anne huffed. "Captain James is a—".

"Is a man of low birth who rose through the ranks by his own merits and served heroically against Napoleon." Miss Bickle clasped her hands to her bosom ever so slightly rapturously. "Were I not certain he favours gentlemen I would marry him myself at once."

This framing forestalled many of Miss Anne's misgivings about the captain, and by extension validated Miss Bickle's warnings about the lieutenant. There was, after all, only room for one villain in a story. "So what should I . . ."

Once again I saw a war raging inside Miss Bickle between the part of her that was addicted to whimsy and the part of her that sincerely wished to advise a young girl well. "Be cordial," she suggested, "and continue to accept his visitations unless your parents object. But—and I want to make this very, very clear—on no account elope with him."

Miss Anne nodded. "I shall not."

"Or go anywhere secluded with him," added Miss Bickle. "Or accept any letters or tokens."

Miss Anne nodded again with the conviction of the young and impressionable.

"Splendid." Miss Bickle beamed her most changing-the-subject beam. "Now, what do you say we go fetch the others, and then I believe Erica might share with us her latest updates to *The Unbeliev-ably Secret Diaries of Georgiana Darcy.*"

This notion appealed to Miss Anne very much. It appealed rather less to me. I have limited patience for mortal storymakers. So I took this opportunity to fade into the darkness and attend to other business.

CHAPTER SEVENTEEN

T HE DAMNABLE THING, READER, ABOUT collecting stories from your miserable species is that you have no inherent sense of pacing, timing, drama, or irony. Try as my kind might to educate you better, you persist in making decisions based on trivialities like "convenience" and "comfort" and "survival" instead. I despair of you, I truly do.

Thus the Caesars and their sometime allies moved to a space of waiting. It was, I assume, a strategically wise decision, but from my perspective it was inestimably tedious. Then again, perhaps I am selling the interlude short. One cannot, after all, tell a tale that hurtles pell-mell from incident to incident without wearing one's reader to exhaustion.

So let us pause awhile and watch the Caesars as they spin on the threads of narrative and fate.

Mr. Caesar still spent much of his time at the Folly, although he (and, perhaps more pertinently, the captain) felt reasonably certain that he was there by election rather than evasion. A man cannot, however, change his entire nature after a single conversation, no matter how handsome and dashing one's interlocutor. Thus, he remained ever so *slightly* given to wallowing.

"Have I," he asked; it was not the first time he asked it, "been a *terrible* brother?"

"Probably," Callaghan told him. "The way my sister tells it, most brothers are."

Mr. Caesar gave him what he hoped was the *friendly* kind of sour look. "I'm not sure that's a comfort."

"It should be"—this was Barryson—"we're all in the same boat where sisters are concerned. Mine never forgave me for not going into the navy."

"Extremely keen to meet sailors?" asked Mr. Caesar.

"'You're a Northman, Barry.'" Barryson's voice was distant and a little rueful. "'You belong on a ship. And magic is woman's craft unless you're fucking Odin, and you're not fucking Odin.' I swear sometimes I think she wants me to sail up the Seine and burn Paris myself."

Not quite sure how to respond to that, Mr. Caesar gave a non-committal nod. "It sounds like you have a complicated relationship."

"Heather's a complicated woman," explained Callaghan. "A fine woman, but complicated."

Still not entirely over himself, Mr. Caesar stared glumly into his drink and said nothing.

From across the bar, Kumar quietly closed his copy of *De re publica* and looked up. "I suspect our friend is suffering from a classical education."

"I probably am," Mr. Caesar conceded, "but I'm not sure I see the pertinence here."

"An English gentleman"—Kumar was leaning forwards now with an almost schoolroom air—"is taught to see himself in the style of the paterfamilias of old Rome. Everything in his household is his and reflects on his personal dignitas. Thus he must extend to each part of it his benevolent guidance, for the prosperity and honour of his least subordinate is *his* prosperity and honour."

Mr. Caesar was about to protest that he didn't see things that way at all, but it would have been hollow. Never especially attentive to his studies, he would not have used quite so many Latin words as Kumar had, but the sentiment spoke to something deep in the part of Mr. Caesar that was indeed an English gentleman, all while drawing sharp reproof from the part that was not. "When you put it like that, it sounds rather selfish."

"That's certainly one way to look at it"—Kumar inclined his head the merest fraction in acknowledgement—"and I'd never call my father a *selfless* man. I might only say that there are . . . advantages and disadvantages to his attentions."

Coming from a world where the space when the other man was speaking was the time to think about what you would say next, Mr. Caesar was not entirely sure how to ask Kumar what he meant without giving offence. Coming from a world where offence is an art form, I was delighted. I was somewhat less delighted when he settled on an artless but acceptable "Oh yes?"

"Few men are educated as we were," Kumar explained, "and that has given me opportunities many lack. But when last I returned home I found Latin came to me more easily than Hindi or Bangla. You worry about being unable to do right by *your* sisters, Mr. Caesar. I can barely speak to mine." As he had been taught, he kept his upper lip resolutely stiff. "Still, neither I nor my father will let them starve. In that regard we are good Englishmen."

Mr. Caesar's gaze drifted forlornly back to his drink. "I'm sorry, I didn't mean to pry."

Grinning, Callaghan leaned in and put an arm around Mr.

Caesar's shoulder. "You're not among the gentry anymore. Prying is encouraged."

"Encouraged by *you*, perhaps." Kumar shot Callaghan a stern look. "Some of us do like to show a *touch* more circumspection. But in this case"—he turned to Mr. Caesar—"there is no need for apology. I could have remained silent had I wished."

"Thank you then," Mr. Caesar tried. "For your perspective. All of you."

Barryson leaned forwards. "You want to thank us," he suggested, "mebbes get the next round of drinks in."

This much, at least, Mr. Caesar felt able to do. I followed him back to the bar where he ordered another of whatever everybody had just had, plus something for the barmaid and something for himself. And there he hovered awhile, wondering a hundred and seven different things all at once.

But, reader, I am not here to watch mortals wonder. Any contemplation Mr. Caesar wished to do in this moment he was more than welcome to do without my observation. Besides, I had other matters to attend to, for his sisters were both still players in this little drama, and it would have been remiss of me to go too long without checking in on them.

I returned, therefore, to the Caesar home where I slid into Miss Caesar's chamber and adopted the role of Ferdinand the puppy. There is, I should stress, nothing unusual about this. It is the kind of merry jape my people play all the time. It certainly bespeaks no undue partiality on my own account. It is no concern of mine if a young woman's choices lead her down a path of heartbreak. Certainly I am not in the business of *comforting* mortals. That would be beneath me.

I nuzzled against Miss Caesar's ankles, and she stooped to pick me up and, in stooping, saw that the cracks were, by now, stretching all the way to her knees.

She remained hard for me to read, being glass and light and hope wrapped in enchantment and the memories of a different girl, but in this I needed few of my ordinary senses to perceive her mood. She carried me to her bed and sat down.

"I feel nothing," she told me.

I *ruff*ed again.

"I think perhaps I should?" Carefully, she ran her fingertips over the spiderwebbing tracery of weakness that was spreading slowly but surely up her body. There was beauty in it still, as there is always beauty in destruction, but now she was looking, she could see how her every movement exacerbated the problem. Not, of course, by any great amount; infinitesimally, but observably.

She was not afraid. Fear is a product of biology, a wash of adrenaline secreted from little mounds of flesh that squat atop your kidneys and tell you that your horrible mortal bodies are worth preserving. When one of my kind takes an interest in one of yours, the capacity for that particular emotion is the first thing we look for ways to circumvent. Still, the new development was concerning to her, and she needed to think. Stretching herself out on the bed and holding as still as possible, she shut her eyes.

"I have not slept," she told me.

"*Ruff.*"

"I used to have such dreams. I would go to so many places and do so many things."

I curled up next to her. She was cold, which a mortal would have found strange but I found merely . . . atypical. "*Ruff.*"

"I suppose . . . I suppose I hoped I would not have to do them alone."

Having only one syllable with which to communicate and being prohibited by strict laws from actually advising her in any way, I *ruff*ed once more.

A glass tear slipped from her eye and fell, perfectly preserved, onto the sheets.

And then I sensed a movement in the air and although I was nowhere near the window, I was certain that a star had fallen. I rose to my feet and growled.

"Oh, don't be so dramatic, Ferdinand," said the Lady, rebuke in her voice and malice in her eye. Or perhaps it was the other way around. "It's only me."

Unable to make an intelligible reply, I left her free to address Miss Caesar at her leisure.

"Why do you weep, child?" she asked once more. "Have I not given you all you asked for?"

A properly brought-up young lady, Miss Caesar could not bring herself to receive a guest—even an unnatural guest—while supine. She sat up and swung herself into a sitting position, wincing slightly at the thought of what the motion was doing to her ankles. "You have," she admitted—never admit this, reader, it's the equivalent of saying sorry after a car accident. "But I find that I am"—she looked at her legs and hoped that the Lady would understand what she meant—"this was not what I expected."

"Beauty is fragile," the Lady replied. "Had you wished for strength, I would have given it to you."

"Then I wish for strength?" Miss Caesar tried.

And the Lady laughed. I have described her laughter many times before, but I shall do so again now. We are a laughing people. Everything you need know about us, you can learn from how we laugh, and when we laugh, and what we laugh *at*.

What I was hearing—what you would be hearing were you

present, though you may trust that my words conjure the sensation quite precisely if you let them—was the *ending* laugh. A laugh like water just the *moment* it falls over the edge of the waterfall. A laugh like a flash flood. A laugh like moonlight on broken glass.

"My dear, wonderful child," she chided, "how many wishes do you think you get?"

With a defiance I could not help but admire, Miss Caesar looked up. "Three is traditional."

"From a different kind of spirit. My people will give you one gift, and what you make of it is up to you."

Miss Caesar stood, and though nothing had changed from the night before, or the night before that, the knowledge that she was falling inexorably into fragments weighed upon her. "I am not ungrateful. I am only learning that there are . . . limitations."

"Every gift is tied with a ribbon."

Looking down, Miss Caesar steeled herself. Or perhaps glassed herself. "Your gift seems slowly to be breaking me."

"That is the ribbon. And if you have no wish to climb mountains or swim oceans, you will not miss the strength of your limbs. The body I gave you is good enough for dancing."

As much as she might have wished to, Miss Caesar had not quite the courage to say that she did indeed wish to climb mountains and swim oceans, that she had not quite realised how badly she might wish to until the chance to was taken from her, or that while dancing was wonderful it was not all she wished to do for the rest of her days. But she began to weep again, sharp crystal tears scattering on the carpet where, had I been a real dog, they would doubtless have stuck in my paws.

Gliding closer to Miss Caesar, the Lady placed two fingers beneath her chin and tilted her face upwards. "Suppose," she said, "I were to bring you to another ball."

"You have brought me to enough balls, I think."

The Lady smiled. Worlds have died for that smile. "Only two. And you said yourself that three is the traditional number."

"Except for wishes."

"Except for wishes. And the ball I intend to bring you to will be one like none you have seen in your lifetime."

Miss Caesar tried hard not to sound tempted. "If you mean the ball for the queen's birthday, that was last month, and Maelys tells me it was dull."

"Your cousin does not know everything. And royal birthdays are not the only cause for royal balls. Nor are *your* rulers the only rulers."

There were a finite number of things that the Lady could have been implying, and I offered a helpful *ruff* to nudge Miss Caesar's thinking in the right direction.

"You are speaking of Titania," she concluded, "of the Other Court."

"It has been too long since there was a formal visitation from our rulers to yours. And at such a ball . . . who can say what manner of gentleman you may meet?"

Miss Caesar blinked. "I am satisfied with Mr. Bygrave, thank you."

"Your sister then."

In the intervening days, the Caesars had been brought at least mostly up to speed on the tiny matter of Miss Anne's new beau being a murderous devotee of a militaristic mystery cult. And while Miss Caesar had initially taken some pleasure in her fortunes outstripping those of her younger, more conventionally pretty sibling, the novelty of the victory had worn off some time ago. "What about my sister?"

"It could be arranged for her to catch the eye of a *real* prize. Of Prince William, perhaps?"

It was a peculiar suggestion, and not one that appealed to Miss Caesar's sensibilities, or that she expected to appeal to her sister's. "He is an old man recently separated from an actress. What could possibly attract Anne to him?"

"He will be king someday."

At this, Miss Caesar laughed. And touched as she was by my people, her laughter likewise spoke volumes. It was a laugh of victory misplaced. "You know little of our courts, I think. The prince regent will take his father's throne, and then if he has no son—which seems ever more likely—Charlotte will rule after he is gone."

The Lady shook her head. "Princess Charlotte will depart this world before her twenty-second year. There will be chaos for a while"—she smiled, as did I—"and then William will be king. And it would take little for Anne to be his queen."

"She is fourteen."

"But for a throne? There is no better way to secure the future of the family."

There were few young women in England—the England of the day, at least—who would not find the offer tempting. "There is no possible way you can promise such a thing."

It was an empty statement, and Miss Caesar knew it, and the Lady knew that she knew it. "'Where the bolt of Cupid fell,'" the Lady quoted, and I yapped at her in protest—she knew exactly what she was doing, "'it fell upon a little western flower. Before milk-white, now purple with love's wound.'"

With commendable pluck, Miss Caesar set her lips into an expression of firm displeasure. "Your proposition, then, is that you *drug* the prince regent's brother, causing him to fall for my sister in the hope that a sequence of improbable deaths will propel her to the throne?"

I *ruff*ed once more in approval.

"Improbable deaths happen all the time. And as for a drug . . . why do you scruple now at attracting a partner by magical means?"

The Lady, I have always felt, is incomparable in her role, but one must be so careful when one confronts mortals with their hypocrisy. They are strangely prone to take it ill. "What do you mean?" asked Miss Caesar, knowing full well the answer.

"'Who that hath an heed of verre, fro cast of stones war her in the werre.'" It was a more acceptable quotation. And since the Caesars had made certain to educate their daughters appropriately, one that was understood. "At the very least you should, perhaps, give your sister the choice. It is, after all, not so very different from the one that you had yourself."

The Lady faded from mortal sight, and I growled at the place where, from Miss Caesar's perspective, she had lately stood.

Absently, she scratched me behind the ears. "Oh, Ferdy," she mused aloud, "whatever shall I do?"

I had no answer. I was not sure what answer I wanted to give.

In the immediate aftermath of the Lady's visit to Miss Caesar I had certain vital duties to attend to. Our kind are inveterate liars, but the bargains we offer are always exactly as stated and if the Lady announced a royal ball three days hence, then such a ball would occur irrespective of the wishes of any mortal agency. It would, I had no doubt, be held at Carlton House (or at least primarily in Carlton House; any event attended by the Queen of Moonlight would extend along at least six axes into realms otherworldly) and my master would expect to be informed.

So I informed him.

The wonder, glory, and honour of being in my master's presence was so great and so unspeakable that I shall not speak of it. Certain things are, after all, too sacred to be shared with mere humanity. My master, in this context, is very much a pearl and you, my gentle readers, are most certainly swine.

Fortunately the natural swiftness, sleeplessness, and efficacy of my people permitted me to resolve all of my courtly duties in the night that Miss Caesar was using to ponder her available options, and to return to the house in time for breakfast.

Matters that morning were subdued, for the family had adopted something of a siege mentality. Not an unexpected outcome, given that they were in many ways being besieged. Captain James had become a near-permanent resident at the house and the various members of the Irregulars visited, well, irregularly to keep him and the family informed of pertinent developments.

It was, therefore, into an already tense atmosphere that Miss Caesar introduced the news of the Lady's most recent offer.

"No," said the younger Mr. Caesar at once, his tone more fearful and less severe than I might have expected from him. Then he looked to his father for reassurance. "It is unconscionable, surely?"

The elder Mr. Caesar set down his fork. "You will be head of this household when I am gone, John, not before. Although I agree that this whole matter should be treated as suspect."

Miss Anne, who had calmed a little since accepting that her latest gentleman was a murderer, was beginning to backslide ever so slightly. "Well," she said, "I don't see that it's so very wrong for *me* to take advantage of the same powers Mary has been employing."

"I don't think it is necessarily an advantage," Lady Mary cautioned. "It seems like it might be——"

"A trap," finished Captain James, whose dashing-ness in the eyes of the Misses Caesar had been elevated by Miss Bickle's approval then subsequently dulled by familiarity. "You want my advice, miss, I'd not trust it far as you can spit."

"A lady," Miss Anne pointed out, "does not spit at all."

Captain James nodded. "Exactly."

Staring blankly into his coffee—now prepared in the English style, which was to say terribly—the younger Mr. Caesar was beginning to lose himself in the pursuit of unknowable contingencies. "But do we know what sort of trap it may be?"

While the company were affirming their ignorance, Miss Caesar looked down at her feet. "I think I may need to do *something*."

The rest of her family followed her gaze. Having no idea what to do about her gradual fragmentation, they had thus far refrained from discussing it, although most of those present had observed the change by now.

"I am in no pain," she clarified, "but I am concerned that if I continue at this rate I may—I do not know *what* I may."

The elder Mr. Caesar turned his attention to the captain. "Would Mr. Barryson know anything about this?"

"No idea," the captain replied. And then, almost as an afterthought, "And he's not a mister; there are no gentlemen in the ranks."

The elder Mr. Caesar's lips curled into half a smile. "Such distinctions mean little in this house, and I prefer to treat men with respect until they prove unworthy of it."

Conscious that the conversation was taking a turn away from her control, and aware that if she did not speak now her courage might desert her entirely, Miss Caesar attempted to moisten her lips, realised that she had no saliva with which to do so, and then said, "I may also know a witch."

"You mean the woman you met after——" Lady Mary began, although she did not quite have the stomach to say *your brother failed to bind the fairy that did this to you in the first place.*

Miss Caesar nodded. "I am not sure if she can be trusted, but she has a house—near Covent Garden, I think——"

On hearing this Captain James turned his eyes skyward in frustration. "Fuck me, she went right past us."

This drew sharp responses of "language" from most of the family and a rejoinder of "It's a large city, she could have been anywhere" from the younger Mr. Caesar.

"She *glows,* John. Even in London a glowing girl stands out."

The elder Mr. Caesar, however, had other concerns. "When you say, Mary, that she has a *house* near Covent Garden."

"I believe it was a gaming hall of sorts?" Miss Caesar suggested. "Although she said also that it was a temple to Isis-Fortuna."

Lady Mary's eyes narrowed. "But not a temple to Venus. There are many temples to Venus in Covent Garden and they are not places a young girl should be wandering."

"Covent Garden after dark's no place for *anyone* to be wandering," the captain told her. "Chancers, bawds, thieves, and theatregoers. And the last lot's the worst."

Miss Caesar batted brittle lashes at the captain. "I am sure I would come to no harm if you were to accompany me."

Unbidden, a light glowed inside her and a music underlaid her voice.

"Hold now, miss." Captain James raised a hand. "I'll have none of your sorcery. But if your family's a mind I'll help you."

Lady Mary and Mr. Caesar exchanged glances. Theirs was not an especially traditional household, and given their own various histories they felt little compulsion to hold their daughters to the arbitrary diktats of the ton. But even they had some compunction about permitting their daughter to consult with a self-confessed witch.

"Is this wise?" asked Mr. Caesar.

"Or safe?" added his wife.

"Or seemly?" put in Miss Anne, who nobody had asked but who was beginning to feel that she had gone far too long without being addressed and sought to rectify that error by the most direct means possible.

Almost unconsciously, the younger Mr. Caesar reached for Captain James's hand. "I think," he said, "that we should probably risk it. We can consult with Barryson also, and anybody else who might have insight into the situation. I am in correspondence with one of the Galli, but she lives in Bath and word would reach her too late. Lady Georgiana has the ear of another witch, but the same problem applies."

Still not content with the response to her contributions thus far, Miss Anne decided to take a different tack. "And suppose I decide I do wish to be queen after all?"

The younger Mr. Caesar sighed. "Anne, have you *seen* Prince William? The man is nearly fifty."

"But a naval gentleman," Miss Anne persisted. "So I am sure he is very dashing."

"He has children who are older than you," added Lady Mary. "And before you say that would be companionable, I assure you it would not."

"And," added Mr. Caesar, increasingly determined to crush this line of reasoning in its infancy, "if the plan is truly to ensnare his affections with witchcraft, it would be profoundly wrong."

At the other end of the table there was a chime of glass as Miss

Caesar clasped her hands together more sharply than she had intended. "That's another thing," she said, hesitantly. "I believe if Papa would accompany me, I may need to pay a visit this morning. To a friend."

The elder Mr. Caesar looked at his children in that planning way that parents sometimes do when they have a strong sense that what they think best will not be that which is best received. "Perhaps John should take you."

This suggestion was taken well by the younger Mr. Caesar, who saw it as a sign of faith in his stewardship, but poorly by his sister, who saw it the same.

"I think John would be quite unsuitable," Miss Caesar protested. "He is not——" But she got no further, because there really was very little he was not. At least very little he was not that was immediately pertinent.

"He is male," Lady Mary pointed out, "and a relative. Whatever disagreements there may be between you, you surely cannot deny he meets those criteria."

And indeed, she could not.

"I am glad you are convinced of my adequacy," Mr. Caesar replied, rather acidly. Which earned him a disapproving look from the captain and a reply of "barely" from his sister. All of which contributed to a beautiful atmosphere of tension when the little party set out visiting a few minutes later: Mr. Caesar, Miss Caesar, the captain, and my invisible self, promenading through the streets of London in an unconvincing facsimile of harmony.

CHAPTER EIGHTEEN

T HE VISIT THAT MISS CAESAR had decided she had to pay
was to Mr. Bygrave. It was, to say the least, forward for a lady
to call upon a gentleman directly. But social convention had started
to fall by the wayside the moment Miss Caesar had materialised
from the fairy realm on Hampstead Heath at dawn and driven two
grown men to their knees with her otherworldly majesty.

Had circumstances not been so dire, the walk from the Caesar
residence to the similarly respectable but not excessively wealthy
abode of Mr. Bygrave and his family would have been a rather
lovely one. Flanked by Mr. Caesar (the younger) and Captain
James (the one and only), Miss Caesar made a picture of maidenly
respectability. Or rather a statue of it. A statue of it carved in crystal glass and dancing with pale light.

Mr. Caesar, being in theory at least the ranking member of the
party, offered his card to the Bygraves' footman, who showed a
commendable lack of concern at being confronted by so atypical a
party. I considered slipping inside and seeing for myself what kind

of home life the tedious Mr. Bygrave had, but since I had no interest in the man, I remained outside with my chosen protagonists.

They were admitted in a timely fashion and shown through to
a tastefully decorated receiving room where a delicate-featured
woman in her late thirties was wearing an unfashionable dress and
an expression of suspicion.

"Robert will be with us presently," she said. "Am I to assume
that this is the"—her lips grew thin—"*glass lady* who has captured
so much of his attention?"

Miss Caesar curtsied, which in her new state was a mesmerising
motion, a ripple of impossible materials and a cascade of white
light. "I am. And would I be right in assuming that you are Mrs.
Bygrave?"

The lady nodded. "It is past time we met, I think."

"Does your son often speak of my sister then?" asked Mr. Caesar, riven somewhat between his desire to support his sibling and
his desire to simplify the complex situation in which his family
found itself.

"Incessantly. Indeed I have found it quite concerning."

While Mr. and Miss Caesar were accustomed to maintaining a
certain politesse, Captain James felt that could very much go fuck
itself. "What do you mean by that?"

As if she'd only just noticed him, Mrs. Bygrave turned her head
the merest fraction towards the captain. "James, is it?" she asked.
"Orestes James?"

"*Captain* James," the captain corrected her.

"My husband spoke well of you." It was a quiet approbation,
almost grudging. "He said you had merit."

From the cannon-smoke of the captain's memory, some patches
of detail emerged. "Your husband was Colonel Bygrave?"

The lady nodded.

"Good officer. Bloody waste."

Before the silence could fully settle, the door opened and Mr. Bygrave entered, shadowed by two younger children.

"But we want to *see*," said the taller, a girl of some twelve years with an unruly tangle of brown hair and more freckles than were considered comely. This sentiment was echoed by her younger brother, still young enough to be composed primarily of mucus and entitlement.

"Miss Caesar is not a fireworks display," Mr. Bygrave chided them. "She is not here to be gawped at."

At which exact moment, because the magics of my people have a strong sense of irony, a beam of sunlight struck Miss Caesar at just the right angle to light her up like a fireworks display. And the whole room gawped.

Once the assembly had recovered their various composures, Mr. Bygrave glanced nervously at Miss Caesar's companions. For her brother to accompany her on a visit was not so very unusual. For him to be accompanied by an officer of His Majesty's army with a reputation for mingled heroism and ruthlessness was rather more out of the way. "Have I"—he hesitated—"have I done something wrong?"

Miss Caesar drifted forward with the endless grace of the Other Court. She looked Mr. Bygrave in the eye and tried to find the words to say the things she very much did not want to say. But at last she had to admit that the words were simple, plain, and unavoidable. "Why do you like me?" she asked.

With almost parodic chivalry, Mr. Bygrave took hold of Miss Caesar's faux-gloved hands. "You are the most beautiful woman I have ever seen."

If there is one thing that my people know, reader, it is that flattery is a drug. Quite literally, for some of us; it can be condensed from the webs of a certain kind of spider and distilled over black fire in the caverns between our world and the domains of the dead gods. But even for mortals it can be intoxicating. And fragmenting as Miss Caesar was, a shard of her wanted to believe that it was enough. "What about me is beautiful?"

Mr. Bygrave was speaking now as in a rapture. "Your beauty," he told her, "defies speech itself."

This was literally true. The Beauty Incomparable is, by its very definition, incomparable. No analogy or simile can do it justice, no adjective can seem anything but scorn compared to its shattering, ensnaring reality.

I will admit, dear reader, that this makes it translate rather poorly to a written medium.

"Then . . . what do you *like* about me?"

Still half-mesmerised, there was only one answer Mr. Bygrave could possibly give. "You are the most beau—"

"About *me*, Robert." Using his given name was an intimacy that should by all rights have been reserved for a far more developed relationship. "About my character, my accomplishments, my connections such as they are."

"None of those things matter," Mr. Bygrave replied. And from his breathless lover's tone he meant it well.

Miss Caesar turned away, crystal tears forming in her eyes. And Mr. Bygrave reached out and placed a hand to comfort her, not seeming to care about the razor leaves that sliced deep into his fingers.

"I have upset you," he said with the typical perspicacity of an English gentleman.

"No." Bewilderingly, Miss Caesar answered truthfully. Touched as she had been by my people, she had yet to acquire our taste for deception. We lie like we breathe. Which is, of course, never.

If I was bewildered by the lady's reply, however, Mr. Bygrave was downright confounded by it. "I must have made some error—I wish only to please you and—"

"Don't."

Mrs. Bygrave and her other guests were watching this little vignette unfold with a mixture of fascination and apprehension. Of the three, it was the hostess who seemed to be handling matters best, but then she had a decade or so on the others and while that is little time in the overall scheme of things, I understand it makes a degree of difference to mortals.

"If you are attempting to say something," Mrs. Bygrave observed, "you are making an ill job of it. Speak plainly, girl."

Though her tears were falling freely now, and bestrewing the carpet like dry dew, Miss Caesar did her best to do as instructed. "I believe that it would be best to end our association."

Neither fully enchanted nor fully free, Mr. Bygrave had little way to process this, and so he made no attempt. He just blinked like he'd been unexpectedly transformed into a rabbit and cast amongst wild dogs. Not that this is the sort of thing that happens to very many people. More's the pity.

Seeking to cover for her son's inarticulacy, Mrs. Bygrave fixed young Miss Caesar with a stern glare. "Would you be so good as to furnish us with a reason?"

"This isn't my society," the captain said, "but where I'm from a lady doesn't have to."

"She does not *have* to," agreed Mrs. Bygrave. "But it is polite for her to do so. Especially when circumstances are so . . . peculiar."

Still weeping glass, Miss Caesar made one more effort. "It

would be best because . . . because this is not me." She flourished her hand with a grace just this side of natural in a gesture that encompassed herself and her situation; light flowed within her as she moved, as if in illustration of the point. "This is an illusion made of stars and mirrors."

A residual loyalty to my people prompts me to disagree with the lady here on behalf of that other Lady whose handiwork was being so disparaged. It was not that she was *wrong* precisely. It could indeed be said with some accuracy that her new status was illusory. But she was making the typical mortal error of thinking illusions are the *opposite* of reality, rather than just another facet of it.

Mr. Bygrave was still looking uncomprehending. "Mary," he said, moved to informality by the intensity of the situation, "you shall break my heart."

On that much, at least, all parties could agree. Miss Caesar gave a solemn nod. "I shall. That is why I must leave."

There was little more to be said, and so the visitors made little effort to say it. Miss Caesar gave a last immaculate curtsey and Mrs. Bygrave, rising, walked the three visitors to the door.

"You never visited me," she told Miss Caesar, only slightly pointedly. "Nor invited me to dine with your family. I confess I thought rather ill of you for that."

With the whirlwind of it all, and the tiny little matter of being physically transformed into a mineral, the specific social niceties had rather slipped Miss Caesar's mind. "I am truly sorry," she said. "For that and—for any other distress I have caused you and yours."

While she was not the one made of unliving matter, Mrs. Bygrave had a rigidity that came from quite a different source. "Thank you. Although given the circumstances I am sure you understand why I am not wholly disappointed at the ending of this connection."

Miss Caesar understood entirely. Ill-chosen connections were preying increasingly on her mind.

The journey back was slightly less pleasant in theory and much less pleasant in practice than the walk over had been. The sun, however, remained bright, which meant that the way it danced through Miss Caesar's body was utterly incongruous with her mood and left her looking a torrent of merry contradictions.

For a while, a pall—not a literal pall, bathed as they were in light and glory—hung over the assembly and they proceeded in silence. But at last Captain James inclined his head towards Miss Caesar the tiniest fraction of an inch and said, "You did well, miss."

"I do not feel I did well." She looked down and away, and the sun gleamed a moment from her eyelashes.

"Had to be done. You did it. And you did it to his face. I'm a simple man, miss, but I know courage."

All in all Miss Caesar did not consider herself especially courageous, and she said as much. "It was fear, Captain. Fear and uncertainty and knowing I could not go on as I was."

And at that, the captain nodded rather more solemnly. "Most courage is."

That evening, Miss Caesar retired to her room early and sat on her bed sobbing. I took the shape of the loyal Ferdinand and curled up next to her and, to my intense chagrin, the Lady took the shape of a faint scent of blood and incense and watched from the shadows.

"You must admit," she told me, knowing full well that I was incapable of replying without compromising my disguise, "she's coming along rather well."

I gave a low growl, which Miss Caesar incorrectly interpreted as addressing her.

"I know, Ferdy," she told me, "I have ruined everything."

"Or," the Lady commented from nowhere, "set everything up *perfectly.*"

There was an element of bravado to this, of course. And an element of circularity. Ours is an anarchic people, so when we say everything is going perfectly what we really mean is that the tumult that has followed from our actions is the kind of tumult of which we broadly approve.

"I have nothing," she continued, a little overdramatically for a young woman still well endowed with friends, family, and social connections to the aristocracy. "And I fear I may soon *be* nothing."

This was perhaps a more serious concern. The fissures that had begun in her feet had of late begun appearing also in her fingers, crossing the palms of her hands like too-short lifelines.

Before she could soliloquise further (people do, you know, at least in my experience), Miss Caesar was interrupted by a knock at the door and her brother's voice asking for admission.

"Come in?" she offered, tentatively. In all her sixteen years on your dull material earth, she could not remember her brother once visiting her in her chamber. It was not unseemly precisely, but they had spent most of their lives in separate spheres and it was strange for them to begin colliding now.

Mr. Caesar entered almost timidly. His attire, for all the pressures acting upon him at that instant, was still immaculate, but his expression was drawn and his eyes downcast. "I wanted to be sure you were all right."

It was churlish to laugh at that, but Miss Caesar was not above a little churlishness. I would offer her youth as defence, but I have never especially felt that churlishness required defending. I have known a great many churls in my time and they are normally excellent value for money.

"You have *never* wanted to know if I was all right," she told him. "Did it really take a bargain with a fairy for you to care about such things?"

The Lady gave a smile of smoke and shadows. "And will she be grateful to me? She will not."

"I have always cared for your well-being," Mr. Caesar told her. "But I think perhaps I have, in the past, had a clearer sense of what that entails."

Miss Caesar's fingers tightened, and a hairline crack spread an eighth of an inch further along her hand. "And what did it entail, in the past?"

"Preserving your reputation," Mr. Caesar replied at once, "helping you seek a husband or, if necessary, some other means of securing a future income. Or of securing an income for myself by which I can support you if the worst befalls."

"The worst"—his sister's eyes were half glaring and half pleading—"being that I remain unwed."

It was a blunt way to put it, but broadly correct. I gave an affirming *ruff.*

Her brother's silence was all the affirmation that Miss Caesar needed. "And you wonder why I did what I did."

Satisfaction gleamed in the Lady's eyes as she watched Mr. Caesar's discomfort. At the back of his throat, the part of him that had been raised a gentleman, that not merely saw the world as it was but accepted it, wanted to protest. To say that yes, he understood, but that things were as they were and though he liked it no better than his sister did, her actions had been rash and selfish. Because that approach had worked so very *well* for him thus far.

"I said clearer," he tried instead. "Not more accurate. I—I may have been trying to help in the wrong ways, I think."

"You think that, do you?" replied Miss Caesar. She did not sound entirely convinced.

"I know it," her brother corrected himself.

"And when did you have this revelation?"

Rationally, Mr. Caesar knew this was a fair response. But rationality was not his first priority. "Mary, must you be difficult?"

The candlelight in the room danced through Miss Caesar's body and gathered at her fingertips. "I'm not being difficult, John."

"You're being a little difficult."

And now the light flared. "I swear, even when you're trying to be kind, you're insufferable."

"Well, perhaps if you'd be a little easier to be kind *to*."

Miss Caesar let out a tiny shriek, which, through a glass larynx, rang like a crystal chime. "That isn't how being kind *works*."

This much Mr. Caesar had to admit was true. After all, the captain had persisted in being kind to him and he'd made that as difficult as humanly possible. So he stopped, took a breath, and said: "You're right. I'm sorry. You're right. And whatever we do from now on about"—he made an inarticulate gesture intended to express *the fact that you have been transformed into a statue*—"we'll do it with you, not in spite of you. I promise."

Miss Caesar remained silent and, inasmuch as she was capable in her new form, looked sceptical.

"Really. I promise. Although in candour I am not certain what we are *going* to do. I fear we have exhausted our options."

There was an opportunity here to turn things against my rival or, at least, to prod the mortals into doing something interesting. I *ruff*ed in a way that I hoped might stir my not-exactly-mistress into action. And it did, in a way. "I could still use my situation to advance Anne?"

"You sincerely think she might be queen?" asked Mr. Caesar, less incredulous than he would have been a year ago. His various encounters since had taught him pleasing respect for the abilities of uncanny beings.

"I think the Lady has great power. And"—she shut her eyes, the light dimming inside her—"I do not think her kind break their promises. Not as they are spoken, at least."

"Such a perceptive girl," the Lady said to me. "Well, perceptive *now.*"

As true as this seemed, Mr. Caesar was not certain that it wasn't a horrendous trap. Which was also perceptive of *him.* "Whatever Anne's wishes may be, and as powerful as your patroness undoubtedly is, we should strive to keep her *out* of her clutches, not to herd her into them."

"And me?" asked Miss Caesar.

Mr. Caesar was silent for long enough that I wondered if he, too, had undergone some manner of transformation. "I do not know. And I cannot help but blame myself."

"Don't," Miss Caesar told him with a gentleness that seemed to rankle at the Lady, who expected better from her protégés. "This was my choice."

It did not escape me that she was now using the past tense.

"Still," her brother replied, "I would free you from it if I could. But I do not know how. We have sent to the Folly for a vitki, but he has limited knowledge of Titania's court."

An air of melancholy was radiating from Miss Caesar, which I would in other contexts have found satisfying, your people's passions being a vintage we savour when we can. But there was a bitterness to knowing that this particular drama had been orchestrated by our rivals, and for the benefit of their queen rather than of my good and noble lord.

"I am sorry, John," she said at last.

"Don't be. You fell foul of an indifferent world. It happens to thousands of people every day, no better or worse than you."

And again, Miss Caesar laughed. But there was affection in it this time, rather than despair. "You're beginning to talk like the captain."

"Apparently he's a good influence on me. Or a bad one. I have yet to work it out." Fearing, perhaps, that he had overstayed his welcome, Mr. Caesar rose and, taking care to avoid the glass roses, laid a comforting hand on his sister's shoulder. "And—if you've still a mind, we will take you to speak with the witch."

When she'd raised the question of returning to Amenirdis, Miss Caesar had not expected her brother to support the notion, or to insist on accompanying her despite his having almost as little experience of the city's worst districts as she had herself. "I do," she told him. "Dangerous as it might be."

Reaching across the narrow space between them, she took her brother's hand in hers, and Mr. Caesar tried not to notice how cold and unyielding they were.

CHAPTER NINETEEN

WHILE MR. CAESAR WAS SPEAKING with his sister, his lover and champion was returning on foot to Lord Wriothesly's Folly to reconnect with his men, and especially with the specific man who had knowledge of magic. And it was as he entered that warren of alleyways that I caught up with him.

Having grown up in St. Giles, he knew these streets well, and there was a tension in the air that he disliked. He knew he was not being followed—at least by any material agent—but still there was a sense that something clandestine and unfamiliar had crawled into the district and was nesting there like a tangle of rats.

The atmosphere in the Folly was subdued when he entered, and Mistress Quickley watched him warily as he made his way to the bar.

"Long day, Orestes?" she asked.

"Went visiting with a young lady."

The landlady stared at him over an imaginary pair of spectacles. "That don't seem your sort of thing. In any way."

A little distance away, Sal and Kumar had been gambling

money they didn't have at a game with crooked dice. Overhearing the comment, Sal turned his head towards the bar. "It's exactly his sort of thing. Forever rescuing people is the captain. It's his worst habit."

"I'll have to find a worse one then," Captain James replied.

Ordinarily, this would have raised a laugh from the company and that would have been the end of it, but Kumar was still looking concerned. "You should, Captain. We may be mere weeks from a fresh war with France and the men need you with them, not off—"

"Off *what?*" asked Captain James with a tone that did not resort to menace, but reserved the option for a later date.

"Off chasing cock," said Sal, flatly.

Callaghan looked up from a corner where he'd been lounging and engaging in idle banter with the locals. "Not that we've a mind to keep a man from his appetites," he explained. "And the Caesar lad seems a pleasant enough sort once you get to know him. But you've put a fearsome lot of effort into this one."

A scowl settled onto the captain's face, decided it was comfortable there, and stayed. "Are you forgetting that an innocent girl has been turned to glass?"

"Bad things happen to innocent girls all the time," Jackson pointed out. He'd been lurking as he usually did in the shadows, waiting for the perfect moment to interject. "Why is this one different?"

"Because her brother had my back," the captain told him. "Same as I've got all yours."

It was hard to watch Jackson move without using the word *slink*, and he slunk out of the shadows now, hands never quite where one could see them easily. "But have you?" he asked. "Because it's beginning to look like you've roped us in to your private battles and we get nothing in return."

Laying his cards neatly face down, Kumar rose and put himself between the two soldiers. "I wouldn't go quite that far," he said in the restrained tones of the Eton-educated, "but while Mr. Caesar seems a fine enough gentleman—"

"Take it from me"—Jackson's voice was low, level, and sneering—"it's easy enough to seem a fine gentleman. That's how half the rackets in the world are run."

Ordinarily, the captain would have taken his men's concerns in the sincere-yet-blunt manner in which they were intended. But ordinarily, he would not have been drawn quite so much into either passion or fairy intriguing. "John's not running a racket. And what I did for his sister I'd do for any as need it."

"Like with that lass in Ciudad Rodrigo," said Callaghan.

"Or the gentleman in Salamanca," added Sal.

"Or that whole business near Talavera," Callaghan continued. "The thing is, Captain, we know you make a habit of this sort of thing"—he was wrong-ish in this regard; the captain's tendency to find those who needed him to find them was far less habit than it was destiny—"but normally it's in wartime."

Jackson nodded. "This though, this is in London. This is coming at us where we live."

"Again, I wouldn't be quite so dramatic"—Kumar raised his hands in the universal sign of placation—"but morale is becoming an issue. The attack rattled people, and the men are saying they don't think that'll be the end of it."

"There's been snooping," Mistress Quickley explained. "Word is a man was pulled out the river with a bullet in his head. Folks are asking questions and I'll not have my customers brung up before the magistrate."

The brave men of the Irregulars, Captain James knew full well, feared not the French, nor the roar of the cannon, nor the cutthroats and partisans that had haunted the hills of Spain. But many of them had a profound fear of the law. "I'll look into it," he assured her. "But you know me. You *all* know me. And when have I ever steered you wrong? Ever let you down?"

"Never," Kumar replied at once, Sal and Callaghan both agreeing in near-unison.

"Then again . . ." Jackson added afterwards, "there's a first time for everything."

And at that, Captain James nodded. He stretched, almost languidly, and then, pivoting sharply, he drove his fist into Jackson's gut, blocked the other man's instinctive counterblow, caught him by the hair, and yanked his head back, baring his throat like a lamb before the knife. "Let me remind you something, Thomas. When we met you were a harsh word and a nod from the gallows, and ever since I've trusted you with my life even though I've heard enough tales to know you deserve to hang six times over. You turn on me now, you'll wish you'd danced with the hemp all those years ago." He shoved Jackson hard away and watched him stumble into his fellow soldiers. "We clear?"

"As a mountain stream, Captain." Jackson's voice always had a whisper of menace in it, but the fact that his hands didn't go *immediately* for a knife suggested that the matter truly was settled. For the moment at least.

With a comradely instinct for defusing tension, Callaghan gave Jackson a hearty slap on the back. "If it's any consolation, I've been wanting to smack you one myself for a while now."

"I hate to say it," agreed Sal, "but you *do* bring it out of people."

While the men debated the finer points of quite how badly Jackson had it coming, Captain James turned his attention back to Quickley. "Where's Barryson? I need him."

"In the back," she replied. "But make it sharp. I'm beginning to think you're bad luck."

Captain James had never been considered bad luck in his life and did not like to be considered it now, but he refrained from passing comment. "Just get him out."

As was typical in the Folly, Barryson was summoned by an informal but efficacious relay of people shouting to people who shouted to people until he at last emerged, dishevelled and drunk, from wherever he had been hiding.

"Need your advice," the captain told him, without nicety or formality.

Barryson pressed his hands to his temples. "Not right now, Captain, it's too early in the morning."

"It's after sunset."

"Is it? Fuck." Then, after a moment's hesitation, Barryson looked suspiciously in my general direction. "Hold up, there's something here."

Around the room the Irregulars reached, quite uselessly, for weapons.

"Is it her?" asked the captain.

Barryson shook his head and then immediately regretted it. "Feels different. Familiar though."

"Something from the men in red?"

That drew a less committal reaction. "I'm a sorcerer, Captain, not a fucking encyclopaedia."

Always more drawn to action than discussion, the captain gestured for Barryson to follow him and led the grumbling vitki out into the streets of St. Giles. I followed, confident now that Barryson's powers would permit him to see me only if he wore the right runes over his eyes.

They darted down a sequence of alleys that would doubtless

have confounded any mortal pursuer but which presented me—swift and airborne as I am—with no difficulties.

"Well?" demanded Captain James.

Blearily, Barryson scanned the skies and the shadows for me. "Still here."

Drawing his sword, the captain addressed a challenge to the night in general. "Show yourself," he demanded. "If you've a scrap of honour, show yourself."

I do not, of course, have a scrap of honour. At least not that I will permit mortals to judge. But it did strike me that it would hinder my collection of the narrative if I did not give these fellows *something* to which to attribute their persistent feeling of observation.

So I materialised.

I elected, in the end, to lean towards the dramatic and the gothic. Soldiers are superstitious folk and take omens and portents very seriously. Robing myself in darkness I took the form of a skeletal crone, traces of skin clinging in places to bones otherwise bleached white with age, eyes still incongruously bright in the sockets.

With commendable fortitude, Captain James levelled his sword at me. "What do you want, ghost?"

By way of answer I let out a long, rattling breath (how did I manage this without lungs? Reader, you take things far too literally) and pointed at an ambiguous space between the two gentlemen.

"It's death, Captain," Barryson declared. "Every soldier's constant companion. It was there when we fought the Lady as well. Looked like a crow then, though."

I had, I confess, been hoping for him to reach exactly this conclusion. The advantage of being thought the personification of an abstract concept was that one could come and go at will and arouse little suspicion. It would, regrettably, oblige me to take on a rather more sepulchral aspect while Barryson was around, in case he had the capacity to detect the inconsistency.

Bold, but not to the point of foolishness, Captain James continued to glare but made no effort to actually strike me.

"Just fuck off," he said at last.

"I think *begone* is more traditional," Barryson suggested.

This did not go down especially well with the captain, but he tried it anyway. "Fine. *Begone.* Leave us alone. We're busy."

Deciding that wordless was the best way to depart, I allowed myself to fade from view, and then to become a faint eddy of cold air, dancing morosely.

"It'll be the lad," Barryson said, once I was gone. "We had none of that until he showed up."

Captain James scowled. "Not what I wanted to ask you about."

"Never ignore an apparition." From how seriously Barryson was taking this, I was beginning to worry I might have overplayed my hand. "If there's death following you, it'll mean something."

"It means I'll be off to war soon," replied the captain. "As will you. But right now we've a glass girl and a blood cult to think about."

In the dark, Barryson shivered, and only partly because I'd blown an icy wind down his spine. "Those could both kill you just as dead."

"They could. But until they do, how about you help me out?"

Drawing himself to a semblance of attention, Barryson endeavoured to look slightly less of a disgrace to the uniform. "Of course, Captain."

"The lad's sister is falling to pieces," Captain James explained. "And she's made contact with a witch lives around these parts. Thought you might be able to help with one or the other."

Barryson picked at a tooth with his tongue while he was think-ing. "Falling apart probably can't be fixed. I can paint her up with strength-runes, but I can't promise it'll work. Glass is still glass and it's made to break. As for the witch"—he gave a loose, insolent shrug—"could be anybody. The slums are swarming with enchant-ers. Most of them are frauds, but it's the ones that aren't you've got to watch out for."

"Come with us," the captain half ordered.

But Barryson responded to the other half. "This isn't my fight, Captain. The king's not asking me to do this."

"No. I am."

The words hung in the night a moment. I confess that I may have facilitated their hanging just a little.

"Fuck," Barryson said at last. "How many times have you saved my life?"

"Three."

"And how many times have I saved yours?"

"One and a half."

Barryson frowned. "You can't save half a life."

"That time at Cádiz was you and Sal together, you get half each."

"Fuck off."

Withdrawing to a more discreet distance, I let the wind die down. Captain James placed a hand on Barryson's shoulder and looked at him with a sincerity that—moving as I do mostly amongst the rich and the otherworldly—I am unused to seeing. "Come with us. Not for duty. Because it's right."

And Barryson sighed. That was the thing about men like Orestes James. They were very, very hard to say no to.

"Absolutely not," Lady Mary was insisting, back at the Caesar residence.

"It is the only way," her son was insisting back, although in truth his knowledge of matters supernatural in no way qualified him to make such an assertion.

"You are not taking my daughter to a gaming hell at this time of night."

"Well, we cannot very well go by day," Miss Caesar countered, still a little unaccustomed to arguing on the same side as her brother. "We are seeking a witch and I understand them to be nocturnal creatures."

Lady Mary frowned. "That is not a good argument for your safety."

"That Captain James will be with us is argument for my safety," Miss Caesar replied, her many recent experiences having rather altered her position on his acceptability as an escort. "And that I have been there before, and the witch did me no harm."

The elder Mr. Caesar, who had been watching the discussion unfold carefully but thus far avoiding comment, now ceased avoiding it. "That somebody chose not to harm you once is far from being proof that they will never harm you."

It was at around this juncture that Nancy entered, announcing the return of Captain James and the strange gentleman with the marks on his fingers. They were welcomed with all due grace and then dropped immediately into the heart of a family debate.

"There a problem?" asked the captain.

"Mama wishes to keep Mary at home," explained the younger Mr. Caesar. "She apparently believes doing nothing about the fact that her daughter is collapsing into shards of glass is the best thing for her welfare."

Raised to impassivity, Lady Mary made no reaction to the

remark, but her husband reacted for her. "John, you will not speak of your mother in such terms."

Although he had learned to be acerbic for a range of very good reasons, Mr. Caesar had enough grace to know when he had gone too far, and too far he had, in this instance, gone. "I am sorry, Mama. This whole business has been hard for all of us."

"Hardest for the young lady, though?" suggested Barryson.

Miss Caesar gasped in adolescent gratitude. "You see how easy that is? Yes, as the gentleman says, this is my affair and I should be free to resolve it as I see fit."

"Resolving matters as you saw fit," the elder Mr. Caesar pointed out, "is what brought us to this in the first place. I do not wish to be harsh, Mary, but trusting unknown magic does not sit well with me."

Ordinarily, Mr. Caesar would have agreed. But if there was ever a time to eschew ordinarily it was when one's sister had been transformed into a rapidly crumbling mineral. "There is simply no way," he said, "that we can free Mary from whatever this sorcery may be if we do not at least consider engaging with sorcery ourselves."

Captain James nodded his agreement. "Barryson, anything to add?"

"Mebbes not that's helpful," Barryson admitted. "Magic can be tricky. I can try to do something about the"—he indicated the cracks that were beginning to creep up Miss Caesar's arms—"but not much, and there's no guarantee any witch'd be able to do more."

"So your advice is that we do *not* trust this enchantress?" prompted Lady Mary, well schooled in the art of telling people that they were saying what she wanted them to say.

"Don't trust her," Barryson agreed. "But see her. You'll never know if you don't, and the captain and me'll be able to keep her safe while we check."

"You promise?" asked Lady Mary, a little breathless and a little hopeful.

Being of an old faith, Barryson took promises seriously. But lacking convenient access to a sacred boar or a silver arm ring, he had little to swear on. "Hang on." He rummaged in one pocket and after a moment's searching drew out a handful of lint and loose musket balls. "Right, what did you want?"

Lady Mary looked—for want of a better word—flummoxed. "For you to promise to look after my daughter."

Nodding solemnly, Barryson closed his fist tightly around the bullets. "By Freyr, Njörður, and the greatest of the gods, I swear on my arms that I will bring your daughter back safe from meeting the witch, or else may my powder fail to catch and may I die on a French bayonet."

"I don't think you have to go quite that far," Lady Mary reassured him.

"He does," explained the captain. "The old gods don't fuck about."

The invocation of direct supernatural retribution against an innocent third party should their daughter come to harm didn't exactly allay the Caesars' fears, but it did at least convince them of the soldiers' sincerity and that they would protect Miss Caesar to the best of their abilities.

Somewhat more difficult for them to accept was the suggestion that Barryson be permitted to paint occult symbols on Miss Caesar's hands and feet in an effort to prevent them from fragmenting further. To this, too, however, they eventually conceded, and a surprisingly timid Miss Caesar—really, what *worse* did she expect?—extended one hand out to Barryson, who had, by this stage, set

himself up in the middle of the parlour with a small parcel of pig-
ments and brushes that he had brought with him for the purpose.

The experiment, however, proved unsuccessful. The surface of
Miss Caesar's hands was cracked and, as the paint was applied,
shifted almost wilfully, causing Barryson to stop before even the
first rune was completed.

"Sorry, lady," he told her. "Magic won't hold. Can't strengthen
glass."

Miss Caesar took her hand back, wiping the traces of paint
away with a handkerchief. "Nevertheless I am thankful for the
effort."

"Proper polite, isn't she?" Barryson observed to the room in
general. "Anyway, can't be helped. We going?"

The finer folk of the family were not accustomed to being hurried, but there was indeed little to be gained by tarrying. And so
Miss Caesar, her brother, Barryson, and the captain set out into the
dark of the London night, intending to visit a sorceress.

Captain James had, in my entirely objective and correct opinion,
been right. Covent Garden after dark was no place for anybody.
The time the party had chosen for their excursion aligned infelici-
tously with the great flux of theatregoers making their various
ways, in disparate states of drunkenness, to their homes or to other
more temporary but perhaps more welcoming lodgings.

The ladies of that district, so infamous in their day and so well
recorded by Mr. Harris in his list, were out in similar force. And
while Mr. Caesar had no especial disdain for that profession nor its
practitioners, their customers were another matter and not people
he wished his sister to be exposed to. At least, not on the streets.

She would meet many of them at balls and salons, but that could scarcely be avoided.

Nor, it was becoming apparent, could the society of rakes and roisters be avoided at their destination. The temple was, after all, a gambling hell as much as it was a house of the goddess, and such places attracted the wealthy and dissolute like iron attracts rust.

So Mr. Caesar was very, very glad of the military men beside him as they pressed through the crowds and into the temple. He had gambled a little, of course, it was the done thing for men of his age, but he had done so more for the appearance of the matter than out of any real love of chance.

Since my exile to the mortal world, I have learned to loathe crowds. The amount of time physical beings spend crammed into tiny, cramped, *hot* rooms that smell of sweat and desperation—and spend in them *willingly* no less—amazes me. Looking back, I can find in myself a profound empathy for what the dandyish Mr. Caesar must have been feeling in this moment. At the time, I was both invisible and immaterial and rose, insubstantial as smoke, to the ceiling, whence I could look down on the throng literally, as well as figuratively.

With as much confidence as she could muster, Miss Caesar walked forwards, hoping that Amenirdis would stop weaving amongst the tables and come to her side.

Captain James, however, was not so patient. He strode through the crowd trailing Barryson and the Caesars in his wake and put himself directly in the path of the hostess.

"You the witch?" he asked. And then when she looked around he followed up quickly with "Nell?"

Amenirdis gave an enigmatic smile. "Not a name I've used in a long time."

"Since when are you a sorcerer?" asked the captain, perhaps slightly more incredulous than was reasonable.

"Since when are you an officer?"

"Fair point."

Feeling, ironically given her predicament, overlooked, Miss Caesar spoke up. "Do you know one another?"

"We both grew up in the rookery," Amenirdis explained. "And both left it. And both returned."

Mr. Caesar cast a weary glance at Captain James. "Does she always talk like this?"

"Always did," the captain replied, "but I think she's got worse."

Doing her best to rise above the bickering, Miss Caesar looked at the witch almost pleadingly. "You said that if I needed you, I could come back."

"What I said," Amenirdis replied, "was that you would do well to stay, and could come back when you wished. I made no offer of aid."

"Then you will not help me?"

A patron, stumbling away from a hazard table, took two steps towards Miss Caesar with an expression on his face that could be best described as hovering between covetous and lascivious. He reached out a hand and had that hand immediately caught by Captain James, who twisted it at a sharp angle and turned the man away.

Amenirdis shook her head. "No."

A tension began in Mr. Caesar's fingertips and ran up his arms to his spine. "So we have entirely wasted our time."

She shook her head again.

"Look here, miss," Barryson tried. "I know how this all works, but it's crowded and we've been on a fuck of a walk, so what do you say we find somewhere to sit down and we can have a proper talk with slightly less riddles."

"If nothing else," I told Amenirdis, "it will make it *far* easier for me to follow what everybody is saying."

Staunchly refusing to react to that particular point, Amenirdis reached out and took Miss Caesar by the hand, leading her through the crowds and the tables and the statues of ancient gods to a narrow staircase and up to a set of rooms far dingier and far less conducive to raucousness than the halls below. They were cluttered with the prosaic necessities of life—cooking pans stacked higgledy-piggledy in a basin and clothes scattered over most surfaces. Only a tiny shrine in one corner of the room suggested its occupier had any tie to the old gods.

Captain James looked around at the chaos. "Fuck me, Nell."

"Amenirdis."

"Fuck me, Amenirdis. You have *not* changed."

Without waiting for permission, Barryson plonked himself down onto the bed that was the only free item of furniture in the room. "Right, let's get down to business. She's falling apart"—he pointed at Miss Caesar—"my gods don't want to do much about it. Yours might. Go."

The bluntness of the common soldier was still unfamiliar to Miss Caesar. "I don't believe we need to be so curt. We are guests here."

Amenirdis knelt with her back to her makeshift shrine and bid the others make themselves comfortable, which led to Miss Caesar perching on the end of the bed while her brother and Captain James spread out somewhat awkwardly on the floor. "You are guests in the house of a goddess, child," she told her. "And goddesses, as a rule, are not patient beings. It is better we speak quickly."

"Even though you've already said you're not going to help?" asked Mr. Caesar.

"You want a quicker answer than no?" Although I mislike mortals, I will confess that Amenirdis, like most witches, had a style I found acceptable.

"I want a quicker answer than 'No, but keep talking,'" Mr. Caesar clarified.

The shrine was lit by candles, and the candlelight framed Amenirdis like a halo. "Then try this. I will not help her, but she will help herself."

The light inside Miss Caesar glimmered. "How?"

"There is to be a ball," Amenirdis began, "and before you ask, I know this because everybody with an eye to otherworlds knows it."

"She's right," confirmed Barryson. "The elf-court makes a fucking racket. They aren't subtle people."

Captain James stretched out his legs and crossed one boot across the other. "We know about the ball. What we don't know is how to play it."

"Like every queen," Amenirdis replied, a little gnomically, "and every goddess."

"But what does that mean?" asked Miss Caesar, half-plaintive half-hopeful.

"If it means anything," added her brother, rather more guarded.

Barryson made a what-can-you-do gesture. "She's a witch, you don't come to a witch for an easy answer."

"Maybe," Captain James conceded, rather begrudgingly. "But we didn't come for no answer either."

A half smile played across Amenirdis's lips. "The army has not taught you patience, Orestes James."

"Wasn't really meant to," the captain replied. "And as good as it's been to catch up, could you *perhaps* just tell us what to do."

"Please," repeated Miss Caesar, with more actual pleading and less frustration.

A deadly serenity crept into Amenirdis's voice. "Very well. Do this, and only this: Know your power."

"I do not *have* any power," Miss Caesar protested. And it was, I had to admit, quite a pertinent point.

"That is not what my goddess tells me."

And although her cousin had been rather burned by her own encounter with the divine, Miss Caesar could not help but be a little intrigued. "What does she tell you?"

"That we are the daughters of Nubian queens. The inheritors of the Mali empire and the legacy of Carthage. That our ancestors made the world quake before there *was* a Europe."

"With respect," Mr. Caesar replied, "I have learned not to trust goddesses. Besides, you're talking about ancient history."

And again, Amenirdis half smiled. "You want to know how to fight a creature made of ideas from a world where time has no meaning, and you think ancient history isn't important?"

"I—" Miss Caesar sounded hesitant at first, but grew surer as she spoke. "I don't see how it's the same as power."

A look that could almost have been pity entered Amenirdis's eyes. "You have the power you take. You traded your strength and your beauty for hands of glass. But you can have them back."

"How?" asked Miss Caesar, her voice carrying the unmistakable and wholly unearned note of hope.

"Can you *please*," I asked from my position in the corner, "give away only *some* of our secrets."

"All magic is woven from stories," Amenirdis said, far more

plainly than she had any right to and over my *vehement* protesta-
tions. "You need to make this story your own. You bargained for
beauty, but you lost more beauty than you gained. Demand redress
from the queen and she must give it to you; the lords and ladies of
the Other Court are cruel and deceitful beings, but their laws are
traps for them as well as for you."

This was . . . half a truth. And if I have to tell you even now that
half a truth is worse than a lie, then I despair at you, I really do.
Not for the first time I found myself wondering what Amenirdis's
game was. To her servants—to some of them at least—Isis was
every goddess and every power, so it was not impossible that the
witch was seeking to serve Titania's ends. But either way I mis-
trusted her.

"That seems too simple," replied Mr. Caesar, edging unconsciously closer to Captain James for support and reassurance.
"What do you think, Barryson?"

"I think you shouldn't fuck with elves," Barryson replied,
although he had the courtesy not to look directly at Miss Caesar
when he said it. "But if you must, then I'd always say to go in
strength. And make an offering to Freyr."

Miss Caesar looked aghast. "An offering?"

"Boar," Barryson suggested. "Or horse. Dog if you have to,
though there's less good eating on them."

Miss Caesar's eyes widened. "I would *never* eat a dog. Or a
horse."

"When you're in the hills of Spain," the captain told her, "without supplies or reinforcements, and the French on every road and
in every village, you'll eat whatever you can damned find."

"There is a reason that ladies do not go to war," replied Miss
Caesar, piously.

Captain James shook his head. "Ladies go to war all the time. Every army drags women and merchants and children behind them."

"Not all women are ladies," Miss Caesar pointed out.

"A poor woman's blood's the same colour as yours," replied Captain James and then, realising that this was not the most sensitive analogy in the context, corrected himself, "as a rich woman's."

Amenirdis had been listening to this conversation with interest and now turned to look Miss Caesar in the eyes. "You have my advice. You may do with it what you will. And if the goddess speaks truly, we will meet again."

"May the goddess *not* speak truly?" asked Miss Caesar.

"She is more rebellious in her heart than a million men," replied Amenirdis, rather gnomically, "more choice than a million gods, more to reckon than a million spirits. Divinities are to be feared, child, not to be trusted."

Mr. Caesar's expression was growing increasingly sour. "That seems perilously close to useless. Must all witches be so vague?"

"Pretty much," said Barryson. "Magic is fucking weird and fucking complicated."

Amenirdis laughed, and for the first time there was the sound of St. Giles in her voice. "He's not wrong. The world is chaos. We try to understand it and to shape it, but we cannot *unsee* it."

Being the ranking gentleman in the group, Mr. Caesar should formally have taken control of the visit. But what should *formally* be, he was beginning to realise, was often not what should *really* be, or what actually was. After all, Barryson, rough though he may have been, understood the old gods as nobody else in the group did; the captain, though he may not have been a gentleman, remained an officer; and Mary, though she was somewhat younger and substantially more female than the rest of the party, was their whole reason for being there in the first place. Mr. Caesar, by contrast, was with them primarily to be supportive. And there was a liberation of a sort in that. So he let his sister take the lead; that, after all, was what the man he was trying to be would do. To his relief and my disappointment, it did not end badly. Rising gracefully to her feet, Miss Caesar bobbed a perfect curtsey to Amenirdis and thanked her for her hospitality. With her heart hidden from me by absence and Amenirdis's hidden by the blessings of the Lady of Ten Thousand Names, I found myself in the narratively uncomfortable position of genuinely not knowing what was going to happen next.

I understand that you mortals relish this feeling. And of all the things I fail to understand about you, this is by far the most perplexing.

CHAPTER TWENTY

T HE TON COULD NOT, ORDINARILY, prepare for a ball in three days, especially not a royal ball, doubly especially not a royal ball with visiting dignitaries, and triply especially not a royal ball with visiting dignitaries that was announced also as a masquerade.

But this was an embassy from the Other Court, and for all their piety and avowed aversion to things uncanny, the ton would move heaven and earth to attend. They would even go so far as to solicit fairy-wrought garments (garments which, I tell you again, are extremely well-made, utterly beautiful, and never ever turn to leaves at dawn) for the occasion in spite of the taboo against such fabrics.

Still the preparation for the event remained complex, especially for the Caesars, who had two daughters and limited funds. Miss Caesar's garments were a part of her and, as such, could not be easily adapted, although she had some expectation that the Lady would assist her in this regard, but Miss Anne and the younger Mr.

Caesar had rather more specific needs. To say nothing of the men of the Irregulars, who it had been agreed would attend in case—as several of them had colourfully put it—of fuckery.

Miss Bickle had, in the end, played the role of—for want of a less loaded term—fairy godmother; being endowed with both wealth and a love of the extravagant she was well suited both to source costumes and to advise on matters of style.

Whether it was the intense flurry of activity preceding the ball or the inherent squeamishness of their set that prevented the Caesars from making the offering to Freyr that Barryson had prescribed I cannot say, but it is worth noting at this moment—as we catch up with our party in the hour leading up to the ball—that the offering had not been made. Whether this would return to bite our heroes in their collective buttocks, we shall see anon.

But what a party it was. Even the costumed nature of the event was not quite able to conceal how eclectic a band they were. Miss Caesar herself was notable by absence, being escorted as always by the Lady, but the rest of the family were a riot of detail. The elder Caesars, accompanying their children on this occasion and fatally determined to let no ill befall them, had chosen simplicity—hooded cloaks and plain black domino masks. Although Lady Mary had signalled her identity to all who knew her by accessorising her cloak with a Wedgwood medallion, depicting a chained and kneeling figure and the words *Am I Not a Man and a Brother?* The others had chosen more complicated attire.

Captain James was perhaps the most straightforward, dressed in court-wear of the like that would have been fashionable two centuries earlier—a heavy doublet with slashed sleeves, and pantaloons in a similar style that gave him the look of a prince from a folktale.

"We all know what we're doing?" he asked, and was answered with a general murmuring of assent. Of course, a good officer never takes yes for an answer. "Barryson?"

"Watching for magic," replied the viking. His attire was furs and steel and topped off with a sword he had acquired from somewhere best not considered.

"Sal and Jackson?"

"Staying out of trouble," said the tallest of the two harlequins. "And reminding you that you don't have to do this."

"Staying back," translated the shorter, "and being ready if help is needed."

"Kumar?"

Constantine the Great—a specific and well-researched Constantine the Great that could have come straight from the walls of the Hagia Sophia—stepped smartly forward. "Communication. Keeping these reprobates clear on what's happening."

"Callaghan?"

The highwayman tipped back his tricorn, although between the kerchief and the mask his face was still concealed. "I'm on Miss Mary," he said with a smile in his voice. "And if I see her break or fall or something try to take her, I'm to act like she was my own sister."

"I've seen how you treat your sister," Sal told him. "Do better."

Callaghan's fist clenched. "That is a scandalous lie and you know it."

"Boy William?" said the captain, cutting across the bickering.

"I'm with Miss Anne," he said. Alone amongst the company he was unmasked, wearing once more the guise of a page boy. "To pay special attention to any man as might try to lead her off. But

CONFOUNDING OATHS 321

don't worry, miss"—he flushed a little as he looked over at Cleopatra beside him—"I'll take good care of you."

Miss Anne, raised to be courteous even if ungrateful, tried not to show that she would rather have been assigned any guardian but him. "Thank you. I am sure I shall be as safe as anything."

The list of assigned roles had, from the perspective of the rest of the gathering, included notable absences. Mr. Caesar, his cousin, her lover, and Miss Bickle all stood unaccounted for.

"And what of us?" asked the younger Mr. Caesar, who, from some imp of the perverse, had chosen to dress as a British infantryman. "This is my sister we are speaking of; I will not be consigned to uselessness."

"Your job is to get us in, and to cover for us if we do something that your lot would never do at a ball," Captain James told him.

It was not busywork exactly, and it was certainly true that it made better use of the expertise of the various members of the group. But it did not feel quite that way to Mr. Caesar. "There *must* be more we can do."

Lady Georgiana, resplendent as Clytemnestra in a bloody gown, contrived to look down her nose at Mr. Caesar despite his slight advantage in height. "There is not. The world is cruel and arbitrary and we can but suffer it."

"*Georgiana*"—Miss Mitchelmore, as Arachne, complete with web, nudged the woman once known as the Duke of Annadale with her elbow—"there is a time and a place."

"And this is both. We are about to walk into danger; I would recommend that we not jump into it headlong."

Miss Bickle, whose milkmaid's outfit (a different milkmaid's outfit and one that, when challenged, she insisted was actually an outfit representing Marie Antoinette *disguised* as a milkmaid) came with an impractically large yoke and two pails that she had, at the very least, this time not elected to fill with actual milk, made a noise best approximated as *pshaw.* "I am certain we can come to no harm while these fine gentlemen are protecting us."

"That," Lady Georgiana replied, "is because you consistently overrate gentlemen."

"I like to think that I overrate everybody," Miss Bickle replied. "It's a much nicer way to see things."

The party had almost finished assembling when the elder Mr. Caesar spoke from beneath his hood. "Captain," he said, "I am grateful to you for all that you are doing, but you should know that when it comes to our daughter, Mary and I will do as we see fit to protect her, irrespective of your instructions."

Captain James gave half a nod. "Wouldn't expect otherwise."

And with that understanding they went to the ball.

Carlton House was the infamous London residence of the prince regent, a sprawling, palatial tribute to art, joy, and vanity. And on this evening it bore also the unmistakable touch of the Other Court. Its Corinthian columns were wound with ivy and its great halls lit with fairy lights. Which is to say, lights provided by fairies, not the strings of tiny bulbs that now bear our name. It is a wholly inaccurate appellation; the things you hang up in the winter have, I am sure, never lured so much as a single traveller to an early death.

The crowds, likewise, bore the mark of Titania's presence. For every masked mortal dressed in outlandish costume there was a creature whose mask was its true face: living dolls and ivy-headed dryads, quick-darting goblins and flower-clad fairies on gossamer wings. Then there were the mortals of the court; the Ambassador was there, representing the king to his queen and not entirely welcome. And alongside him, those who had walked deeper or made stranger bargains, those whose transformations—like that of Miss Caesar—marked them out as clearly belonging to *elsewhere*.

Miss Mitchelmore—not my primary focus in this tale but still a lady around whom interesting things happened—found her eyes drawn inexorably to one of these demi-mortals, a woman with cold eyes and an aquiline profile, with talons of steel and wings of beaten copper, with a bearing and demeanour that seemed somehow familiar. And whispering a gentle word to Lady Georgiana she led her lover away from our present story into another that I shall not tell you.

The Irregulars proved less prone to distraction, keeping to their assigned roles and their positions, letting the crowds swallow them and watching, always watching, for whatever danger might present itself.

For danger, or for wonder.

The queen herself (the queen who mattered, which is to say Titania, not the Queen of England, who was indeed present and holding court in her own pedestrian manner) had yet to arrive, but while she was the guest of honour, she was not the creature at the heart of this glittering web.

That distinction was reserved for Miss Caesar. Although a dispassionate observer might account her more fly than spider.

The Lady and her charge arrived an hour to the second after the official commencement of the ball. Crystal trumpets and spindle-limbed servants heralded her arrival, and she entered the ballroom in a cascade of white light.

Like everybody else, Miss Caesar was costumed. Unlike everybody else (at least everybody else who remained nominally human), her costume was her body. She wore a gown of no cut ever seen in that age or prior, a wild thing of cracked and shifting glass. Her shoulders were bare and transparent, her hair worn high and fused with her headdress into a spire that would have graced any fairy princess. A mask covered her face, a plain oval with tiny, stylised lips, empty holes for the eyes, and, on its left cheek, a single sculpted tear.

The whole room fell silent at her entrance. The queen, the prince regent, and even the young Princess Charlotte—permitted out of seclusion this once at least—watched her in awe as she walked the length of the grand hall, her footsteps echoing like bells. The Lady trailed behind her and, seeing her protégé in no further need of support, cut to one side to collect Miss Anne, who she had, after all, promised an introduction to royalty.

This being a fairy ball, I was entirely within my rights to attend physically, and even invisible I was plainly present to a sizeable minority of the attendees, but provided I retained my bird's-eye view (occasionally literally; that was the other helpful thing about this kind of ball, the occasional live songbird was very much to be expected) they mostly wouldn't try to talk to me.

Thus I was able to watch the proceedings from several angles at once, to see Miss Caesar stride confidently to the centre of the hall and be flooded immediately with admirers from whom she selected her first dance partner seemingly at random, and, at the same time, to see Miss Anne—with Boy William following sheepishly in tow and her entire family watching anxiously from the sidelines— follow the Lady to where Prince William was standing, masked only in a plain black domino in order that he not be mistaken for an ordinary person.

I did not hear what words passed between the prince and the girl, but he took her hand for the dance, and the band struck up a waltz. Descending to the crowd, I listened in to what her family were saying.

"It could be worse," Lady Mary was observing dryly. "He may be four times her age, but we can be relatively confident he has no wish to murder her."

The younger Mr. Caesar nodded but didn't take his eyes off his sister. "It is only one dance, and if nothing else it should elevate her status in the eyes of others."

Captain James, more accustomed to surveying the whole field of view than the Caesars, replied with half his attention elsewhere. "Will it? I thought masques were meant to be anony— Hang about."

Cutting off his instinctive desire to explain that yes, strictly at a masquerade nobody knew who anybody else was, but in practice everybody did and had a lifetime's experience of showing they did while pretending they didn't, Mr. Caesar followed the captain's gaze to two men on the opposite side of the ball.

The first, the elder of the two, was dressed as a Roman emperor, complete with toga and laurels. By his paltry attempt at a mask and his distinctive whiskers, he was plainly Major Bloodworth. The second was more concerning. He wore the attire of a legionary, lorica segmentata across his chest, his head covered by a Gallic helm. In deference to the British climate and the sensibilities of the day, he had chosen to wear woollen braccae covering his legs to the greaves rather than leaving his knees exposed as Augustus might have. The most peculiar part of his outfit, however, was the mask, which was pure gold—or gilt at least—and covered his entire face in a façade of eerie serenity. Mr. Caesar and the captain were both certain that he was watching Miss Anne.

Balls in general, and masquerades in particular, were supposed to be carefree occasions. An opportunity to let down one's hair (figuratively at least; to actually let down one's hair would be the height of unseemliness) and live, for a while at least, in the moment. Which meant of course that in *practice* they were a tangle of white-hot thorns made from petty resentments, old tensions, and new intrigues. The dances changed, and the revellers switched partners. To the Caesars' relief, Miss Anne had not stood up with the prince twice in a row—there was seeking royal favour and then there was shameless social climbing, after all.

With commendable alacrity, Boy William had noted the Roman legionary approaching Miss Anne to ask her for the next dance and had taken it on himself to point her in the direction of an older gentleman masked as a fox rather than let him sweep her up at once, but he had not quite had the strength, in the space between dances, to stop the gentleman marking her card.

"Perhaps the next set, then," the legionary said—his voice was soft and by now, to the Caesars at least, unmistakable, "if you would so honour me."

"The lady is—" Boy William had begun, but the legionary had ignored him, and made it quite plain that if Miss Anne wished to refuse him, she would need to do so publicly, thereby giving him great insult.

And given the choice between protecting herself from a man she knew to practise human sacrifice or protecting her reputation, Miss Anne made the only choice she could.

I observed the whole exchange, of course, for such is my function. But Kumar observed it also and circulated at once back to Mr. Caesar and the captain to inform them of the problem.

"He has her for the next dance," he explained. "The boy did his best, but this isn't his battlefield."

For all of fourteen seconds, Mr. Caesar had been letting

himself relax. One sister was awaiting Titania and could do nothing truly ill-advised until she arrived; another was with royalty and thus as safe from scandal as she could possibly be, so long as she remained in public. The sneaking in of Lieutenant Reyne—for it had to *be* Lieutenant Reyne, did it not—was a setback he kicked himself for not anticipating.

Sensing his lover's unease, Captain James laid a hand on his shoulder. "Don't worry," he said. "I'll have a word."

"What sort of word?" asked Mr. Caesar, suddenly full of yet more trepidation.

"The kind that he won't ignore."

Before Mr. Caesar could ask him for any more details, the captain was gone, prowling his great cat's prowl through the crowd and circling towards the legionary from the last angle he'd be watching.

The helm, in this case, was a help. It meant that Lieutenant Reyne had little to no peripheral vision. Which in turn meant that the first he knew of the captain's approach was when a voice in his ear whispered: "This costume comes with a nice thin knife, and we both know that armour is for show."

"And you'd stab a man in the middle of a royal ball?" the lieutenant whispered back. "You'd be lucky to hang."

Captain James kept his voice low. "Way I see it, you've tried to kill one person I care for and are planning to kill another. Reckon stopping you's worth a hanging."

"Then strike."

"Could do. Or we could take a walk."

To my fairy sight, the hall was a cacophony of mortal wanting and striving and yearning, much of it concealed, but with my attention all focused on the two gentlemen and the blade, I saw their hearts beat three times in indecision and watched the captain's fingers play lightly along the hilt of a dagger that was far less costume than it appeared.

They walked.

As much as I wished to keep observing the dancers, the confrontation between the two military men looked likely also to be fruitful, narratively speaking. So I followed them, taking the advantage of breaks in their conversation to flit back like moonlight into the hall and watch for developments.

And I had time. A ball of this nature spilled over most of the house, and so it took some while for the captain and his companion, moving as they were at implied knifepoint, to find somewhere they could talk openly. They settled at last on the library, which even the revellers of Carlton House would be unlikely to disturb and which was situated a convenient floor below the main attractions.

There, far enough now from crowds that in many ways each man was entirely at the mercy of the other, they moved to a respectable, non-knife-appropriate distance and, watching one another with utter suspicion, settled into two conveniently separated armchairs.

"So," asked the lieutenant, "what did you wish to say?"

I took advantage of the pause to check that nothing new had happened in the hall. It had not, but the band had struck up a popular piece called "The Fairy Song" and it was fast approaching midnight, both of which pointed to the queen's arrival being imminent. But not so imminent that I could not return to the library.

"How about you take off your mask first?" the captain was saying. His own mask had already been removed; it had been a silly ornamental thing that kept well with the princely image but had otherwise not suited him.

Whether out of curiosity, coercion, or simple courtesy between military men, Lieutenant Reyne obliged, removing his legionary's helm and the mask with it, setting the headpiece down on the floor.

"In a more civilised world," he said, "we would share a brandy."

"I'm not a civilised man."

Lieutenant Reyne gave a soft, almost apologetic smile. "You are not a *refined* man," he said, "but you are a civilised one. After all, you are a British officer."

"Barely."

"My father was barely a gentleman. I barely scraped together the coin for my commission. We live in a world of barelys."

The captain's lips curled into an expression of profound unimpressedness. "If this is the part where you tell me we're not so different, I've heard it."

"No, no, I am quite aware of the dissimilarities between us. I am from the country, you are from the streets. I paid for my place, you won yours. You are a captain, I am a lieutenant. And your skin, of course, is darker than mine." His tone was conversational, almost breezy. "Still, I am more of your sort, I think, than the major's."

"How'd you figure that?"

The lieutenant's smile grew cold. "Because neither of us are fools."

Another lull, time enough for me to check on the hall (still nothing, the fairy dance still playing; it would be last dance of the first set, just in time for the queen to make her entrance).

"What do you want with Anne?" asked Captain James, force-fully changing the subject.

"You know what I want with her."

"I might, but I don't think I'll believe it unless I hear you say it aloud."

The lieutenant let that hang awhile, then leaned forwards, almost conspiratorial. "I want her blood. She's the highest-born virgin that the fewest people will miss."

At this, Captain James nodded thoughtfully. "You're right," he said. "You're not a fool. You're just a murdering bastard."

"We're both murdering bastards, Orestes. May I call you Orestes?"

The captain sneered. "Fuck off."

"I'll take that as a yes. But you and I both know that war is a murdering business."

Another silence. Back in the hall, a clock was close to chiming midnight.

"Not like this," the captain replied.

"*Exactly* like this. Are you aware of the name of my order?"

From the way he shrugged, Captain James could not conceivably have cared less. "Cult of Something? Servants of Somebody?"

"We call ourselves the Iphigenians."

The captain looked blank.

And the lieutenant laughed. "Sorry, it never occurred to me that a man named Orestes wouldn't *know.*"

"Know what?"

"Just as the Greeks were making war on Troy, it so happened that Agamemnon slew a deer in a grove sacred to Artemis. In pun-ishment, she stilled the winds so their fleets could not sail."

"Sounds like Artemis could have saved a whole lot of pointless death."

That earned half a nod from the lieutenant. "It seems the gods rather *like* pointless death. To return the winds, Artemis demanded that Agamemnon sacrifice his daughter Iphigenia. Sources are rather varied on whether she went to her death willingly, but it is a lesson that my order learned well."

"We don't sacrifice people in this country. Haven't for centuries."

"Quite right." Lieutenant Reyne nodded. "To sacrifice a human being to a god is accounted a terrible crime by all the laws of England. But Orestes, what do we do in war that would *not* be accounted a terrible crime, were it to happen in peacetime?"

Captain James thought about that. "The waiting," he said, "and the digging. And the walking. Which makes up most of it in my experience."

"And the killing?"

"Some of that as well. I'm not saying all of it's right, but there's times when it's needed. There's rules and you stand by them. Soldiering is soldiering and murdering is murdering. I'll not pretend they're the same just to sound clever."

A melancholy chuckle escaped the lieutenant's throat. "How little you must think of me."

"Telling a man you want to cut an innocent girl's throat will do that."

Another silence, just barely broken by a clock beginning to chime the hour. "What is it that you love, Orestes?"

The clock struck once.

"Family, and them that are like family. The regiment."

Twice.

"Shall I tell you what I love?" Three times. "I love only two things: England, and the men who fight for her." Four. "Tell me, how many deaths is one girl worth?"

The clock struck a fifth time. "It's not a quartermaster's list." A sixth. "You're not weighing out rations."

"Oh, but I am." A seventh. "That girl's death might save a ship of the line"—eight—"or squadron of rifles."

"Or nothing"—nine—"and you're just a killer"—ten—"fuck, you killed a man you knew."

"Like a brother," the lieutenant agreed as the clock struck eleven. "But war is sacrifice."

Twelve.

In the hall—of *course* I checked the hall, what kind of storyteller would I be had I not?—things were changing. The fairy dance had ended and the partners were separating. The first half of the evening was over and refreshments were about to be served. But as they began to move from the dance floor, buds, then whole leaves, then branches decked with thorns began to break through the far wall. . . .

"Don't give me that," Captain James was saying. "You can't really believe—"

. . . And the leaves were joined by a light, here golden, there silver, the sun and the moon in harmony, or a fine pretence of it. . . .

"But I do. How can I not? The power of the gods is undeniable."

. . . And bricks crumbled and paint peeled and the wall drew aside to reveal the path to that Other Place where my kind dwell where stars dance by daylight, where the ocean is above and the sky is below, where all is possible but nothing actual. . . .

"And if the other side have it too?" asked the captain. "If they offer up their children to whatever they have over there."

"Teutates," said the lieutenant quite matter-of-fact, "Taranis, the Neptunian beast that sired Merovech. And believe me, they do make such offerings. So we must make ours or we will *fall*."

. . . From the light came Titania. . . .

The captain stood, one hand drifting towards the cuirassier's sword he still wore at his side. "I'll not kill you," he said, "not here. Like I said, murdering's not the same as soldiering. But stop this, or next time we meet it'll be a different story."

. . . She was garbed all in white, and rode a white horse with fifty-nine silver bells on its rein. . . .

Lieutenant Reyne bowed his head. "As you say, Captain. And, for what it's worth, I've always considered you a fine officer."

. . . Clarions announced her coming; her courtiers were dressed in spiderwebs and morning dew. . . .

"Heard good things about you too," the captain admitted, a little grudgingly. "Known men who served under you. Said you never flogged a man as didn't deserve it or sent a man to die for nothing. Not long ago I'd have said that made you better than most."

Unmasked, the lieutenant looked almost melancholy. "Yet you fail to understand the calculus."

"Never had no schooling. Didn't learn calculus, but I learned right from wrong."

"It is right to save lives." Lieutenant Reyne rose and tucked the helmet and mask under his arm. "But the bells have struck. And if the rumours about this evening are to be believed I suspect that you will have other matters to deal with very shortly." He smiled, and his smile was almost wistful. "I am sorry we met as enemies, Orestes. In another life you would have been a great asset to the order."

"In another life you'd have been a great asset to the army."

Since mortal pleasantries are of little interest to me, I left the men to part with whatever vague threats or promises they felt appropriate and returned my whole attention to the hall where, her grand entrance being made, Titania was circulating now amongst the mortal noblesse.

Our court is, you should understand, far older and more essential than your fragile, artificial social structures. But the mortal mind cannot comprehend the truth of us, and so when we present ourselves to your world we do so through the lens of your own culture. Thus in the partially demolished ballroom of the Prince Regent of England she wore the mien and raiment of a European queen, or at least a recognisable parody of one. A crown of spun silver and living laurels graced her brow, and her gown was sewn with a hundred thousand diamonds, kobold-mined in the places far beneath. All about the room, gentlemen kissed her lily-white hand, and the queen herself curtseyed when her unearthly parallel approached.

Showy. That was Titania's problem. Unlike my fine and noble lord Oberon, who is extremely understated and down-to-earth. And looks extremely dignified in his crown of antlers that I have never once seen become unfortunately entangled with a light fitting.

The plan for Miss Caesar to confront the fairy queen for redress stumbled a little here. Crowds are selfish entities and even the wonder of the Beauty Incomparable could not quite clear a way through the throng that now surrounded the Queen of the Other Court.

Matters were proving equally frustrating for Miss Bickle, who had certainly not come to a fairy ball only to leave without so much as glimpsing the queen clearly. Abandoning social convention, she managed—with some effort, and at considerable cost to her dress—to climb the tangled arch of life and marble which now replaced the far end of the hall. This put her perilously close to fairyland proper, which lay a few short meters behind, but for the moment mist shrouded it, and not even Miss Bickle's boundless curiosity would quite let her wander unprepared into the unreal realm.

While the Queen of Light and Glory was distracting the rest of the room, the captain took the opportunity to pull the younger Mr. Caesar out of the ballroom and into a secluded alcove behind an arras.

"Get her out," he told him, breathless and still furious.

"Mary?"

"Anne. Reyne's after her, and I'm sure the fucker is moving tonight. I'll send the lad with her."

Mr. Caesar froze. "Here? What do we do?"

"We move fast," the captain said, "and we move quiet."

"Will it work? There's still Titania to reckon with."

The look in the captain's eyes was steel, which, contrary to myth, is a far greater danger to my kin than iron is. "Right now she doesn't matter. Do the first thing. Live. Do the next thing. That's how it works."

In the shadows, Mr. Caesar's hands shook and his spine tensed. He gazed at the captain with that mix of admiration and yearning he always had. "In case we don't. Live, I mean, then I should say—"

Catching Mr. Caesar about the waist, Captain James pulled him in and kissed him, quick and fierce and burning. "Save it. We're not done yet and nobody's dying tonight."

The talk of death was not doing much to assuage Mr. Caesar's temptation to stay in that alcove with the captain and pretend none of the rest of it was happening. Except pretending was what he'd been doing his entire life, and he was sick of it. So he nodded as decisively as he could manage. "Let's go."

The advantage of a masquerade was that two gentlemen

appearing from behind an arras was no great cause for speculation, or at least no greater cause than anything else that went on at such an event. Doing their best to look the acceptable kind of disreputable, the captain and Mr. Caesar went at once in search of his younger sister.

With commendable social instincts, Miss Anne had returned to her family once the dance had ended and was now standing demurely alongside her parents, engaging in light small talk with a distracted-looking Miss Mitchelmore. The younger Mr. Caesar burst into the group with tremendous urgency and broke up the conversation with only the most distant pang of embarrassment.

"Orestes says we need to get you out," he told his sister. Over his shoulder, the captain nodded his affirmation.

"Will she not be safer in a crowd?" asked the elder Mr. Caesar.

Captain James nodded in a *yes, but* sort of way. "She was, but this"—he indicated the tide of revellers that still flowed (appropriately enough, given her occasional lunar associations) towards the lady Titania—"is not a normal crowd. This is turning into cover. My advice is take her home now before we start seeing real chaos."

Never one to keep her opinions to herself, Lady Georgiana sidled over to interfere. "I'm inclined to agree with the soldier. I have never known an otherworldly being to appear and make things *safer.*"

The assembled extended family discussed this matter a few moments more, but, as they did, Captain James took it upon himself to signal to Kumar, who in turn signalled to Boy William, who had positioned himself such that he could keep watch on both the lieutenant and Miss Anne without drawing too much attention to himself. Which meant that by the time the group had decided what was to be done, the Irregulars had moved seamlessly to cover their sight lines and the new plan could be implemented immediately.

"Right." Captain James set everybody their assignments and, despite his misgivings about taking instruction regarding his children's welfare, even Mr. Caesar acquiesced to the arrangement. "I'll spot Reyne to make sure he doesn't go anywhere. Boy William, you take these three"—he indicated the elder Mr. Caesar, Lady Mary, and Miss Anne—"get them home safe, especially the girl."

Miss Anne did not especially enjoy being referred to as *the girl*, but having at least some sensibility of the danger she stood in, she accepted it.

"The rest of us cover the exit, make it look like everything's normal, and remember there's still the queen, the Lady, and Miss Mary to think about."

Few if any of the assembly were in any danger of forgetting the fact, but with the Irregulars running interference, the elder Caesars, backed by Boy William, navigated Miss Anne from the building with no fanfare and with few any the wiser.

There were, after all, far more interesting things for the guests to be looking at.

CHAPTER TWENTY-ONE

T HE QUEEN OF THE OTHER Moon was, at last, coming to the end of her circuit. She had accepted the greeting and tributes of princes, dukes, earls, and counts and was beginning to turn her attention to the lesser members of the company. Which was to say, the people who hailed only from the kingdom's thousand wealthiest families, rather than its thirty wealthiest.

So at last Miss Caesar had an opportunity to speak her piece. And although she was now merely the second most radiant being in the hall (the Beauty Incomparable was a wondrous gift, but Titania would permit nothing to outshine her, although my lord would—of course—do so on many occasions despite her best efforts), when she and the queen came face-to-face they amplified one another. The queen was all light, and Miss Caesar all glass, and so the one poured into the other and danced and shifted and spilled out again across the ballroom, bathing the onlookers in a radiance the like of which mortal eyes saw once in their lives, and then only if blessed with remarkable fortune—of one sort or another.

And when the queen at last spoke, her voice was like hearing the dawn. Like children laughing on a battlefield. Like a storm in a heat wave. "What do you want, child?"

A glass face behind a glass mask, Miss Caesar had never looked, nor sounded, less like herself. But she spoke the words clearly enough. "I want redress."

"Redress?" The queen's tone was carefully neutral.

"I bargained for beauty," Miss Caesar echoed, trying to keep as close to Amenirdis's phrasing as she could. Which was a good instinct; words are magic and changing the words changes the spell. "But I received less than I gave away."

Like the Lady, like most of her courtiers, Titania had a remarkable laugh. One that held only kindness, even when used for cruel purpose, that offered hope even as it stole choice, that took all you had and left only happiness behind it.

"I received less than I gave away," Miss Caesar repeated. And there was strength in that repetition. Few would make the same petition to the Queen of the Wrong Mirrors twice.

But our kind grow bored easily, and the queen was growing bored now. She turned her face from Miss Caesar and began to walk away.

"I received," Miss Caesar said for the third time, "less than I gave away."

The laws that bind our people do not bind yours. You may lie about a thing any arbitrary number of times, though you somehow persist in believing repetition is truth anyway. But while we know that your laws are not ours, we sometimes live in the spaces between them. What we tell you three times is true, and what you tell *us* three times we must heed, whether we wish to or not.

Whether you would wish us to or not.

Titania turned back, a new menace in her aspect. Her gown of diamonds shimmered white with anger and the laurels on her crown curled back to reveal thorns. "That is a grave accusation, child, and must be answered."

With no spoken signal, Titania called the Lady to her side. The Lady herself, perhaps conscious that her relationship with Miss Caesar was reaching its conclusion in one way or another, had been touring the party in search of fresh clients. Now she went obediently to her queen. "Majesty?"

"This girl charges that she bargained for beauty, but that what was given did not outweigh that which was taken."

"No price was stipulated," the Lady replied, coolly. "And that beauty was granted cannot be denied."

This seemed to satisfy the crowd, whose vulnerability to the Beauty Incomparable was surely proof enough for any reasonable person.

Not that being reasonable is ever truly a requirement amongst my kind.

But just as the matter seemed settled, a rough, northern voice called out from the back of the room. "I deny it."

The whole crowd turned, and Barryson pushed his way forwards. "I am Barry," he said, "son of Barry, son of Bob, keeper of the old ways, and I demand that this matter be tried at the Althing." This was an interesting gambit, although the laws of the Old North were of limited sway in either the English court or its fairy echo.

Titania turned her head to face Barryson. "Are you a lawspeaker?"

Barryson shook his head. "There's none in the south, as I'm sure you know."

"Then you have no authority." She turned and walked back towards the far wall, where now the mist was receding to reveal a long colonnade of trees stretching endlessly into a distorted distance. "If you wish to make your case, child," she called to Miss Caesar without so much as looking at her, "then make it. But you will not make it here."

And so as the queen retreated and her court went with her, Miss Caesar followed. Although neither I nor the crowd nor her family nor, perhaps, she herself could tell if she went from her own will.

"Fucking stop her," called the captain to whichever of his men could hear him. The cry was passed on as effectively as it could be and, on the periphery of the room, Sal and Jackson, still masked as harlequins, did their best to flank the queen's procession, but the crowds were too thick and her fairy courtiers too canny to permit interference. As the Irregulars and Mr. Caesar tried to fight their way to the queen and her petitioner-captive, the mists rolled back and the far wall of the great hall of Carlton House began to rebuild itself with uncanny speed.

The majority of the mortal attendees had the foresight to stay well clear of the aperture as it closed, and to make no effort to follow Titania into her place of power. This was sensible of them, but their presence as spectators still proved an impediment to those attempting a more reckless pursuit, meaning that by the time Mr. Caesar reached the aperture-that-was, it wasn't.

"Come back," he yelled at the unyielding brickwork. "Come back here and . . ." He wasn't quite sure what the *and* was, and so he left it forever uncompleted. And when Captain James's hand came down gently on his shoulder, he put his own hand over it and let it rest for a moment in comfort.

"We need to go," the captain whispered. "Barryson did his best, but it's clear he's not a real toff. And the magistrates will not take us sneaking into a royal ball lightly."

He was right, of course. And even had he not been, what

reason was there to stay? Mr. Caesar had lost track of both his sisters, and while he had reason to hope Anne would be well, he could not be certain of it. His first instinct was to hang his head in shame, but shame had bought him nothing so far. So he swallowed his fears, fell in behind Captain James, and trusted not to fate, but to action.

"No fucking authority?" Barryson was saying as they assembled outside. "I'll give her no fucking authority."

"And how, pray, will you do that?" asked Lady Georgiana, who had left alongside the Irregulars, reasoning that little would happen that evening that topped an otherworldly intervention and an abduction.

"Be nice, Georgiana," chided Miss Mitchelmore. "We're none of us planning to give up on Mary, are we, John?"

Mr. Caesar agreed in theory but was having trouble in practice. He did not lack for determination, but he sorely lacked for ideas. "No," he said somewhat unconvincedly. "Although since she just walked through a wall into a world that is not on any map, I fear we may need to regroup at least."

"Situation like this," Captain James told him, "you need to follow quick. We don't know what's happening to her."

"Follow *how*?" asked Mr. Caesar, not quite despairing but not far from it.

All eyes turned to Barryson. "There's a way," he confirmed. "But you won't like it."

Mr. Caesar's jaw grew tight and his lips grew thin. "This is going to involve blood sacrifice, isn't it?"

"Doesn't everything?" asked Lady Georgiana.

Very much not in the mood, Mr. Caesar was reduced to an inartful but expressive: "No, it fucking doesn't."

"But this will. You want to get into Alfheimr, you need to talk to Freyr." This was . . . only partly accurate. The hidden truths of the cosmos are what you mortals might call syncretic, and so while Freyr is one name by which one god who claims dominion over one part of my people's realm is sometimes known, he hardly holds a monopoly on ingress. "You want to talk to Freyr," Barryson continued, "you need to offer him a boar, a horse, or better still both."

"And where are we going to get a boar and a horse at this time of night?" asked Mr. Caesar, increasingly convinced that the world was spinning, or had long spun, off its axis.

From his instinctive place in the shadows, Jackson gave a low chuckle. "This is London, Mr. Caesar. You find it the same way you find anything else. You put the right coins in the right hands."

Barryson gave a sharp nod. "Give me an hour and I'll have something. Meet me on Hampstead Heath, where you were going to duel the major."

Mr. Caesar rested his head in his hands. "And then what? We slaughter some animals, walk into another world, and then tell the Queen of the Other Court 'Excuse me, I want my sister back'?"

"I hate to say it." This was Callaghan, who'd been holding his peace thus far and seemed able to hold it no longer. "But the lad's right. This isn't a plan, it's fearsome close to being a trap."

"Did I ask for your opinion, Infantryman?" replied Captain James, sharper than Mr. Caesar had heard him since they'd met.

Eerily monochrome in his harlequin's garb, Sal slinked forwards. "We're not in the field now, Captain. Every man here is with you because you've earned as much, but don't throw it away on a fool's errand."

"Saving my sister is not a fool's errand," insisted Mr. Caesar with far more conviction than he felt.

"It will be if it fails," Callaghan pointed out. "We're not talking about some village full of Frenchmen here, we're talking about strange magic and otherworlds. I'll have your back, Captain, but sure and I'm taking a lot on faith with this one."

Captain James stared at his men, hesitant for the first time since I, at least, had known him. "Kumar? What about you."

"I trust your judgement," the scholar told him, "and I wouldn't ask any man to abandon his sister. But you have to admit, you'll be risking all of us for one girl."

"When you put it like that," said Lady Georgiana, "it does seem rather foolish."

Miss Mitchelmore aimed a sharp kick at her ankle. "*Georgiana.*"

"She's *sixteen,*" pleaded Mr. Caesar. And he was, now, pleading in a manner that an uncharitable observer might almost consider unmanly. "You know her." He turned to Jackson. "*You* know her. You've been to my house. You've fed us your terrible coffee."

"No offence," Jackson replied calmly, "but you're nothing to me. And though I'm sure you're too polite to say it, I'm nothing to you."

A week ago, this would have been the exact truth. Now . . . now, like so much in Mr. Caesar's life, things were more complicated. "Mary is my first priority," he said—and of that much he could be entirely certain. "But I believe I am beginning to count you as . . ." The stumble was not quite fatal, but a lifetime of dancing around propriety could not be erased overnight. "I mean, I would not presume to call you friends, but I would not put you in harm's way save for very great purpose."

Jackson, however, did not seem convinced. "Those are very

fine, words, sir. But I've heard fine words from a lot of men in my life, and most of them would see me hang in a heartbeat if it would profit them."

"And what about me?" asked Captain James. "Am I such a man?"

Still masked, his face still painted all in white, Jackson smiled. "You said yourself I deserved to swing."

"You do. But you've not."

I watched with interest as Jackson and the captain squared off against one another. There was a chance, just a chance, that this would end with somebody getting stabbed, and while it was looking increasingly likely that the evening would end in *some* kind of bloodshed whatever happened, a little appetiser never goes amiss. "I'm your man, Captain," said Jackson at last, thwarting my desire for violence. "And if you say we're doing this, we'll do it. But I'll tell you now you're being a bloody fool."

Captain James nodded once, slowly. "Barryson, go get the sacrifices. We're doing this. Men, fall in."

The Irregulars, save Barryson, fell into a column, with Mr. Caesar bringing up the rear.

"Much as I hate to play the part of the weaker sex," observed Lady Georgiana, "I think I *might* suggest we leave this to the professionals. I've had a rather confusing night."

Miss Mitchelmore laid a hand on her lover's arm. "Whatever that lady was, I am sure we will find her again. But for now I agree we should leave things in the hands of—" She looked around at the assembled soldiery and a look of dark realisation crossed her face. "Um, John . . . have you seen Lizzie?"

You might, perhaps, have expected me to tell you now what had become of Miss Bickle. As accustomed as you must now be after two volumes (you did read the first one? Yes?) of my brilliantly observed and artfully constructed narration, you must have the expectation that I would have flitted across nine worlds and located the good lady in order that I might assure my readers that she would do nothing entertaining without its being relayed to them.

Alas, even I have my limits. And Miss Bickle, it seemed most likely, was already within the court of Titania. And there I go only when sorely pressed.

Of course, I am writing this novel in retrospect, so I *could* tell you where precisely she had gone and how, when, and if she returned to the mortal world. But I choose not to.

Instead we follow Mr. Caesar, Captain James, and the Irregulars as they make their way across Hampstead Heath to their appointed meeting place. And having followed them, we watch them standing around waiting in the cold and the dark. I confess that I, too, am disappointed, but when one is setting up a magical working, one needs to consider all manner of logistical elements that do, in fact, take time to arrange.

I mean, I say *needs to.* But actually I would heartily recommend winging it. After all, what could possibly go wrong?

After longer than I would have liked but approximately as long as was expected, Barryson arrived in company with two men of unsavoury demeanour, the elder leading a brown draft horse that looked two days off from the knacker's yard and the younger dragging a boar that looked rather more energetic.

"And who are these?" asked Mr. Caesar, not welcoming the intrusion.

The older of the two men smiled and stuck out a hand, which Mr. Caesar shook out of sheer social inertia. "Jim Cooper," the stranger said. "Butcher, slaughterer, and victimarius. Think of Cooper's for all your sacrificial needs. The lad's my apprentice and won't be no bother. You got your own knife"—he drew a long, brutal-looking blade from his belt—"or do you want to use mine?"

Mr. Caesar winced. "Could somebody else not do it?"

"She's your sister," Barryson pointed out. "You don't want the gods thinking you're afraid to get your hands dirty."

As it happened, Mr. Caesar was, in fact, afraid to get his hands dirty. After all, for most of his life he had moved in circles where getting your hands dirty was punishable by immediate expulsion. But those circles held less power over him than once they had and besides, he owed his sister a little fear. He just thanked the fates that his costume hadn't included expensive gloves.

"This pair for the gods of the north?" asked Cooper, indicating the animals.

Barryson nodded.

With the appraising eye of a professional, Cooper looked at the beasts, then the landscape, then back at the beasts. "Reckon them two trees'll take the weight."

"What weight?" asked Mr. Caesar, whose evening was spiralling from disaster to pure gothic horror.

"The bodies," explained Barryson. "The gods'll want them hung from the trees for a bit. We could just let 'em choke out without the knife-work, but then they thrash something awful."

This was starting to go too far for Mr. Caesar. "I am not leaving two dead farm animals hanging from trees in a public woodland. It's unseemly."

"Don't worry about it, mate." Cooper waved Mr. Caesar's concerns off with a morbid cheeriness. "We won't leave 'em to rot, that'd be a waste of good meat. Once the gods've had their share me and the lad'll take 'em down, stick 'em on the cart"—he pointed down the hill to the little path where, sure enough, a cart was waiting—"and they'll be sausages by lunchtime."

With a fatalistic suspicion that he already knew the answer, Mr. Caesar asked, "Who's going to buy horse sausages?"

"The unsuspecting," replied Jackson.

Privately vowing never to eat a sausage again, Mr. Caesar turned quickly to Barryson. "Let's get this over with. What do I actually have to do?"

Wordlessly, Barryson nodded to Cooper and his apprentice, who led the sacrifices each to their separate tree. When both were in place, the attendants binding their back legs with long ropes, Barryson called on the men to gather around the horse and place their hands on it. The places either side of the head, Mr. Caesar noted, were reserved for him and the captain.

"Freyr, Lord of Alfheimr," Barryson intoned from his position at the rear of the horse, "bountiful one, take this offering and, y'know, just let us in because we've got a job to do and time's wasting."

It did not, to Mr. Caesar's ears, seem an especially respectful way to address a deity, but he took it as his cue to act.

Which he would do. Any moment now.

Gently, Captain James closed his fingers over Mr. Caesar's and held his gaze steady. "You can do this, John. Strike hard and strike true."

So Mr. Caesar struck. With Captain James guiding him he cut stronger and deeper than he might have otherwise, but it was still a messy blow and the horse bucked wildly. Then the victimarii hauled on their ropes and, with the assistance of Callaghan and Sal, raised the unfortunate creature into the branches where its blood continued to stream down onto anybody who wasn't quick enough to get out of the way. And also onto Barryson, who seemed to be deliberately trying to catch it in his bare hands.

Once he'd bloodied himself enough, Barryson paced between the two trees and smeared the bark of each with horse blood before bringing the group to the boar and repeating the same ritual.

"I"—Mr. Caesar's voice quavered—"I think I should do this one alone."

Captain James stepped back. "You sure?"

Once again, Mr. Caesar chose honesty. "No. But I think— Barryson, it's . . . it means more, doesn't it? If you do it yourself. It's more likely to . . . work?"

And, much as Mr. Caesar hoped he wouldn't, Barryson nodded.

In his mind, Mr. Caesar had been carefully telling himself that it would be easier this time. That the boar was smaller, and a smaller animal would *obviously* be easier to stab forcefully in the throat.

He should have remembered that he knew nothing about livestock.

Smaller it may have been, but it was angrier, stronger, its hide tougher and its throat harder to find. A gentleman, Mr. Caesar was at once sure, would never dream of performing such an action unaided.

But a soldier would. A brother would. His cousin, come to think of it, had. And so he struck.

The beast struggled forcefully, wrenching the knife and his wrist both, and tossing its head in a way that Mr. Caesar would insist for all of the next eight minutes had cracked one of his ribs.

But it died. And the offering was accepted. And once more the beast was hoisted into the tree, and once more Barryson soaked his hands in the blood, mingled it with the blood of the horse, and then, when he was satisfied with his preparations, stood in the space between the trees and said in a loud, clear voice: "I'm waiting, Freyr. I stand before you with blood on my hands and blood in my hair and ask passage. Now open the *fucking* door."

And to Mr. Caesar's sincere surprise, he did.

Between the hanging corpses of the horse and the boar, the air swam and mist rolled in and then away to reveal a path lit by a very different moon.

Barryson turned to his companions in triumph. "Gentlemen, shall we go?"

The men fell in and, cautiously, Captain James in the lead, they stepped through into fairyland.

CHAPTER TWENTY-TWO

ONCE MORE I TOOK THE shape of a songbird, for in my native land I am not invisible, even to mortals. Fortuitously, Titania's kingdom (which is also Alfheimr, which is also several other worlds known by several other names; reality is a jewel of which you mortals see only facets) is densely wooded and the path on which the company now walked was lined by black-and-silver trees, bare-branched and beckoning. So I perched myself amongst the thorns and watched.

Sensibly, the Irregulars and their aristocratic associate proceeded through the woods as though the trees themselves were self-aware beings of limitless malice. And while they were, in this instance, incorrect (the malice of the trees was, in the strictest sense, limited), it was a very reasonable precaution.

The colour scheme of this particular end of Titania's realm being distinctly monochrome, anything that fell out of its distinct silver-grey spectrum stood out some way, and so it was for the flash—caught through the trees—of golden hair just off the path.

"Look lively"—this was Callaghan—"that might be the Bickle girl."

"Or it might be a trap," warned Jackson, though he fell into position regardless.

"Do we actually have any weapons with us?" asked Mr. Caesar. "I for one did not go armed to a costume party."

Around him, the Irregulars demonstrated all the various ways they had violated this basic precept of masquerade etiquette, from the simple expedient of incorporating a sword into their outfit to more complex arrangements of knives in boots and pistols in concealed pockets.

"Clearly a foolish question," Mr. Caesar conceded.

At a silent command from Captain James the unit, with Mr. Caesar bringing up a decidedly ununitary rear, crept through the otherworldly woodland towards the entity that might have been Miss Bickle.

"Careful," whispered Barryson. "Some of the things in this place are shape-changers."

That, of course, was slander.

As the Irregulars crept forwards they saw that the shape in the distance was indeed Miss Bickle, or looked like her (and therefore definitely was; if you are ever lost in fairyland the first and most important piece of advice I can give you is to trust absolutely *every-thing* you see). And she was in what to any other mortal would be distress, slender creatures of split bark and dead sap inching ever closer to her, grasping hands extended.

"Are you dryads?" she was asking. "I have always yearned to meet a dryad."

They were not, strictly speaking, dryads. Dryads are a species of nymph and so tend to adopt more pleasing aspects in order to better tempt mortals to leave them offerings. These beings were something slightly other, fairy-folk making a game of being trees.

And our games seldom end well for humans.

I flitted to a nearer branch in the hope of seeing better and, as I encroached, I noticed something else moving amidst the treetops. Not a bird but a winged woman, a sly and nimble figure with steel at her fingertips.

The not-dryads, to nobody's surprise but Miss Bickle's, made no response to her enquiry. Instead they drew closer, until their spindled twig-hands clutched at her bodice and their jaws lolled open to reveal thick, vine-like tongues.

"Could still be a trap," said Jackson.

To which Sal nodded and pointed into the canopy, where the steel-fingered woman was waiting. "Seems like."

"But if it *is* Lizzie," Mr. Caesar replied, whispering less naturally than the others owing to a marked lack of relative practice, "we can't just leave her."

Kumar looked apprehensive. "We *can*," he said. "But I agree it would be a trifle unsporting."

While this debate was, if not raging, then at least gathering impetus, the steel-fingered woman swooped, and Miss Bickle looked up at once startled and delighted.

"Leave this one," the steel-fingered woman said. "She interests me."

The wood-things turned hollow eyes to her and made sounds like dry brush cracking underfoot.

"That is no concern of yours," the steel-fingered woman replied.

The creatures crackled back, but withdrew despite their objection. I should say, readers, that I am of course fully able to comprehend the speech of the wood-things, but I endeavour to give you the experience of witnessing these events through limited mortal perspectives, not my own.

Miss Bickle gazed at the steel-fingered woman with a sort of general gratitude that I was certain had no basis in any sense of her own mortality. "Thank you," she said, "but I am sure they did not mean me harm."

"They did."

Never one to let go of her good opinion of terrible things, Miss Bickle brushed the comment off. "I find that very hard to believe."

"Duly noted."

"For all I know," Miss Bickle continued, "*you* mean me harm."

"Perhaps I do." The steel-fingered woman reached out a hand and traced a single knife-edged talon along Miss Bickle's cheek. "You would do well to treat me as if I do."

Miss Bickle shuddered. "If you intend to seduce me, you should know that I have firmly established that dallying with ladies is not to my tastes."

Of all the responses the steel-fingered woman had been expecting, that was none. "You are a peculiar creature."

"People keep telling me that. I think they just lack imagination."

The character of the exchange was not absolute proof that Miss Bickle really was herself rather than a shape-shifting imposter, but to Mr. Caesar at least she sounded so familiar that it seemed worth the risk.

And the captain concurred. The Irregulars fanned out into flanking positions and then, once there were at least one or two pistols trained on the newcomer, he approached. "And what do you want with the lady?"

The steel-fingered woman turned her head towards the captain, leaving the rest of her body eerily still. "What do you want in this place?"

"Rescue mission."

"Noble, but foolish. As for what I want, I have questions."

While Captain James had the attention of the steel-fingered woman, Mr. Caesar took the opportunity to sidle around towards Miss Bickle. "Lizzie," he stage-whispered, "walk towards me, slowly."

It had been a valiant effort, but a doomed one. "And what will that achieve?" asked the steel-fingered woman, her gaze lighthousing around to fall on Mr. Caesar. "Were I any danger to the child, I assure you distance would not ameliorate it."

"Perhaps not," agreed Captain James. "But I've armed men with me, and a sorcerer amongst them. I fancy we've a fairer chance than you think."

The steel-fingered woman twitched her beaten-copper wings. "Do you now?"

"Perhaps," ventured Miss Bickle, "I could simply answer her questions?"

"That *would* be simplest all round," the steel-fingered woman agreed.

Mr. Caesar did not appear convinced. "She's a fairy. You can't trust them."

"Actually," the steel-fingered woman replied, "I'm as human as you. Or perhaps more pertinently as human as your sister."

The response silenced Mr. Caesar momentarily, but Captain James stepped, as he was so often wont to do, into the breach. "What do you know about Miss Mary?"

"What say you answer my questions first, and then I consider yours?"

"What say," replied the captain, "we answer your questions first and then you *answer* ours?"

The steel-fingered woman drummed her claws together with a

faint rattling sound. "That seems a bad deal. I know much more than you do."

"Then we'll take our friend and go."

Whether by instinct or experience, Captain James had played his hand well. My people—and those mortals who live long amongst us—are insatiably curious beings, and we will agree to all manner of inadvisable things if the alternative is to let something go unknown. "Why was I being followed?" the steel-fingered woman asked.

"No idea," replied the captain. "Is that all you wanted to ask?"

Miss Bickle, who was less cautious about such things and so less inclined to keep to the letter of a bargain, tried to be helpful. "Perhaps we might be able to tell you more if you explain who was following you. And perhaps also when they were following you and maybe what exactly you're talking about."

"A girl," the steel-fingered woman explained. "Slender, pretty, dressed as Arachne. She was . . . hovering the whole ball but never actually approached me."

"That was Maelys," Mr. Caesar explained. "My cousin. Whatever she was doing I assure you she meant no harm."

The steel-fingered woman glared. "You will learn that such assurances mean little here. Tell me who she *is*."

Although not wholly without empathy, Mr. Caesar was finding himself at something of a loss to think his way into the mindset of a metallically augmented woman who had lived for an unknowable duration in the midst of an inhuman court. "She is the lady who achieved a little notoriety last year as a consequence of a curse levied by Sulis Minerva?" he offered. "And presently she is a close friend and associate of the Duke of Annadale."

"The Duke of Annadale," the steel-fingered woman replied, "is dead. That much I know well."

Mr. Caesar internally reprimanded himself. He had tried to stop using the nickname for Miss Mitchelmore's sake. "Of Lady Georgiana Landrake," he clarified.

The steel-fingered woman blinked once. Her eyes, like her fingernails, were brushed steel, bright but cold. "Neither name means anything to me." This, like so much else in the world, was a lie. "But you have answered, and so I shall return the favour."

Captain James gave a sharp, no-nonsense nod. "Good, where's the girl?"

"With the queen, in the Dancing Hall."

"Which is where?" asked the captain.

They had answered one question and had a single answer in response. Nobody in Titania's court would have counted it at all amiss if the steel-fingered woman had considered the debt paid and taken off on her wings.

But she did not.

"Follow me."

To my surprise, they did. To my still greater surprise, I did also. And to my greatest surprise of all, it did not turn out to be a trap.

Despite her wings, the steel-fingered woman kept to a pace that the Irregulars, Miss Bickle, and Mr. Caesar could easily match, and led them through the hazards of Titania's land with remarkable good faith. Frankly it was enough to make any native of the fairy realm suspicious, because we as a rule *never* treat so straightforwardly. Of course, the steel-fingered woman was human by birth and so she perhaps had human frailties still holding her back.

The Dancing Hall was located in the beautiful, impossible palace at the heart of the realm. From the angle at which the Irregulars approached—for the palace, like most everything in the Other Court, varies dramatically depending on how you reach it—the building was a cascade of delicate spires, as though a rainstorm had been frozen in time and built by some artful magic into a dwelling-place. And for all I know that was exactly what had happened. Titania would certainly have been capable of such things.

Although she had been more helpful than was strictly *necessary*, the steel-fingered woman had not wholly abandoned the instincts that had let her survive the past decade or so in the Other Court. So she did not *enter* the palace, but she led the party as close to it as she could manage. "There"—she pointed at a silver-white archway leading into the halls themselves—"take only right turns, follow the sound of music, and when somebody tells you to leave, do what they say."

"Are you *sure* about that?" asked Mr. Caesar. "It doesn't sound entirely . . . intuitive."

Captain James seemed inclined to agree. "You've been helpful, but if you're trying to fuck us at the last minute—"

"Oh *no*." Miss Bickle rallied at once to the steel-fingered woman's defence on the basis of no evidence. "These are *exactly* the kinds of instructions that one must follow in this sort of place. I expect, for example, that some way into the castle we will encounter a passage with only a left turn, and we will be required to walk down it backwards. Or else there will be a junction and there will be the sound of music coming from the left passage and we will be required to turn right through"—she made a brief, not entirely silent calculation on her fingers—"four hundred and twenty degrees in order to find ourselves facing in the right direction."

"Are you sure, lass?" asked Callaghan. "Because if you ask me that sounds a whole hell of a lot like bollocks."

Begrudgingly, Mr. Caesar gave his friend his support. "Actually, from personal experience, it really does seem to work like that."

"One can't help wishing," Kumar mused aloud, "that it felt a little more magical, and a little less asinine."

Barryson shrugged. "That's the thing about magic, it doesn't give a shit what you think of it."

Suspecting that the shape of a songbird would be too conspicuous once the merry band of mortals was wandering lost through the halls of Titania's palace, I became a spider and lowered myself into Miss Bickle's hair, reasoning that of all those present she was the least likely to object to my presence. She was shorter than most of the company, which meant my view was a little limited. But she moved about with such fleetness that I was afforded a range of angles from which to watch a band of grown men failing to follow basic instructions.

"She said *only* right turns," Sal was explaining the first time the path branched—a sheer marble corridor to the right, a hall lined with strange geometries ahead, "not *every* right turn. We can still go straight on."

"The music's coming from the right," replied Callaghan.

"It's not, you've just let off one too many muskets near your ears."

Captain James, speaking as mellowly as he could given the situation, moved to intervene. "Everybody just be quiet. Give us a moment and we'll listen carefully."

"Does that sound even qualify as music?" asked Kumar. "It's more of a hum."

"Which part of quiet didn't I make clear?"

After a few moments' listening they decided that yes, the slight hum did count as music but that no, it wasn't coming from the right and that therefore yes, Sal had been correct that only right turns did not mean every right turn and so they should go straight ahead.

Miss Bickle spun 360 degrees to her right anyway, which I found a little disorienting, but when she was done we kept good pace with the group.

Ahead, as Miss Bickle had predicted, they were indeed faced with a pure left turn, which they did indeed navigate by walking backwards, although Jackson did make a point of reminding them that it might just have meant they'd gone the wrong way.

"So what would happen," wondered Callaghan aloud, "if we walked this corridor forwards?"

"Maybe nothing," Barryson replied. "Or maybe we get our skins ripped off by things with knives for faces. Want to give it a try?"

To my disappointment, nobody did.

At the end of the corridor in question they found themselves at a T-junction, and the question of whether they needed to turn right as they were *facing* or right as they were *walking* came to occupy them for several minutes.

"It seems terribly unjust," said Kumar to nobody in particular, "that something this undignified should have such a high chance of killing us."

Mr. Caesar nodded grim approval. "Ever since I have become familiar with magic I've come to dread the thought of dying a farcical death. And Orestes"—the captain had looked as though he was about to say something—"don't you dare tell us that all war is farce because while I admit I have never served my country, I doubt you have ever done anything as undignified as walking backwards through an enemy stronghold in fancy dress."

"Yeah, fair point," the captain conceded.

"Though we've come close a few times," added Sal. "We've done some fucking ludicrous things down the years."

The Irregulars all agreed to this, just as they all eventually agreed that they needed to turn right as they were *facing* in this instance.

As they crept further into the palace, down passages made of rough stone or living wood and through doorways curtained with a thousand moths, the thought occurred to several of the company that they had thus far seen nobody in their travels. Although whether this meant that things were going very well or very ill they could not say.

Two turnings and a bridge across a river of wine later, the party came at last upon the first living thing they had encountered. Well, the first living thing save for your humble narrator, who was still perched unnoticed atop Miss Bickle's head.

The thing in question was wearing human shape, or human-like shape, although its fingers had an extra joint, and when it spoke an astute observer would note that it had a second row of needle-sharp teeth set just behind the first. For reasons best known to Titania and her servants, it was wearing the uniform of the Coldstream Regiment and bearing a musket tipped with a green glass bayonet.

"Halt," he demanded, "who goes there."

For so many reasons, dealing with this new eventuality fell to the captain. "Orestes James," he said with military formality, "Captain, Third Foot Guards."

"Leave," said the creature, its voice oddly thin and its eyes oddly gleaming, "or be run through."

Captain James cast a look over his shoulder at his men, and at Mr. Caesar. "Then I guess I'll be run through."

The creature struck. The bayonet, sharp in that deceptive fragmenting way that only glass can be, bit into Captain James's breast. And then the blade shattered, and the creature shattered, and the world shattered.

As I said. She's showy.

It said something—not necessarily something good or something bad, but something distinctly notable—about Mr. Caesar's priorities that as reality tumbled in fragments around him he ran first and fastest to the side of Captain James, who staggered into his arms from shock.

The uniformed creature was gone, as was the corridor, and in their place was the Dancing Hall. Contrary to the sometimes whimsical naming conventions of my species it was not a hall that itself danced (we have those also, but they go by different names). It was a wide, gilded space and it was filled with dancers, each alone, each glass, each a mortal who had bargained for the Beauty Incomparable.

And they were beautiful by any objective standard, exquisitely crafted and delicately detailed. The light shone through and in and off of their bodies, and even in their imperfections—the places in which they had cracked or splintered, or where they were missing fingers or in some cases whole limbs—they possessed a kind of chaotic wonder.

They were each and every one of them masked, and they danced a perpetual spiral for the pleasure of the Queen of Elsewhere.

The queen, I should add, was very much present, enthroned on a dais at one end of the hall. Her seat was wrought of silver mined by spirits of the deep earth, her gown was sewn from moonbeams by pixies with deft needles, her crown had been spun from gold and gossamer by the finest goblin-smiths. And she watched now with detached beneficence.

Still bleeding from a wound above his heart, but active and alert for all of that, Captain James steadied himself, although Mr. Caesar continued to stand close in case he should stumble again.

Keeping his eyes on the queen, he spoke to his men. "Fan out. Find the girl."

The Irregulars needed no further instruction, although the process proved more taxing than they had expected. The dancers did not deign to stop for identification, many of them were sharp at the edges, and, en masse, they were nigh impossible to distinguish from one another.

While the gentlemen in the group were searching the crowd for one flawless masked dancer amongst a hundred, Miss Bickle walked slowly but purposefully towards the throne, carrying me with her.

Since I was technically a spy from a rival court, I was not wholly comfortable at being drawn so close to the Queen of Sun and Storms. In theory, chroniclers such as myself enjoy certain privileges much as mortal diplomats might, but in practice our rulers, like yours, can be a little testy. Reasoning that my best hope lay in openness, I took the shape of a fly, left Miss Bickle's hair, then became a bird once more and alighted on the queen's hand.

She glanced down at me. "Ill met by moonlight, emissary."

I trilled my own greeting and let her return her attention to Miss Bickle.

"Approach, child." Titania's voice was fire in winter and rain in summer.

With more caution than she normally displayed, but still less than the situation warranted, Miss Bickle approached. "If it please your majesty," she said with a pretty curtsey, "I am looking for my friend."

"Your friend is where she wishes to be." Titania's voice was promises and secrets and two truths and a lie.

"I don't think she is," Miss Bickle hazarded. "She seemed quite adamant at the ball."

Titania smiled. "Girls are fickle."

A contemplative expression crossed Miss Bickle's face and her brow furrowed sceptically. "I'm not sure that's true. My friend Miss Mitchelmore, for example, has always been quite devoted to her family and to her lover, and I account myself extremely constant in my affections. My affection for the anonymous lady author of *Sense and Sensibility*, for example, is abiding and—"

"Nonetheless," Titania interrupted. As Queen of the Other Court she was not accustomed to people, especially mortals, speaking at such length to her. "She may leave whenever she wishes."

"And she is definitely *here*," Miss Bickle persisted—and this was a good question, one that many mortals would have forgotten to ask. "In this room?"

The smile had never left Titania's lips, but now it broadened just a fraction. "Oh yes."

"And she isn't the room itself? Or otherwise transformed in any way? She still appears as she did when we last saw her?"

We do not, as a rule, like it when mortals are exhaustive in their questioning. But the Queen of Both Evers gave a slow, grudging nod. "She does."

Miss Bickle turned to look out over the dance floor, where Mr. Caesar and the Irregulars were searching every dancer and getting precisely nowhere. There was, she felt certain, a solution. The queen herself, after all, had told her that Miss Caesar was in the room, and this was not the kind of thing she would lie about.

She looked up.

Suspended from the ceiling, impossibly high above the ground, was a silver hoop twined with white flowers, and reclining, impossibly balanced, within that hoop was a figure. From this distance and at this angle it was impossible to know who that figure *was*, but Miss Bickle had a strong sense of narrative fitness, and in this place narrative fitness was a surer law than gravity.

"John," she called across the hall, "I think it very likely that she's up *there*."

Mr. Caesar, Captain James, and the rest of the Irregulars stopped and stared upwards. And as they did, the dancers—responding to some imperceptible signal—moved into a wide circle with the suspended figure at the exact centre. From everywhere and nowhere, violins played a sweeping crescendo, and the silver hoop, along with its occupant, descended to the floor.

Even up close, Mr. Caesar could not quite tell if it was his sister. She was still masked, still dressed in the same incongruously flowing glass as everybody else. The only real clue as to her identity was the pattern of fissures that spread across her legs and arms, which seemed familiar but not conclusive.

"Mary?" he tried.

And the girl in the hoop turned to look at him.

"Mary, are you well? Are you yourself?"

Slowly, she slid herself out of the hoop, stood, but said nothing.

"Mary?"

"John?" The answer came soft and uncertain.

"We need to get out of here."

From the dais, Titania gazed down with emotionless grace. "You do not *need* to do anything. The child came here for a reason."

"You came here," Mr. Caesar reminded her, "because you did not want this. You've gone your whole life ignoring me for—now I look back—very good reasons. *Please*, Mary, ignore her as well."

Somewhere in the recesses of her mind—and a mind she still had, that being an immaterial thing not transmutable by our magics—Miss Caesar tried to remember. "I came for redress."

"And do you still feel you need it?" asked the Queen of All Seasons, innocent as summer.

Only silence answered.

"This might be out of turn," said Captain James, moving to Mr. Caesar's side. His hand, I could not help but notice, was resting lightly on the hilt of the cuirassier's sword. "But it don't seem to me like the lady's in much of a place to make decisions."

"Because the decisions she makes may not please you?" asked Titania. Her voice was a cool spring in a desert, virgin snow in a garden.

"Because she can't say two fucking words together."

"Perhaps she chooses not to." The queen's eyes were all compassion, or some beast pretending to be compassion. "I assure you I have placed her under no enchantment."

From just within the ring of dancers, Barryson spoke up. "Say that twice more."

"A little knowledge," the queen replied, "is a dangerous thing. But since you insist. I assure you I have placed her under no enchantment. I assure you I have placed her under no enchantment."

And that, reader, was entirely true. She was indeed giving them such assurances.

Mr. Caesar, taking care not to cut himself on the increasingly jagged and splintered roses, placed his hand on his sister's shoulder. "Mary, please."

As if in a dream, which in many ways she was, Miss Caesar looked at her surroundings. And like a dreamer she found herself hard-pressed to think of anything outside of the unreal present.

"You can stop this," Mr. Caesar told his sister, with a conviction born from desperation. "Whatever has happened to you, you can overcome." He took her hand. "I'm here, but I need you to be here too."

Behind her mask, Miss Caesar shut her eyes and tried.

"I am beginning to feel," the Queen of Promises said, "that you are wasting my time."

There was an irony to this, of course. If there was one thing that the Other Court did not have to worry about, it was time.

The music died away and Miss Caesar stood transfixed under the gaze of the Queen of Never and Always. And at last she said, voice near broken, "I have come for redress."

Titania nodded. "Then speak your case."

"I bargained for beauty."

"And you were given it."

Miss Caesar raised her fragmenting hand, almost as though seeing it for the first time. "This is not beauty."

Enthroned on silver and enrobed in starlight, the Queen of Light and Wonder leaned forwards. "The world disagrees."

"The world—" And at this she stumbled. The world, at least the world she had been wont to move in for most of her sixteen years, had always called her unworthy. Always overlooked her. Always dangled riches in front of her and then told her *not for you*. "The world . . ." she said again, "does not matter."

An edge of amusement was creeping into the queen's voice like a fox creeping into a nursery. "And who are you to speak so boldly?"

If my people have one weakness, it is that we cannot resist a challenge. And I might almost have believed that the queen was baiting the child to defy her. We so seldom taste defeat that it becomes a dish that some of us perversely savour.

For a long moment or a short age, Miss Caesar considered the question, and in the end gave the only response she could. "I am Mary Caesar."

Titania, however, was not impressed. "That is no answer at all."

"It is the only answer I can give. It is the only one I care for. I bargained for beauty, but you do not get to tell me whether I received it."

"Inconstant creature." The Queen of Twelve Winters spoke with a new contempt. As though she had hoped for more. "You were rewarded amply, and you took that reward freely."

"I no longer want it."

"Then," said the queen with a glimmer in her eye like a dying star, "you may give it back."

I thought, at first, that Miss Caesar's failure to respond at this juncture came because she was, in the depths of the heart she no longer had, still tempted by the power of the Beauty Incomparable. It was, after all, an objectively wondrous thing whose power she had barely begun to draw upon.

I thought incorrectly.

The mask that Miss Caesar now wore protruded just fractionally from the edges of her head, although since it was contiguous with the structure of her body this delineation was purely cosmetic. Still, it was enough for her to dig in her fingertips. And to pull.

It began with a sound like a finger on a wineglass, a high, keening noise that set teeth on edge and sent sympathetic vibrations resonating through the other dancers. Then came the cracking, the sound of glass in pain. A sharp, jagged fissure spread from Miss

Caesar's forehead to her chin and at last she screamed. Her voice began sharp and otherworldly, but as she pulled her tone softened and grew more natural, more human.

With a decisive snap, a long, wide shard of glass came away and beneath it was skin, fresh, deep brown, and living. On her hands as well, flakes and fragments were falling away, revealing mortal flesh, as weak as glass in its own way, but held together with sinew and hope and will.

Half-mortal now, Miss Caesar found that the glass cut as she pulled it away, blood running from her forehead and slicking her palms as she ripped herself free of that vitreous cocoon.

Looking back, in possession now of a physical body, I have more sympathy with the way that so many of the mortals present looked away. Even Miss Bickle, who ordinarily had a strong stomach for disquieting magic, averted her eyes as Miss Caesar's bloody work progressed from her face and throat and head to the rest of her body. Only her brother and the captain watched the entire transformation. I could not say why they did. Duty perhaps. Or love.

As she had torn and fought and bled, Miss Caesar had been walking slowly forwards until at last she stood at the foot of the dais, staring up at Titania with fury. Her gown was ragged where the glass had pierced it. Her skin was cut in a hundred places. Her hair curled free about her head, and her eyes blazed.

I could not help, in that moment, finding her just a little majestic. For a human.

"You gave me nothing," she said, "and I have returned it. You have no more hold over me."

The Queen of Here and Nowhere held Miss Caesar's gaze. "Pretty words. But suppose I were to keep you here. What would you do?"

"I am not alone."

Behind her, the Irregulars formed up into a slightly shabby rank.

"A half dozen human soldiers?" Titania's smile shifted once again, wry and unforgiving. "Do you truly think I fear swords or bullets?"

"I think," Miss Caesar said, "that I am not alone."

Captain James began drawing his sword, but Mr. Caesar checked him. At the four o'clock position of the circle, one of the dancers had raised her hands to her mask and was beginning to tear.

Titania froze. "These are *mine*."

"They are their own. As am I."

Once more the singing-glass sound filled the air.

"Stop this," demanded the Queen of Oaths and Figments.

Miss Caesar shook her head. "I cannot."

"Then begone."

And the world fell down.

Titania was a showy creature, but when pressed she could act quite decisively. No sooner had she told the mortals to leave than they had left, the court and the Dancing Hall and the glass women collapsing and Hampstead Heath reappearing between eyeblinks. Back in the mortal world at last, I perched inconspicuously on a tree branch and watched.

It came as some surprise to most of the assembly, although not to me or to Barryson, that the sacrifices were still bleeding and the victimarii still present. Jaunts to the Other Court took place on an unpredictable timeline, and those who encroached on the lands of my people could return to find that no time had passed at all, or that a century had gone by.

"Go all right?" asked Cooper, apparently as used to other-worldly comings and goings as I was myself.

Mr. Caesar looked at his bloody, bedraggled sister who, despite everything, still stood rather prouder than she had in recent weeks, and at his lover who, although he remained on his feet, was still bleeding from a deep cut to the chest. "All right," he confirmed.

"Don't suppose you want to give us a hand with the carcasses?"

Under other circumstances, the Irregulars at least might have agreed. Theirs was a culture of mucking in and helping out and their instinct was to be involved with anything that needed doing. But it had been a long evening, and they had an injured young woman with them. So they made their apologies and left, save Barryson, who could less afford to offend providers of sacrificial offerings.

As I watched them go, I saw a single star streak across the heavens and heard the chime of silver bells.

"I suppose," the Lady said beside me, "that you are rather pleased with how this has ended."

"If your queen chooses to collect the wrong mortals," I told her, "it is no concern of mine. My lord, on the other hand, will I am sure find this endlessly amusing."

The Lady gave me a cold look. "Your lord has had his own share of embarrassments."

Aghast, I pressed my fingertips to my breast and adopted an attitude of scandal. "Never *once*. As his chronicler, I would be sure to know of any."

"There will come a time," she warned me, "when you have to stop dining out on a chance acquaintance with an influential playwright."

"Perhaps." I shot her my most endearing smile. "But until then, you know what they say. History is won by the writers."

But sadly the witticism was lost on the Lady, who turned and vanished back into her mistress's realm. And our paths did not cross again for some while. Or for no while. Or they had already crossed.

Time does not mean for my people what it does for yours.

CHAPTER TWENTY-THREE

I EXPECTED NO FURTHER CHAOS THAT night. In retrospect this was foolish of me, for the circumstances required to *produce* chaos were well established. I can assume only that my time amongst mortals had made me grow complacent.

Whatever the reason for my casual attitude, it remained justified for a few hours at least. The little band of adventurers parted ways after leaving the heath, the bulk of the Irregulars returning to the Folly while the captain and Mr. Caesar escorted the newly organic Miss Caesar back home.

They arrived at the Caesar house in the small hours of the morning to find the entire family waiting up for them, even Miss Anne, who would often not have bothered.

Frustratingly, at least from my perspective, the reunion was almost entirely lacking in coherent speech. The Caesars expressed their joy at their daughter's devitrification through a round of cautious embraces, followed by an apologetic rousing of Nancy, who was charged with the necessary but somewhat arduous task of assisting her mistress with her many cuts.

"I am well enough, I assure you," Miss Caesar told her servant and parents both. "I know it looks"—she gazed down at herself—"rather ghastly, but truly it is good to *feel* again. I could not, you know, for so long. Nor have I slept. I should so like to *sleep.*"

"Not covered in blood you won't, miss," Nancy insisted. "It's me as'll have to clean the sheets after."

So at considerable effort from the sleep-deprived and long-suffering Nancy, a bath was drawn for Miss Caesar, and the rest of the household retired to their various bedchambers. I was about to follow the captain and Mr. Caesar when I noticed Miss Anne reaching her own room and then hesitating at the door, turning, and making for the room where her sister was bathing.

This I *had* to observe.

As I think I have explained many times over the course of these volumes, I have no interest in mortal bodies, and watching humans bathe is no more interesting to me than watching them walk. It is substantially less interesting than watching them die. But this seemed unusual, and I *do* like things that are unusual.

In the bathing room, Miss Caesar was wincing as Nancy tried to clean the most visible of her lacerations. When the door opened she whipped her head around with visible irritation.

"What do you want, Anne?"

Miss Anne paused in the doorway. "Just to see you."

"Well, you've seen me."

"To speak with you then."

Miss Caesar looked pained. "Whatever you have to say can surely wait until morning?"

"I wanted to say I've missed you."

"I've been right here," Miss Caesar replied, although even she knew that was a lie.

Miss Anne drew a stool across the room and sat by her sister's side. "You can miss a person who is present, I think."

Trailing her fingertips in the bath, Miss Caesar watched blood colour the water. "True. Perhaps I missed me too. Perhaps that's why I came back."

"Did it hurt?" asked Miss Anne.

"Being glass? Or not being?"

"Both?"

Miss Caesar frowned. "Yes. Still, I suppose it means you can have Mr. Bygrave now. It was never really me he wanted."

"I'm not sure it was ever really me he wanted either," replied Miss Anne, her eyes downcast. "Surely a gentleman who truly cared for me would not have had his head turned so easily."

A rueful smile disturbed Miss Caesar's lips. "There was magic involved. I do not think he can be held entirely accountable. But even if he does not come back, you will find other gentlemen. You are very beautiful, Anne."

Miss Anne nodded, uncertain. "The wrong sort of beautiful, I think. I do not believe I will grow into the kind of woman gentlemen marry. I saw the way they looked at you while you were"—she did not finish the sentence—"and I misliked how familiar it was. I do not think either of us wish to be baubles."

"You would rather we were old maids together?"

Still averting her gaze just the slightest amount, Miss Anne replied, "I can imagine worse fates."

I understand litotes, reader, I truly do, but to one of my kind, *I can think of worse fates* is seldom anything but a threat. We can, after all, think of so very many fates and they are most of them terrible beyond your comprehension.

"We could read to one another," Miss Caesar suggested. "And I could teach you to play pianoforte."

Miss Anne's demeanour shifted somewhat towards its natural "I *can* play pianoforte."

"Yes, but you play it very ill."

"I have changed my mind," Miss Anne declared. "I wish you to return to the fairies." It had been intended as lighthearted, but Miss Caesar tensed. And to her credit (at least by mortal standards), Miss Anne noticed. "Oh, Mary, I'm sorry. I didn't mean—that is, I really am glad to have you back. Truly."

Letting her fingers play a little in the water, Miss Caesar gave a soft smile. "I know you are. It's just—those words have more meaning for me than they used to."

"'I wish'?" asked her sister.

Miss Caesar nodded. It was a good lesson to learn, although I knew from experience that mortals seldom held to it entirely. Common phrases slip out so easily, and it can be such fun when they do.

Satisfied that I had heard all I could from the young women and only slightly disappointed that they appeared, for the moment, to have ceased quarrelling, I resumed my original intent and went to call on Mr. Caesar. Like Nancy, he was in the business of cleaning wounds; unlike Nancy, the wound he had to deal with was singular, long, and deep.

"It's fine," Captain James was insisting despite its being clearly not. "I've had worse from the French."

"You should see a doctor."

"Didn't need a doctor in Spain, don't need one now."

Acutely aware that he had no idea what he was doing, Mr. Caesar did his best to bind a dressing over the captain's wound, still deeply concerned at how much it was bleeding. "Are you not worried about infection?"

"Broad and shallow," Captain James replied. Which, yes, contradicts my narration, but who are you going to believe? An all-seeing fairy or a man who wishes to reassure his lover? "There's a reason we don't make bayonets from glass. It'll stay clean enough. Besides, I heal fast."

Not entirely convinced, Mr. Caesar finished the job as well as he could. When the captain lay down, he lay beside him, keeping a cautious distance but playing his fingertips over the man's arm. "Penny for your thoughts."

"Not sure they're worth that much," Captain James replied. "Not sure I'm thinking so much as . . ."

"So much as what?"

"Wondering."

That was no answer at all. "Wondering *what?*"

"Suppose it had gone worse."

"You mean suppose we'd lost somebody." Mr. Caesar's hand grew still and his mouth grew dry. "One of the men?"

Captain James nodded. "Yeah."

It would have been false to suggest that Mr. Caesar had never considered the possibility, but he didn't quite want to think it through to its end. "If you're asking whether I'd have thought it was worth it . . . whether I'd have traded one of your people for my sister."

"I think I might be asking exactly that."

"In a heartbeat," Mr. Caesar admitted. "I'm sorry, Orestes. I—whatever Jackson says, I would spare your men harm if I could—but we're talking about my *sister.*"

"And my brothers. Brothers I took into the fire for you."

Mr. Caesar shifted his weight, conscious all at once that they were, yet again, in his house, on his bed, on his terms. "You said you'd do the same for anyone."

"I would. But"—he shook his head—"I don't know. Sometimes I worry you've made me forget where I'm from."

Mr. Caesar looked over at the captain, who might still have been dressed as a fairy-tale prince but who looked, in his eyes at least, every inch the soldier. "I don't think there's much danger of that."

Raising a hand to his chest, Captain James traced the outline of his most recent wound. "You know what Reyne told me?"

"Does it matter? Whatever he said you stopped him. You kept Anne safe tonight."

"He told me it was for them. For the regiments."

"And you believed him?"

The captain was still looking grave. "He said one girl's life could save a company. And I'm not even sure he was wrong."

"You don't think he was wrong to want to *murder my sister*? Or me, for that matter."

There were some questions you absolutely did not want your lover to hesitate in answering and this was one of them. "I don't know," the captain said at last. "Maybe he's full of shit. But he sounded like he meant it and I—I knew *what* he meant."

"What did he mean?" asked Mr. Caesar, suddenly tense and more than a little concerned.

"I'm not a scholar," the captain evaded, "Kumar could probably put it in prettier words. I just know that when it comes down to it, when you're there, on the battlefield, and all you can smell is powder and all you can see is smoke and all you can hear is the shot and the cannon and the drums so they all wind up one sound in your head—when you're *there*, there's only one thing you're really fighting for."

Havering between alienation and empathy, Mr. Caesar wasn't quite sure what to say. "I assume you don't mean the king?"

"You fight for each other," said the captain, talking to nobody in particular now. "You've got no quarrel with Napoleon, not really.

In a different world you'd share a drink with a Frenchman without a second thought. But still you do your part because if you don't, another man'll have to do it for you. A man you've lived and marched and fought beside for a month or a year. And who might die because of you if you're not where you're meant to be and doing what you're meant to do."

The profession of arms had never called to Mr. Caesar and he had never once considered taking up a commission. And he would have gone to his grave never once regretting that choice were it not for how distant it made him feel in that moment.

"I'm not about to start slitting throats for Mars," the captain went on, not totally reassuringly. "But I can't shake the feeling that I chose your family over mine. And while Reyne's a shit, that's one line I'm sure he'll never cross."

Gently, so as not to disturb his wound, Mr. Caesar leaned over and kissed the captain on the forehead, then the cheek, then the lips. "I'm sorry," he whispered. "I'm grateful and I'm sorry and"—reaching down, he twined his fingers through the captain's—"I can't promise that I'll ever see the men the way you do. I don't think I ever could without living through what you've lived through. But please don't think I took what you did lightly. What any of you did."

I had seldom seen a man want to believe something as much as Captain James wanted to believe Mr. Caesar in that moment. And he *mostly* did. "Still," he said, "it's over now. And I've known plenty of men as felt different once the gunsmoke died down and they could go back to their old lives."

"My old life," replied Mr. Caesar, "was flitting from salon to salon, trying to out-poison people who despised me. I have no wish to return to it."

Captain James drew in a deep, slow breath. "You might change your mind. I'll always be a soldier, and running from war to war or waiting for a man to come back when he may never. That's—well, that's not much of anything."

In the candlelight, Mr. Caesar reached up to brush a hand across the captain's cheek. "This felt like something," he said. "This feels like—"

He got no further because a commotion from downstairs woke the whole household.

Sal and Jackson, both back in uniform, stood in the Caesars' parlour, each looking like rage in a red jacket.

"What's all this about?" asked Captain James, the elder Mr. Caesar, and Lady Mary simultaneously.

"You have *fucked* this," Jackson told the captain. "You have *proper* fucked this." Usually carefully mannered, his accent was slipping noticeably closer to the streets.

"Fucked what?" asked the captain. "And how?"

"Boy William didn't make it back to the Folly," explained Sal, the more composed of the two if only slightly.

The young Misses Caesar, still dressed for bed and so not at all in a seemly state to be seen by the soldiery, made their way into the parlour to discover what the matter was. Seized by a moment's caprice, I took on the shape of the dog Ferdinand and nuzzled myself against Miss Caesar's freshly human ankles.

"What's wrong?" asked Miss Anne, wide-eyed and timorous. "Did you say something had happened to William?"

Jackson rounded on her with a menace more properly reserved for bailiffs or professional criminals. "He's gone. What do you know?"

"Nothing." She quailed back, trembling, and Sal placed a hand on Jackson's arm to restrain him.

"Don't let him worry you, miss," Sal said as gently as he could manage. "But if you could tell us when you last saw him, it'd help."

Having no wish to subject her daughter to any more questioning, Lady Mary cut in. "He saw us home a little after midnight," she told the soldiers. "We asked if he wished to stay, but he said he should return to your . . . your inn. He said he would be missed else."

"He was fucking right," replied Jackson. "Did you see anything on the way back?"

"Any men in red?" added Captain James.

Lady Mary shook her head. "Nobody. Not that I saw."

"Nor I," added the elder Mr. Caesar. "I should not have let him go if I had thought it unsafe."

"At least tell me," said the captain in a voice that was practically a growl, "that he wasn't a virgin."

Miss Anne stiffened. "I'm not sure what that has to do with—"

"*Somebody*," Captain James went on, "must have thought to take him out and make a man of him." He glared at Sal.

"Firstly, Captain, you know as well as I do that fucking isn't what makes a man a man. Secondly, we'd considered it, but he didn't seem ready. And I agree with the lady, why does it matter?"

The younger Mr. Caesar moistened his lips. "It matters because if he's a virgin, they'll sacrifice him to Artemis."

A pall fell over the room.

"We're finding him," declared the captain. "Now."

"And how are we doing that?" asked Jackson. "That dog a tracker?" He nodded derisively in my direction.

The younger Mr. Caesar looked down at me. "Where did you get that animal exactly?"

"He was a gift from the Lady," Miss Caesar explained, looking appropriately sheepish. "I don't know why he hasn't gone."

"Then you can't trust him," warned Lady Mary. "Surely if there is one thing we have learned it is that nothing good comes from that place."

Mr. Caesar looked doubtful. "I fear it may be more complex than that, Mama. We received assistance in the Other Court, although why it was given I still do not know."

Gazing wistfully down at me, Miss Caesar sighed. "Oh, Ferdinand, Ferdinand, Ferdinand, I do so wish you could help us."

The words and the name snagged at my spirit like hooks, although any fisherman will tell you that a hook can bind both ways if you are not careful. I yapped once, capered to the centre of the floor, ran around chasing my tail for a moment, and then, aided by a wholly unnecessary swirl of crimson mist, I took on the shape of a fresh-faced youth in the attire of a page boy.

"My lady," I said with a smile, "I thought you would never ask."

CHAPTER TWENTY-FOUR

I AM ACCUSTOMED TO MORTAL AMAZEMENT, for I am quite exceptionally amazing, but even by my high standards the astonishment I engendered by my appearance was gratifying. It was even more gratifying that Sal and Jackson both drew pistols on me.

"Give me one reason I shouldn't shoot you," Jackson demanded in a tone that would have chilled me to my bones if I had bones, or could feel chill, or had been in any danger whatsoever.

"Because we both know it wouldn't stick," I told him. "Now"—I turned back to Miss Caesar—"you have two more wishes. And I do suggest you word them *carefully.* You don't want a repeat of your recent travails now, do you?"

"And what would you know about that?" asked Captain James. Like Jackson he had adopted a threatening tone, and unlike Jackson I wasn't totally convinced he couldn't hurt me. Certain mortals are gifted in these areas. It's the gods' way of regulating us and, I suppose, each other.

"Fairies gossip. Now, what about your second wish?"

Miss Caesar looked at me with an admirable wariness. "What about my first wish?"

"You wished that I could help you."

"But you didn't."

I tutted. "Dear me, child, did nobody ever teach you the difference between *can* and *will*?"

"That seems needlessly pettifogging," observed Lady Mary.

"Welcome to wishcraft. Your daughter may ask me for two more things, and when she does I am bound to give her *exactly* what she asks for."

"Just *don't*," the younger Mr. Caesar told her. "It isn't worth it."

Miss Anne, recovered from Jackson's interrogation, spoke up. "But if it helps us find William . . ." Tears were beginning to form in her eyes. "Whatever they plan to do to him they once planned to do to me."

"It's your choice, Mary," said the elder Mr. Caesar. "I would like to assist these people, but I will not ask you to put yourself in danger."

I sincerely hoped that the mortals weren't going to start being sensible. "A little word to the wise," I offered, "unless this delightful child can be certain she will never say the words *I wish* carelessly ever again for the rest of her life, I *highly* recommend she find some way to be useful now."

"And why should we believe you?" asked the younger Mr. Caesar.

"You shouldn't. Especially not when I'm telling the truth."

Miss Caesar turned—quite impertinently, I thought—away from me and towards her family. "Suppose I were to ask for him to take us to—"

"Not *us*," her father interrupted. "You aren't coming."

"What if we need another wish?" asked Miss Caesar, which from my perspective was an excellent point.

Jackson nodded. "She's right. No sense leaving the magic behind."

"We are leaving her," the elder Mr. Caesar insisted, "and that is final."

"Thought it was her choice," Sal pointed out.

On this, however, the elder Mr. Caesar remained firm. "Wishing is her choice. She's not racing after a gang of armed cultists."

"Time's wasting," Jackson complained. "If they've not cut his throat already they might while we're standing here arguing. Make the fucking wish."

Miss Anne didn't quite stamp her foot, but she rallied to her sister's defence anyway. "Don't rush her."

Sal lowered his head. "I'm sorry, sweet thing, but we may not have much time."

With a decisiveness that I hoped would spill into foolishness, Miss Caesar turned back to me. "I wish," she began, and what a promising beginning it was, "that you would guide all those people here—"

"And at the Folly," added the captain.

"—and at the Folly who want to rescue Boy William to wherever it is he's being held."

I bowed. "Done."

And then I disappeared. I had been commanded, after all, to guide two separate groups of people beginning at different locations to a single place the location of which I did not actually know.

Fortunately, as I believe I may have pointed out once or twice, I am exceptional.

I found Boy William himself quickly enough. There were only

one or two places in the city that one could appropriately make a sacrifice to Artemis, and it was not hard to check all of them.

It might have been slightly more difficult to guide the rescuers to the appropriate place before the boy was eaten by a bear, but that was not remotely my concern.

In order to actually guide the parties to their destination, I conjured each group a classic will-o'-the-wisp and hoped the mortals would have the wit to follow them. I will confess that it was not the *best* image to call up, given its association with being lured to a murky death in a swamp. But it seemed to work. The band at the house were already expecting something, while the ones at the Folly were at least somewhat willing to track a witch-light through the night on a hunch and a hope.

Because I am at *least* as skilled in my area of expertise as the Lady is in hers, the scheme worked perfectly. So perfectly, in fact, that both sets of mortals arrived at the exact same time despite leaving from radically different parts of the city. Of course, even if they had *not* arrived simultaneously and the closer party had been required to spend a half hour standing around bickering about whether this whole affair was a windup, I could simply have lied and told you otherwise.

But that, reader, would be quite beneath me.

I had led the rescue party to the gates of the Tower of London and when I appeared once more before them, I was getting some very suspicious looks.

"He's in there?" asked Captain James, only too willing to believe his ill fortune.

"I fear so," I told him. "But that should be no difficulty for such a fine body of men, surely."

The elder Mr. Caesar, who had been quite unwilling to be left behind, looked at Captain James, who still moved a little stiffly from the glass bayonet. "He is injured," he said. "And I am old, and my son takes too little exercise."

"Excuse me," the younger Mr. Caesar protested, "I walk quite regularly."

"Can you not just"—Callaghan waved his hands in a gesture indicating magic—"hop us over the walls?"

"I *can*," I told him. "I *choose* not to."

Captain James scowled. "Barryson, can you make this fucker be less of a fucker?"

"Sorry"—Barryson gave an apologetic grin—"don't know the right words. Everything's worse in the south, elves included."

Kumar rested his chin on two fingertips and pursed his lips contemplatively. "If the men in red really *are* in there then they must have got in somehow, and they might not have closed the door behind them."

"And they'll have left it unguarded?" asked the captain in his most expecting-the-negative tone.

"Guards," said Jackson, "we can deal with."

"What about bears?" asked Barryson.

The younger Mr. Caesar raised a hand in a just-a-moment gesture. "I don't believe anybody mentioned bears."

"As I see it," Barryson explained, "they'll be here for two reasons: because it's a symbolic place for a sacrifice, and because bears are sacred to Artemis and this is the only place in London you'll find one."

The elder Mr. Caesar began loading and priming a pistol that his son had never realised he owned. "It seems like we have a plan. Where do we think they went in?"

On this, Barryson was surprisingly certain. "Traitor's gate. Matches the symbolism, and they must've known we'd follow, and a water gate makes it a pisser to keep powder dry."

"And so resolved," I said, "our intrepid heroes set——"

"Sorry," asked Captain James, "what do you think you're doing?"

It was, I will confess, an embarrassing moment. "My apologies, I occasionally narrate mortal actions."

A look of realisation crossed Barryson's face. "Fuck, you're one of *those*."

"Excuse me, I object to the designation *one of.* I assure you I am quite unique. Having no time for such distractions," I said as I slid into mists and shadows and out of mortal sight, "Captain James took charge of matters."

"Right," he said, "let's go."

Sal and Jackson, handing over their muskets and pistols , slipped away from the rest of the group, moving with as much stealth as was possible for people dressed in bright red jackets and gleaming white breeches. As they approached the water gate they slipped from the shadows to the cut in silence and vanished beneath the surface. The rest of the Irregulars, along with the Caesars, hugged the line of the wall and waited. I, having the virtue of invisibility, did not.

There had been two guards posted to watch the traitor's gate. Each bore a rifle. Each had been charged with watching the waters to ensure nothing disturbed the sacrifice. And each was woefully unprepared for an attack from beneath by a seasoned murderer with a knife.

Two bodies vanished into the murk and a few minutes later Sal and Jackson reappeared with the message that the coast was clear.

So the Irregulars and the Misters Caesar slipped into the water, making certain to keep heads and powder and firearms above the surface. They emerged into the outer ward of the tower and progressed as quickly and as quietly as they could manage to the inner courtyard.

And there was Boy William, bound and kneeling in the shadow of the White Tower. Lieutenant Reyne stood beside him, robed but unmasked, his hood down and a blade in his hand. A little way off was Major Bloodworth, who watched the whole affair with a mix of disdain and impatience. A scattering of masked men stood around the little vignette; most carried muskets, some carried pistols. One was holding a bear on a chain and didn't look entirely like he knew what he was doing.

"Artemis," Lieutenant Reyne was incanting to the sky, "daughter of Zeus, slayer of wild beasts, you that spin the silver light at night, receive this sacrifice which we offer to you."

"Rush them?" suggested Callaghan. "Or one of us can probably put a bullet in his head."

The lieutenant's invocation continued. "We the British army and King George offer to you the pure blood that flows from a virgin's throat."

"Might miss," the captain replied.

"Grant our ships an untroubled journey. Grant that our—"

With a low murmur of *fuck it* Captain James strode out into the courtyard. "Here for my man, Reyne."

The lieutenant lowered his knife just a fraction. "It wouldn't have come to this if you'd let me take the girl."

"*Let* you?" sputtered the major. "You're an officer of the British army, you don't need permission from the likes of him."

Serene in the moonlight, Lieutenant Reyne turned his attention to the major. "You could have seized her yourself."

"I'm here to give orders," the major replied, "not to grab hold of silly chits."

"Afraid to get your hands dirty?" asked the captain.

The major's expression of contempt somehow managed to deepen, a process that took it from "utter" to "absolute." "How typical of your sort to mistake dignity for fear."

At the foot of the tower, the lieutenant's hand tightened on his blade, and he twisted Boy William's head back to expose his throat.

"I've men behind me," Captain James warned. "Do this and you won't walk away."

Neither Lieutenant Reyne's hand nor his voice wavered. "After everything I have done, do you really believe I am unfamiliar with sacrifice?"

I am scarcely a judge of these things, reader, for I am not—or at least was not at the time I made these observations—vulnerable to mortal weapons, but I could not help but feel that the advantage in this standoff lay all with the lieutenant. He had position, numbers, and a complete disregard for his own life and the lives of others. It was a winning combination.

But then even in so dire a circumstance, the unexpected can happen.

"We'll trade." The voice was not the captain's. It belonged to the younger Mr. Caesar, dashing forth from the shadows with an air of panicked heroism and addressing himself to the major directly. "You're not here for the gods, you're here because I made you angry. You want to cut a throat, cut mine."

"John," the captain said with affectionate weariness, "don't be such a fucking—"

"*Done*," said the major. "You"—he indicated one of the masked soldiers—"seize him."

The man did as commanded, but got only about halfway towards the younger Mr. Caesar before the elder, striding from the

increasingly empty hiding place of the Irregulars with pistol unerr-
ingly levelled, intercepted him. "Touch my son," he said with the
same level but authoritative tone that had made him so popular on
the speaking circuit, "and you will die."

All around the courtyard soldiers were raising muskets, but thus
far nobody had risked being the first to fire. And despite the major's
bargain Lieutenant Reyne had yet to set down his knife. "The sacrifice," he explained with the timeless patience that has, throughout history, characterised those shackled to incompetent superiors,
"must be a virgin, and that man *decidedly* is not."

The major sneered. "Really? Way I hear it he's never been with
a woman."

"In the eyes of Artemis, that is not the criterion."

And then, to my overwhelming joy, the major said: "Fuck
Artemis."

The bear growled.

"Major Bloodworth," pleaded Lieutenant Reyne, striking a
practised balance between entreaty and calm, "I strongly suggest
that you recant that. Quickly."

Strong suggestions, however, did not go over well with the
major. "Fuck Artemis," he repeated, "for a Grecian whore. I'm not
here to play your petty games, Reyne. I'm here to teach *that
man*"—he pointed an accusing finger at Mr. Caesar—"a lesson,
and I will do it with or without your pagan bitch goddess."

Readers, you know that I love chaos. And what happened next
I loved a great deal.

With a roar to shake rooftops, the bear—a vast American grizzly gifted to the king some years prior—broke free of its handler
and rushed to defend the honour of its patroness as only a six-
hundred-pound omnivore can. Several of the masked soldiers

attempted to stop it, but, having no tools at their disposal save notoriously inaccurate black powder weaponry, they succeeded only in
provoking a firefight.

The man who had been charged with apprehending the
younger Mr. Caesar moved to make good on his orders and progressed a full two paces before the elder Mr. Caesar made good on
his word and shot him full in the chest.

A volley of musket fire rang out from the Irregulars and then,
through the smoke, they charged with war cries and bayonets. Boy
William, hands tied, squirmed wormlike towards his companions,
but Lieutenant Reyne—abandoning his knife and drawing a
sword—reared above him like a praying mantis. This left me with
something of a dilemma. I so enjoy seeing mortals dismembered,
and now I needed to decide whether I watched a young boy get run
through with a blade or an old man get ripped apart by a bear.

I chose bear, and I was not disappointed. The major had never
insulted me personally, but he was such a *rude* gentleman and
watching King George's pet grizzly bear him—my apologies, the
pun in this case was truly unintentional—to the ground, clamp its
jaws around his head, and then bite with a pressure in the region
of a thousand pounds per square inch was eminently satisfying. Of
all the Hellenes, I have always had a quiet respect for Artemis.
Insult most gods and they will spin elaborate schemes of vengeance
involving falling in love with your own reflection or being transformed into a spider or having your whole city burned down by
men hiding inside a big wooden mammal. But sweet Artemis will
usually just fucking kill you.

The bloody matter of the bear had distracted me just long
enough that when I returned my attention to Boy William I
expected him to have been stabbed already. Which would not necessarily have been a total loss; he might still have wriggled in an

amusing fashion. But I had reckoned without the innate love of drama amongst almost all of the conflict's primary belligerents. So Lieutenant Reyne had felt it necessary to repeat his dedication to the goddess before he struck, which had permitted Captain James to intercept his blade just in time, which had in turn allowed the younger Mr. Caesar to dash towards the boy, seize his hand, and drag him to safety. Or at least to something resembling safety given that they were still, variously: surrounded by armed men who wanted them dead, under the watchful gaze of a bloodthirsty deity, and eight feet from an angry grizzly.

"I said things'd be different if we crossed paths again," said the captain in a matter-of-fact tone.

"They're certainly more wasteful." The lieutenant aimed a cut at Captain James's head, but the captain turned it aside easily. "How many of my men have you killed already?"

"As many as it took. You shouldn't have come for one of mine." The captain fought with untutored grace and a strength born of something purer than vengeance. He thrust clean at the lieutenant's throat, making him spring back.

With an almost piteous expression, Lieutenant Reyne shook his head. "If only you'd been a man of vision. We could have done remarkable things."

The lieutenant was keeping a cautious distance from Captain James, which I thought showed a rather unsporting commitment to self-preservation. He circled widdershins to put allies behind him. And, perhaps more important, to turn the captain's back to the bear.

An experienced swordsman, if an unpolished one, Captain James was keenly aware of the risks of being outflanked, but with the rest of his men engaged elsewhere there was little he could do about it. He risked a glance over his shoulder to make certain that he wasn't about to be torn apart by an enraged ursine, and in that moment of less than complete focus, Lieutenant Reyne was on him.

Watching from a scant few feet away with Boy William at his side, Mr. Caesar felt a deep swell of nausea. Despite all he'd been through, he still wasn't used to the sound of gunsmoke, nor the sounds of men screaming, and most certainly not the roars of wild beasts, and it was a mystery to him how the captain and the others could go so heedless into danger.

Biting his lip and trying to do something, anything, to feel less helpless and useless, he did his best to untie Boy William's hands, but he had never been good with knots. As it turned out, however, he was far better with knots than he was with bears.

The American grizzly, having had all it needed of the major, was returning to the fray guided by its hunger and the will of a goddess. It had avenged the insult to Artemis quite adequately, but there was still the matter of the sacrifice, of virgin blood offered up to the weaver of moonlight. And so it paced now towards Boy William with hunger in its eyes and a feral piety in its heart.

Barely able to move, Mr. Caesar had just the wherewithal to take two steps forwards and place himself between the beast and Boy William, although how much protection he expected his squishy mortal body to offer against the bulk of an apex predator I do not really know. Whatever his intended outcome, the tableau of the younger Mr. Caesar standing as tall as he could manage betwixt the boy and the bear was striking enough that it struck Captain James a fatal distraction.

Turning his eyes from his own enemy for just long enough to utter a frankly uninspired cry of "John," the captain was knocked at once to his knees by Lieutenant Reyne, too close to bring the point of his sword to bear but well placed to drive the pommel into the back of the captain's skull.

Whatever distress Mr. Caesar may have felt at watching his lover fall was swamped by the still greater distress of being charged by a third of a ton of fur, fangs, and flesh. With one hand he shoved Boy William backwards as far as he could while with the other he covered his eyes so that he would not need to look death in the face.

Thus he did not see the bear barrelling towards him, nor did he see Barryson charging past him in the opposite direction, his hair wild and his eyes wide and a war anthem of the old north on his lips.

On his own duelling ground in the shadow of the White Tower, Captain James had been equally expecting of death, but the lieutenant's blade had never fallen. Turning his head cautiously he saw what I had seen myself far better and far sooner: the lieutenant standing still, his hands raised, the elder Mr. Caesar behind him with a pistol.

"Put the sword down," he was saying, "and call off your men and your beast."

The beast was having more difficulty with Barryson than it had with the major—the initial charge had put a bayonet into its neck below the jawline and it was losing blood by the moment. But bears, dear reader, bears are large and strong. And courage will take a man only so far.

The lieutenant's command to stand down came as the first rays of dawn crested the battlements of the tower, as the bear fell, and as Barryson fell beneath it.

In the end the battle had been short-lived and with mercifully few casualties, one of them nonhuman. The major was gone, of course, and several of the men in red had suffered wounds that put their odds of survival into the realm of card turns and coin tosses. Sal had taken a shot to the arm and Callaghan a cut to the face, but otherwise the Irregulars emerged intact.

Save Barryson.

He was still alive when the captain and Mr. Caesar reached him, though his arm was mauled past using and his chest streamed blood from deep gouges. And Mr. Caesar mouthed a silent *thank you* while Captain James offered a louder and less civil "You stupid bastard."

Barryson laughed through blood. "Fancied a fur shirt," he said. And then he said nothing else.

What remained of this encounter was a tedious mixture of emotion and logistics. The sun having risen, a sacrifice to Artemis was now impossible and thus the Iphigenians had little to gain by further resistance. Captain James saw them rounded up and, after seriously entertaining the suggestions from Sal and Jackson that they just be gutted and dumped in the river, instructed his men to deliver them to the Mithraeum where they might face military justice. While the stronger, more martially inclined men were taking care of this matter, Boy William and the Misters Caesar took steps to disentangle the bear from Barryson's body and to arrange for a coroner to be called.

They made a melancholy scene, for though the Irregulars had seen a great deal of death, it is not something mortals ever truly grow accustomed to, at least not when it comes for their own. For the sake of his men, and perhaps for Mr. Caesar, the captain kept a bold face on matters for as long as there remained enemies to be watched over, but Callaghan and Kumar kept vigil over Barryson's body while the others worked, and offered what words they could for the departed. Even Sal and Jackson, who had the least aversion to blood of all the company, took solace in one another, stood side by side, their arms about each other's waists and their heads inclined together.

For my personal tastes, I must say it all got rather mawkish. I began to feel an increasing desire to leave them to it. Besides, I had one more loose end to deal with.

Miss Caesar was in her room, still not sleeping, although this state was at least now attributable to anxiety rather than her utter transfiguration into an inorganic substance. Not bothering with my dog's guise, I appeared to her as I had after her first wish, all dash and charm.

"It is not done," she said, "for a gentleman to be alone in a lady's room."

"I am not a gentleman," I told her.

"You are certainly no lady."

"Quite so. I am neither or both. I am birdsong and sunlight. I am a dream."

Miss Caesar gave me a look that, in a different era, in a different context, would have very clearly expressed that she was tired of my shit. "I am weary," she said, "and I would know if my brother and father are well."

"They are," I told her, quite truthfully. I never lie, readers. Never ever. "As are most of the men. And the sacrifice to Artemis was prevented"—I cocked my head in a quizzical gesture—"which I suppose means that your king's armies will be disadvantaged relative to those of Napoleon, but I'm sure that will have no wider consequences."

Perhaps it was her recent experience with the Other Court, but Miss Caesar seemed quite immune to my efforts to get, as you mortals might say, inside her head. "Then," she said, "you are here for my third wish."

"Quite so."

"And if I choose not to make one?"

"Then I will wait."

She nodded, understanding. "And if I ever utter the words at any time in the future, you will take whatever I say as opportunity to toy with me, as your friend did."

There is little mortals can say to us at which we will take true offence, but I could not stand for being called a friend of the Lady. That would be to deny my fealty to my lord Oberon, which is, of course, absolute and unfailing and wholly deserved by his great wisdom, majesty, and glory. "She is no friend of mine," I said without hesitation. "We serve different masters. But otherwise yes, you are correct."

"Then . . ." Miss Caesar looked down at herself. She looked, to my wholly inexpert eyes, rather lovely in that moment. Whole and mortal, her cuts already healing. "Then I wish you well."

I was uncertain that I had heard her correctly. "I am sorry, what do you mean precisely?"

"I didn't think what I meant mattered. Don't you just take my words and make whatever you will of them?"

"It is a little more complicated than that," I protested. Although not too strongly, because in candour it was not *very much* more complicated.

"Then I am sorry if I have made things difficult. But that is my wish: I wish you well. It is a mortal pleasantry, and the most harmless wish I could think to make."

This was growing vexing. I had no particular desire to ensnare the girl in a net of her own words and drag her through blood and darkness with it, but I would have liked the *option*. "You could have had wealth," I told her. "Long life, happiness, love."

She nodded her agreement. "I could. But I have learned the hard way not to wish for things I do not need, or that I already have."

"'I wish you well,'" I murmured. "You realise I can do nothing with that?"

"Might you not do whatever you want?" the lady ventured. "Albeit for yourself, rather than for me."

The thought galled me. I am a loyal servant of the Other Court, after all. I am a being defined by my function and my place and have never once harboured any secret desires for a different life. "You are a strange child, lady."

"And you are a very strange dog. But I think I am glad I met you."

I did not return the compliment. I said simply: "I wish you well," and permitted myself to fade from her sight.

CHAPTER TWENTY-FIVE

B ARRYSON'S FUNERAL WAS A FEW days later. It was to be a small affair, just the Irregulars, the Caesars, and a few people from the Folly.

He was a heathen, of course, and so was not to be laid to rest in a churchyard. The mourners gathered on a jetty jutting out onto the murky waters of the Thames and his body was laid in a cheap rowboat piled high with kindling, a musket laid beside him. A musket that technically remained the property of His Majesty's army but not a single person there gave a damn about His Majesty in that moment.

No priest was present—the faith of the old north was not popular in London and there was no time to bring a specialist from Newcastle, which meant the service such as it was fell to Captain James.

"I'm no man of God," the captain said, his back to the water and his eyes to the crowd. "Nor of any gods. Nor words, now I think of it. But I fought with Barryson five years and so there's that."

In the run-up to the event, Mr. Caesar had offered to help him prepare a more polished speech, as had Kumar, but he'd rejected their help. Not how it was done, he'd said.

"He told me once," the captain continued, "that his family went back to Ragnar Lodbrok, who I'd never heard of. But he said the name meant *hairy trousers*, and I thought that fit. And if his ancestors really did come from the north in long ships and burn Northumberland then, well, I reckon he went out in a way they'd be proud of."

There were murmurs of agreement from the Irregulars.

After a moment's reflection, the captain went on. "He was loyal. He was a laugh. He had my back. And most importantly, at the very end, he took the fucker with him."

This last phrase passed around the Irregulars like a chorus or a prayer. A low, sincere echo of *he took the fucker with him.*

Once the captain had finished speaking, the assembly took turns to say their personal farewells. When Miss Caesar and Miss Anne made to approach the boat, their father checked them.

"Best not to," he whispered. "He fought a bear and lost. You should not have to look."

Miss Caesar and Miss Anne exchanged glances, and then took one another's hand.

"I think," said Miss Caesar, her words less certain than her tone, "that we might have to, in fact. We are old enough to see terrible things."

The elder Mr. Caesar was not wholly convinced by this, but his wife laid a hand on his shoulder and nodded. So the sisters joined the line of mourners and approached the body.

A human corpse holds no horror for me personally. I am uncomfortably aware that you are all made of meat and mucus and so having that reality exposed to daylight in no way serves to heighten my disgust at corporeality. For mortals, however, things are different. And so it was that the Irregulars, in preparing Barryson's body for its send-off, had done their best to conceal the ways in which it had been mauled and mutilated by the beast he had reciprocally slain. A clean jacket had been fastened neatly over the wreckage of his chest, and his mangled arm had been severed from the few threads of sinew that were holding it in place, leaving a sleeve pinned smartly in place in a manner much reminiscent of the late Admiral Nelson.

Still, he was dead, and his body substantially less complete than when they had last seen it, so it remained something of a shock for the young ladies.

"I didn't really know you," Miss Caesar said to him—it seemed a poor opening but had the virtue of being an honest one. "But you helped me anyway. And I'm—"

"I'm sorry you're gone," Miss Anne filled in.

There didn't seem much else to say. Still, the girls lingered at the back of the line and thought, as all young things must do eventually, about death.

"If it pleases you, ladies," said Boy William, appearing at Miss Anne's elbow. "We're about to fire the boat. You might want to stand clear."

There were, in theory, ordinances against launching flaming barques onto the Thames, but in the opinions of all those there gathered, those laws could go fuck themselves. Captain James set sparks to the tinder—which in the absence of matches took slightly longer than was dramatic or decorous—and, when it caught at last, pushed the boat out into the water.

It was not, in the end, so very spectacular. Setting an inferno on water is difficult and unlike my own homeland, the physical laws of

your world give no weight to theme. The boat burned, but by daylight the fire was pale and it quickly grew small on the river. By the
mercy of whatever god was overseeing such things that day it did
not rain, but the sky was grey and around the little band of mourners the business of London went on quite as normal. You mortals
are insignificant things, and your deaths are insignificant. Especially when viewed from above.

Eventually, Barryson drifted out of sight, and the mourners
turned away. Mr. Caesar, however, kept watching until Captain
James laid a hand on his shoulder and drew him away.

"It's over, John."

"I know. I just—he saved me."

"He did what any of us would do. You stand where you can and
hold off what you can and hope whoever's behind you has better
luck. That day you had better luck."

A thought was niggling at the back of Mr. Caesar's mind. Well,
in fact, several thoughts were niggling at the back of his mind; this
was, after all, the first time he had attended the funeral of a man
he had personally watched die. "He had a sister," he said at last.
"He told me once. I'm not sure they got on, but will—that is, is she
going to be . . ."

"Where Barryson comes from," replied the captain, "sisters can
take care of themselves." His gaze landed for a moment on the
Misses Caesar, who were walking away with the crowd and speaking politely but appropriately with the soldiers. "As can yours, most
of the time. But the regiment'll see she's told what happened. She'll
know he died a Northman. And we'll not let her starve, if that's
ever a danger."

There was, Mr. Caesar reflected, much that was not right with
the world. Like, for example, the fact that a good man had been

eaten by a bear while attempting to prevent a murderous cult from performing a blood sacrifice to Artemis. But there was a rightness to *this*, to the captain and the Irregulars and the way they rallied to one another in a crisis. The way his family did the same. And the way that—when the captain was beside him—those things fit, however imperfectly, together. It had a sense of fragility still, *they* had a sense of fragility, that Mr. Caesar could not entirely trust. But, for the moment, if only for then, it made sense. It was enough. When so much wasn't.

The wake was held at the Folly, and Mistress Quickley, with typical wherewithal, was charmingly vague about who would end up being saddled with the bill for the drinks. The air filled with stories and with soldier's songs about leaving home and returning home and a certain amount about drinking, fucking, and killing.

In other circumstances, Mr. Caesar would have been concerned at his sisters hearing such things, but it seemed asinine after the events of the last few weeks to think they were in danger from unseemly words. Still, he kept a weather eye out for anybody who might be making untoward advances. As fond as he had grown of the Irregulars, they had not quite grown so close that he would trust them implicitly with a gentlewoman's virtue.

They—or at least Mr. Caesar and the captain—had entered a melancholy phase of the evening. The celebration of Barryson's life was winding down and the reality of his death was bubbling up in people's minds. Especially since the man responsible for the whole thing would, it seemed very likely, go back to his life with no consequences.

"We should've shot him there and then," Captain James said to his tankard. "Surrender or no surrender, and friends at court or no friends at court."

"You'd have regretted it." Mr. Caesar and sincerity were nodding acquaintances at best, but on this at least he felt oddly certain.

"I'd fucking not."

"You're a good man, Orestes. And as twisted as he might be, Reyne is a fellow soldier. He may have dishonoured himself, but you'd never dishonour him."

"Could have turned my back," the captain mused. "Let Jackson deal with it."

"Or Papa could have shot him." It was intended as a contribution, rather than a contradiction. "But he did not, because it would have been wrong."

"You think it's that simple?"

Mr. Caesar looked across the room to his father, who was engaged in an animated discussion with Callaghan about—he suspected—something political. "Honestly, I don't know. I like to think it is. For him."

"If you say so"—the captain shrugged—"I barely know the man, but from what I've seen he's not afraid of complicated."

Leaning back on his elbows, Mr. Caesar tilted his head back and stared despairingly at the ceiling. "Please don't. It's been a trying time and I don't think I'm ready to start thinking of my father as having layers just yet."

"You've seen him shoot a man, John. If that's not a layer, I don't know what is."

This was, Mr. Caesar had to admit, a fair comment, although it sat uncomfortably. His father had always been *there*, as immovable as you mortals think mountains. And given the choice between reexamining that assumption or changing the subject . . . "The men aren't too angry?"

Always a fast learner, the captain had grown accustomed to Mr. Caesar's segues, but was having trouble following this one. "About what?"

"One of you died because of me. Because of us. Because of everything between you and me and Mary and the Lady and the major and . . . all of it." It was a lot, when laid out like that, and Mr. Caesar was not quite sure what answer he was expecting.

The answer he got, however, was: "Nah."

"What do you mean *nah*? You can't just *nah* something like that."

Captain James took a swig of his beer. "Can and did. The men know right from right. You came through for us and they respect that."

"Even Jackson?"

The captain cast a wary eye across the bar to where Jackson and Sal were sitting in a corner deep in what can only be called cahoots. "Even him. He's a shit, but he's our shit. And he saw you put yourself in front of the boy."

"I don't think I even remember doing that."

"Doesn't matter." The captain kept watching as Sal and Jackson parted ways and went to find sport amongst the other guests. "He remembers. Got a long memory has our Jackson. Not saying you've got a friend for life, but you don't need to watch for glass in your food or knives in your back."

Mr. Caesar was about to say that he'd take his victories where he could, especially where Jackson was concerned, when the door to the Folly opened and a woman entered. She was tall, dark-skinned, and wearing a dress of cheap, fairy-woven cloth in shades of red and blue. Her hair was wound into a series of tight buns close to her head that looked, from any given angle, like a crown. Without her headdress and her ritual garb, it took Mr. Caesar a moment to place her.

"Amenirdis?"

She nodded.

Captain James looked up at her only *slightly* challenging. "Back to the old stomping grounds?"

"Paying my respects," she replied.

"Didn't know you knew him."

"I know *you*."

"It was good of you to come," Mr. Caesar told her. It wasn't entirely his place, but the division of labour between him and the captain gave him a certain amount of leeway in social situations. "I suspect Mary will want to see you."

Miss Caesar was sitting with her mother and sister, talking politely with Boy William, who seemed to have grown very attached to the ladies, and Kumar, who was taking advantage of slightly more refined company. When Amenirdis approached her, she rose, bid a courteous farewell to her companions, and went to speak with her.

"I feel I should thank you," she said. "Although I confess I am unsure what you actually did."

Although she was no longer dressed in the aspect of a priestess, Amenirdis gave a smile so enigmatic she may as well have been. "That is how the best magic works."

They sat down together in a corner of the Folly and Miss Caesar cast about for something appropriate to say.

"Do you miss it?" Amenirdis asked. She didn't need to say what *it* was.

Miss Caesar shook her head. "It's like you said. It wasn't really anything. A fairy trick. I just wish I hadn't caused so much trouble."

Laying a hand on Miss Caesar's arm, Amenirdis shook her head. "You did not. Trouble came to you. And it will come to you again."

A stillness fell over Miss Caesar and she felt momentarily cold. "That sounds like a prophecy."

"Just a guess. This is a hard world for a young woman."

They fell silent again, just a moment. And then Miss Caesar looked up. "Would you teach me—"

"No."

"You don't know what I was going to ask."

"The same thing everybody asks," said Amenirdis. "I am a witch. You want me to teach you witchcraft. I will not, it is a difficult life. I would rather you went on to be happy."

Miss Caesar smiled like she'd won a bet. "Actually, I was going to ask if you could teach me to do my hair like yours."

Ordinarily, witches are outwitted even less often than my kind, although when they are it is usually by children. At any rate the novelty was enough to make Amenirdis laugh. "Did you never learn?"

"Who would I have learned from? I know no women who look like me."

"True. And yes, that much I will teach you."

And so the evening wore on, and to my great disappointment no fights began and no gates were opened into otherworlds. Funerals, in my experience, have a tendency to go one way or the other, something about grief either brings mortals together or tears them apart. I had of course been hoping for tearing, but I was, on this occasion, disappointed.

There are disadvantages, reader, to my reliance on stories that are in no way made up or embellished. In an artificial narrative I could easily arrange for events to tie up neatly at the end, for every thread of the story to weave together like some great and perfect tapestry. Reality, however, has the awkward habit of playing Penelope and unpicking that which a narrator would sooner have left intact.

Worse, mortals have no innate sense of pacing.

The elder Mr. Caesar, along with Lady Mary, left the wake early and took their daughters with them. Respect for the dead was all well and good, but St. Giles was not without its dangers, especially for young women. Even young women who enjoyed the goodwill of a small band of armed bastards. The younger Mr. Caesar, on the other hand, remained behind. A funeral, after all, was a time to be with family, and in that moment, in that exact context, the family that mattered were the Irregulars.

It would be neater if all my principals had come together for some manner of curtain call, but, alas, they thwarted me. And so I found myself for the last time having to divide my attention between goings-on on opposite sides of the city.

On the bright side, it was the third time I would need to do so in this tale. And some numbers are auspicious.

The Caesars had, at least, managed to secure the earl's carriage for the evening, meaning that they did not need to walk their children through a rookery by night. And it had been a long day, so as they rattled through the streets they let the motion of the vehicle rock them into a quiet somnolence.

. . . In the dark of the Folly, Mr. Caesar and the captain lay together, breathing in time and eye to eye across the shadows.

"Thank you," whispered the captain. "For coming. And for staying." . . .

"Would it be very terrible," Miss Anne asked the carriage as a whole, "if I did not marry immediately once I am out? I am beginning to think that men are more complex than I had expected."

"That," her father replied, "would be very wise. Indeed your mother and I would be quite happy if you would not marry at all."

"Oh no." Miss Anne looked aghast. "That would be most dreary. But I am beginning to see that finding a truly *good* man may take more work than I anticipated."

. . . Mr. Caesar pressed his lips lightly to the captain's and whispered against them. "We don't have to, you buried a friend today."

But Captain James drew him closer, turned him gently onto his back. "I'm a soldier, John. I've buried friends before and will again, but life has to go on." . . .

As the carriage moved out of the worst parts of the city's underbelly into those with better lighting and more socially acceptable crimes, Miss Caesar looked sleepily at the faces of her family and let her thoughts wander.

Miss Anne's thoughts remained rather more focused. "I think it ill of John not to return with us. Now is surely the time to be with family."

"Family," Lady Mary pointed out, "can mean more than one thing."

. . . Sex and death have walked hand in hand for millennia, and it can be a terrible pairing or a beautiful one. As I have said many times and will continue to say for as long as I fear mortals will fail to believe me, I find little beauty in mortal flesh, but I can find great poetry in mortal feeling.

So it was with some care that I watched the captain and Mr. Caesar tell one another, through the lyrics of fingertips and ragged stanzas of breath, a story of wanting and keeping and hoping that even now neither could quite articulate with something as vulgar as words. . . .

Miss Caesar's thoughts, which had been straying across the city and the world, meandered back to the present and formed themselves, quite without her permission, into a question.

"Papa," she asked, "what was Grandmama like?"

. . . Mr. Caesar lay still with his head on the captain's shoulder. And his thoughts, which had been wandering past and future and flesh and blood, formed themselves, without his permission, into a request.

"Don't go." . . .

"You know your grandmother," Mr. Caesar replied, genuinely perplexed.

"Not Lady Elmsley," his daughter clarified. "Your mother."

Mr. Caesar grew very quiet and then said, softly, "I find it harder and harder to remember."

. . . "What do you mean, don't go?"

"To France. To war. I don't want to lose you."

"It's what I do, John." There was no anger in the captain's voice. But nor was there longing. "It's dangerous, but it's the life."

Mr. Caesar shifted, apprehensive. "And what do I do?"

"Wait. Like all the rest."

"You want me to stand on the docks and sing melancholy songs until you return?"

Captain James rolled over. "You wanted to be a soldier's man. That's how it goes." . . .

"Then . . ." Miss Caesar was saying in the carriage. "I should like to know what you do remember."

Settling back in his seat, the elder Mr. Caesar shut his eyes. "It is a long story. And there are reasons I have not told it to you."

Miss Caesar lowered her gaze. "Even so, I should like to hear what I can."

For a moment, it seemed her father would say nothing. "I was born," he began hesitantly, "more than fifty years ago in the Kingdom of Cayor. . . ."

And that, readers, is where I stepped away. I am a collector of stories, not a thief. I speak of things I have seen, not things I have heard from other narrators.

CHAPTER TWENTY-SIX

DESPITE MR. CAESAR'S ENTREATIES, CAPTAIN James and the rest of the Irregulars did indeed go back to war. The British army was mustered by early June and, although hostilities did not begin in earnest for another two weeks, Mr. Caesar, as a consequence, spent a number of days standing on the docks, looking out towards the sea, perfecting his air of aesthetic melancholy.

"Perhaps," Miss Bickle told him—she had taken to keeping him company since the regiment had gone, "we should go to the seaside. It seems rather more fitting to be gazing out at the sea rather than the Thames. The Thames is so smelly."

"Would it greatly surprise you," Mr. Caesar replied, "to know that the smell is not my primary concern?"

"Not at all." Miss Bickle was largely immune to sarcasm. "I am sure your largest concern is that Captain James might get shot by a Frenchman."

The wind off the Thames which, now Miss Bickle had mentioned it, *did* have a certain element of the open sewer to it, blew cool on Mr. Caesar's face. "Would it surprise you yet more greatly," he said, "to know that my greatest concern isn't that either?"

The vast majority of the time, Miss Bickle was a portrait of obliviousness. She had her ideas about how things were and should be, and had trained her mind to systematically edit the world to preserve those ideas in the face of all evidence. This, however, was not the majority of the time. "Are you concerned he'll forget you?"

"He's in *France,*" Mr. Caesar declared, as though it were the end of the world. "Or Belgium. Fuck, I hope he's in Belgium. I can't imagine Belgian men are anywhere near as interesting as French men."

Miss Bickle frowned. "Even if French men are very, very interesting they can't be as"—she looked up at him with wide eyes and the conflicted expression of one whose kindness is matched only by her honesty—"well, I'm sure you're more interesting than *some* French men at least."

"Oh, thank you very much."

"I just mean, well, you know, the French. They do have rather a reputation."

"True." With a sigh, Mr. Caesar turned back to the river. "And—even without, you know, the French and the Belgians and the Dutch and the Danish and the Prussians and all of them—"

"Gosh." Miss Bickle mentally enumerated the various nations of the Seventh Coalition. "Aren't wars complicated?"

"Even without all of them," continued Mr. Caesar, who had known Miss Bickle for long enough to have learned that speaking over interjections was a necessary survival strategy, "I . . . I also very much do not want him to be killed."

In defiance of all laws of propriety, Miss Bickle took Mr. Caesar by the hand and they stood together awhile watching the ships on the river. And for a while there was nothing but the lapping of the

water and the—admittedly rather intrusive—cries of street ven-
dors to disturb the moment.

Then, Miss Bickle raised her voice in a soft, strong, and profoundly off-key melody. " 'I would I were on yonder hill,' " she
began, " 'tis there I'd sit and cry my fill.' "

Mr. Caesar glared down at her. "No."

" 'And every tear would turn a mill . . . ' " She met his gaze, challenging him to respond.

"I'm not singing a mournful song with my own bloody name in
it."

" 'And every tear would turn a mill,' " Miss Bickle repeated. I
should, as a responsible peddler of influences, remind my readers
that there are definitely circumstances in which an inability to take
no for an answer is a decidedly *negative* quality in a person. But this
was not one of them.

"All right. You win." He cleared his throat and continued in a
rather better voice. " 'Johnny has gone for a soldier.' "

Any hope Mr. Caesar may have had of that being that was
dashed at once. Miss Bickle carried on warbling. " 'I'll sell my rock,
I'll sell my reel, I'll sell my only spinning wheel.' "

"Oh no, we're not doing all of it. The verse about dyeing my
petticoats red at the very least I reserve the right to veto."

"Oh, but John." Miss Bickle frowned. "You'd look so fine in red
petticoats."

He had known the argument was useless before he had begun,
but he'd needed to try anyway. They did, in the end, sing all of it,
even the verse about the petticoats, as they walked away from the
riverbank.

And Mr. Caesar, who was not ordinarily given to sentimentality,
found tears pricking his eyes. Then more than pricking, so that he
needed to stop in the shadow of a doorway and compose himself.

"I could have gone with him," he said. "I could have enlisted or followed with the wives and children. I didn't. He'd be right to abandon me."

Miss Bickle extended one finger and jabbed Mr. Caesar firmly in the arm. "Don't be silly, John. Soldiers leave their loves at home all the time, and they come back all the time. Anyway, fate would not be so cruel as to snatch Captain James away from you so swiftly."

From anybody else it would have been malice, or at least wilful obstinacy. From Miss Bickle it was just what she was like, and Mr. Caesar took it in the spirit it was intended. "You and I have personally met a goddess and the queen of the fairies and they were both terrible people. Why would you expect fate to be any less vicious?"

Miss Bickle considered this. "Because I am a foolish girl who prefers to choose hope."

When she said it, it seemed easy. And so Mr. Caesar delicately dabbed his tears away with a handkerchief. And chose.

I will admit, reader, that I have (or I suppose from another perspective quite literally *am*) an imp of the perverse that urges me to leave the story here. As I intimated at the end of my last novel, once the central conflict is resolved, I like to bring things to an end as swiftly as possible. Ordinarily, I lose interest the moment everybody has been turned back from whatever they've been turned into and everybody is in love with the right person (by my standards, at least, I will freely admit that I am not wholly above leaving a gentleman under the effects of a love potion if it will lead to his making better choices—this happened once in Athens, as I am sure you remember).

But narrative convention, in this instance, dictates that I should provide you with just slightly more information.

Of course, what narrative convention demands is not always within my power to give. Since I collect these stories by observation, I could not simply *invent* details in order to provide closure to a reader some two centuries after they took place. I would have needed to be present at some event at which I could authentically observe that, for example, Captain James either did or did not die at the end of a French sabre at the Battle of Quatre Bras.

By great good fortune, however, I was present at just such an event.

Napoleon had fallen once again, to the great joy of all those who cherished freedom from tyranny and the rights of hereditary aristocrats, and the ton was alive with celebration. And with the Bourbon monarchy restored to their definitely entirely rightful throne, the great and the good of England were once again able to engage their passion for the Parisian without feeling like traitors to their nation and their class.

Thus, the Vicomte de Loux was able to host another ball and was, once again, somewhat incentivised to invite as much of the army as he could, in order to remind everybody that he'd been on the right side all along.

There had, initially, been something of a question over whether the Caesars would be invited at all, given the fracas that had unfolded last time. But since the man most likely to make a scene at their inclusion had been eaten by a bear, it did not in the end prove much of an issue.

"For the hundredth time," Miss Caesar was telling her brother, as they rode in a still-borrowed carriage to the vicomte's new let, "go and speak to him."

It was not a conversation Mr. Caesar wished to repeat. But then he hadn't wished to repeat it any of the other times either. "He hasn't come to speak to me."

"He's been at war. He's probably had other things on his mind."

"Then I should not intrude."

Miss Anne, who had been watching the countryside roll by outside, gave her brother a sharp look. "You need to be bolder, John."

"I'm really not sure I do." This was a lie. He was very sure he did indeed. It was just so much harder on his own.

The carriage rolled to a halt alongside a dozen others and the Caesars alighted. Mr. Caesar made his habitual scan of the crowd and noted that his uncle had yet to arrive, which he counted as a small blessing, and that the regiment had yet to arrive, which he counted very much otherwise.

But he pushed the thoughts aside. Either the captain would be there, or he would not. Either he would have returned from the war still wishing to be part of Mr. Caesar's life, or he would not. In the meantime there were still Miss Caesar and Miss Anne to consider. And here Mr. Caesar consoled himself with the thought that at the very least it would be hard for things to go worse than they had last time.

Even so, the spectre of recent events hung over all three of the Caesar children as they made their way to the ballroom. The ton had a frankly inconsistent record when it came to supernatural scandal. At times they would do their best to forget it lest they be uncomfortably reminded of their own cosmic insignificance. And at times they turned sharply against the victims for essentially the same reason.

"And you're sure," Mr. Caesar checked with his sister for the hundred and third time, "that you want to risk this?"

She nodded. "I have tried being ignored, and I have tried being what society asks. Tonight let them take or leave me as I am."

So Mr. Caesar led his sisters to the ballroom and, once they had been announced, he let Miss Caesar lead the way.

Her demeanour had changed greatly since her return from the Other Court. She had taken to dressing more brightly, and in styles that better suited her. This evening she wore a white chemise beneath a gown of red draped asymmetrically over one shoulder. She looked almost classical, at least to her brother's eyes. To her own eyes she looked only like herself, and that, she felt, was enough. For the past several weeks she had taken to wearing her hair tied in styles she'd learned from Amenirdis, but for the evening she had let it loose, and free, framing her head like a sunburst. As she walked into the ballroom with eyes—some cruel, some welcoming—turning towards her, she felt like every queen and every goddess.

She was not sure if she had *hoped* that Mr. Bygrave would be the first to approach her. But he was.

"Miss Caesar." He bowed stiffly. "You—that is, I—it has been some time."

Changed as she had been by her experiences, a lifetime of training could not be overwritten in a hundred days. Miss Caesar dropped into a flawlessly executed curtsey. "It has, sir."

"I confess," he went on, "my memory of the last few months is a little . . . muddled?"

That, Miss Caesar had expected but did not like to hear. "It was fairy magic," she said. "I believe it clouds the mind."

Mr. Bygrave developed a sudden and intense interest in his own shoes. "I suppose I am feeling less muddled now."

"Then I shall be happy to introduce you to my sister."

At that, Mr. Bygrave coloured. "No. I mean, your sister is lovely also and, well, it wouldn't do to dance with only one lady at a ball. But, well, would you . . ."

It would have been the easiest thing in the world to say yes. But it was also the easiest thing in the world to say *I wish*, so Miss Caesar had learned to be wary of easy things. "I have had many unusual experiences lately," she explained. "And I am not sure I am quite ready to begin looking for a gentleman. Not quite yet."

Mr. Bygrave nodded, sharp and resigned. "I understand."

"But"—Miss Caesar bit her lip—"there can be little danger, I think, in *one* dance."

The music struck up and Miss Caesar let Mr. Bygrave lead her onto the dance floor.

"I believe," Miss Caesar told him, "it is expected that we should converse."

Mr. Bygrave flushed a little, not quite certain what to converse about. "Have you . . ." he tried, "have you read any good books lately?"

"Yes," replied Miss Caesar. "Shall I tell you about them?"

"Well, isn't that sweet," said a voice at Mr. Caesar's ear.

Wrapped up in observing his sister as he had been, Mr. Caesar jumped half out of his skin as he turned to see a smiling woman whose gown, if he looked closely, didn't look entirely made-to-measure. "Sal?"

"Captain thought it was best if a couple of us went in quiet. Reyne's mob are still out there and they've still got guns."

Now he was looking still closer, he noticed that Sal's makeup was a little heavier than it once had been, and that it seemed to be covering a fresh scar on her right cheek. "Are you well?" he asked.

"Well enough. Always did my best to take the fuckers with me. And this'll fade." She touched her face, a little self-consciously. "But it's not me you want to ask about really, is it?"

"How are . . . all of you?" Mr. Caesar asked.

"Alive."

"Good." A prickling sensation began to gather on Mr. Caesar's spine. Perhaps it was just the thought of the Iphigenians, still active, still sharpening their knives. "And is Orestes . . ."

With surprising polish, Sal pointed with her eyes towards the entrance to the ballroom, and Mr. Caesar turned just in time to see Captain James arrive.

He looked much as he had ever done, much as Mr. Caesar suspected he would ever do. There is a kind of immortality that comes with confidence, and a kind of timelessness. He still belonged more to the battlefield than to the ballroom, but he brought his world with him.

While Mr. Caesar's brain was debating with itself over whether he should approach the captain or let the captain approach him, his feet were making the decision on its behalf. He crossed the floor with an almost unseemly directness until he found himself face-to-face with Captain James.

"Thought I'd find you here," the captain said.

"I should have . . ." Mr. Caesar cast his eyes down. "I knew when the regiments were returning, but I didn't know if you'd . . . if you'd want me to."

"As a rule," replied Captain James, looking playfully aggrieved, "a man comes back from war, he wants you to."

"Sorry."

The captain patted Mr. Caesar on the back in a way that could easily be mistaken, by a casual observer, for companionable. Then he left his hand in place in a way that certainly could not. "Do better next time."

Mr. Caesar's mouth was going a little dry, which was only about the third on the list of things making him feel foolish. "There'll be a next time?"

"And a time after that. I'm still a soldier, John. Going away is part of the life. That okay with you?"

It wasn't a question that he'd ever imagined having to answer, but Mr. Caesar found it easier than he might have imagined. "As long as you come back."

There was little that could pass between them at a public ball, the laws and the state of society being what it was, but Captain James's fingertips shifted just slightly along Mr. Caesar's shoulder blade. "Always."

And that, reader, is where we shall leave them. Surrounded by the wealthy and oblivious, frozen like butterflies in glass in a moment where we may pretend, in the face of all conceivable evidence to the contrary, that all is right with the world.

It is also where I shall leave you.

We have walked together awhile now, and I do not do this for fun but because I am stuck in your reality and driven to it by penury. Besides, I can give you no assurances about the future of our heroes. After all, the captain is a military man, and military men have such eventful lives so who, truly, can say what the future (*their* future, I should say—and your past, and my eternal present) may hold. Perhaps he and Mr. Caesar found themselves travelling the globe and witnessing wonder after wonder, Mr. Caesar learning eventually to cherish the rough sleeping and hard living that comes with being a soldier's lover.

Or perhaps the opposite is true. Perhaps in the end their lives could never quite merge, the gentleman and the warrior being, at last, too different to really belong in each other's worlds. And perhaps Captain James, for all his great potential, died at last in some squalid colonial battle for the glory of a king who could not possibly have cared less for him.

Then again, the captain is a hero, and heroes seldom end so poorly. And there will be a revolution, shortly, in Greece that will draw so many fascinating people together. So who knows what marvelous adventures the captain and Mr. Caesar may have before them. Or how they might change the fates of empires. Or what Lord Byron may have to do with matters.

I do. Obviously.

Have I whetted your curiosity? Well then, perhaps you will need to continue reading my books. I have little else to do with my time in exile and your support gratifies me greatly.

And the gratitude of the fair folk is a fine thing.

As fine as it is terrible.

Your friend,

R

ACKNOWLEDGEMENTS

I acknowledge no debt to any immortal being save my lord Oberon, ever kind, ever wise, and ever merciful. I acknowledge no debt to any mortal being whatsoever but I will grudgingly admit that despite the shortcomings of their species my editor, Emily Archbold; my agent, Courtney Miller-Callihan; the sensitivity reader, Helen Gould; and my assistant, Mary, are perhaps intermittently helpful on rare and specific matters.

ABOUT THE AUTHOR

Alexis Hall is the mortal pen name of a wandering fairy spirit cruelly exiled to the physical world for reasons that were not at all his fault. He is slowly coming to terms with his predicament and feels fortunate that he has found a way to monetize his contempt for humanity.

ABOUT THE TYPE

This book was set in Baskerville, a typeface designed by John Baskerville (1706–75), an amateur printer and typefounder, and cut for him by John Handy in 1750. The type became popular again when the Lanston Monotype Corporation of London revived the classic roman face in 1923. The Mergenthaler Linotype Company in England and the United States cut a version of Baskerville in 1931, making it one of the most widely used typefaces today.